Susanna Kearsley was a museum curator before she took the plunge and became a full-time author. The past and its bearing on the present is a familiar theme in her books. She won the prestigious Catherine Cookson Fiction Prize for her novel *Mariana*, and was shortlisted for the Romantic Novel of the Year Award for *The Winter Sea*.

www.susannakearsley.com

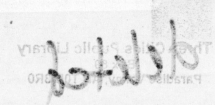

By Susanna Kearsley

Mariana

The Splendour Falls

The Shadowy Horses

Season of Storms

Every Secret Thing
(*previously published under the name Emma Cole*)

Sophia's Secret
(*also published as* The Winter Sea)

The Rose Garden

THE
SPLENDOUR
FALLS

SUSANNA KEARSLEY

First published in Great Britain in 2012 by
Allison & Busby Limited
13 Charlotte Mews
London W1T 4EJ
www.allisonandbusby.com

A CIP catalogue record for this book is available from
the British Library.

10 9 8 7 6 5 4 3 2 1

ISBN 978-0-7490-4031-4

Typeset in 10.5/15.5 pt Sabon by
Allison & Busby Ltd.

The paper used for this Allison & Busby publication
has been produced from trees that have been legally sourced
from well-managed and credibly certified forests.

Printed and bound by
CPI Group (UK) Ltd, Croydon, CR0 4YY

For my wonderful agent Felicity.

The morning we first met you said this was your favourite of my books, and all these years I've thought of it as 'yours', and I have nothing else to give you that you need, so here you are: this is officially Your Book now, with my love and heartfelt thanks for all you do.

The splendour falls on castle walls
And snowy summits old in story:
The long light shakes across the lakes,
And the wild cataract leaps in glory.
Blow, bugle, blow, set the wild echoes flying,
Blow, bugle; answer, echoes, dying, dying, dying.

This and all other quotes contained herein are taken from
Alfred, Lord Tennyson's 'The Princess'.

PROLOGUE

. . . when all was lost or seem'd as lost . . .

The first night had been the worst. They had come on so violently, and without warning. One moment she'd been peacefully at prayer within the chapel, and the next the captain of her guard was pounding at the door, with orders she should seek in haste the safety of her chamber. And then someone had whispered 'siege'. . .

It had been dreadful, that first night – the darkness and the shrieking of the wind and the fires burning everywhere, it seemed, upon the plain below. But daylight came, and still the castle held. Of course it held, thought Isabelle. This was Chinon. Like the Plantagenet kings it sheltered, Chinon Castle had a will of iron. It bowed before no man.

At first, she had not wanted to believe that Guillaume des Roches could be so bold, so callous, as to try to hold her hostage. He'd been an ally of the king her husband, and in return he had been used most fairly. Had John not made des

Roches warden of Chinon? And yet she'd seen the evidence with her own eyes, she'd seen des Roches himself among the men, striding freely through their ranks as though such treason were a thing to make him proud.

If John were here, she thought, he'd teach the traitor otherwise. If John were here . . .

She drew the velvet robe more tightly round her shivering body and looked again towards the west. The sun had slipped much lower, now. Already it had flattened on the purple haze of hills, spilling its brilliance into the darkly flowing river. Soon, she knew, there would be only darkness left. Four nights now she had stood here in this high and lonely tower, watching while the dying sun sank weakly in the western sky. This time she found herself looking for the fires, her own eyes seeking out the places where the rebels kept their camps.

'They are quite close, tonight,' she said aloud, and one of her women stirred beside the hearth.

'My lady?'

Isabelle glanced round, her long hair tangling on the crimson velvet. 'I said the fires are close, tonight.'

'Yes, my lady.'

'It must be very cold . . .' She looked away again, thinking on the madness that might drive a man to leave the comfort of his own warm hearth in this, the depth of winter.

Her women were watching her, she could feel their eyes. Her calmness, she knew, surprised them. They thought her still a child, as she had come to them three years ago, when John had brought her here, to Chinon, for the wedding. He'd scandalised the court that summer – she had heard the whispers. A man past thirty marrying a girl of twelve . . .

But even then, she had not been a child. She had already been betrothed to Hugh of Lusignan when John had met her first at Angoulême. No matter. As in the game of chess, a king outranked a knight, and Isabelle had known from their first meeting how the game would end. Some said that she yet wanted Hugh, but they were fools who thought so. In all her fifteen years, she had loved one man only – a quiet man, a caring man, with midnight eyes that smiled for her alone. And had it been her choice to make, three years ago, she would have chosen John.

He was not like his brothers, not like Richard. She'd met the fabled Lionheart – an armoured giant with a beard of gold. The image of his father, people said, the image of the Lion himself, King Henry, that raging intellect who, with indomitable Eleanor of Aquitaine, had bred a line of princes unparalleled in time.

It was, thought Isabelle, the strangest family. They loved and hated one another, wept and warred and plotted, moving always in a weird diagonal between deceit and truth. It had left scars on all of them, especially John. He did not speak of it, but many times she'd seen him standing silent in the chapel here at Chinon, brooding on the very spot where old King Henry, sick at heart, had finally died.

'Twas rumoured it was John's fault that the Lion ceased to roar – John's fault because he had been Henry's favourite, and because the king had seen John's name upon a list of those who stood against him. But Henry's heart was not so weak, thought Isabelle. He'd fought his sons before, unflinching. He'd dungeoned up his wife. He'd played John and betrayed him until no one could with any certainty say how his feelings lay. And yet John loved him. When he stood so sad and solemn in the chapel, Isabelle had but to look upon her husband's face to know whose heart had broken there those many years ago.

Still, people would persist in rumours. They whispered now about young Arthur of Brittany, held captive in Rouen for laying siege to the old queen at Mirabeau. John had once been fond of Arthur, his brother Geoffrey's only son, and Geoffrey, who died young, had been of all the brothers closest in both looks and age to John. But Arthur was not Geoffrey. Where his father had been cunning, Arthur failed to think at all, and his rash behaviour left John with no option but to take him prisoner.

And so the rumours shifted, day to day. Arthur of Brittany was free . . . he was in fetters . . . he was planning his escape . . . he was too weak to raise his head . . . he had been moved in secrecy from Rouen . . . Some said – she'd heard it only yesterday – that Arthur was already dead, that John had had him killed. What foolishness, thought Isabelle. John could not kill the boy.

She might have told that to the men camped now around the walls of Chinon Castle, if they had been like to listen, since it was for Arthur's sake that they had come. They thought to hold her hostage for the freedom of the reckless young pretender. Fools, she thought. They knew John not at all.

The wind struck chill through the high narrow window. It had a voice, that wind – half human and half demon, that numbed the soul and turned the heart to stone. Isabelle turned slowly from the dimming view and crossed the great round room to where a smaller window gazed upon the north. The northern sky was deepest blue and full of cloud, without a star to pierce the gloom. Did they have stars, she wondered, at Le Mans? Her message would, by now, have surely reached him. Le Mans was not so very far away. She had but to hold out a few more days, and help would be at hand. Isabelle smiled faintly in the firelight. Even if John had loved her not at all, she knew he would not lose his precious Treasury. Indeed, she might have thought he loved his Treasury above all else, had it not been for the day she'd teased him about it and he'd caught her to him, there in front of everyone, and told her: '*You* are my treasure.' She could still taste his kiss upon her lips . . .

Her hand moved, unthinkingly, to the gold and pearl pendant at her throat, and she frowned. 'Alice,' she said quietly, over her shoulder, 'I would have my jewel casket.'

'Yes, my lady.' The woman by the fire rose obediently.

'And Alice . . .'

'Yes, my lady?'

'Which of the servants knows the tunnels best?'

They did not need to ask which tunnels she was speaking of. Chinon Castle was riddled with them. John often said it was a mystery that the walls did not collapse.

'Old Thomas, my lady,' came the answer, finally. 'He works in the kitchens.'

'Then I would have him brought to me,' said Isabelle, 'without delay. I have need of him.'

The women stared at her, and murmured, but they knew better than to question her wishes. For all her youth, this waif-like figure by the window was yet Isabelle of Angoulême; she was their queen, and she would be obeyed. Old Thomas would be fetched with haste.

Content, Isabelle turned back to the small window and the fires burning brightly on the blackened plain below. She did not hear the door behind her close, nor hear the footsteps of the women ringing down the cold stone passage. She only heard the wind. She was still standing motionless, her eyes upon the northern hills, when Alice came to set the small jewel casket down beside the bed.

Alice was the oldest of her women, and her gaze fell very gentle on the sad-eyed little queen. 'He will come, my lady,' she said softly, and they both knew it was not Old Thomas that she meant.

Isabelle nodded, without words, and blamed the stinging winter wind for the sudden trail of dampness on her face . . .

CHAPTER ONE

. . . and thus a noble scheme
Grew up from seed . . .

'And did he come?' I curled my feet beneath me on the sofa, and poured another cup of tea.

My cousin was idly contemplating my sitting-room window, where the raindrops chased one another down the panes in ragged paths. He pulled his gaze back to mine, with an effort. 'What?'

'John,' I prompted, patiently. 'Did he finally come to rescue Isabelle?'

'Oh.' He smiled. 'Naturally. He sent his best knight, Jean de Préaux, with a group of mercenaries, to bring poor Isabelle back safely to Le Mans.'

I pulled a face. 'How very noble of him.'

'You would have seen the romance in that, once,' Harry said, passing me his own teacup to be refilled. It was a gentle reprimand. He was quite right, I knew, but I pushed the thought aside.

'So tell me,' I said, 'about this new theory of yours.'

'My dear girl, it isn't theory – it's been published in three quite prestigious journals.'

'Sorry.'

He forgave me, leaning back. 'Well, you remember when they turned up that new chronicle last year, at Angoulême?'

'By William de What's-his-name? Yes, I remember.'

'Right. It tells us Isabelle hid something when she was besieged at Chinon, something so valuable that she didn't want the rebel barons to find it. At least we can infer that much. She asked for her jewel case, and then she asked for someone who knew the tunnels, and then she disappeared for nearly an hour with this Old Thomas, to where, nobody knew.'

I frowned. 'But surely when the threat was over, she'd have got back what it was she hid.'

'Not necessarily. Chinon was hardly secure, remember, and John lost it completely not long afterwards, so Isabelle might never have had the chance. The chronicle,' he told me, 'clearly states that in her later years our Isabelle spoke often of the "treasure without price" she'd left in France. Put two and two together—'

'—and you've got your lectures packed with students for the term,' I teased him, smiling.

He grinned. 'Not this term. I'm on half-time now, remember? One term off, one on. And this one's off.'

'Nice work if you can get it.'

'Well, I need the time for writing. I've been working on this book . . .'

'Let me guess. Plantagenets.' That was no great effort to

16

deduce. My cousin Harry had been potty for Plantagenets since we were both in the nursery. I'd paid the price for his obsession many times in childhood games, condemned to die a Saracen at Richard the Lionheart's crusading hand, or playing Thomas à Becket, a role I thought was rather fun until I learned the fate of the Archbishop. The only truly juicy part I'd been allowed to play was that of Eleanor of Aquitaine, which I'd played often, until Harry one day locked me up in 'Salisbury Tower' – an old bomb shelter at the back of his neighbour's garden – and left me there till dinner time. To this day, it was all I could do to force myself to take the tube in London, or to spend more than ten minutes in my own basement.

My cousin smiled. 'Not all of the Plantagenets – just John. A sort of revisionist approach to his biography. The misunderstood king. Which reminds me, did I show you what your father sent me?' Without waiting for my answer, he dug into his pocket and produced a circle of hard plastic, within which nestled a small and perfect silver coin. 'That's John himself, in profile. Must be worth a bloody fortune, but your father just put it in the post.'

I took the encased coin from him, turning it round. 'Wherever did Daddy pick this up?'

'God knows.' My cousin shrugged. 'Uncle Andrew has so many friends in odd places, doesn't he? I sometimes think it's better not to ask too many questions.'

I agreed. 'He doesn't answer questions well, at any rate. He'd likely say he bought it at a car boot sale.' He'd say it with a straight face, too, I thought. My father was a charming liar when he chose – a trait that he'd acquired through his lifetime in the diplomatic corps. I'd learned the trick of it myself, these past few years.

'He says,' my cousin informed me, 'you ought to ring him more often.'

I looked up, eyebrows raised. 'I ring him every month. He *is* in Uruguay, you know – if we talked any more frequently I'd drain my savings, such as they are.'

'I know. I just think he worries about you, that's all.'

'Well, there's no need.' I flipped the coin over to study the reverse. 'You'll be off to France then, I expect, to do more research?'

'Yes, at the end of the month.'

'Just in time for the wine harvest.'

'Precisely.'

I took a sip of tea and sighed. 'I'm envious, I really am.'

'So come with me.' He dropped the comment casually, then slid his eyes sideways to watch my reaction.

'Don't be daft. You know I can't.'

'Why not?'

'Some of us,' I explained mildly, 'do work for a living, you know, and I can't just pick up any time I like and leave.'

'Give over,' was my cousin's blunt response. 'You work for my dad, for heaven's sake. I'll not believe that Braden Glass would fall to pieces if you took a fortnight's holiday. Surely Dad or Jack could answer their own telephones . . .'

'And then there's the house to think of,' I went on stubbornly. 'I'm supposed to be looking after it for Daddy, not leaving it unattended so some burglar can break in and strip the place.' I saw his unconvinced expression, and I frowned. 'Look, I'm sorry if you think I'm boring . . .'

'It's not that you're boring, exactly,' Harry corrected me, 'it's just that you're not very exciting. Not any more. Not since . . .'

'This has nothing to do with my parents' divorce. I'm just getting older, that's all. Taking some responsibility.'

'There's responsible,' said my cousin drily, 'and then there is responsible. Mother tells me it's been six months since you so much as stopped in at the pub for a drink.'

I rolled my eyes. 'The curse of living in a small community. What else does your mother tell you?'

'That she hardly ever sees you smile, and that last month in London you walked straight past the fountains in Trafalgar Square without tossing in so much as tuppence.'

I looked down. 'Yes, well. Only tourists throw coins in fountains.'

'That never used to stop you.' He set his empty teacup on the table at his knees. 'Which reminds me, may I have my King John coin back? Thanks. You might have stopped believing in good luck pieces, Emily Braden, but I haven't. I'd rather lose my right arm than this little chap. So,' he said brightly, tucking the silver coin safely back into his pocket, 'that's settled, then. You're coming with me to Chinon.'

I shook my head. 'Harry'. . . '

'Cheap flights right now, out of Heathrow, but you'll have to book this week I think. Dad says the end of September would be fine with him, just so he knows . . .'

'Harry . . .'

'And I've found the most wonderful hotel, sixteenth-century and right on the main square, with a view of the castle.'

'Harry,' I tried again, but he'd already pulled out the brochures. The photographs made Chinon look like something from a childhood dream – pale turreted houses and winding cobbled streets, with the castle rising like a guardian from the cliffs against a lavender sky, and the river Vienne gleaming like a ribbon of light at its feet.

'There's the tower where Isabelle would have waited out the siege,' Harry said, pointing out a narrow crumbling column at the castle's furthest edge. 'The Moulin Tower.'

I looked, and shook my head with an effort. 'I can't come with you.'

'Of course you can.'

I sighed. My cousin had the rare ability to solve the whole world's problems single-handed. My father did that too, sometimes, and my Uncle Alan. At the moment, I sensed I was the victim of a triumvirate of conspiracy. I hadn't changed that much, I reasoned . . . had I? It was just that when one's parents, after thirty years of marriage, chose to go their separate ways, it made one view life rather more realistically. So what, I asked myself, was wrong with that? So my parents' happy marriage hadn't been so happy after all. So love was never meant to last for ever. It was better that I'd learned that lesson young, instead of making their mistakes all over again.

And I didn't carry any bitterness towards my parents. A little disappointment maybe, but no bitterness. My mother was . . . well, she was just my mother – vibrant, headstrong, independent. Every now and then she sent me postcards from Greek ports or Turkish hotels or wherever she and her latest boyfriend were at large. And Daddy . . . Daddy went on working as he always had before, only now instead of his London office he had his office at the British Legation in Montevideo. He'd hardly seemed to notice the divorce.

But then, he'd never really grown up, my father. Like all the Braden men, my father had a child's innocence and simple faith and depthless well of energy. My Uncle Alan was the same, and Harry too. It made them all three rather charming, and I loved them for it, but it put them on a plane of life one couldn't always reach, or share.

Harry was the worst of them, come to that. Though I was terribly fond of my only cousin, he'd driven me to the brink of murder more times than I cared to remember. Unreliable, my mother called him. I might instead have termed him 'easily distracted', but it amounted to much the same thing when one was left stranded at the airport because Harry had gone off exploring, somewhere. The memory made me smile suddenly, and I looked across at him with affection.

'I'd be a proper idiot to go on holiday with you,' I said. 'God alone knows what trouble you might lead me into.'

He grinned at that. 'Maybe that's what you need, a good adventure. Bring you back to life.'

'I'm perfectly alive, thanks very much.'

'No you're not.' His eyes were serious behind the smile. 'Not really. I miss the old Emily.'

I looked down at the spreading tangle of coloured brochures. It was a trick of light, I knew, that made me see the shadow of a woman waiting still within that tower at the ruined castle's edge, yet for a moment she was plainly there. A young woman, staring blankly out across the years, waiting, wanting, hoping . . . For what, I wondered?

Brave Prince Charming on his pure white charger, riding to the rescue? More fool her, I thought – he wouldn't come. *You're on your own, my girl,* I told the shadowed figure silently, *you'd best accept the fact. Those happy-ever-afters never stand the test of time.* The shadow faded and I looked away, to where the raindrops were still dancing down my window panes.

Harry poured the final cup of cooled tea from the pot, and settled back in his chair, his blue eyes oddly gentle as he tapped my thoughts with maddening precision. 'If you don't believe in fairy tales in Chinon,' said my cousin, 'then there's no hope left for any of us.'

CHAPTER TWO

Arriving all confused . . .

I should have known better. Experience, as everyone kept pointing out, had taught me nothing. Even my Aunt Jane had raised her eyebrows when I'd told her I was going on holiday with Harry.

'My Harry? Whatever for?'

'He thinks I need a holiday,' had been my answer. 'He's promised me adventure.'

'How much adventure,' she had asked me, drily, 'were you planning on?'

I'd shrugged aside the warning. 'I'm sure we'll do just fine. Besides, I do like Harry.'

'My dear Emily, that's hardly the point. We all like Harry. But he has a habit of being, well, rather . . .'

'Unpredictable?' I'd offered, and she'd smiled.

'That's being kind.'

I'd reassured her it was only France that we were

going to, not darkest Africa. What could possibly happen in France? And if something were to happen I was well equipped to handle it – French was at least a language I could speak, thanks to my father's years of service at the Paris Embassy. Besides, the thought of spending two whole weeks in Chinon was terribly seductive.

Aunt Jane had listened to it all, her blue eyes twinkling, and quirked an innocent eyebrow. 'You've taken out insurance, have you?' And then she'd laughed and turned away to make the tea.

My Uncle Alan had been less cynical. 'Just what you need,' he'd pronounced with satisfaction. 'Change of scenery, eh? Bit of romance.' He'd winked at that and nudged my arm, and I had smiled as I was meant to, thinking all the while that romance was the last thing that I needed. A holiday fling perhaps, quick and painless, but real romance . . . well, that proved as reliable as Harry himself, and, like my cousin, it could only lead one into trouble.

Harry, for his part, had done his level best to confound our suspicions these past weeks. He'd gone ahead of me to do some of the 'boring bits' of research on his own – I never had liked reading rooms. But he'd been almost conscientious with our travel plans, had sent me maps and confirmation of our reservations at Chinon's Hotel de France. He'd even telephoned on Sunday last from Bordeaux, with my final instructions.

'Not the Gare Austerlitz, love,' he'd corrected me cheerfully. 'Montparnasse. You still know your way around Paris pretty well, don't you? Just take the bus in from the airport, and then the TGV from Montparnasse to St-Pierre-des-Corps, that's the quickest way to do it. You'll be there before lunchtime.'

I'd stopped scrawling down directions and tapped the pen against my notepad, frowning. 'And you *will* come to meet me?'

'Certainly. I'll be driving right across the top of Tours – that's where St-Pierre-des-Corps is – so I'll pick you up right at the railway station. I've got the red car; you shouldn't have any trouble spotting me. Shall we say noon?'

'That's noon on Friday?' I confirmed. 'Friday the twenty-fourth?'

'Don't worry,' he'd said, sounding amused. 'I won't forget. I'm not a total idiot, you know. Besides, I've had this letter, did I tell you?' He hadn't, as it turned out, so he went on to elaborate. The writer of the letter was some fellow history buff who'd read one of my cousin's academic journal pieces on the lost treasure of Isabelle. 'So presumably he reads English,' said my cousin, 'though his letter was in French. He's rather cryptic, but it seems he has some information that might interest me, about the tunnels underneath the castle. Asks me can I get in touch with him. It's wonderfully intriguing – just like that Watergate informant chap, you know the one . . .'

'Does your man have a code name, as well?'

'No.' Harry had sounded a shade disappointed. 'No, just his real name . . . Didier . . . Didier something. I'd have to look it up, I don't remember. Well anyway, he lives in Chinon, so that's why you needn't worry I'll forget to pick you up. I'm rather keen myself to get up there and find out what this fellow knows.'

'Fine, then I'll see you on Friday.'

'St-Pierre-des-Corps at noon. I promise.' It had been that final word, oddly enough, that struck a warning note, but the phone line was already crackling, breaking up. I'd heard my cousin's voice saying, 'Must dash, sorry,' and something that sounded vaguely like 'Till Friday', and that was that.

I should have known.

'Bloody Harry,' I said aloud. The young woman seated at the table next to mine looked up, surprised, then glanced away again discreetly as she raised her dainty cup of coffee. My own cup was long since empty, and cold against my fingers. I pushed it away with idle irritation and, resting my chin on my hands, stared out through the wall of windows in front of me. The view from the cafe of the rail station was less than inspiring – a wide sweep of concrete slabs set in a square geometric pattern, curving rows of futuristic lamp standards perched on thick concrete pillars, and a long low concrete fountain filled with foaming white jets of water that only emphasised the coldness of the architecture. Across the street three large blocks of flats rose like blemishes from the landscape, pale and impersonal, with rows of windows staring blankly back at me through the prison railings of their balconies.

I sighed.

This section of the city of Tours was depressingly modern. Chinon itself lay somewhere to the southwest – not far, though at that moment it seemed a thousand miles away. I could almost hear it beckoning, that lovely castle in the river's curve, beneath a violet sky. 'The flower of the

Garden of France', the brochures had promised me. I sighed again, with feeling. Because I wasn't in Chinon – I was here, and St-Pierre-des-Corps looked nothing like a flower.

He wasn't coming, I thought glumly. Harry never came an hour late. He either showed on time or not at all.

'Well, bother it,' I said, and once again the woman at the next table turned her eyes upon me warily. She seemed relieved to see me counting out the change to pay my bill, and even more relieved a moment later as I took a firm grip on my suitcase, pushing back my chair. I felt like telling her I didn't normally talk to myself; that it was all the fault of my rotten bounder of a cousin . . . but then it didn't really matter what she thought, as I was leaving anyway. Harry or no Harry, I would find some way to get to Chinon.

Outside, the air was cool against my heated skin. The skies had threatened rain all morning and the breeze was brisk, but still one wistful, optimistic patch of watery blue had broken through the unrelenting grey. With lifting spirits I headed for the taxi rank.

There were three taxis parked along the curved arcade of concrete columns in front of the station, but only one of them – the one at the rear of the rank – appeared to have a driver. He was standing not ten feet away from me, leaning against the bonnet of a smoke-grey Renault Safrane, eyes fixed upon the fountain in mild contemplation. One hand was thrust deep into the pocket of his tailored wool trousers, while the other held a half-finished cigarette. He wasn't tall, but the dark and handsome labels certainly applied. He wasn't young, either – perhaps a decade older than my own twenty-eight years. Distinguished, my mother would have branded him, and rather elegant in that unaffected way that the French alone seem to have mastered.

As I drew closer, his gaze slid sideways from the fountain to my face, and something flickered behind the dark eyes before they drifted on, taking in my clothes and, most tellingly, the British Airways tags still dangling from my suitcase. Before I'd had a chance to use my French he spoke to me in flawless fluid English. 'May I help you, Madame?'

He knew I wasn't married. His glance had rested on the fingers of my left hand – more from habit than anything else, I imagined, as I never looked my best when travelling. But it was a matter of politeness, to address me as 'Madame'.

'Well, yes. I need a taxi, please.'

He frowned. An odd response, considering he was leaning against one. It wasn't until he cast a quick glance along the taxi rank that I understood.

'I know you're last in line,' I told him, 'but the other taxis don't have drivers.'

He looked back at me and smiled. 'Where do you wish to go, Madame?'

'To Chinon.'

'Chinon?' He lifted the cigarette, narrowing his eyes against the smoke. They were very thoughtful eyes. 'But it is almost an hour away, Chinon. An expensive trip by taxi.'

'Oh.' I tried to look as if it didn't matter, but of course it did. I couldn't throw my budget out of whack.

Again he glanced along the idle taxi rank, then back at me, as though he were trying to decide something. I saved him the bother.

'Is there a train to Chinon, then?' I asked him.

'Not from this station, no.' His face cleared. 'But there is the *autocar* . . . the bus. I think that it departs at thirteen hours and a half, from over there.' The dark head nodded once, towards the fountain. 'You can buy a ticket from inside the station, there is time.'

I checked my wristwatch, making the conversion to the French twenty-four hour system. I had fully fifteen minutes to buy my ticket and catch the *autocar* – plenty of time. 'Thank you, Monsieur,' I said, lifting my single suitcase from the pavement. 'Thank you very much.'

'You are welcome.' He inclined his head gallantly, then leaned back against the sleek grey Safrane and looked away, lifting the cigarette. When I came out of the station the second time, he was deep in conversation with an older red-faced man sweating beneath the burden of a rich-looking set of luggage.

I passed by swiftly, without looking up, and scurried on towards the waiting *autocar,* where I settled myself in the vacant front seat behind the driver. I had every intention of enjoying my clear view of the passing scenery, but the rolling motion of the bus defeated me, and before we'd even driven the few miles to the centre of the city of Tours I was asleep. It was wholly understandable – I'd been up before the birds that morning, caught the plane to Paris and endured a bumpy bus ride, high-speed trains, and two full cups of railway station coffee the consistency of river mud.

I might have kept on sleeping straight to Chinon, but for the sudden blare of a car horn directly beneath my window. The second blast of sound brought my head round with a jolt that rattled my teeth, and my eyes flew open in time to see the Safrane cut smoothly in front of us, travelling at twice the necessary speed. So, I thought smiling, my dashing taxi driver had found himself a fare after all. Good for him. He had long disappeared down the road ahead by the time the bus reached the next town.

'Azay-le-Rideau,' the driver announced over his microphone. Fully awake now, I held my breath as the bus folded itself around the narrow, sharply twisting streets, pressing pedestrians back against stone walls or into the shelter of doorways. Down we went at a dizzying angle, disgorged a handful of passengers in front of a row of shops, and swept on over a bridge that offered an intriguing glimpse of a jewel-like château that seemed to have been built on water, a perfect island perfectly reflected in a pale quiescent lake.

Here at last, I thought happily, was the Loire Valley of the brochures and guide books – and the France that I remembered from my childhood. The town gave way to forest, and the forest fell in turn to field and vineyard. I sat forward in my seat, reading the passing signposts with interest, and then with eager recognition. *La Devinière* . . . surely that great block of a building was the birthplace of the writer Rabelais. I remembered reading about it in one of my brochures, somewhere. Which meant that Chinon itself must be just around that . . .

'Oh,' I said suddenly, and with rather more force than I'd intended.

The bus driver smiled at my reaction, understanding. He slowed his speed a little. 'It is your first visit to Chinon?' he guessed, in French.

I somehow managed a nod in reply, and the bus slowed still further.

'It should be savoured, then, this first approach,' he told me.

Savoured indeed. The yellow-white ruins of Chinon Castle rose majestically above us like the crumbling scene of some great Shakespearean tragedy, an unbroken sweep of blind wall and decaying towers bleached with age, jaggedly spearing the grey and ever-shifting sky.

Despite the bus driver's best efforts, I barely had time to register the image before the road tipped sharply downwards, hugging ancient walls hung thick with ivy as we dropped towards the level of the town. The castle hung high on the cliffs above us now, all but forgotten in my first view of the river Vienne and the wide avenue of towering plane trees that ran along the riverbank, marking the approach to the town centre. Nothing – neither Harry's descriptions nor my own faded memories of the French countryside – had prepared me for such a sudden, breathtaking explosion of sheer beauty.

'Oh,' I said again.

It was, I realised, an inadequate sort of comment to make, but the bus driver seemed quite pleased by it.

'It grabs, does it not? It grabs you here,' he said, making a fist with one hand over his heart, to illustrate.

I found my voice at last. 'Yes, it does.'

And it did. It grabbed me so completely, in fact, that when the driver announced: 'Place Jeanne d'Arc' and another handful of passengers filed off the bus, I scrambled off after them without thinking, bumping my suitcase down the steps. It was only after everyone had scattered purposefully that I realised I hadn't the faintest idea how to get to the Hotel de France.

I stood for a moment with the river to my back and the plane trees stretching off to either side, and looked for someone to direct me. The square across the street was, I presumed, the Place Jeanne d'Arc, a great broad crossroads filled with a confusing swirl of bodies and faces and the half-familiar sounds of speech and laughter. I'd just prepared myself to grab the nearest person when, quite by accident, I saw a face I recognised.

He had parked the Safrane in a no-parking zone beside the curb, and was leaning up against the bonnet as before, frowning slightly as he watched the milling crowd. I don't know what impulse it was that made me cross the street towards him – simple weariness, perhaps, or maybe just his handsome face. I caught him this time unawares.

'Is it also an expensive taxi ride,' I asked him, in English, 'to the Hotel de France?'

His head came round, startled, and the frown dissolved into a genuine smile. 'No,' he conceded. '*That* is not expensive. I will take you.' He pitched the stub of his cigarette into the street and levered himself away from the car, coming round to open the passenger side door for me. 'You have only the one suitcase?' he asked, taking it from my hand.

'Yes.'

There were already suitcases in the back seat of the taxi, the same expensive cases that I'd seen the round and red-faced man struggling with at St-Pierre-des-Corps.

'But you already have a fare, Monsieur,' I said, looking at the suitcases. 'I'm sorry, I didn't realise . . .'

'It is no problem,' he assured me. He shoved the costly luggage aside, unconcerned, to make room for my less impressive bag. 'The gentleman has business to attend to. I will return for him. He will not miss me; your hotel is not so far.'

It was, in truth, the shortest ride I'd ever taken in a taxi. A few moments along the river, back the way I'd just come, then up a narrow square wedged tight with plane trees to a still smaller square shaded by leaning acacias.

'The Hotel de France,' my driver announced, with a smile that was wholly understandable. I could probably have walked the same distance myself in less than five minutes, and for free. I looked at the metre on the dashboard, and his smile deepened. The metre was blank.

'There is no charge, Madame,' he told me.

'Of course there is.' I reached for my wallet. I didn't like to be in debt.

'But I insist. The taxi, it has hardly moved at all.'

'How much do I owe you?'

He looked at me a long moment, silently weighing my will against his, and then he tipped his head, considering. 'Ten francs.'

'A cup of coffee costs ten francs,' I reminded him.

'Fifteen francs, then.'

I handed him twenty-five, and he took it with a thoughtful glance at my face. 'I hope that you enjoy your stay in Chinon, Madame.'

I'd have no problem doing that, I thought a moment

later, as I looked around the quiet hotel lobby. For all my cousin's failings, he did have his brilliant moments, and he'd chosen the Hotel de France in one of them.

It was an older hotel, lovingly restored and decorated in rich classic tones of rose and cream, with an elegant hardwood staircase spiralling upwards from the entrance hall. To my left a few steps led up to the sunlit breakfast room, while on my right a door stood open to the bar. Both rooms were empty.

The young woman at the front desk was amiable and pretty, if a little dim. No, Monsieur Braden had not yet arrived, but our rooms were all prepared . . . two rooms . . . I was sure that we wanted two rooms? *Very* sure, I told her, and with a small, perplexed shrug she handed me the key. 'Your room is on the second floor, Madame. Room 215.'

And so my holiday begins, I thought drily, with Harry, as I'd half expected, nowhere to be seen. I could almost hear Aunt Jane's mild voice saying, *Didn't I tell you, dear?* as I climbed the two flights of curving stairs to the second floor.

My room, at least, was all that I'd been promised – bright and fresh-smelling, with a soaring, white-painted ceiling and walls papered in a soft, restful gold. And best of all I had a window, a huge casement window that looked out over the square and the clustered rooftops of the old medieval village.

Swinging one half of the window inward on its hinges, I leaned out as far as I dared and inspected my view. There was a fountain nestled among the acacia trees in the square below me. I hadn't noticed it on my arrival, but there it was, a large bronze fountain ringed by sculpted figures. Even above the confused noise of the street and square I could hear the steady dancing splash of water cascading from the two-tiered basin into the gathering pool below. The sound set off a rush of memory, and for a fleeting moment I was five years old again, my fingers trailing in another fountain while my father urged me, 'Make a wish . . .'

I pressed the memory firmly back, and focused. A man was sitting on the rim of the fountain's pool with a spotted dog sleeping at his feet, and beside them a flower-seller was starting to dismantle his display of drooping marigolds and roses. I was drooping a little myself. Another wave of weariness swept over me, and I pulled myself away from the open window, turning my wrist to see the time. Three o'clock, nearly. Fifteen hours, I corrected myself with a faint smile. Time all travellers were at rest.

It was sheer heaven to crawl between the sheets of the sprawling bed and draw the blanket to my chin. I was so completely and utterly exhausted that I would not have expected to dream. But I did dream, all the same. I dreamed that an angel was playing the violin outside my open window. It should have been a lovely dream, but it wasn't.

The angel wore my cousin's smiling face.

CHAPTER THREE

We were seven . . .

I awoke refreshed, completing my revival with a half-hour in my private bathroom. The small tiled room was thick with steam when I finally switched off the shower spray and emerged, my skin the colour of a boiled lobster above the plush white hotel towel. The steam followed me in a swirling great cloud as I dripped my way across the carpet and round the corner of the rumpled bed to push the window open wider.

I had only slept an hour or so, but it might have been a different day. The grey sky had broken to reveal a clear, unblemished field of blue, through which the sun blazed its determined way towards the west. Bright sunlight touched the feathered tops of the acacia trees in the square below and glittered in the pools of the fountain. In the place where earlier I'd seen the flower- seller, a weary trio of tourists now sipped demis of beer at a little white table with red plastic chairs, one of a dozen or more such tables that seemed to have sprouted from nowhere in the square.

I drew back again from the window, combing my fingers through my drying hair. The air was biting still, despite the sun – too cool, perhaps, for an outdoor table, but the idea of a drink appealed to me.

Downstairs, I found the hotel bar no longer empty. A handful of people were taking advantage of the invitingly intimate modern decor – sectioned seats and ottomans arranged round tables of pale laminate, the rich terracotta tones of the upholstery glowing against grey linen walls and charcoal carpet. Enormous plants and artwork softened the modular angles, and the late afternoon light poured slanting through the floor to ceiling windows facing out upon the fountain square.

The conversation dipped, paused, and began again when I walked in, and I found myself facing the not unfriendly stares of two young men who sat together by the nearest window. One of them, a black-haired lad with gentle eyes, smiled cautiously and greeted me in French.

'Would you care to join us?' he ventured. 'There's plenty of room.' At my hesitation his smile grew charming. 'We're quite well-behaved, I promise. It's only that we've been travelling together for four months, now, and we're tired of hearing each other talk. Please,' he urged me, indicating the vacant seat across from him. 'Let us buy you a drink.'

His companion sent me a vague but pleasant smile as I took the offered seat, reminding me a little of a chap I'd known at school – he, too, had worn tie-dyed shirts and let his hair grow straggling to his shoulders, and he'd carried with him something of the same distracted aura of a young man who has chosen to remain young, like the hippies of the sixties. The dark-haired lad, by contrast, was cleaner-cut, conservative, and better-schooled in manners. He raised his hand to get the bartender's attention. 'You're new at the hotel, aren't you?' he asked me. 'I haven't seen you before.'

I nodded, trying without success to place his accent. Not Provençal, I thought – it was lighter than that. Not Breton, either, but something decidedly rustic, rather loose about the vowel sounds . . .

'I've only just arrived,' I said, 'this afternoon. From England.'

He lowered his hand and grinned. 'You're English?' he said, in my own language. 'I should have known. Every time I try to start up a conversation with someone—'

'Good heavens,' I cut him off, astonished. 'You're American.'

The long-haired youth winced visibly. 'Canadian, actually,' he corrected me. It was the sort of stubborn, pained response that Hercule Poirot made in the detective books, when someone called him French instead of Belgian.

His friend forgave me my mistake. 'The accent sounds the same, I know.'

'The hell it does.' The hippie grinned. 'We don't sound like the Whitakers.'

'Well, true. But then, they're from the deep South, so that's hardly surprising.' The dark young man glanced over at the gleaming oak-topped bar, where a middle-aged couple sat in conversation with the young bartender.

Middle-aged, I decided upon closer examination, was

perhaps the wrong label for them. The woman would certainly have resisted it. She was quite pretty, in a brittle sort of way, with artfully arranged auburn curls and fluttering hands that glittered with rings. At first her husband looked much older, until one noticed that his silver hair was not matched by his tanned and vital face.

'I'm sure you'll meet them,' the long-haired youth assured me. 'Garland likes to keep up to date on new arrivals. She's kind of . . . well, kind of unique.'

'Her husband's really nice,' the dark one added. 'His name's Jim.' Which reminded him he hadn't yet introduced himself. 'I'm Paul, by the way. Paul Lazarus. And this is my brother Simon.'

'Emily Braden.' I shook hands with each of them in turn, relaxing back into the thick cushioned seat. Dark-haired Paul, I decided, was the younger of the two, despite appearances. I'd found that between siblings there was always a clear pattern of interaction, of deference and command, that set the first-born apart. Simon Lazarus might look the less mature but he was restless, more aggressive, and now that our conversation had switched to English he assumed the role of spokesman for both of them – assumed it with a natural ease born of long familiarity and habit.

He sent me a friendly grin. 'We're doing the Europe thing. Paul finished university last spring and neither one of us could find a job, so we decided to squander our savings instead. We're planning to go all the way around the world, if the money holds out. And if I can ever get Paul away from this place.' Simon grinned wider. 'I had a hard enough time dragging him out of Holland, and now here we are,' he told me, 'stuck again.'

Paul smiled and would have said something, but he wasn't given the chance. The bartender, having excused himself from the American couple, descended upon us in a whirl of youthful vigour.

Seen at close range, the bartender appeared even younger than I'd first suspected. He couldn't have been above twenty, but it was easy to see how I'd been deceived. Only in France, I thought, could a teenager look suave, even worldly. He would break a lot of hearts, this one. He probably had already.

I watched in open admiration as he exhaled the expressive 'pouf' of breath that was so undeniably French, muttered some brief comment about *les américains*, and winked conspiratorially at Paul Lazarus. 'What can I bring you?' he asked, in flowing English.

'Thierry will tell you,' Simon said positively, his accent anglicising the bartender's name so that it came out sounding like 'Terry'. 'Thierry, tell Miss . . .'

'Braden,' Paul supplied.

'Emily,' I said, over both of them.

'. . . tell Emily what the difference is between Canadians and Americans.'

The bartender looked down at me with a serious expression. 'The Canadians, Madame, are much more difficult,' he confided. 'They are impossible. This one,' he pointed at Simon, 'makes always the curtain in his room to fall down, and always I must get the ladder to replace it.'

'Twice,' Simon defended himself. 'I've only done it twice.

41

And it's your own fault for putting a curtain in front of that window to begin with. Windows like that are meant to be opened, to be enjoyed. I can't help it if your stupid curtain rod gets in the way.'

'You see?' Thierry winked again. 'Most difficult, these Canadians. But you, Madame, you are not Canadian?'

'Worse.' I smiled up at him. 'I'm English.'

'*Non!*' He clapped a hand to his heart in mock agony, but his eyes twinkled at me. 'You would like a *café au lait*, Madame? All the English, they enjoy the *café au lait*.'

Only, I thought, because that's what we learned to say at school. Until I'd lived in France I hadn't known there were so many different kinds of coffee, from thickly fragrant *café* on its own, to the decadent richness of *café crème*. I considered my options. 'Could I have a *crème* instead, please?'

'*Bien sûr,*' he said. 'With pleasure.'

'Thierry,' Simon informed me, as the bartender left to fire up the gleaming monster of a coffee machine sitting behind the bar, 'is the nephew of the proprietors, Madame and Monsieur Chamond. Have you met them yet? No? Well, don't worry, you will. They're terrific people, very easy to talk to. I'm surprised they're not in here now, they usually are. Anyhow, Thierry's their nephew. He's a bit of a drain on them, I think, but he's lots of fun. Just don't let him know you speak French,' was Simon's advice, 'or he'll talk your ear off. He kept Paul going for three hours our first afternoon here.'

'You don't speak French?' I guessed, and Simon shrugged.

'Just the basics. Hello . . . where's the bathroom . . . I

have a blue hat – that sort of thing. Paul's the expert. He spent a year in Switzerland, on a Rotary exchange.'

I assured Paul that he'd done his sponsors proud. 'You sounded terribly French, just now.'

He smiled. 'So did you.'

Thierry had returned with my *café crème*. He set it with a flourish on the table in front of me, sent me a thoroughly disarming smile, and swept off again to take the order from a clustered group of older tourists – Germans, from the snatches of their conversation I could overhear. It wasn't easy to hear things at a distance. The radio crooned steadily above our heads, not loudly but persistently, and Edith Piaf had just begun to sing 'La Vie En Rose' when my wandering gaze came to rest upon the solitary figure in the far corner.

Had I been drinking anything but coffee I'd have blamed it on the drink – that blinding moment of illumination that made time, for one long heartbeat, cease to be. It was as if my mind said, see now, *this* must be remembered . . . this single moment, with Piaf's voice rasping out the haunting lyrics and the clink of glasses fading to a far-off sound no louder than the trickle of a fountain.

Time blinked. The moment held. There was no reason for it, really – none at all. None, at least, that I was willing to admit. The world, I thought, was full of handsome men.

This one sat close against the tall French windows that opened to the street and fountain square. He looked German too, I thought, or maybe Swedish. His hair was so amazingly fair, the same whitish-gold colour that one sees sometimes on very young children, and where it brushed against the collar of his crisp white cotton shirt it seemed to blend into the fabric. His eyes looked oddly dark in contrast, though of course I couldn't tell their colour. He looked too handsome to be human, really, sitting there – like some youthful middle-aged pop star, narrow-hipped and long-limbed, his classic face unlined.

Simon Lazarus caught me staring. 'That's Neil,' he told me helpfully. 'He's English too, like you. He's a musician.'

I'm sure my face must have shown my reaction because Paul laughed, a short soft laugh of understanding. 'No, not *that* kind of musician,' he said. 'He's a violinist. Plays with a symphony orchestra, I think. You'll hear him practising if you're around the hotel in the afternoon.'

So this, I thought, was my mysterious angel with the violin. He certainly looked the part, with that face and his loose white shirt and the sun turning his hair to a halo of light.

'I think I heard him playing earlier,' I said, to Paul. 'I was half asleep at the time. I thought I'd dreamed the music.'

'He sounds like a recording when he practises,' Simon put in. 'He's that good. His room's right underneath ours, on the first floor, so we can hear him pretty clearly. Hang on, I'll introduce you.'

There wasn't time to voice a protest, he was already taking charge, turning his head to call across the bar, and a moment later I was being introduced. 'Neil Grantham,' Simon said, 'meet Emily . . .'

'Braden,' Paul supplied, for a second time.

'Braden,' Simon echoed. 'Emily, this is Neil.'

I had to look a long way up. He was older than I was, though I couldn't have placed his age with any certainty.

Thirty-five, perhaps? Forty? I watched his smile cut a cleft in one clean-shaven cheek, and crinkle the corners of his eyes. Black eyes. How odd, I thought. Like his hair, they seemed to glow with some strange inner radiance. I mumbled something banal and shook his outstretched hand.

'She heard you practising this afternoon,' Simon went on, conversationally.

'Did you really? I hope I didn't disturb you.'

I shook my head. 'It was lovely, actually. I like Beethoven.'

The crinkles round his eyes deepened, and he took the seat beside me. 'I'm flattered you could recognise it,' he said. 'You've just arrived?'

'This afternoon.'

'From England, I gather?'

'Yes.'

It was difficult to carry on small talk with a man who looked at you like that, I thought. This was not the sort of man that one could flirt with. Those eyes were far too level, far too serious, and because of that they made me feel uneasy. I smiled at him even as my own defences slammed down stoutly into place, and to my relief Neil Grantham didn't try to bridge the distance. He rubbed an absent hand along his outstretched thigh and shifted his gaze to a thick paperback novel sitting on the table next to Simon. I'd noticed it earlier myself, and smiled at the title: *Ulysses*. The sort of book, I thought, that young men like Simon Lazarus went in for – the sort of book that thumbed its nose at polite convention. Which is why I was surprised when Neil addressed his question, not to Simon, but to Paul. 'Haven't you finished that, yet?'

45

Paul smiled lazily, but it was once again big brother Simon who answered for him. 'Give him a chance.' Simon's grin was broad. 'He's only been reading it for two years.'

'Experiencing it,' said Paul. 'I'm experiencing it. You don't just read James Joyce, you know.'

Simon seemed ready to make some argumentative reply, but something he saw over my shoulder distracted him. 'Damn.' He glowered into his wine glass. 'Don't look now,' he muttered, 'but we're about to be invaded.'

It must be the couple from the bar, I thought – the couple from America. Either that, or Scarlett O'Hara herself had just snuck up behind my back. 'Hel-*lo*,' drawled the feminine voice at my shoulder. 'Is it all right if we join your little party? I was just saying to Jim how *tiring* it is to have to speak in French all the time. Boys, you don't mind, do you? Hello, Neil. I heard you playing this afternoon and I said to Jim it's just like being in Carnegie Hall – no, really, it *is*. Hello, I don't believe we've met. I'm Garland Whitaker.'

'Emily Braden.' I briefly clasped the ring-encrusted hand, feeling somewhat dizzy after that introductory speech. Jim Whitaker shook my hand firmly and sat down beside his wife, facing the window to the street. His solid, almost stoic figure made an intriguing contrast to his wife's gushing mannerisms. They were both in their mid-forties, I decided, although Garland fancied herself younger.

'The boys have picked you up, I see,' she said to me. 'You have to be careful with these two, you know. They look harmless, but they're really *not*. Oh, Paul,' she shifted in her seat, '*do* you think you could be a dear and make that Thierry understand that the heater in our room is just too hot for us? I tried to explain it to him, but I don't think he knew what I was saying and his English is really *so* awful . . .'

It hadn't sounded awful to me, but then the French did have a mischievous tendency not to speak well when it suited them. I'd watched many a Parisian waiter play the game with unsuspecting tourists, particularly tourists who were difficult to deal with. Garland Whitaker, I thought, might just qualify for that distinction.

Her husband, on the other hand, appeared to be a different sort of person entirely. He had kind eyes. 'Thierry speaks English perfectly well,' Jim Whitaker informed his wife in a calm voice. 'If you'd stop talking to him like he was a two-year-old with a hearing problem, you'd find that out.'

Garland Whitaker ignored the rebuke and smiled brightly at all of us. 'Jim's mother was French, you know. Or so he says.' She cast a teasing eye upon her husband. 'I never met your parents, darling, so I have to take your word. But really,' she told Paul, 'Jim can only speak a little French, and you get along so well with Thierry, I'm *sure* you'd have no problem . . .'

'I'll see what I can do,' Paul promised.

'Oh, wonderful. Now, listen,' she continued, leaning forward in her seat, 'while everyone's here . . . I'm thinking we should all take Christian out to dinner tonight. You know, a sort of going away party.'

Paul looked surprised. 'Christian's going away?'

Neil Grantham smiled, and answered, 'Not exactly. He's moving out of the hotel, though, into a house.'

'The house *her* husband used to live in.' Garland flashed a gossip's eyes. 'Can you believe it? Apparently she owns it, though she hasn't lived in it herself for ages. She let *him* use it, instead.'

I didn't know who 'him' was – 'her' husband, obviously, but that hardly helped. Still, I didn't think it polite to ask.

'I suppose it will be nice for Christian, having a whole house to himself,' Garland went on. 'Mind you, I wouldn't want to live where somebody had *died* . . . can you imagine how awful? And in a sense it's kind of tasteless, don't you think, for Martine to even offer? Out with the old, in with the new. I mean, her husband isn't even buried . . .'

'Ex-husband,' Simon cut her off abruptly. 'He was Martine's ex-husband.'

Paul finally looked across and noticed I was all at sea. 'A woman that we know,' he told me, quietly. 'Her ex-husband killed himself night before last, by accident. He tripped and fell down the stairs.'

'Not down the stairs,' Simon made the correction in authoritative tones. 'Over the bannister. Broke his neck.'

'Ah,' I said.

Garland Whitaker smiled slyly. 'Maybe it wasn't an accident. Maybe Christian did it, just to make sure . . .' She broke off suddenly and twisted round in her seat as the hotel's front door slammed. 'Why Christian, darling, we'd almost given up on you! Come on in and join the gang.'

I had the distinct impression that the man hovering in the open doorway would have preferred to face a firing squad.

He appeared to be around my own age – a lanky, soft-eyed man with rough blonde hair that looked as if he'd cut it himself with a pair of garden shears and a beard that seemed more the result of simply forgetting to shave than of any concerted effort to grow one. His clothes, too, were rather rumpled and oddly matched, his denim jeans stained with small splotches of bright colour.

'I must go and change my clothes,' he excused himself self-consciously. His voice was quiet, edged with a German accent that kept it from being soft. 'I have missed the bus connection back from Saumur, and it has made me late.'

'You will join us for dinner, though?' Garland Whitaker pressed him, then turned her smile on all of us. 'We are going for dinner, aren't we? To give Christian a proper send-off?'

It wasn't so much an invitation as a stage direction, I thought. The man named Christian wavered a moment longer in the doorway, then gave in like the rest of us.

'Of course,' he said politely, and faded into the hallway. The heavy clump of his shoes on the stairs had a faintly defeatist sound.

Simon slouched back in his seat, scowling blackly, and opened his mouth to say something. I didn't actually see Paul's elbow move, but I did see Simon jump a little in his seat, and whatever he had meant to say he kept it to himself. Garland Whitaker, triumphant, turned her attention back to the rest of us, and started talking about some day trip she and her husband had taken, or were planning to take . . . I'll admit I didn't really listen.

She just went on talking anyway, red curls bobbing with the motions of her head, that honeyed Southern voice giving way to grating trills of laughter. Like Simon, I was not impressed. I felt the frown forming on my own face, and could have used Paul's elbow in my own ribs to remind me of my manners. Instead, some instinct made me glance upwards, at the face of the man sitting beside me.

The look Neil Grantham slanted back at me was privately amused.

But he wasn't smiling, and he didn't say anything to me. So there really was no reason why I should have looked away as quickly as I did, face flaming, like some prudish Victorian spinster. Or why I should have felt, all of a sudden, a ridiculous urge to run.

CHAPTER FOUR

. . . let the past be past; let be . . .

The restaurant was packed to the rafters with the Friday night supper crowd, but I didn't mind waiting for a table. It was a cosy sort of restaurant – small and warm, filled with glorious smells and furnished with a tasteful eye for detail. Besides, I thought, one had to like the name: *Le Coeur de Lion*. In honour of Richard the Lionheart, I presumed. Plantagenets again. Harry, when he stayed in Chinon, probably ate here every night.

While the seven of us waited, packed like sardines by the door, I introduced myself to the shy young German. His name was Christian Rand, he told me, above a firm but fleeting handshake.

'Christian's an artist,' said Simon, who had dressed up a bit for dinner, topping his T-shirt with a thick black jumper and smoothing back his hair into a sailor's pigtail. 'He's not a tourist, not like us. He's lived in Chinon for . . . how long, Christian? Five years?'

'Six.'

'Really?' I looked at Christian Rand with interest. 'At the Hotel de France?' I'd read of all those great composers, poets, writers, who had lived in hotel rooms, of course, but I'd never actually met someone who . . .

'No.' He shook his tousled head and smiled. 'For these past two months only. I had until July a small house, not too far from Chinon, but my neighbours they were not so good. And so my friends the Chamonds said that I could stay at their hotel while I am looking for another house.'

It was the longest speech I'd heard him make, and the effort appeared to leave him exhausted.

'And now you've found one,' Garland piped up, her tone bright.

'Yes.' Christian looked down silently. He wasn't as slow as he looked, I thought. He knew quite well that Garland Whitaker was dying to draw him into conversation, to learn as much as she could about his dealings with this Martine woman, whoever she was. But Christian Rand was not prepared to play.

The waiter finally managed to find us a table tucked well away from the other patrons, where we wouldn't disturb the quieter, more reticent French at their evening meal.

Garland Whitaker perused the menu with an expression of vague distrust. 'Maybe a pizza,' she decided. 'Though they're not *real* pizzas here, you know. Not like we get back home. Jim ordered a pizza here a couple of nights ago and when it came to the table it had an *egg* in the middle of it. Can you imagine? A runny egg. I tell you, I nearly *died . . .*'

52

'Sounds kind of good, actually,' Simon mused, leaning forward. 'Which one was that, Jim?'

Garland was mortified. 'Oh, Simon, *don't*. If there's anything I can't stand, it's the sight of a runny egg.' She looked away, missing Simon's smirk, and turned enquiring eyes on Christian Rand. 'You'll be moving into your new house tomorrow, I take it?'

'Yes.'

Garland turned to Neil and smiled sweetly. 'Then I guess you'll be our only artist left in residence, darling.'

I'd been trying, since we left the hotel, not to notice Neil at all. For reasons I chose not to explore, I found it easier to talk to Simon or to Paul – or even to the taciturn Christian – than to meet those quietly intense dark eyes. But I couldn't keep it up for ever, especially not since he'd taken the chair directly opposite mine. I glanced up, in time to see him shrug off Garland's comment with a small, indulgent smile. 'I'm hardly in Christian's league.'

'Nonsense,' Simon said. 'You had Paul reciting poetry today, in the stairwell.'

Neil's eyebrows lifted. 'Poetry?'

'Yeah. In French, of course, so I didn't understand it. What was it you said, Paul?'

Paul lifted his head, looking faintly embarrassed, and shrugged. 'Just a quotation I remembered. Not poetry. Just something George Sand wrote in her diary about Liszt.'

'What was it?' I asked him, curious myself now. He sent me such a look as Caesar must have given Brutus, and repeated the quotation out loud. It was a lovely phrase, almost lyrical in its sentiment, and it told me rather more about the boy

53

Paul Lazarus than it did about Neil's violin playing.

'Are you going to share it with the rest of us?' Garland Whitaker prompted, a trifle impatiently.

It was only when I looked up, into Neil Grantham's blank expectant face, that I suddenly realised Paul and I must be the only ones who understood the French language on that level.

'Sorry,' I apologised. 'It means: "My griefs are etherealised, and my instincts are . . ."' I faltered, and looked to Paul. 'How would you translate that last word?'

'Exalted?'

'That's it.' I nodded. '"My instincts are exalted."'

'How pretty.' Garland eased back in her chair, satisfied.

'Indeed.' Neil looked sideways at Paul. 'Thank you.'

Paul shrugged again. 'It's what I felt, that's all.'

'Well, it's no small praise, that, for a musician. I can't say as I've ever etherealised anybody's grief before.'

'Do you practise every day?' I asked Neil.

'Every day. Not as much as I ought to, of course, but as much as I'm able.'

'Neil's not really on vacation,' put in Garland. 'He's recuperating. He broke his hand.'

'Tell her how,' Simon dared him.

Neil grinned. 'Stupidity. I let myself get dragged into a fist fight, in some bar in Munich.' He held his left hand up to show me. It was a nice hand, square and long-fingered, neatly kept. 'It's getting better, but I can't do all my fingering properly yet. So my employers kindly gave me some time off. On the condition,' he added, 'that I don't enjoy myself too much.'

54

'And is this your first trip to Chinon?' I asked him.

He shook his head. 'No. This would be my eighth visit, I think – maybe even my ninth. It's an addiction, really, Chinon is. You'll understand, if you stay long enough.'

Beside me, Simon nodded. 'Monsieur Chamond says once you've been to Chinon, you're hooked for life. He says you'll keep on coming back.'

'He sounds like a wise man,' I said. 'I haven't met him yet.'

'I'm sure you'll meet them eventually,' Jim Whitaker assured me. 'They're nice people, both of them.'

'*They* speak English,' Garland said. 'Not like that nephew of theirs. Honestly, you'd think with all the tourists they get around here, more people would take the time to learn English. It's so *frustrating*, trying to communicate.'

At the far end of the table, Paul smiled gently. 'I'm sure the French feel the same way,' he said, 'when they visit America.'

Our waiter seemed to understand us well enough. He took Paul's order first, then Neil's, then waited while Garland tried to choose a wine and Simon tried to learn which pizza had the egg on it. I settled on a galette for myself – a buckwheat crêpe filled with cheese and mushrooms – washed down with a half bottle of sweet cider.

The food, when it arrived, was excellent, and yet the meal itself was slightly off. I tried, and failed, to put my finger on the cause. The atmosphere around our table was, at its surface, entirely normal for a group of people who'd just met on holiday – a little forced, perhaps, but normal. And yet, I thought, there was a tension here . . . a tension spun from more than my awareness of the man across the table. One couldn't shake away the sense that something deeper flowed beneath the smiles and salt-passing, some darker conflict hinted at but never quite revealed. It made me feel excluded.

I ate my meal in silence, for the most part, and let the others talk. In time the conversation dwindled to a kind of battle between Simon and Garland Whitaker, both of whom seemed fully capable of carrying the standard single-handed. Garland proved the more experienced combatant, and more often than not her voice came out on top.

She had remarkable stamina, I had to admit. The table conversation had exhausted several topics, and still she showed no sign of wearing down. Her husband, though, I noticed, had stopped listening. He went on eating quietly, his gaze occasionally focusing with mild interest on someone or something at another table – a laughing child, an old man eating alone, a frilly woman slipping titbits to a poodle underneath her chair . . . But he'd tuned his wife's voice out completely. It was, I assumed, a defence mechanism he'd acquired over the years.

Garland chattered on about the château that they'd visited that morning. 'We stay in one place,' she said to me, 'and take our day trips out from there. So much easier than jumping from place to place, don't you think? And I can actually unpack my clothes, which is a blessing. This time we're doing all the Loire châteaux. We always like to have a theme for our vacations, don't we, Jim? Always. We did the D-day beaches on our honeymoon.'

'How romantic,' muttered Simon. He tore a piece of

bread in half to mop up what remained of his runny egg, and looked towards Jim Whitaker. 'Were you in the Army, during the war?'

It was the first real smile I'd seen from the American. He looked rather nice, when he smiled. 'I'm not that old, son,' he said. 'I wasn't even born until after the war ended.'

'Oh,' said Simon. 'Sorry.'

Garland laughed her tinkling laugh. 'Your father fought in France, though, didn't he?' she asked her husband. 'That's how he met your mother.'

'Yes.'

'And Jim was in the Army, Simon, when I married him. We lived in Germany for two whole years.' She shuddered. 'God, that awful little apartment, darling, do you remember it? But then I guess it was just fine, for Germans.'

Christian flicked a brief look down the table, but made no comment. It was Neil who asked the Whitakers just where in Germany they'd lived, and nodded when they told him. 'I do know it,' he said, smiling. 'There's a wonderful music festival not far from there, every June. Lovely place.'

'I hated it,' said Garland with a shrug. 'The people were so unfriendly. Nazis, probably, most of them.'

Her husband pushed his empty plate away and smiled at her with patience. 'Now come on, honey, you know they weren't.'

'Darling, it's *true*. Don't you remember all those little holes someone kept digging, all over town? Mrs Jurgen's dog fell into one, and the police got suspicious? Well, *that* was Nazis, the police proved it.' To the rest of us she explained: 'There'd been money hidden there, or something,

57

at the end of the war, and these people were coming back to find it thirty years later. Incredible. And then there was the time . . .'

She was still going, like a wind-up doll on overload, when we finally paid the bill and rose and wound our way through the labyrinth of tables to the front door.

It was heavenly to breathe the outside air. The restaurant fronted on the long and narrow Place du Général de Gaulle, and against the dark green trees the streetlamps glowed a softly spreading yellow. Further up the square the fountain gurgled merrily, and I saw the sign of the Hotel de France illuminated through the shifting leaves.

Christian apparently saw it too. He mumbled some faint words of thanks for dinner, and wandered off towards the beckoning lights. A moment later Neil Grantham followed suit. He had a long unhurried stride, and watching him I felt again that strange unbidden twinge of interest. I pushed it back, and tried to hold my thoughts to what was going on around me.

Simon and Garland had switched from Nazis now to neo-Nazis, and the rising tide of tension in Europe. 'It's all the immigration,' Garland was saying. She tossed her auburn head. 'It's the same everywhere, I think, all these foreigners moving in and taking over. It's like the Jews all over again, isn't it? I mean, you can't *condone* what the Nazis did, don't get me wrong, but you can almost understand it. These immigrants can get so uppity . . .'

It was an ugly thing to say. I stared at her, and Jim burst out: 'God, Garland, *honestly* . . . !' and then to my delight Simon recovered from his own stunned silence with a vengeance and began to give her proper hell. In the midst of all this Paul turned placidly to me and smiled. 'Feel like taking a walk?' he asked.

'Sure.'

I don't think anybody even noticed us leaving. Paul turned towards the river, away from the hotel, and I ambled along beside him, content to let him set the pace.

We walked past a statue that I recognised from my travel brochures – a seated figure of the great humanist Rabelais, once a traveller and a lover of life, now confined to one small patch of garden at the end of the Place du Général de Gaulle. Bathed by floodlights, the seated scholar seemed immense, brooding in gloomy silence as the river murmured on behind him.

Paul sauntered across the road and round the far side of the statue, where a narrow breach in the river wall revealed a long fall of sloping stone stairs that vanished into the dark water below. On the seventh stair down, he sat and waited for me.

'I lied,' he confessed, with a sheepish smile. 'I didn't really feel like a walk. I felt like a cigarette.' He shook one loose and offered the pack to me, but I declined, watching his face in the brief flare of the match.

'I didn't know you smoked,' I said.

'Only when Simon's not around. He's got opinions on all kinds of things, and smoking's one of them. I try to avoid arguments when I can. In case you hadn't noticed.' He grinned suddenly, and I knew that he was thinking not of his brother but of Garland Whitaker, and the little scene we'd just escaped from.

I envied him his self-control, and told him so. 'I'm afraid she makes me lose my temper.'

'Bad luck to lose your temper on the Sabbath – that's what my mother always tells me.'

'I'm safe, then. It's only Friday.'.

'After sundown on Friday.' He smiled. 'My Sabbath.'

It took me a moment to digest that. 'You're Jewish?'

He shrugged, still smiling. 'With a name like Lazarus I'd better be.'

To be truthful, I hadn't noticed his surname at all. But then, I fancied myself a different sort of person than Garland Whitaker. I thought again of what she'd said, of how she'd said it . . . 'She really is a hateful woman.'

'No she isn't. Not really. She just gets a little bit much sometimes, that's all.' His eyes touched mine briefly, warmly, then drifted away again, out across the wide expanse of river to the shadowed line of trees that rimmed the opposite shore. 'She doesn't mean anything by it. It's simple ignorance with her, not spite.'

I wasn't convinced. 'Sure about that, are you?'

'Pretty sure. Besides, you get used to it, after a while.' He paused, drawing deeply on the cigarette, still gazing out over the swiftly flowing water. 'You see those trees over there? That's not the other side of the river, it's an island. You can't tell, really, unless you see it from the cliffs, or walk across the bridge, there.' His voice was soft and even, storytelling. 'They burned the Jews of Chinon on that island in the fourteenth century. Accused them of poisoning the town's wells. It didn't just happen here, of course, it happened everywhere. Women, children, no one cared.

They just burned them.' He glanced at me and half smiled in the darkness. 'The Nazis weren't the first, you know. It's been around for ever, prejudice.'

'That's hardly an excuse for it.'

'No,' he agreed, exhaling a stream of smoke that caught the shifting light from the street behind us. 'But sometimes taking the historical perspective helps you understand a little better why people do the things they do. That's what life's all about, I think – understanding each other. Now Simon,' he told me, his mouth curving, 'sees things differently. If someone spits at Simon, he spits right back. An eye for an eye. But that doesn't accomplish anything.' He turned his head to look at me. 'People hate too much, you know?'

His face, in that instant, seemed suddenly older than my own. Centuries older. And then he laughed and looked away, and the moment passed.

'God,' he said, 'I sound like my father.' He pitched the stub of his cigarette away, and it died with a hiss in the dark water. 'Come on, I'll take you for a real walk, across the bridge. You get a great view of the château from over there.'

He rose, the boy again, and led the way. The bridge was an impressive one, a gentle arc of pavement raised on heavy piles sunk deep into the river Vienne, and the river seemed to be doing its level best to wear away the unwanted obstacle. From the arched openings beneath us the roar of the rushing water rose fiercely to our ears.

I saw what Paul had meant about the island. It was a small island, to be sure, little more than a wedge of trees and scattered houses stuck oddly in the middle of the broad river, like the lone oaks one sometimes sees stranded in the ploughed stretches of a farmer's field. It looked quite peaceful, really, pastoral, as if its murderous past had never been. And yet, and yet . . .

'There,' Paul announced proudly, 'now turn around and look at *that*.'

It was spectacular, as he had promised. The soaring walls of Chinon Castle rose in floodlights from the cliffs, its long majestic outline standing sentry over the huddle of ancient houses below. In the river at our feet, the blinding image was reflected clearly, with scarcely a tremor to disturb its still perfection.

'Beautiful, isn't it?' Paul asked me.

I nodded dumbly, gazing up at the pale outline of the tower that marked the furthest jutting corner of the castle walls. The Moulin Tower. Isabelle's tower. Again I saw the shadow moving softly past the window, but before the shadow formed a shape, a wind arose and rippled down the river, and the bits of bright reflection broke and scattered on a rolling surge of darkness.

CHAPTER FIVE

'Come out,' he said . . .

The telephone was ringing as I stepped from the shower early next morning. Still dripping, I grabbed a towel and made a lunge for the receiver.

'Hello?'

The line crackled unhelpfully for a few seconds, and then a deep familiar voice came booming down the line. 'Emily? Is that you?'

'Daddy?'

It would have been difficult, at that moment, to judge which one of us was more surprised to hear the other.

'What the devil are you doing in France?' demanded my father. 'You ought to be in Essex.'

'I'm on holiday,' I told him.

'What?'

'Holiday,' I said, raising my voice above the static of

the transatlantic line. 'In Chinon.' I frowned. 'How did you get my number?'

'Didn't know it was your number, did I? They must not have heard me clearly at the front desk, I suppose . . . put me through to the wrong room.'

My frown deepened. 'What are you talking about?'

'I was trying to reach Harry.'

'Harry?' My voice was swallowed by a sudden burst of static that didn't quite disguise my father's sharp oath.

'Blast these telephone lines,' he said. 'We can put a man on the moon, but we can't *talk* to him, there's the tragedy. Can you hear me now? I was saying,' he went on, speaking more distinctly, 'that I was trying to reach Harry. Trying to return his call, rather.'

'Harry telephoned you?' I repeated, stupidly.

'Apparently. He left a message on the machine.'

'When was this?'

'I've no idea, love. Yesterday, I suppose, or perhaps the day before. I've been in Buenos Aires for a few days, on business.'

'What, golfing with Carlos again, you mean?'

'Carlos *is* business, my girl, so don't you go sounding all superior,' my father set me straight. 'Anyhow, I've not rung to talk to you, now have I? So fetch me Harry, will you? Put him on the phone.'

'He isn't here.'

'He's not out in the ruins at this hour, surely? It can't be breakfast time there, yet.'

'Half six,' I told him. 'And he really isn't here. He was supposed to meet me yesterday, but he hasn't turned up yet.'

'Hasn't turned up?' My father feigned surprise. 'Our Harry? Now, there's an item for the evening news.' His voice was dry. 'We are talking about my nephew, aren't we? The same boy who kept you waiting seven hours at the airport because he wanted to see where a footpath went?'

I smiled. 'Yes.'

'The same boy,' my father went on, 'who was supposed to meet you at the festival in Edinburgh, that one year?'

'The very same.' I'd gone to Edinburgh, as it happened. Harry had made it as far as Epping, where he'd met up with an old girlfriend . . . but that was, in itself, another story.

'Well,' said my father, 'when he does turn up, tell him I'm waiting with bated breath to find out why he rang.'

'I will.'

'Mind you, he didn't sound too urgent in his message. He's probably forgotten all about it, now. Gone off on the trail of King John's coat buttons, or some such other nonsense.'

I smiled. 'That reminds me . . . wherever did you find that coin for him? That King John coin?'

My father coughed, pretending not to hear me, and asked a question of his own: 'What *are* you doing there on holiday? You haven't gone on holiday in years.'

'It was Harry's idea. He thought it would do me good to get away.'

'Well,' said my father, faintly pleased, 'he might be right at that. The village life's no good for you, you know – not healthy, stuck down there away from everything.'

I could have reminded him that he had turned out healthy enough, having grown up in that same village, and that I'd only gone there in the first place because he'd asked me to mind the house for him, but I wasn't given time to answer back.

'Must go now, my dear. Enjoy your trip.'

'Daddy . . .' I said, but the line had already crackled and gone dead. With a sigh, I set the receiver back in place. Honestly, I thought, they were all the same, the men of my family. Cut from the same cloth.

I shrugged my arms into my dressing gown and yanked my window open to let out the steam from my shower. Leaning out across the sill, I drew a deep breath of the morning air, drinking in the peaceful scenery.

I couldn't see the castle from my room – that view was blocked by another building squared against the hotel wall, its windows tightly shuttered still against the morning sun. But if I leaned a little further out and looked off to my left, across the tops of the trees that filled the square, I could just see the river, shining silver, beyond the head of the Rabelais statue.

Somewhere close by a bell was counting out the hours. Seven times the bell rang out, then silence. I was straining further across the sill, trying to get a better view, when the silence was abruptly shattered by a reverberating crash from the room next door. The window just beside mine on the left had opened inwards, and after a long moment's pause I heard a burst of helpless laughter followed by a cheerful curse that floated out into the clear morning air.

I must have made some sound myself, because Paul's dark head came round the painted window frame, his expression apologetic.

'Sorry,' he said, in a hushed voice. 'Simon's knocked the curtain off again. Did we wake you up?'

I shook my head. 'I was awake already.'

Simon's head joined Paul's at the window. 'Some crash, eh? I swear Thierry hangs the thing low on purpose, just to make life difficult for me. Don't you have any problem opening yours?'

'No.' I glanced upwards at my own curtain rod, which hung a good inch clear of the top of the frame.

'I told you,' said Simon to Paul, his chin defiant. 'It's only us. He does it on purpose.'

Paul shrugged and grinned. 'Yeah, well, you're on your own this time. You can tell him yourself.'

'I don't know the word for curtain,' Simon hedged, a little hopefully, but Paul stood firm.

'So go look it up in the dictionary. It's the only way you'll learn the language.'

After a final glance at his brother's face, Simon withdrew from the window, and Paul turned back to face me, still grinning.

'Beautiful day,' he commented. 'You must have brought the sunshine with you; we've had nothing but rain for three days.'

It was beautiful, I conceded. The shadows hung sharp and clear on the turreted houses and tightly clustered rooftops of the medieval town centre, and the pale stone walls gleamed brightly above the tufted green tops of the acacia trees. Two cars swung round the square below us, but the noise of traffic was muffled in the distance and the cheerful gurgle of the fountain carried over everything.

A second bell began to chime, quite near and rich and ringing, and I looked at Paul in some surprise.

'I thought the bell just went,' I said.

'There are two bells. I've been trying to figure out exactly where the second one is – it's either at the Church of St Maurice, just up the rue Voltaire, or it's at the City Hall, which is that big building over there.' He pointed out the large square building to our left, at the spot where the fountain square narrowed into the Place du Général de Gaulle. 'I can't quite make it out. But the first bell, the one you heard a few minutes ago, that's up at the château.' He used the proper French word for the castle. 'Which reminds me,' he went on. 'Do you have any plans for this morning? Because Simon and I are going up to the château to putter around for an hour or so, and we thought if you didn't have anything else to do . . .'

Well, I certainly wasn't going to waste my first full day in Chinon hanging about the hotel in the hope that Harry would show up. He'd be here soon enough, I thought drily, and in the meantime there was no law that prevented me from touring on my own. 'I'd love to come,' I told Paul. 'Thanks.'

'Terrific. It's really something to see, and you shouldn't waste this sunshine. The weather here can be kind of unpredictable.'

We both heard the stern knock from the corridor.

'That'll be Thierry,' Paul said, with a wink. 'He'll be irritated.'

'Wouldn't it be simpler to just leave the curtain off, instead of always hanging it back up again?'

'Oh, sure.' He shrugged. 'But it's sort of a game for them, I think, and Simon considers it a personal challenge. Simon,' Paul told me in a positive tone, 'loves a challenge.'

Which was, I learned as we set out after breakfast, quite a thorough summing up of Simon's character.

He took charge of our impromptu tour party the moment we passed through the front doors of the hotel and stepped onto the pavement. 'OK,' he began firmly, 'since this is Emily's first real day in Chinon, I think we should take her down the rue Voltaire first, and then up to the château from there. It's a lot easier than going straight up those steps, anyway.'

He meant the broad, inviting flight of cobbled steps that cut between the buildings to our right, in a direct line with the fountain. The steps themselves didn't appear to be particularly steep, but it looked a long way up. I could just see the small cluster of yellow-white houses peering over the edge of the cliff that rimmed the town.

'What is this stone, do you know?' I asked my self-appointed guides. 'All the buildings here seem to be made of it.'

Simon proudly supplied the answer. 'It's tufa-stone. *Tuffeau* in French. It's the same stone they used to build Westminster Abbey, as a matter of fact.'

'He's been reading the guide books,' Paul explained. 'It's just a porous limestone, really. That's what the cliffs round here are made of.'

Tufa-stone. I filed the name away in my memory. On some of the buildings it almost looked like marble, hard and smooth and faintly reflective, cut in enormous blocks

69

that had been fitted so expertly one could hardly spot the seams. Coupled with the slate-blue pointed roofs, it gave the town a certain unity of colour and style that lovingly embraced the eye. Most of the shutters were open, now – painted metal shutters stained with rust, and older wooden ones, unpainted, that hung unevenly on their hinges, fastened back against the walls of their respective houses by ancient iron latches. I could understand why Simon found his curtain rod such a nuisance. French windows begged to be flung wide – it seemed a crime somehow to keep them closed.

The rue Voltaire led off the square as well, a narrow cobbled street that cut a line between the cliffs and the river. It was a lovely street, tastefully restored and rich in atmosphere, but I only caught the briefest glimpses of its tight-packed houses as Simon drove us past them at a breathless pace.

'And here,' he said, coming to a full and sudden stop where a narrow street angled across the rue Voltaire, 'is the Great Crossroads. Well, it was a lot greater in the old days, I guess. This,' he told me, pointing up the smaller sloping street, 'was how people used to get to the château back then. And that well over there, against the wall, is where Joan of Arc got off her horse when she came to Chinon to see the Dauphin.'

'Ah.' I smiled. It wasn't that I didn't like Joan of Arc – I had in fact been fascinated by her in my younger days, but having lived in France I'd gorged myself on Joan of Arc relics and Joan of Arc books and Joan of Arc historic sites until, in the end, it had produced the same effect as had the one too many Rusty Nails I'd drunk the night of my twenty-first birthday. All these years later, I couldn't face a Rusty Nail without a shudder.

Still, so as not to ruin Simon's tour I dutifully inspected the well and made the proper noises. Satisfied, he turned to lead the way up the tilting little street. 'We go up here. Just watch your step, it's pretty rough.'

And pretty steep, in spite of the fact that the road bent back upon itself several times in an attempt to soften the grade of the ascent. Halfway up I stumbled on the jutting cobblestones and paused to catch my breath.

'Small wonder Joan of Arc got off her horse,' I said, between gulps of air. 'No self-respecting horse would want to make this climb.'

Paul laughed and moved steadily past me. 'You get used to it.'

I wasn't so sure. 'Is this really easier than going up the steps?'

'Yes,' both boys averred, in unison.

Simon grinned, and pushed the hair back from his face. 'Neil goes up and down those steps a few times a day,' he informed me, 'for exercise. He says musicians need to keep in shape.'

'Bully for Neil,' I muttered, and forced my wobbling legs to push onwards. Just when I thought they couldn't possibly carry me any further, we cleared the final corner and found ourselves gazing out across the rooftops to the gently snaking river. It was a breathless view. The gardens of the closer houses had been terraced upwards to the level of the cliffs, a chequerboard of trees and flowers hemmed

71

by ivied walls turned crimson in the autumn air.

A final slope, five paces more, and out we stepped onto a modern road that ran along the level of the cliff. Facing us, a cracked and crumbling wall rose starkly up one level more, its sheer bulk draped with clinging clumps of ivy broken here and there by leaning doors that marked the entrance to some long-abandoned dwelling.

'There's the château,' said Simon, pointing.

'Give us a chance,' I pleaded, slumping back against the wall. 'Wait till my vision clears.'

Simon wasn't listening – he was already several steps ahead, walking with a brisk and purposeful step, but Paul hung back to wait for me. 'Not far now,' he promised. 'We're almost there.'

I glanced after Simon, noticing not the soaring narrow tower that served as gateway to the château, but the alarming slope of the black asphalt road ahead. 'More climbing?' I asked, weakly.

Paul laughed again. 'I thought you Brits were used to hills.'

'Yes, well,' I excused myself, 'I'm from the flat part.'

Simon finally noticed we weren't keeping up. Frowning, he turned and called, 'Come on, you two.'

Paul shot me a rather paternal glance. 'You ready?'

'Have I a choice?'

The final approach wasn't all that bad, as it turned out, mainly because my attention was focused on the strange tower ahead of us. The *Tour de I'Horloge,* Paul told me when I asked him – the Clock Tower. It was tall and curiously flat, like a cardboard cut-out of a tower, with a blue slate roof and wooden belfry. The bell that chimed the hours, I thought, must hang within this tower.

A stone bridge spanned the grassy moat that once had barred invaders from the tower's high arched entrance gate. Today, the wooden doors stood open wide, inviting us to leave the road and cross the narrow footbridge to where Simon waited by the postcards, impatient.

'They do have guided tours,' Paul said, as we paused at the entrance to pay, 'but Simon and I usually just wander around on our own. It's up to you, though, if you'd rather take a tour . . .'

'I hate guided tours,' I assured them, 'thanks all the same. Much more fun to wander.'

And wander we did. I'd always liked castles. I'd expected this one to be little more than a ruin, but many of the rooms and towers had been preserved intact within the shattered walls. One could almost hear the footsteps of brave knights and ladies, kings and courtiers, echoing round the empty rooms. The white stone, bathed in light from mullioned windows, lent a bright and airy feel to the sprawling royal apartments and made them look much larger than they were. From every corner twisting stairs led up to unexpected rooms with hearths and windows of their own, small private sanctuaries where a queen could comfortably retire to do her needlework or dally with her lover . . . at least, I thought, until the king found out, and had the lover killed.

In the next tower on, Simon pointed to a large framed painting of the château, just like the view Paul had shown me from the bridge. 'That's one of Christian's paintings. Pretty good, eh?'

'It's marvellous.' I leaned closer, amazed. 'Christian did this, really?' It was a bold and sweeping painting in the true romantic style, and he had caught exactly the unusual pale colour of the tufa-stone gleaming bright against a stormy violet sky.

'He's incredibly talented,' Paul said, beside my shoulder.

'So I see.' With a vague prickling feeling of being watched, I slid my gaze from the painting to the figure looming in a shadowed recess of the tower wall. Not a real person, thank heavens – just a statue, and a massive one at that. 'Good heavens,' I said. 'It's Philippe.'

Paul looked up as well, at the young heroic face. 'Who?'

'Philippe Auguste. One of the early kings of France. He was the first real French king to own this château, actually,' I went on, recalling Harry's countless lectures.

Simon frowned. 'Who owned it before?'

'The counts of Blois and Anjou, I believe. And then the Plantagenets.'

'What, like the Black Prince, you mean?'

I smiled. 'A little earlier than that. Richard the Lionheart and that bunch. Richard's brother John was the last to own Chinon.'

'As in Robin Hood?' Simon checked, his eyebrows lifting. 'Bad Prince John? That guy?'

'The very same.'

'Neat.'

Paul looked at me with quiet interest. 'You know a lot about the history of this place, then?'

My smile grew wider. 'Rather. I'm lectured on it constantly. My cousin,' I explained, to both of them, 'is something of an expert on Plantagenets. It's his fault, really, that I'm here at all – he talked me into coming on holiday with him.'

The brothers exchanged glances. 'But he isn't here,' said Simon, pointing out the obvious.

'Not yet, no. But then, that's not unusual for Harry. He does race off on tangents when he's working on a theory. Which reminds me,' I said, turning, 'how does one get to the Moulin Tower?'

Someone was coming. Isabelle raised her head, all thought of sleep forgotten, as the heavy stamp of boots on stone drew nearer. Oh, please, she prayed, dear Mother of God, please let it be John.

Beside her, the old woman Alice roused herself, alarmed. 'My lady—'

'Hush.' The whispered word held urgency. The boots were at the door now. She held her breath.

A rough knock, and a rougher voice . . . a voice she knew. 'Your Majesty, are you awake?'

He hadn't come. She swallowed back the bitter taste of tears and felt in darkness for her gown. He'd promised he would always come, whenever she sent word . . . with solemn eyes he'd sworn it, always. But the man who stood outside her chamber now was not her husband. She stood, shivering in the velvet gown, and crossed to unbolt the door, raising a hand to shield her eyes from the sudden glare of torchlight. The tall man in the passage looked more fierce than she remembered. He frightened her, he'd always frightened her, and yet she'd rather die than have him see it. By force of will she kept her voice composed. 'My lord de Préaux.'

'Majesty.' He knelt, and took her hand. The torchlight traced an old scar on his cheekbone as he raised his head. She saw no mercy in his eyes, no warmth – they were the hard eyes of a ruthless man who made his living by the sword. 'You are to rise, and come with me,' he told her. 'I am to bring you safely to Le Mans.'

'John sent you?'

'Yes.'

She only had his word, she thought, and the word of such a man was hardly comfort in these troubled times. If he'd turned traitor, like the others . . .

Still, she was alone, with John not here – she had no choice but trust. Besides, she thought, de Préaux was a soldier – soldiers had no cause to lie. To take her hostage, he had but to seize her where she stood. And if he desired her dead he'd simply kill her and be done with it. The fact that he'd done neither proved de Préaux spoke the truth.

She raised her chin. 'My lord,' she said, 'the rebels do surround us.'

'Yes, I know.'

'May I ask, how did you . . . how . . .'

'With difficulty.' He stood, impatient. De Préaux never stayed long on his knees. 'Do you come or no? I've twelve men freezing round the fire in your courtyard. They've ridden long and hoped for sleep, but I'd think it less than wise to wait till morning.'

She shivered in a draught of air that swept along the passage. 'What would you have me do?'

'Dress you warmly, and make haste.'

'My women . . .'

'Only you.' He shook his head. 'We have but one horse spare. Your maids must wait.'

She glanced at Alice. 'But my lord—'

'Queen Isabelle.' He was not moved; his ugly face was resolute. 'Upon your life my own life hangs. I am not sent to save the household – only you. It is yourself the rebels seek,' he reminded her, 'and once they learn their prize is flown, the castle will be safe. The siege will end.'

'There is the Treasury, still.'

'These men have no desire for treasure.'

No, she thought. They had one cause, and one cause only – to force John to release his nephew Arthur. And so he would, in time. Frowning, she drew back, gathering the folds of her robe about her. 'What news of Arthur of Brittany?' she asked, slowly. 'Is he well?'

The eyes that touched hers held a fleeting trace of pity. And then he looked beyond her to where Alice stood in silence by the bed, and for a moment understanding passed between the dark knight and the old woman. 'See that your mistress dresses warm,' he said. He bowed and turned away.

Watching the last faint flickering of torchlight vanish down the twisting stairs, it seemed to Isabelle that every stone around her breathed a sigh of cold despair, as if by sorcery her own bedchamber had become a prison . . . or a tomb.

CHAPTER SIX

From all a closer interest flourish'd up . . .

'You've done it now,' said Paul, as we watched Simon bounding off away from us.

'Whatever do you mean?'

'That story you just told us, about Queen Isabelle. You mentioned treasure. *Big* mistake.' With Simon safely out of sight, he rummaged in his pocket for his cigarettes, shifting clear of the shadow cast by the tower at his shoulder. It was in ruins now, the Moulin Tower – an empty hull of stone with dark weeds sprouting in the roofless chambers. And no one walked those chambers, any more. A sign beside the bolted door said sternly: *Danger!* so we leaned instead against the low lichen-crusted wall that formed the western boundary of the château grounds. Behind our backs the slumbering Vienne flowed seaward, unconcerned.

Paul cupped the match against the breeze. 'Telling a story like that to Simon,' he advised me, 'is kind of like waving a red flag in front of a bull. He's all fired up, now.'

'He's only gone to find the toilet, Paul.'

'Don't you believe it. Not my brother.' He grinned. 'He has the bladder of a camel. No, you wait and see – he's sneaked off down to the entrance booth to see what he can learn about the tunnels.'

I looked along the empty path, intrigued. 'But he doesn't speak French.'

'That wouldn't stop him.' Stretching his legs out in front of him, Paul dug his feet into the gravel and braced his hands beside him on the sun-warmed stone. 'So,' he said, 'what happened?'

'When?'

'To John and Isabelle. You never finished the story.'

'Oh, that.' The breeze blew my hair in my eyes and I pushed it back absently. 'It's not the happiest of endings, I'm afraid. John did kill Arthur, or at least he had him killed, depending on which chronicler one reads. The King of France – Philippe – you remember the statue? Well, Philippe went rather wild. He'd raised the boy, you see. He'd been great friends with John's big brother Geoffrey, Arthur's father, and when Geoffrey died Philippe took Arthur back to Paris, brought him up. John might as well have killed Philippe's own son.'

'So he started a war.'

I nodded. 'A terrible war. It cost John nearly everything. Chinon was one of the first castles to be captured, actually – it fell to Philippe not long after Arthur died.'

'And Isabelle?'

I looked up at the Moulin Tower, lonely and abandoned,

the green weeds grasping at the crumbled window ledge. 'He lost her too, in the end. John had foul moods and jealous rages, like his father. He even followed in his father's footsteps in another way – kept Isabelle locked up and under guard, just as his mother had been kept.'

Paul frowned. 'How sad.'

'Yes, well,' I shrugged, 'it's not a fairy tale, I'll grant you. But then real life never is.'

He turned his head to look at me, squinting a little against the sun. 'You don't believe, then, in a love that lasts a lifetime?'

'I don't believe,' I told him drily, 'in a love that lasts till teatime.'

'Cynic,' he accused me, but he smiled.

We sat on several moments in companionable silence while Paul smoked his cigarette, his eyes half narrowed, deep in thought. I couldn't help but think again how different he was from his brother Simon. One had room to breathe, with Paul.

'Tragic,' he said, quite out of the blue.

'I'm sorry?'

He shrugged. 'It's just a kind of game I play, finding the right adjective to suit a place. I try to distil all the feeling, the atmosphere, down to a single word. Château Chinon's been a tough one, but I've got it now – it's tragic.'

He'd hit the nail precisely on the head, I had to admit. In spite of all the sunshine and the blue sky, and the brilliant golden walls, the place did seem to be pervaded by an aura of tragedy, of splintered hopes and unfulfilled desires.

The swift breeze stole the sunlight's warmth and, shivering, I glanced up.

'Simon's coming.'

'Damn.' Paul stubbed his cigarette against the wall, setting off a shower of red sparks that died before they reached the ground. By the time Simon reached us, the telltale evidence lay crushed deep in the gravel underneath Paul's shoe.

'I got a map,' said Simon cheerfully.

Paul's eyes were knowing, but he held the innocent expression. 'Map of what?'

'The tunnels, stupid. Now, according to the woman at the gate, there should be something we can *see*, just over here . . .' And off he went again, with purpose, heading for a spreading box tree several yards away. 'Come on, you two,' he called back.

With a sigh, Paul straightened from the wall arid stretched. 'I told you so.'

I smiled. 'Well, not to worry. When my cousin turns up he'll be glad of the help.'

It took us some few minutes to find Simon, round the far side of the box tree. At first it seemed he'd vanished into thin air, until we stumbled on the narrow shaft sunk deep into the well kept lawn. A flight of stairs, worn smooth with age and damp with fallen leaves, descended here to end abruptly at a blank stone wall. And at the bottom of those steps stood Simon.

'Hey, come down here,' he invited. 'This is really neat.'

I frowned. 'But it doesn't go anywhere.'

'Of course it does.' He pointed off to one side, into darkness. 'Come and see.'

I wasn't really going underground, I reassured myself. The sky was still above me, calmly blue. But when I reached the bottom step the air was dank, and the only thing that kept me from bolting right back up the steps was the fact that I'd have flattened Paul in the process. He leaned in now, behind me, looking where Simon had pointed. One had to focus past the iron bars to see the dimly stretching corridors beyond. 'You're right,' he told his brother. 'This *is* neat. Where does it lead?'

Simon consulted the hand-sketched map he held. 'I'm not sure. The woman at the gate said there are tunnels all over the place, not just under the château but all around Chinon. I think she said Resistance fighters used them in the war.'

It was easy to imagine that. Easier still to imagine the echo of earlier times. I could almost see the torchlight casting shadows on the arched stone walls, and hear far off the furtive rustle of a velvet gown against the eerie silence. I wondered if this was the tunnel Isabelle had passed through, on her way to hide her treasure . . .

I was so deep in my imaginings that the sound, when it came, caught me unawares. A sound quite real and not imagined: the quiet closing of a door, somewhere in the dark and stretching shadows.

I cleared my throat. 'Did you hear that?'

'Hear what?' Both brothers looked at me blankly.

'It sounded like a door.'

Paul tipped his head and listened, but the dusty walls stayed silent. 'Maybe the château workers use the tunnels,' he suggested, 'to get around the place. Or for storage.'

It seemed logical enough, I thought. But I felt a good deal better when we'd clambered up to ground level again, up in the sunshine where the breeze could blow the shivers from my skin.

'Oh, hey,' said Simon, looking at his map, 'I think that might have been the tunnel that goes to the vineyard.' Brow furrowed, he followed the tracing on the map and tried to match it with his own steps, so deep in concentration that he didn't seem to notice when he left the grass and walked onto a broad paved circle that jutted out from the château walls. It might have been a tower once, or some such other fortification, but time had worn it level with the lawn. And Simon might have kept on walking, clear off its edge, had Paul not whistled sharply.

'What?' Simon raised his head, enquiring. He stopped two inches from the railing and leaned over, with a nod. 'Yeah, that's where it leads, all right. If Isabelle hid her treasure there,' he told me, as we joined him at the railing, 'your cousin can kiss it goodbye.'

Below us ran the road that had brought me into Chinon yesterday, now busy with a blur of passing traffic. And on the other side of the road was the most incredible estate I'd ever seen. It was a vineyard, a huge and wealthy vineyard – so huge, in fact, that the rows of dark green vines rose up the rolling slope to the horizon and beyond, protected by a tall unbroken boundary wall that ran along the road. Well, almost unbroken, I corrected myself. There was a gate, a great iron thing that would have suited Buckingham Palace, and from the gate a broad drive swept imperiously up the hill to meet a Grecian mansion, gleaming white.

Above our heads a cloud raced underneath the sun and sent a shadow swiftly up the deeply furrowed hill, as the shadow of a hawk might chase its prey across a trembling field.

Paul understood my awe. 'The *Clos des Cloches*. It's really something, isn't it? I'm told they make the best wine in Chinon.'

The *Clos des Cloches* – the vineyard of the bells, I translated in my own mind. 'It's beautiful.'

Simon shifted closer. 'Martine says they give tours in the summer, and wine-tastings, but it's out of season now. Everyone's too busy with the harvest.' Elbows on the railing, he hung forward, heedless of the dizzying drop. 'Hey, look,' he said, 'there's Neil.'

I looked. The bright gleam of Neil Grantham's hair made him easy to spot on the narrow path beneath us, by the road. Two other men were with him, and a woman with short dark hair. I couldn't see their faces from that angle, but Simon gave a low whistle.

'Damn Neil,' he said, good-naturedly. 'He always beats my time.'

Paul smiled. *'That,'* he told me, with a downwards nod at the dark-haired woman, 'is Martine Muret.'

Martine Muret. I frowned. Oh, right . . . the woman Garland had been gossiping about in the hotel bar yesterday afternoon. The one whose former husband had just died . . . what, three days ago? I watched her now lean close to Neil, her hand possessive on his arm. She had a quick recovery time, I decided drily.

Simon shouted down and waved, and I pulled myself up quickly, taking a step back from the railing. 'Listen, it must be nearly lunchtime. I'd better go back down, in case my cousin's come.'

'Are you sure?' Simon turned around, distracted. 'Because there's a Joan of Arc museum in the Clock Tower, if you'd like to . . .'

I hastily assured him I'd seen plenty for one day, and it was always best to leave something for the next time . . .

'Well, it is your first day,' Simon conceded with a shrug. 'We probably shouldn't wear you out.' He checked his watch. 'And you're right, it is lunchtime. Hey, Paul, let's go ask Neil and Martine if they want to try that Chinese place across the river.'

Paul smiled. 'She's too old for you.'

'Age,' his brother said, indignantly, 'is completely relative. You're the physicist, you ought to know that.'

He bounced off, energy renewed, and Paul sighed. 'You're sure you don't want to join us?'

'Well . . .'

'Joke,' he said. 'I wouldn't do that to you. Two hours with us is long enough for anybody. Just don't forget to warn your cousin.'

'Warn him?'

'That Simon's after Queen Isabelle's treasure.'

'Oh, that.' I promised him I'd not forget. 'I'll see you later, then.'

I left him on the road outside the château. Instead of going back the way we'd come, along the path that wound down through the ancient part of town, I walked a few steps

86

further on and found, as Paul had promised, the entrance to the *escalier de la brèche,* a steep flight of stairs that led back into the fountain square.

It was far easier going down, I decided, although the steps were too broad to take at a normal pace. I had to take them like a child would, one foot down and then the other, following their steeply twisting course between stone walls hung thick with ivy. Here and there a wooden door gave a glimpse of someone's terraced garden, or a fruit tree leaned across the wall to drop its leaves.

One final twist, a straight descent, and there I was, safely back at the fountain square with the hotel angling off beside me, its fanciful wrought-iron balconies webbed like pure black lace against the yellow-white stone of the facade.

The fountain sang and beckoned from the centre of the square. I stopped and paused, and took a step towards it. But the man sitting on the edge of the fountain's basin changed my mind.

He had been sitting in that same spot yesterday, when I arrived – I'd seen him from my window. There couldn't be two men in Chinon with a dog like that, a little spotted mongrel curled around its owner's feet. And he wore the same clothes, leather jacket over tattered shirt, his blue jeans soiled and frayed. He looked, I thought, a shade less than respectable. Not threatening, exactly, but . . . something in his roughened face, some quality I couldn't place, put me on my guard.

The man himself appeared to take no notice of me. He went on smoking, gazing placidly at nothing in particular.

At his feet the small dog shifted, raised its head, and pricked its ears up, suddenly alert. It stared, I thought, directly at my face. And as I crossed to the hotel I felt those silent eyes upon me, watching steadily, as a hunter sights its prey.

CHAPTER SEVEN

Nor knew what eye was on me . . .

Monsieur Chamond rose from behind the reception desk to greet me with a smile smooth as silk. In middle age he was a handsome man, neat and compact with an efficiency of movement that I much admired. In his youth, he would have rivalled his nephew Thierry as a breaker of women's hearts. Most certainly he would have broken mine.

We exchanged our formal greetings, and because I answered him in French he kept on in that language, a little cautiously, poised to switch to English at my first sign of difficulty. 'I'm sorry that I was not here to meet you yesterday, myself. You are enjoying your stay in our hotel, I hope?'

'Very much.'

'And your room, it is satisfactory?'

'It's lovely, Monsieur,' I said, and was rewarded with a warm smile of pleasure.

'I'm glad. Room 215, is it not?' He handed me the key. 'And you have another message, Mademoiselle. Just this morning.'

I took the narrow envelope he handed me and turned it over, frowning slightly. It was addressed, quite simply, 'Braden', in a bold black hand I didn't recognise. 'Another message . . . ?'

Monsieur Chamond proved most perceptive. At the tone of my voice his eyes moved with sudden apprehension to one corner of the desk, below the counter, and whatever he saw there made him shake his head. 'I am so very sorry, Mademoiselle, I had assumed . . .' With the shrug of one resigned to suffering, he retrieved a small square notepad with a message scrawled upon it. 'Our regular receptionist Yvette, she is on holiday for two weeks, and so her sister Gabrielle is filling in. She tries, poor Gabrielle, but she is not Yvette. She is . . . easily confused, and sometimes when I tell her things, she forgets.' His smile held an apology. 'Your cousin telephoned last night, while you were out at dinner.'

Wait for it, I thought drily. 'Oh, yes?'

'He speaks good French, your cousin – like yourself. He said he would be late, perhaps a few days. If you did not mind . . .'

'I see.' My host, I knew, had made that last bit up. Harry would hardly have cared whether I minded. 'And did he say where he was ringing from?'

'No, I'm afraid not.' He looked at me more closely, perhaps surprised that I'd received the news so well. 'This will not spoil your plans, I hope? Your holiday?'

'Good heavens, no.' I'd rather expected it. In fact, when Harry hadn't met me yesterday, as promised, I'd braced myself for the inevitable. My cousin rarely kept to schedules. Hours turned into days with him, and days to weeks, and by the time he did show up in Chinon I might well be safely back in England, sorting through my holiday snaps. I smiled at Monsieur Chamond. 'I'm sure I'll manage, on my own.'

'But I am sorry that you were not told last night. We might have saved you worrying.'

Worry? About Harry? Hardly likely, I thought. 'No harm done,' I said, looking down at the envelope he'd given me. 'And is this from my cousin, too?'

'No, Mademoiselle – that came this morning, as I said. By hand.'

'How curious. I wonder who . . . ?' I tore the flap, and drew a printed card from the envelope. It was an invitation, of all things. I was invited to a guided tour and wine-tasting, the card informed me, at a time of my own choosing, although a written note along the bottom edge asked would I please be kind enough to telephone for an appointment. How *very* curious.

Monsieur Chamond was watching me. 'It is from the *Clos des Cloches,* I think?'

'Yes.' I showed it to him. 'That's the vineyard on the hill, isn't it? The one behind the château? I saw it just this morning.'

'Yes. The white house.'

'Odd. I wonder where they got my name.'

'Ah, no,' he said, 'that is my writing, Mademoiselle, on the envelope. The boy who brought it told me it was for the

English lady staying here. And you,' he explained, with a small shrug, 'you are the only English lady that we have.'

'But surely . . .' I let the protest hang, unfinished. I could hardly accuse my host of making a mistake – that would be rude. And anyway, it hardly mattered. It was just an invitation; probably some sort of marketing ploy delivered round the hotels. Come and taste our wines, and bring your wallet with you – that sort of thing. Strange, though, that they should still be holding tours at harvest-time. I dropped the square card into my handbag and forgot about it.

Well, *nearly* forgot about it. One couldn't quite forget about the *Clos des Cloches* in Chinon, I discovered. The name leapt out at me again half an hour later, from the menu of the restaurant where I'd chosen to eat lunch. 'May we suggest,' the menu read, 'a red wine from the *Clos des Cloches*?' Why not, indeed? A half bottle of the youngest vintage could be squeezed within my budget, I decided. The waiter took my order down approvingly, then vanished, leaving me to watch the ebb and flow of passersby along the narrow cobbled street outside the window.

The restaurant was tiny, just six tables and a narrow bar, but Monsieur Chamond had recommended it so strongly I had gamely searched the streets until I'd tracked it down. The French, I reasoned, knew their restaurants. And lunches were a serious affair. Most businesses closed down in France from noon till two, so everyone but cooks and waiters could observe the ritual. I had forgotten how enjoyable it was to sit and eat at leisure, not to hurry, with the warm smells swirling lazily around me and the hum of conversation drifting past from nearby tables. I'd forgotten how wonderful the food in France could be – how even a salad could be stunning, filled with unexpected textures and a subtle trace of spice. And I'd completely forgotten about the wine.

At home I rarely drank wine with my meals, but here in France it seemed so natural, and the half bottle seemed so harmlessly small, that I'd already drunk three glasses by the time I thought to count. And by then I couldn't do much, anyway – I was feeling quite pleasantly foggy.

So foggy, in fact, that when I'd finally paid the bill and stepped outside, I found I couldn't quite remember just which way I ought to go. Looking round, I tried to get my bearings. There was the château, off to my right, which meant I should head that way, surely . . . except it seemed to me I'd come along a wider road than that one . . . and I had changed direction twice . . . or was it three times? *Blast,* I thought, *you're lost.*

The tourist map I'd tucked into my handbag proved no help at all. It only showed the central part of town, and the unnamed streets and alleys formed a mysterious web on the glossy paper. It was no use, I decided – I'd have to ask someone.

It was no small thing, here in France, to ask someone directions. The rules of etiquette were very clear – the person you asked was obligated to help, even if they didn't have a clue, themselves, exactly where to send you. Wrong directions, to the French, were better than no directions at all. When all else failed, they'd pull another stranger into the discussion to assist. I'd caused a pile-up on a Paris pavement, once, by asking someone where to find the nearest bookshop.

So it was with a certain caution that I scanned the passing faces now, waiting for the proper sort of person. The morning's sun had disappeared behind a swell of slate-grey cloud, and people walked by briskly with their collars pulled tight against the damp. I chose a woman slightly older than myself, smartly dressed and carrying a briefcase. She glanced with mild horror at my map, and I remembered how the French disliked maps – they preferred to ask a person. Calmly, I refolded it and stuffed it in my handbag, listening in patience while she told me how to get back to the Hotel de France.

It sounded rather more complicated than I remembered, but I thanked her, careful not to slur my words, and toddled off in the appropriate direction. The problem with medieval towns, I thought some twenty minutes later, was that the streets all ran whichever way they wanted. Which meant, I thought as the asphalt gave way once more to cobblestone, that following directions proved nearly impossible.

The pavement shrank until there was barely room for one person to walk, and I crowded close against the leaning buildings. These houses had not been scrubbed clean like the houses on the rue Voltaire, and the passing centuries had weathered their walls to a sort of uniform dun colour. Here and there, where the houses didn't quite meet one another, a darkened crevice lay concealed by broken boards, or a snatch of garden glimmered through the narrow opening.

An old woman with suspicious eyes, her thick, shapeless

94

body lurching from side to side, passed by me in indifferent silence, and I felt bolder stares from a cluster of young men who moved more swiftly and with purpose.

Around the corner, the street was quieter. The human noise of shouts and speech and motors grew steadily more faint behind me, until my own footsteps sounded intrusively loud. On every house the shutters were pulled back and fastened; lace curtains fluttered at the open windows. Painted doors sagged on their ancient hinges, over steps that had been swept spotlessly clean. The evidence of human life was everywhere, but I saw no one. The twisting street was empty, lonely, silent.

I might have been the only soul alive.

And so the cat, racing past me in a sudden blur of black and white, nearly scared me to death. I jumped aside as a great lolloping mongrel of a dog came tearing up the street in hot pursuit, but the cat was even quicker. In the blink of an eye it hurled itself over a high stone wall, leaving the dog standing in frustration on the other side. After barking its displeasure, the dog slunk sourly off in search of a more co-operative quarry.

The wall over which the cat had vanished formed part of a narrow alleyway whose name, *Ruelle des Rêves,* was plainly marked for all to see. The Lane of Dreams. It seemed too grandiose a name for such a tiny thoroughfare.

Curious, I crossed the street. Standing in the lane, one could easily see how the cat had managed its escape. The wall was thickly hung with ivy – not the dark English ivy to which I was accustomed, but the other kind so common here in Chinon, a tangled mass of paler green that brightened at its outer edge to crimson, where the smaller leaves spilled down in curling tendrils.

No windows peered into the little lane, and there appeared to be just one door, painted green and set so deep in ivy that one almost didn't notice. It would open, I thought, into the garden of the house that rose behind the high stone wall.

The house itself looked less than friendly. Even as I took a step backwards to view it from a proper angle a window slammed above my head, and looking up I saw a face against the glass. Only for an instant, the briefest glimpse, and yet I recognised the face and knew the man who owned it: the young German artist, Christian Rand.

This must be his house, then. The house that had been loaned to him by Martine . . . what was her name? Martine Muret. The house in which, three days ago, a man had died. I remembered Garland Whitaker saying cattily, *Maybe it wasn't an accident. Maybe Christian did it* . . . One wouldn't need much fancy to imagine murder here.

It was enough to give one the creeps, really – the silent street and the dingy, claustrophobic Lane of Dreams, and the touch of death still hanging heavy round the house. Like ivy, I thought, dropping my gaze to the wall.

The cat's unblinking eyes locked with mine. I hadn't heard a sound, yet there it was, settled comfortably among the red-tinged vines that rustled along the top of the high wall. After a moment's hard stare the cat, like Christian, chose to ignore me. The pale eyes closed.

Twice snubbed, I turned away. Since I was, by this time, quite hopelessly lost, it hardly seemed to matter which direction I chose, and so I walked on through the narrow lane and came into another street as quiet as the one I'd just been on. Unlike the first street, though, this one was packed with cars and people, and the silence made me curious until I saw the cause of it.

At the street's end stood an old church, pale and plain and solid. And in front of the church, almost blocking the road, a long hearse stretched dead black against the yellowed walls of the houses. The mourners, sombre in their dark overcoats, milled about the pavement, exchanging subdued kisses and handshakes.

One face among the many drew my gaze. It was the smoothly handsome face of my taxi driver, his classic profile turning a fraction away from me as he bent his head to say something to the young woman standing by the church door – a young woman with short black hair and fragile features that were almost tragic in their beauty. I frowned. I'd seen her somewhere, too, just recently . . . but where? And then she placed her hand upon his sleeve and I remembered.

I looked with deeper interest at Martine Muret. This morning, from the château walls, I'd seen her laughing, leaning close against Neil Grantham, full of life. She looked sedate now, solemn, though I couldn't find much sadness in her lovely face. But then, I thought, perhaps she wasn't sad. Paul called the dead man her ex-husband, so they must have been divorced. She might have hated him, for all I knew. She might have wished him dead.

Respectfully, she looked down as they carried out the flowers – great elaborate racks of flowers, red and gold, that were laid with care inside the waiting hearse. A woman, not the widow, started weeping audibly, and not wanting to intrude further I pulled my gaze away.

And then I froze.

Across the narrow street, not ten feet from me, the dark, unshaven man from the fountain square leaned one shoulder against the stuccoed wall of the house behind him, and calmly lit a cigarette. Expressionless, he met my eyes. For a long unnerving moment we just stood there, staring at one another, and then the church bells set up a great clanging peal of sound that made the dog at his feet throw back its head and howl, joining the general lament.

The burst of noise broke the spell. I turned and walked on rapidly, away from the church and the press of mourners. Foolish, I thought, to be nervous of a stranger in broad daylight, in a public street. Foolish to find myself listening for a sinister fall of footsteps on the pavement behind me. Still, foolish or not, I kept on walking faster and faster, and I was very nearly running by the time I reached the river.

CHAPTER EIGHT

. . . on the spur she fled; and more
We know not, –

I would have walked straight on past Paul, had he not called to me. He was sitting where we'd sat last night, near the top of the steps leading down to the river, his body folded in unconscious imitation of the brooding statue behind him. Resting his book face down upon his outstretched leg, he called again and waved.

Even with the zebra-striped pedestrian crossing, it took some minutes for me to cross the busy street and join him.

'You've been drinking,' he said, in a brotherly tone.

'Only a little wine with lunch.' I raised one hand to touch my flushed cheek. 'Is it really that obvious?'

''Fraid so. Your eyes are kind of glazed.'

'Oh, well.' I took the news in stride, not overly concerned. Stepping with care over his leg, I settled myself on the next step down and linked my hands around my knees. It was a lovely place to sit and watch the world go by, to watch the river coursing past and hear the ducks call out to one another as they paddled round the reeds that edged the sloping river wall. One could sit here all the afternoon, and never be disturbed.

I sighed, my worries sliding from me as I smiled up at Paul. 'And how was your lunch?' I asked.

'Don't ask.' He grinned. 'The Whitakers decided to go for Chinese food today as well.'

I laughed. 'Oh, Paul, what rotten luck.'

'You're telling me. Martine and Garland spent the whole meal taking shots at one another – all terribly polite, you know, and smiling – and when Martine started scoring points Garland suddenly developed one of her headaches and made a big dramatic exit. You should have been there.'

'Just as well I wasn't,' I replied. 'Theatricals don't impress me.'

Paul tucked one hand inside his jacket, searching for his cigarettes. 'I don't think they impress Jim much, either. He didn't seem too upset when Garland left. He just ordered another drink.'

They were a most unlikely couple, Jim and Garland Whitaker. When I said as much to Paul, he smiled in agreement.

'I like Jim, though,' he said, placing a cigarette between his lips. 'He's a lot smarter than he lets on. And he really takes an interest in things.'

'What sort of things?'

'Oh . . . history, architecture, local food. He's the one who wanted to tour the Loire Valley, you know – not Garland.

Garland couldn't care less. And this trip is definitely not her style.'

'Oh?' I looked up, interested. 'In what way?'

'Every way. Garland stays at the Ritz when she's in Paris. Christmas in the Swiss Alps. Easter on the Italian Riviera. Chinon,' he told me, 'would not have been her first choice for a holiday.'

'Are the Whitakers rich, then?'

'Disgustingly rich.' He nodded, blowing smoke. 'Of course, they'll never say as much directly, but Jim's clothes aren't off the rack, they're tailor made. And he's got one suit that's worth at least a thousand dollars.'

My expression must have been questioning, because he laughed and, mimicking a New York Yiddish accent, said: 'My family's in the garment business, *Mäusele*. I know from menswear.'

'What's a *Mäusele?*' I wanted to know.

'Little Mouse.'

'Oh.' Is that what I reminded him of, I wondered? A little mouse, afraid to come out of her hole? But I didn't ask him that. Instead, I asked: 'What does Jim Whitaker do, anyway? Do you know?'

'He says he works for a private engineering company, but Simon thinks that's just a smokescreen, a cover story to hide Jim's real occupation.'

'Which is?'

'CIA, of course.' He winked. 'Simon gets a little paranoid sometimes – he's studied politics too long. He sees conspiracy in everything and everybody, and the worst part is that it's contagious. I've spent so much time listening to

Simon that even *I* look at Jim sometimes and think, yeah, he does look kind of secretive, you know? It catches.'

'Maybe that's my problem, then,' I said, hugging my knees more tightly. 'My own imagination's been working overtime this afternoon. It must be Simon's paranoia rubbing off.'

'Why? What have you been imagining?'

'I rather fancied I was being followed.' Said like that, I thought, it sounded ridiculous. I smiled.

'Who was following you?'

As I described the man, Paul's eyebrows drew together in a frown of recognition. 'What, the gypsy, you mean? The one with the little dog about that big?' He held his hands a foot and a half apart, to simulate the size of the dog.

'That's the one. He's a gypsy, really?' I'd never seen an actual gypsy before – only fake ones in films.

Paul nodded. 'There are a lot of gypsies around here. Some of them live in campers – caravans, I guess you'd call them – down by the beach. They're not the cream of society, to be sure, but that guy you saw is pretty harmless. At least, he's always been nice to Simon and me,' he said, shifting his legs. 'Simon always stops to pet the dog. So I wouldn't worry about . . . oh, damn, there goes my book!'

I caught it for him as it came bouncing down the steps beside me. 'There,' I said, handing it back to him. 'No damage done. But you've lost your place.'

'That's OK, I can find it again.' He grinned. 'I have a very intimate relationship with this book.'

'Well, I should think so, if you've been reading it for two years.'

102

He turned the paperback over, balancing it carefully in his hand. 'That was always my favourite poem, you know, when I was a kid. Tennyson's *Ulysses*. I used to know it by heart.'

From what I'd seen so far of his memory, I was willing to bet he knew the poem still. I'd memorised it once myself, years ago, at school. I remembered how romantic it had seemed – the aged Ulysses throwing off the chains of boredom, leaving his dull hearth in search of new adventure. To *sail beyond the sunset* . . . I'd thought that beautiful, once. But now I knew it was a wasted effort, chasing sunsets. There was nothing on the other side.

Paul was watching me with those wise eyes that saw too much. I glanced away, quite casually, and asked him: 'But however did you make the leap from Tennyson's *Ulysses* to James Joyce? They're not a bit alike.'

'That,' he told me, 'was my sister's fault. She saw this book in a used bookstore a couple of summers back, read the title, and bought it for me. She thought one Ulysses was the same as the next. I didn't want to disappoint her, so I started reading it.' He smiled again, and set the book aside. 'It's become sort of an obsession. I won't be able to rest until I've finished the damn thing.'

I was vaguely surprised to learn that Simon and Paul had a sister. Not that it mattered, but for some reason I'd thought there were only the two of them. The curious thing about meeting people on holiday, I told myself, was that one formed opinions based on first impressions, or past experience. And one was so often wrong. I looked up at Paul. 'How many brothers and sisters do you have?'

'There are six of us, altogether.'

'Six!'

'Yeah. Simon's the oldest, then Rachel, Lisa, Helen, me and Sarah. Sarah,' he added, having counted everyone off in order on his fingers, 'is the one who bought me the book.'

'Six,' I repeated, incredulous.

My reaction amused him. 'Let me guess. You're an only child.'

I admitted that I was. 'But then my cousin was usually around at holidays and half-terms to keep me company. People used to mistake us for brother and sister, we looked so much alike.' We still did, come to that. Especially around the eyes. The thought of Harry triggered a more recent memory. 'I've had a message from him, by the way. He'll be a few days late.'

'Don't worry,' Paul said. 'Simon will have the next few days planned out for us, just watch. He's a man with a mission now.'

'Queen Isabelle's treasure, you mean?' I smiled. 'Well, he can hunt if he likes, but I doubt he'll find it. Harry says the research alone could take years.'

'God, don't tell Simon that. The more impossible something is, the more he wants to do it.' He stubbed out his cigarette, fraying the end of it, and lit another. 'And don't tell Simon you saw me doing this, either. He'd have my hide. He thinks I just come down here to feed the ducks.'

There were an awful lot of ducks, now that I noticed it. They seemed to be clustered mostly upriver, where a cobblestone ramp for launching boats slanted gently down to meet the water, although a handful of adventurous ones had ridden the current down to where we sat and were paddling now around a flat-bottomed punt moored by chains to the river wall. The ducks were noisy little creatures, scolding and complaining as their feet beat time against the dragging river.

I'd often fed ducks myself, as a child, but now I simply put my chin on my hands and watched them, while Paul smoked his cigarette in mellow, undemanding silence. At length he stood and stretched, picking up his book. 'Come on,' he said. 'Let's go and see if Thierry's got the bar open yet. I could use a coffee or something.'

I walked back with him, but when he would have bought me a drink I shook my head, yawning. 'Have a heart,' I begged him. 'I only got here yesterday, remember, and I've been on the go ever since. I'll never make it through to suppertime if I don't have a nap.' The thought of supper made me frown. 'Do you all eat together, every night?'

He laughed, and shook his head. 'No, we usually end up doing our own thing. Why, did we scare you last night?'

'Well, I wouldn't want to . . . heavens, is that Neil?' I broke off suddenly to stare in wonder at the floor above us.

'Yeah. He's good, isn't he?' Paul listened for a moment, then flashed a sympathetic smile. 'And he's just getting started, from the sounds of it. I hope you can sleep through Beethoven.'

I couldn't, as it happened, but it was my own fault more than Beethoven's. My restless mind would not keep still enough for sleep to settle on it. It conjured images of gypsies and of castles and of dark-eyed men with blindingly fair hair. In the room below, Neil finished playing the symphony's opening *allegro,* and moved smoothly on into the funeral march. A new set of images rose to join the ones already swirling behind my closed eyelids – a black-and-white cat and a mournful church and a spray of flowers, red as blood. And through it all, the gypsy's face turned, watching me with a strange and secret smile.

I opened my eyes, and sat up.

It was no use, I thought. I wasn't going to sleep. I might as well go down and have that drink with Paul. What happened next, I later decided, was *entirely* Beethoven's fault. If he hadn't written such a beautiful piece of music, I wouldn't have paused on my way downstairs to listen to it. And if I hadn't paused, there on the first floor landing, I wouldn't have been anywhere in sight when the Whitakers' door opened further down the hall, and Garland came out into the passage. She hadn't seen me yet – she was looking down, one hand shielding her forehead – but I felt a moment's panic. I didn't like the woman, didn't want to be drawn into conversation, didn't want Neil Grantham to hear her piercing voice and know that I was standing there, outside his room . . .

I looked round, seeking some escape. Not down the stairs, I dismissed the obvious. There wasn't time, and she was bound to see me. But beside the stairs a glass door stood propped open to the outside air, and, feeling a proper coward, I ducked my head and darted through it. Behind me, the rustle of footsteps swept by without stopping, and a heartbeat later I heard a sharp knock. The violin fell silent. Cautiously, I edged along the wall, away from the open doorway, away from the murmur of voices.

I hadn't picked the best of hiding places, really. I was standing on a sheltered terrace, built upon the flat roof of the hotel's garage – a broad, square stretch of pavement bordered by a wooden portico and hugged on three sides by the bleached stone walls of the hotel. One couldn't truly hide, out here. All someone had to do was poke their head around the door, and there you were, in plain view. But for the moment, at least, the terrace was deserted, except for me.

The voices stopped. A door clicked shut. The rustling steps retreated down the corridor. But instead of going back inside, I crossed on tiptoe to the centre of the terrace, where a neat grouping of table and chairs basked in the fickle sunlight of the afternoon. Wiping the dampness from a chair. I sat down. From here I had a panoramic view along the cliffs, from the wedge-shaped Clock Tower guarding Château Chinon to the wilder fringes of the hills beyond the town.

High above me on the cliff path a small cluster of sightseers had paused against the waist-high wall, and their red and purple jackets made a splash of welcome colour on the drab white rise of rock behind them. One of the couples was holding hands and laughing, and I hated them without reason.

The violin began again. I closed my eyes against the beauty of it, settling back with a sigh. He wasn't playing the Beethoven any more. No, this was stranger music, sweeter, more seductive . . . yet familiar. I searched my memory for it. Elgar, I decided. That was it. Edward Elgar. The *Salut d'Amour*.

Neil played it beautifully, with such emotion that the air around me trembled from the sound. I remember wishing he would stop, because I didn't want to think of love just now. I remember squeezing my eyes shut tighter still, and feeling the sudden damp of tears upon my lashes. And after that, I don't remember anything.

I hadn't meant to sleep. But when I next opened my eyes the terrace was in darkness, and a scattering of stars gleamed faintly where the clouds had been before. The chill had penetrated to my bones. I rose and flexed my stiffened shoulders, picking my way cautiously across to the glass door into the hotel. Someone, while I'd slept, had closed that door. I tried the handle. 'Damn,' I said, aloud. They'd locked me out.

Hugging my arms to ward off the cold, I pressed my face against the glass and peered along the corridor. I knocked twice, loudly. No one came. 'Damn,' I said again, cursing my own stupidity. And then, quite by chance, I saw the stairs. It was a narrow flight of stone stairs, nearly invisible in the dark, curving downwards from the level of the terrace. Remembering that the hotel's garage was underneath me, I plucked up my courage and started down, my hand clutching at the railing, expecting at any moment to miss my footing on the uneven stone. It was a relief to feel the ground again, safe and solid beneath my feet and, after a moment's search, to find the door that I had hoped would be there.

It didn't open into the garage, as I'd expected, but straight onto the street itself. The fountain gurgled placidly in front of me, bathed in the golden glow of street lamps, and the hotel's front doors, brightly lit beneath the awning, beckoned me from several yards away. I shivered again and headed for those doors.

But before I reached them, I saw the child.

I stopped, and hovered, hesitating. *It's not your business,* I warned myself. *Don't get involved.* But I couldn't help myself.

She was so young, I thought, no more than six or seven years of age, and so pitifully alone. A miserable figure all in black, sitting still as a statue on the bench at the far side of the fountain square, her large eyes fixed upon the doors of the hotel. She looked up as I approached, and my heart turned over tightly. She'd been crying.

Hunching down on my knees, I spoke to her as gently as I could, in French, and asked what was the matter.

'I can't go home,' she said.

'Why can't you? Don't you know the way?'

She shook her head, setting her short cap of dark brown curls bouncing around her pale face. 'Papa will be so angry.'

Tears swelled again in the big eyes and I rushed to reassure her. 'I'm sure he won't be angry, really he won't. You can't help being lost.'

'I'm not lost, Madame,' she said, with another toss of her head. 'I know how to get to my house. But my papa, he will be angry.'

'Tell me why.'

'Because I left them. They looked the other way, and so I left them. Papa, he said I was to stay with her until suppertime, but they did not want me there, you see . . .'

'I see,' I said, although of course I didn't. 'And who are "they"?'

'My aunt and her friend. Her man friend.'

'Ah,' I said, comprehension dawning.

'I was sorry, afterwards, for leaving them, but when I went back they had already gone, and so I came here to wait for them. My aunt's friend stays at this hotel, and so I thought . . . I thought . . .' Her lower lip quivered. 'But they have not come. And I cannot go home.'

'Nonsense.' I rose to my feet, stretching out one hand. 'Of course you. can. I'll take you home.'

The big eyes were imploring. 'But my papa . . .'

'Just you leave your papa to me.'

She sniffed and thought a moment, and then the small cold fingers curled around my own, trustingly.

'Now, where is your house?'

'It is up there,' she said, and showed me. 'Behind the château.'

She was pointing at the steep stairway leading upwards from the square. Wonderful, I thought with an inward groan. Why couldn't I have been called to play the Good Samaritan to a child who made her home on street level? With sinking heart I started up the steps, the little girl in tow.

Simon and Paul had been quite right, I decided – the stairs were definitely more difficult to manage than the more gradual ascent from the rue Voltaire. By the time we neared the top my lungs were burning, and my heart was pounding wildly against my ribcage. I felt an old woman beside the child, who climbed with irritating ease. At the summit of the steps I paused, trying desperately to buy a moment's rest. 'Where now?' I gasped.

'This way,' she said, and pointed. I let her lead me up the long slope to the château, then round the sheer and silent floodlit walls and down again. I would have gone on further but she held me back.

'No, Madame,' she told me, 'it is here. This is my house.'

'*This* is your house?' My jaw slackened. I felt rather like someone who'd become lost and was wandering now in circles, forever coming round again to the same familiar spot. It was, after all, beyond the bounds of mere coincidence . . . wasn't it? 'This is your house,' I echoed, as if the repetition might convince me, and I lifted disbelieving eyes to stare at the great imposing gates that rose before us – the gates of the *Clos des Cloches,* the vineyard of the bells.

Chapter Nine

A feudal knight in silken masquerade . . .

The gates were locked. I would have pressed the buzzer, but the child stopped my hand.

'No, no, Madame – this way,' she said, and led me through a smaller door set in the high stone wall. We came out in a dark and peaceful garden, heavy with the scent of roses. Still slightly dazed, I let my young friend pull me up the wide well-groomed approach to the white mansion, shining whiter in its floodlights, looking nearly as impressive as the château ruins that it faced.

With every step the house grew larger, and I felt smaller by comparison, scarcely taller than the child who held me by the hand. Even the front door, when we finally reached it, looked disproportionately huge.

'The door, it will be locked,' the girl informed me, matter-of-factly. 'You must push the bell, just there.'

She pointed, and I pushed.

After what seemed an eternity of silence, the door swung open on its hinges, trapping us in a slanting slab of blinding yellow light. The face of the man who stood in that doorway was faintly grey and sternly lined, his mouth a deep horizontal slash beneath a hawk-like nose. It was easy to see why the child had feared his reaction, I thought. I rather feared it myself.

Which was why, when I finally found my voice, I heard myself stammering out the little girl's predicament, or at least the essence of it, in a rapid rush of speech, ignoring the persistent tugging at my sleeve.

'. . . and so naturally I assured her, Monsieur, that you would not be angry,' I concluded, rather lamely.

Beside me the child gave another tug. 'But Madame,' she hissed, in a stage whisper, 'this is not my father. This is only François.'

I looked in surprise from the tall grey man to the child, and back again. 'Oh,' I said.

The man had been staring at me steadily, his eyes in shadow, but now, as if awaking from a trance, he bent his head, the corners of his hard mouth lifting in a smile that surprised me with its kindness. 'It is true, Madame,' he told me gravely. 'I am not the father of Mademoiselle Lucie. But please, do come in.'

Numbly, I stepped into the brilliantly lit foyer, and felt the child's fingers loosen from my grasp. The man named François shut the door firmly behind us, and I noticed for the first time that he was an older man, in his sixties, perhaps, or even early seventies. Old enough to be the child's grandfather. He drew himself up gravely and looked down at the small figure beside me.

'So, Mademoiselle, you have had an adventure tonight, have you not? A bath, I think, and then to bed.'

'I have not had my supper . . .'

'Just water and dry bread, tonight,' he threatened her, but he didn't look as if he meant it, and she wasn't a bit fooled. 'Say thank you to the kind lady, Lucie, for bringing you home.'

She turned to me, her dark eyes noticeably clearer and less miserable. 'Thank you, Madame.'

'You are most welcome.'

I solemnly accepted the kiss she gave me, before François sent her off with a playfully imperious sweep of his hand. Giggling, she galloped up the elegant staircase that curved upwards from the foyer, her small feet making no noise on the thick red carpet as she trailed her hand along the painted wrought-iron railings of the bannister.

I felt the man's eyes on my face again, with a curious intensity, but as I met his gaze the impression vanished. He cleared his throat and spoke. 'This is a very kind thing you have done, Madame. The streets can be quite dangerous for a small child, and her adventure might not have ended so pleasantly. I am grateful to you for bringing her home.'

'It was no trouble, honestly.'

'You will wait here, please, Madame,' he commanded me, as I turned to leave. 'Monsieur Valcourt, I am sure, will also wish to thank you.'

My hesitation must have shown, because he said to me again: 'Wait here, please,' before he finally left me. The tone of his voice left no room for argument. I linked my hands behind my back like a chastened schoolgirl and did as I was told, feeling a childish twinge of apprehension, as though it had been myself and not the girl Lucie who'd gone wandering off against the rules. This was, I thought, what happened when one got involved in other people's problems.

Still, I had to admit that my situation was not entirely without interest.

The inhabitants of the *Clos des Cloches,* like Jim Whitaker, evidently bought their clothing tailor made. The tangible evidence of wealth met me here at every turning. Not only wealth, but old and polished wealth, generations of it, handed down with pride from time immemorial. The plush red carpet, the marble floor on which I stood, the golden sconces on the white-painted walls, the rich, dark tones of the gilt-framed portraits – all this spoke to me of money and of privilege.

A portrait by the staircase drew my eye, and I moved closer to examine it. It showed a boy just entering his teens, a boy with thick black hair and great dark eyes that watched me, lifelike. Those eyes, I thought, were faintly familiar . . .

'Good evening, Madame.' The deep voice spoke suddenly out of the air behind me.

I had not heard him come into the foyer, but my startled reaction was not due solely to the unexpected nature of his entrance. Pulling my eyes away from the portrait, I turned slowly round to face Monsieur Valcourt, and had the satisfaction of seeing his own features change abruptly.

'You . . .' he said, the flash of surprise in his dark eyes quickly swallowed by a spreading warmth.

I lifted my chin a fraction and summoned up the brightest smile I could muster. 'You owe me twenty-five francs, Monsieur,' I told him.

I ought to have been furious, I told myself. No doubt he had thought it a marvellous joke to be mistaken for a taxi driver, and he had certainly enjoyed that joke at my expense. It was a rotten thing to do, and I should have despised him for it. But the best I could manage was a kind of limpid irritation, and even that would not hold up beneath the smooth persuasion of his smile.

'I owe my daughter a debt, I think,' he said, coming forward. 'I am Armand Valcourt.'

'Emily Braden.' I shook his hand stiffly, keeping the contact as brief as possible.

'You're angry with me.' I did not answer, and his breath escaped him on a sound that wasn't quite a sigh. 'I never said, you know, that the taxi was mine. If you had asked, I would have told you no, I was just waiting for the driver to collect my luggage from the train, that's all. But,' he spread his hands, in self-defence, 'you didn't ask.'

'You might have told me, later. When we met the second time.'

'I might have, yes. But by that time you were convinced I drove the taxi. I thought it would embarrass you to find out who I was. And it was no great sacrifice for me to drive you to your hotel.'

'You took my money,' I reminded him.

'You were most insistent, as I recall.' His eyes were gently mocking above his smile. 'I did not keep your money, Mademoiselle. I gave it to my friend, Jean-Luc, who owns

117

the taxi. And if it matters, he also was not pleased with me, when he found I'd taken his taxi. So I have been twice reprimanded.' Not that he looked particularly remorseful. He thrust his hands in his pockets and tilted his head to one side. 'Am I forgiven?'

'Possibly.' I softened, noting he had switched to calling me 'Mademoiselle' in place of the more formal 'Madame'. The change implied a subtle move in our relationship as well – no longer strangers, but acquaintances.

'But you are right,' he said, 'I must repay you. Have you eaten yet?'

'No, but—'

'Then please, you must dine with me, tonight. François always cooks far more than I can eat alone. Do you like veal?'

'Yes, but—'

'Good. You can leave your coat there, if you like, beside the door. Here, let me help you.'

I hesitated, and he smiled again. It was a damnably persuasive smile. 'Please,' he said again. 'I've upset you, and my daughter has dragged you across half of Chinon. The least that I can do is give you dinner.'

It would be harmless enough, I thought, to accept the offer. I *was* rather hungry, and the fact that he was flirting with me openly convinced me just how harmless it would be. Flirtatious men I could handle. It was the serious ones, like Neil, who made me nervous – the ones who looked straight at you and spoke simply and had no use for games. Men like Neil, I thought, might talk of love and mean it, while flirtatious men demanded nothing, promised less, and never disappointed. There could be no danger, I decided, in a dinner with Armand Valcourt.

'Of course,' he said, 'if there is someone waiting for you back at your hotel . . .'

I shook my head. 'No, I'm all on my own.'

'Good,' he murmured, cryptically, as I followed him from the foyer into a long, expansive room half shadow and half light, its understated elegance both soothing and surreal. It had been decorated with an eye to detail – the artistic arrangement of chairs and sofa, the graceful antique writing-desk, the swan-like pair of table lamps . . . but it looked more like a stage set than a sitting-room. A place where no one really *lived*. The image was compounded by the fact that one whole wall seemed made of windows, black as pitch at this late hour. As we moved, the glass threw back our images, distorted.

'I eat in here,' he told me. 'It's my habit, when I'm alone. Unless you would prefer the dining-room?'

I shook my head. 'Here is fine.'

He must have already been sitting down to dinner when François had interrupted him. A table at the far end of the room was set for one, its polished surface scattered with an odd assortment of china bowls and chafing dishes.

I'd seen so many films about the rich that I was half expecting serving maids in starched white caps, but it was Armand Valcourt himself who fetched me an extra plate and cutlery, and filled my wine glass from the open bottle on the table.

'It's last year's vintage,' he explained, as he poured. 'Not a great wine, I'm afraid, but sufficient for François's

119

cooking. The real cook is off this evening.'

He took the chair across from me and raised his own glass in a toast. 'To small deceptions,' he said, with a slow deliberate smile.

The wine, to my untrained palate at least, proved excellent, as did the meal itself. I thought François a smashing cook, and said so.

'François has many talents,' my host told me. 'He's a good man and a loyal one. But you will learn this for yourself, I think.'

'What do you mean?'

'You've made a friend of him tonight, make no mistake. He does not forget a kindness, and he's very fond of my daughter.'

'Oh, I see.' I nodded. 'Well, that's understandable, Monsieur. She is a charming child.'

He smiled a little, lowering his eyes to the food on his plate. 'Her mother's doing, and not mine. Brigitte was much more sociable than I am.'

I thought it impolite to ask the question, so I didn't, but he answered it for me anyway. 'My wife had a weak heart, Mademoiselle. She died three years ago.'

'I'm sorry.'

He was still looking down, and I couldn't see his eyes. 'Life moves us onwards, does it not? More wine?'

I held my glass out while he poured. 'How many children do you have?'

'Just Lucie. I think it must be lonely for her, sometimes.'

'I rather enjoyed being an only child, myself,' I confessed. 'I was spoiled rotten.'

Briefly, his enigmatic gaze touched mine. 'François tells me I'm not to be angry with my daughter. Your words, I think.'

'Yes, well . . . I did rather promise her that you wouldn't be.' I suddenly developed an intense interest in my own plate, pushing my vegetables round with the fork. 'I shouldn't have interfered, perhaps, but if you'd seen her you'd have understood. She looked so small, and so unhappy, I thought surely no parent would want to . . .' My voice trailed off and I speared a carrot with my fork. 'Besides, she wouldn't have come with me, otherwise. She was afraid.'

He raised an eyebrow. 'Afraid of what?'

'Of your reaction, naturally.'

That surprised him, and he frowned as he dismissed the notion with a classic Gallic 'pouf'. 'I don't beat my daughter, Mademoiselle.'

'Of course you don't. But your daughter was very tired,' I reasoned, 'and upset. And things always do seem quite a bit more frightening when one is lost. Not that she was ever lost herself, really, but she'd lost the people she was with, which rather amounts to the same thing.'

His mouth curved, and I had the distinct impression he found me amusing, but the tone of his voice betrayed nothing. 'She would not have lost anyone if she had done as she was told. I gave her clear instructions to remain with her aunt.'

'Yes, but she told me . . .' I broke off suddenly, realising my error. It was really none of my business, I thought. This was a family matter, and I ought not to get involved.

Armand Valcourt raised his eyebrow a second time, expectantly. 'Yes?'

'Nothing. It's not important.' I scooped up a forkful of seasoned meat and tried to ignore his suddenly curious eyes, watching me across the table.

'Where exactly was my daughter, Mademoiselle, when you found her?'

I glanced up, saw he wasn't going to let the matter drop, and sighed. 'She was sitting by the fountain just in front of my hotel.'

He frowned. 'And did she tell you why she went there?'

'She told me her aunt's . . . friend was staying there. I think she hoped they'd come back to the hotel, so she was waiting for them. Forgive me for asking, Monsieur, but the child's aunt . . . .your sister . . .'

'My wife's sister,' he corrected me.

'Shouldn't someone notify her that your daughter is safe? She must be frantic with worry by now.'

My statement was punctuated by a loud bang from the front hallway, and Armand Valcourt reached, smiling, for his wine glass. 'I don't think that will be necessary,' he said. 'This will be Martine now.'

Martine . . .

At first I thought, *it couldn't be,* and then an image flashed into my mind of Armand Valcourt standing close beside the widow at today's funeral, and I thought, *of course it must be,* and I turned expectantly as Martine Muret burst in upon us.

I believe I'd been preparing myself to dislike her, for her beauty if nothing else, but the moment the door from the hallway flew open all my preconceived notions went out of the window. In place of the coldly glamorous woman I'd expected, I saw someone who seemed scarcely older than her wayward niece, with cropped black hair and large eyes liquid in her bloodless face. And 'frantic with worry', I now saw, was an understatement. Martine Muret was terrified.

'Armand, I cannot find her,' she broke in, ignoring me completely in her distress. 'Lucie, she is gone. I have looked everywhere, but—'

'Calm yourself, Martine,' her brother-in-law said, raising one hand to stop the woman's flood of speech. 'Lucie is fine, she's safe in bed.'

'Oh, thank God.' Her knees caved weakly in relief and she dropped suddenly onto a tapestry-covered chair by the long windows. Touching a hand to her brow, she seemed to notice me for the first time, and the look she sent her brother-in-law was faintly quizzical.

In a few brief, unembellished sentences, he explained who I was, and how I'd come to be there.

'I am so grateful to you, Mademoiselle.' Her smile was a fleeting shadow on that lovely, fragile face. 'You cannot know how I have suffered these past hours, searching for my niece. One reads such horrible things in the newspapers, you know, and I was so afraid . . .' She couldn't even finish the thought out loud. Her pale hand brushed her temple once again, and she said quietly: 'I would never have forgiven myself.'

I mumbled once again that it was nothing, that I'd been only too glad to help Lucie, that they'd already been too kind . . . And pushing aside my empty plate, I glanced down at my wristwatch. 'But I'm afraid I really must be getting back to my hotel.'

'I will drive you,' Martine said, as if determined to repay the debt. 'Where are you staying?'

'The Hotel de France.'

I caught the flicker of surprise, the too-bright smile. 'Oh, yes?'

'Martine has friends there,' said Armand Valcourt. Leaning back in his chair, he lit a cigarette, and the lighter's click was as violently loud as the cock of a loaded gun. 'But I think, perhaps, that I should drive you down myself. To see you get back safely.' He stressed that last word, 'safely', and Martine's eyes flashed a quick response.

I glanced from one face to the other, sensed the coming storm, and diplomatically excused myself to use the bathroom. In spite of the fact that arguing was to the French what complaining about the weather was to the English, I'd never learned the knack of it. I hated arguments. I particularly hated being in the middle of them, and so I loitered as long as I could in the little toilet under the front stairs. Which rather backfired when Martine and Armand came into the hall. Trapped, I could only stand and wait, pretending not to hear the angry voices.

'I've already told you I was sorry,' snapped Martine Muret. 'What more do you want?'

'I want you to behave responsibly, to show some consideration for my feelings, Lucie's feelings, instead of thinking only of yourself.' He wasn't really shouting, but his voice was cold and hard and carried clearly. 'Do you realise what can happen to a child, alone at night? Do you?'

'Of course I do,' she shot back. 'What do you think, Armand, that I wasn't worried myself? That I wasn't sick with fear when I realised she was missing? Is that what you think?'

'I think you were too occupied with other things to notice she was gone. Which one was it, this time?' he asked her. 'The German or the Englishman? Or have you grown bored with them already, and found someone else?'

'I don't see that my private life is any of your business.'

'When it affects my daughter, it's my business. My God, Martine, what were you thinking of? We buried him today, or have you forgotten this?'

A silence followed, stung by the echo of those words. 'I forget nothing,' said Martine, at last, in a calm and quiet voice. 'And how dare you judge my feelings, Armand. What do you know of love?'

I heard her cross the foyer and start up the staircase, her footsteps treading lightly over my head. Still, I waited until those footsteps were completely out of earshot, until I'd heard the click of Armand Valcourt's cigarette lighter, before I decided it was safe to emerge.

He was standing at the foot of the stairs, his expression quite relaxed and natural. Only the jerking movement of the hand that held the cigarette betrayed his anger. By the time I reached him, even that small action had been brought under control. His eyes, on mine, were normal. 'Ready?' he asked me. 'Yes? Then let us go.' And handing me my jacket, he ushered me out into the waiting night.

CHAPTER TEN

. . . the Graces, group'd in threes,
Enring'd a billowing fountain . . .

He drove a Porsche. That didn't surprise me overmuch –
the flashy red sports car rather suited him – but it did set
me wondering. If Armand Valcourt owned a car, why had
he taken a taxi from the station yesterday morning? Come
to think of it, why had he taken the train? I only wondered
for a moment, then I asked him.

He shrugged. 'I always take the train when I go to Paris.
Martine might need the car, you see, if there were some
emergency with Lucie. And anyway, I'd be a fool to drive
the Porsche in Paris.' He shot a sideways glance at me.
'Why the smile?'

'Was I smiling? Sorry. It's only that I used to
live in Paris, so I understand completely. My father
once backed into a Mercedes. The owner wasn't
very . . . understanding.'

Armand laughed. 'No, I don't suppose he would have

been.' I felt again the flashing glance. 'How long were you in Paris?'

'Five years. But it was ages ago. I was only twelve when we left.'

He smiled and swung the Porsche round the hairpin bend that plunged towards the river. 'I had wondered,' he confided, 'where you learned to speak your French.'

It took a minute for his words to hit their mark. I'd spoken French to little Lucie, when I'd first approached her in the fountain square, and then . . . well, I suppose I'd simply gone on speaking it. In all the confusion, I hadn't really noticed. I shrugged now, suddenly self-conscious. 'My father's in the foreign service,' I explained. 'He wanted me to have a second language.'

'You have one. Your French is very beautiful.'

'Thank you.'

He didn't ask me what I did for a living, but then the French didn't ask such things, as a rule. It was considered impolite, a means of pigeonholing people before one really got to know them. Since the Revolution, everyone was meant to be equal anyway. *Almost* equal, I amended, leaning back against the glove-soft leather of the Porsche.

Armand Valcourt had missed the Revolution. There was a certain feudal gallantry about the way he dropped me at my hotel door, coming round to help me out of the car as if I were royalty. His handshake lingered, by design, and his smile was deliberately charming. 'You have your key?' he asked me.

'Yes.' I rummaged for it in my handbag, pushing aside a stiff white card with printing on it. 'Oh,' I said. I'd

128

quite forgotten, in all the confusion, about my mysterious invitation to taste wine at the *Clos des Cloches*. 'This was from you, then, I presume?' I held it up to show him. 'It was left for me this morning.'

'Was it?' The charming smile broadened, refusing to take responsibility.

'Yes.'

'Ah. That is very curious, you know, because we don't give tours this time of year.' Taking the card from my hand, he assumed a mock-serious expression. 'Still, it appears quite genuine. I am sure,' he said, as he gave it back, 'that we would honour it.'

'So you did send it, then.'

His dark eyes held a deep amusement. 'Well, if I did, I could have saved myself the trouble.'

'Why?'

'Because you came to see me anyway.'

Definitely a flirt, I thought, as he walked back round to the driver's side of the car. Smiling faintly, I watched the Porsche's back lights twinkle out of sight along the Place du Général de Gaulle.

It was a lovely night for late September, crisp and clear, filled with the drifting scents of autumn – pungent leaves and petrol fumes and slowly burning coal. My watch read ten past eleven, but there were still people passing me by on the pavement – young people, mostly, in boisterous clusters, making their way to the lively bar on the nearest corner. The mingled sounds of dance music and laughter spilled out across the square. Saturday night, I thought. I thrust my hands in my pockets, feeling suddenly at a loss.

I could almost hear my cousin's voice reminding me, in disapproving tones: *It's been six months since you so much as stopped in at the pub for a drink.*

Frowning, I hovered there a moment, trying to decide whether to go out for a drink or go up to my room. In the end I did neither. I crossed to the fountain and sat on the bench where I'd found Lucie Valcourt.

Here, beneath the whispering tangle of acacia branches, it was easy to go unnoticed. I sat back, facing the brilliant glow of the Hotel de France and the bustling bar on the corner, and focused on the pleasantly murmuring fountain in front of me.

The bottom pool was perhaps two feet deep, a stone hexagon raised on a sloping step. Water cascaded into it from a bronze basin set high overhead like an upside-down umbrella, and that basin in turn was fed by the overflow from a smaller bronze bowl above *it*. From the centre of the fountain rose three women, cast in bronze, supporting the entire structure. Back-to-back the women stood, arms lowered to their sides, their fingers linked in an eternal show of sisterhood. There was no mistaking their classical origins – even without their flowing draperies and tightly coiled hair, there was a depth of beauty to their faces that told me they belonged in ancient Greece.

A hopeful nudge against my legs disturbed my contemplation. It was a cat, a rather familiar-looking black-and-white cat, and when the green gaze locked expectantly with mine I fancied that I recognised it. It was the same cat, surely, that I'd seen that afternoon perched on the high wall of Christian Rand's house. It rubbed itself against my legs a second time, more demanding now than hopeful, and I tapped my fingers on my lap. 'All right, then,' I coaxed it, 'it's OK.' Pleased, the cat leapt up and padded round in circles on my knees, pausing once to sniff my face in a delicate sort of greeting.

It was clearly a stray – one stroke of my fingers along the dirt-encrusted back told me that – but it was nonetheless affectionate. And trusting. It stopped circling and curled itself inside my jacket, claws working against the stiff fabric, and within seconds the green eyes closed. Head nestled heavily against my breast, the cat breathed deeply with a steady, rumbling purr that vibrated up through the thick fur to my caressing hand. Surprised, and oddly moved, I crooked my neck to stare down at the sleeping animal.

I ceased to be aware of time. I don't know for certain how many minutes had passed before I heard the footsteps coming down the steps from the château, between the shuttered buildings.

Neil Grantham's hair was almost white beneath the street lamps, white as his shirt beneath the soft brown leather jacket he was wearing over faded jeans. *Oh, damn,* I thought, feeling again the unwanted stirring of emotion, like a persistent hand tugging at my sleeve. I shrank back further into shadow, hoping he'd go straight into the hotel without seeing me. His head came round as if I'd called to him, and with easy strides he crossed the square to join me on my bench beside the fountain.

'You'll get fleas,' he said, looking at the cat.

'I don't care,' I tightened my hold protectively, lifting my chin. 'He just wants some attention, poor devil. I've a soft spot for strays.'

He smiled and stretched his long legs out in front of him, elbows propped against the top rail of the bench's back. His presence, like the cat's, was very peaceful, but for some reason that only made me more nervous. If only he would flirt, I thought, like Armand Valcourt had, then I'd be fine. But Neil was not Armand. He just went on sitting there, perfectly still, as though he were waiting for something.

I stroked the cat's head, and cleared my throat. 'Were you just up at the château?'

He nodded. 'My nightly walk. It's the only exercise I enjoy, really – walking. You ought to come with me some time.' I glanced at him then, but he still wasn't flirting. His face was dead serious.

I made a non-committal noise and swung my eyes back to the trickling fountain with its trio of lovely bronze women.

Neil followed my gaze. 'Enjoying the fountain, are you?'

'Yes,' I said, and then because the silence stretched so long I cleared my throat again and told him, childishly: 'There used to be a fountain in our garden when I was very small. My father worked in Rome, then, and we had this marvellous house, with a courtyard and everything, and the fountain in the middle of it. A wishing fountain, my father called it – he used to give me a coin at breakfast, every day, for me to make a wish with. Anything I wanted.'

Now why, I thought, had I told him that? It was a foolish thing to tell a total stranger.

Neil went on looking at the dancing fall of water. 'And did it work?'

Did it work? I remembered the day I wished for a kitten, and found one wandering in our back lane. And the day the horrid girl next door fell off her bike. I tucked my jacket round the sleeping cat and shrugged. 'I don't remember.'

He brought his quiet gaze back to my face, and I hastily changed the subject. 'Are these women in the fountain sculpture Greek?'

'That's right. Splendour, Joy and Beauty. The three Graces.'

'Oh, I see.' I peered more closely at the downturned faces. 'Which one is which, do you know?'

'Lord, no.' His smile was disarming. 'I only know their names because I looked them up last Tuesday. Simon asked me, and I didn't want to appear ignorant, not when I've been coming to Chinon for so long.' His eyes slid from me, looking at the figures with new interest. 'Still, I imagine there's some way to tell them apart, if we approach it logically. Splendour means brilliance, doesn't it? So the lady facing into the sunset would be my choice for Splendour – she'd get the best light, vivid colours. And the prettiest one is round the other side, facing the hotel, so I'd say she's Beauty. Which leaves Joy, and that fits,' he decided, 'because she's got the widest smile.'

I frowned. 'She's not smiling.'

'Of course she is. They all are. That's what Graces do, you know. They smile upon you and make life beautiful.'

'Oh.' The man was seeing things, I thought, as I stared back at the nearest statue, the one Neil had pegged as Splendour. She certainly wasn't smiling. Not at me.

High above, in the ruined château, the midnight bell

began to toll, disturbing the sleeping cat. The green eyes opened and stared at me with a deeply disappointed air, then in one fluid motion the cat rose and stepped, stretching, from my lap onto the pavement. Stiff-legged, it wandered off into the shadows.

Neil watched it go, then looked across the square at the noisy corner bar. 'Listen, since we're both still up, can I buy you a drink?'

Five years ago, I would have told him yes. Five years ago, I would have done a lot of things.

Tonight I stammered some excuse about being tired, and faked an unconvincing yawn.

'Another time, perhaps,' he said.

'Perhaps.' I rose from the bench, and said goodnight, and his dark eyes gently called me coward.

'Goodnight, Emily.'

It seemed a long walk across the little square to the hotel door, mainly because I felt those eyes upon me every step of the way, but when I turned at the door to glance back, Neil wasn't watching me at all. He wasn't even looking in my general direction. His face was turned the other way, towards the château steps.

The black-and-white cat had returned, weaving itself nimbly around Neil's outstretched ankles. As I watched, he leaned forward and scratched the animal's ears absently, but he didn't look down. He just went on looking with narrowed eyes at something . . . or someone . . . I couldn't see.

CHAPTER ELEVEN

'O long ago,' she said, 'betwixt these two
Division smoulders hidden;'

Next morning the young bartender, Thierry, looked a little the worse for wear. He set the basket of croissants and bread between the boys and me, and leaned against the spare fourth chair at our breakfast table.

'. . . but no,' he went on, 'they do not come down for breakfast today. Madame Whitaker, she has the headache since yesterday afternoon – the migraine. She stays in bed today. And Monsieur Whitaker, he went out very early.'

It was still only nine o'clock, and Simon looked with interest at the empty corner table where the Whitakers liked to sit. 'By himself?'

Thierry admitted that he didn't know. 'But then, I do not always pay attention. I think that he is gone to hear the Mass somewhere.'

'I'm surprised you haven't gone to Mass yourself,' Paul said. 'You could use a confession, my friend.'

Thierry merely grinned and raised his shoulders in a carefree shrug. 'But I must work on Sundays,' he excused himself. 'Who else would serve your breakfasts?'

Which was probably just as well. Judging by the shadows beneath his dark eyes and the rather wickedly rumpled look he was sporting after what had obviously been a wild Saturday night, I decided Thierry's soul was very likely past redemption.

'He's superhuman,' Simon said, with grudging admiration, as Thierry left us to attend an older couple seated by the window. 'He wore us out completely last night, at the disco. You should have been there, Emily.'

I pulled a face. 'I'm much too old for discos.'

Paul stopped pouring his second cup of coffee long enough to roll his eyes. 'Oh, right. What are you, thirty?'

'Twenty-eight.'

'Positively ancient,' he said drily. 'They'll be fitting you for false teeth next, I guess.'

'Besides,' Simon added, 'age is no excuse. Neil's come out with us a couple of times, and he's forty-something. He dances pretty good for an old guy.'

'Pretty well,' Paul corrected him, automatically.

'Whatever.' Simon grimaced. 'Remind me to get some aspirin later.'

'I've got some,' I offered, reaching for my handbag. 'Somewhere, that is. I don't know why I carry all this, I can never *find* anything.' Rifling through the overstuffed bag, I started to remove things, one by one, piling them beside my empty plate. My bulging wallet, sunglasses, two pens, a packet of tissues, a crinkled tourist map of Chinon, a square of thick paper with printing on it . . .

'Hey,' said Simon, pouncing on the latter. 'What's this? You've been holding out on us.'

I glanced up. 'What? Oh, it's just an invitation.'

'Yeah, right.' Simon flipped the card around to show his brother. 'To the *Clos des Cloches*.'

Paul whistled, impressed. 'Who'd you have to kill to get that?'

'No one.' I smiled. 'They just gave it to me. Aha!' I found the aspirin at last, and handed the bottle to Simon.

He took it absently, tapping the edge of the card with one finger. 'The *Clos des Cloches* is where that tunnel leads, from the château.'

Paul caught my eye. 'Oh, here we go.'

'No, no,' said Simon, 'I was only thinking that it might be kind of neat to get inside, you know. To find out what the tunnel looks like at that end.'

'I would think it looks a lot like a wine cellar,' was Paul's dry comment. 'And they probably would have noticed by now if Queen Isabelle's jewel box was lying around.'

'Not if she buried it.'

'You are not,' Paul said firmly, 'going to dig up the poor guy's wine cellar.'

Simon ignored him and rocked back in his chair, deep in thought. 'I wonder if there's any place in town that rents out metal detectors.'

Paul looked at me. 'I told you this would happen.'

I laughed. 'I don't mind, honestly. And Simon, if you want to use the invitation—'

'Oh, no, it's yours, I wouldn't steal it from you. But,' he

added, with a grin, 'there's nothing here that says you can't bring guests.'

He was quite right. The card wasn't even addressed to a specific person. A small, mischievous thought began to glimmer at the back of my mind. Armand Valcourt had flung a challenge down last night – he expected me to come. I didn't doubt that he was used to having women swoon in all directions when he smiled. He was probably sitting up there now, waiting for me to ring him, and feeling smug about the whole affair. And I knew just the way to wipe that smug look off his face. 'All right. I'll ring the *Clos des Cloches* and arrange a tour for the three of us. For today, if you like.'

'But no metal detectors,' Paul instructed, turning knowing eyes on his brother. 'And no shovels.'

Simon promised nothing. 'This morning would be good,' he said. 'We don't have anything planned for this morning.'

Indulgently, I checked my watch. 'I'll see what I can do.'

Paul had been right about Simon, I thought – once he set his mind to something, he was rather like a great shaggy dog with a bone. When I would have dawdled an extra minute over my coffee cup, he pushed and prodded me up the stairs instead. He would probably have followed me right to my room, to see that I dialled the telephone properly, if he hadn't been distracted by the sudden, shocking oath that greeted us on the first floor landing.

'Careful, Neil,' Paul called out. 'It's Sunday.'

'I don't bloody care,' Neil's voice came back, and then his head came round the open door to his room. 'Do any of you know anything about hi-fis?'

138

Forty-something? I thought, looking at his longish hair and unlined face. I'd not believe it. He looked half that age this morning. Something had clearly irritated him – his mouth was set in a thin, tight line, his dark eyes narrow with impatience.

'Stereos, you mean?' Simon asked. 'What kind of stereos?'

'The kind that don't bloody work.'

Paul couldn't keep the smile from showing. 'Yeah, I have a little experience with those. Want me to take a look?'

'Please.' Neil relaxed a little in response, pushing the door wider to let the boys in. Catching my eye, he flashed a brilliant smile. 'I don't bite, honestly.'

I hung back, and was relieved when Simon boldly came to the rescue. 'She has to make a phone call.' One couldn't argue with that tone of voice, I thought, and with a tiny shrug that absolved me from blame, I turned my back on Neil and continued up the stairs.

The man at the *Clos des Cloches* picked up the phone on the second ring. It wasn't Armand Valcourt. The older man, perhaps – François. At any rate, his voice was kind. Yes, he assured me, it was possible to take a tour that morning. Would ten-thirty be agreeable? That gave them nearly an hour to prepare. And for one? For *three*. That threw him for a moment, and he asked again, just to be sure.

'Three,' I repeated, and thanked him. Replacing the receiver, I sat back and waited for Simon and Paul to come upstairs.

The minutes stretched.

Finally I crossed to my door and opened it a crack,

listening. They were still one floor down, in Neil's room – I could just hear the murmur of voices. I was about to close my door again when I remembered what Paul had called me, yesterday: *Mäusele*. Little Mouse. *I'm not afraid of anything*, I told myself stoutly. Convinced of that, I stepped into the corridor and headed downstairs.

The door to Neil's room was wide open, as he'd left it, and I could see the three of them inside, clustered round what looked like a chest of drawers.

'Well, that's not it,' Paul was saying, his own voice losing patience. He shifted and I saw that he was frowning at a great gleaming metal hi-fi system. It was truly a monster – all dials and wires and separate components. Neil rummaged among the wires, pulled out a red connecting line and plugged it in somewhere else.

'What about that?' he checked.

Simon slotted a cassette tape into the machine and pushed a button. Nothing happened. 'Nope. I hate to say it, Neil, but I think you're out of luck.'

I hadn't made a sound, but Neil looked up and over his shoulder, his eyes seeking mine unerringly. 'Hullo,' he said. 'I don't suppose that you . . .'

'Sorry.' I shook my head. 'I'm hopeless with electronics.'

Simon grinned. 'Well, you can't do any worse than the three of us.'

Neil's mouth curved wryly, and he dropped the wires, admitting defeat. 'Come in,' he invited me. 'Don't be shy.'

I came a few steps into the room, keeping the door to my back. It was a larger room than my own, with a soaring ceiling and cool shadows dancing on the papered walls. It was quiet, like him, and it smelled of him – of soap and freshly-ironed cotton and the faintly woodsy scent of aftershave. I concentrated fiercely on the window facing on the fountain square. His window, too, was more beautiful than mine. It was a door, really: arched glass panels that touched the floor, swinging inward on their hinges so that one could walk straight out into the narrow balcony beyond. The rustling branches of the acacia trees seemed near enough to touch.

Neil followed my gaze, understanding. 'Nice, isn't it?'

'And you'll notice,' Simon pointed out, 'that Neil doesn't have any stupid curtains blocking his view.'

Neil smiled at that. 'Yes, well, I'm afraid I had Thierry take them down. It improves the acoustics when I practise.'

'You hear that?' Simon asked his brother. '*Thierry* took them down. Favouritism,' he pronounced. 'That's what it is. Though I don't imagine Thierry'll be too happy when he finds out you busted his stereo.'

'Probably not, but I'm sure he'll find me another. I'd just as soon have a smaller one, anyway,' he confessed. 'This one's rather too powerful for my needs. Can't set the volume higher than three, or it makes your ears bleed.'

'That's your age showing, old man,' Simon teased.

I looked from the jumble of cassette tapes on top of the hi-fi to the sleek violin case propped on a corner chair. 'Do you tape your practise sessions, then?' I asked Neil.

'Lord, no, I spend enough time listening to myself. No, my orchestra in Austria is learning a new piece,' he explained, 'by a young composer – very strange stuff, very difficult. And with a newly written piece I find a tape more helpful than just looking at the score. Actually,' he said, rubbing the back of his neck, 'this is the second system I've ruined. I brought my own portable one with me, but it barely lasted two days.'

'Maybe someone's trying to tell you something,' Paul suggested, tongue in cheek.

'Maybe. But if it keeps up, it'll drive me to drink.'

'Hey!' Simon suddenly remembered his treasure hunt. He turned to face me, hopeful. 'Did you get through to the *Clos des Cloches*?'

'Yes.'

Something chased across Neil's face, some flicker of emotion that was gone before I could identify it. 'The *Clos des Cloches*?' he echoed, lightly. 'Why were you ringing there?'

Simon answered for me. 'They gave Emily an invitation for a tour and wine-tasting. So we're all going.' Cheerfully, he looked in my direction. 'Was this morning OK for them?'

'Yes. Ten-thirty.'

Paul glanced at his watch. 'God, that's only half an hour from now. We'd better get a move on.'

Neil folded his arms across his chest and looked down at me, his eyes faintly searching. 'They gave you an invitation?'

I nodded. 'I met the owner, you see, quite by accident, and—'

Simon cut me off. 'You met the owner? Really? Great! Then you can ask him for me.'

Neil pulled his eyes from mine, eyebrows lifting. 'Ask him what?'

'If I can see his cellar.' I was watching Simon's face when

the next thought struck him, and my heart sank, because there wasn't a thing I could do to prevent it. 'Hey,' he said brightly, turning to Neil, 'why don't you come with us? You know the guy, too, don't you?'

Startled, I glanced up at Neil, and he met my eyes with a curious smile. 'Yes, I know him,' he said, sliding his gaze to Simon. 'And thanks. I'd be delighted to join your tour.'

Armand Valcourt didn't look especially delighted when he met us at the gate. He hid it well, but I caught the hard line of his smile as he returned Neil's handshake.

'It's been a long time,' Armand said.

'Yes.'

'Martine told me you were back. I was surprised you did not come earlier, to the house. You are avoiding us, perhaps?'

'Not at all.' A curious tension grew and stretched between the two men, like a tightly strung wire, until the air around us fairly hummed with silent friction. It felt, I thought, almost like hate . . .

Paul must have felt it, too. Ever the peacemaker, he took a step forward and introduced himself, and the moment of unspoken combat passed.

Armand shook Simon's hand next, then mine, his dark eyes knowing. 'So,' he said, in French, 'you decided to use your invitation, after all. And you have brought your friends. How . . . nice.'

I smiled up at him, innocent. 'Did I mention, Monsieur, that my friend Paul can speak the most beautiful French?'

'Can he?' The dark eyes laughed, left mine and looked

at Paul. 'Can he, indeed?' He let go of my hand, and took a step backwards. He looked different again by daylight. The working man's outfit of chinos and sweater suited him rather well, I thought.

Simon nudged me. 'Ask him.'

Armand arched an eyebrow, intrigued. 'Yes? You have a question, Mademoiselle?'

Again I smiled. 'More of a request, actually. Simon here was hoping to see your wine cellar.'

'Ah.' He looked from me to Simon, and back again. 'Naturally, the cellars are included in the tour, but at the end, yes? For the tasting. We must follow the process in its proper order, beginning, I think, with the vines.'

He turned to lead us along a narrow, straight-edged path, cool in the shadow of the high stone wall that bounded the vineyard. Simon, impatient as always, kept close behind Armand, and Paul ambled along behind. Neil fell into step beside me, matching his pace to mine.

We walked in silence to begin with, but then my own awareness of him made the silence uncomfortable, and I tried to think of something neutral to talk about. 'You've been here before, then?' I asked.

'Yes. I knew his wife.'

I bent my head hurriedly. 'Oh, I see.' So much for neutral, I told myself.

'Brigitte, her name was,' he went on, in a mild tone. 'We had mutual friends in Vienna. I knew both the sisters, Brigitte and Martine.'

Curiosity pricked me then, and against my better judgement I asked: 'And were they very much alike?'

144

I felt the glancing touch of his eyes on my downturned face. 'That's right, you've met Martine, haven't you? Yes, Brigitte was very like her to look at, but as far as personality . . .' He smiled a little, thinking back. 'Brigitte was wild. Unpredictable. She met Armand and married him, all in one weekend. Destiny, she called it. She believed in destiny.' He spoke the word almost as if he believed it, too. He cast a quick glance up the ridge towards the white house, remembering. 'She used to hold these huge dinner parties,' he told me, 'all artists and writers and poor musicians like myself, and she'd fill us full of food and wine and set us talking. Bright minds and brilliant conversation, that's what Brigitte wanted. Like Madame Pompadour.'

Still looking down at the path, I stole a sideways look at the denim-clad legs striding evenly beside mine, and the beautiful, long-fingered hands, and I thought I knew exactly what Brigitte Valcourt had wanted from Neil Grantham. The sudden stab of feeling rather shocked me. I hadn't felt jealous in years. Aloud I said: 'It must have been fun.'

'It was. Brigitte brought us all together, Christian and myself and . . . oh, there was a gang of us, in those days. I don't know what happened to most of them. When Brigitte died the group just fell apart, stopped meeting.'

I kicked a pebble on the dirt path. 'How did she die?'

'Heart failure.'

'Oh. I'm sorry.'

'It happens. She'd been in and out of hospital since giving birth to Lucie – she used to make a new will nearly every week, I think,' he said, with a brief smile. 'I don't think any of us was particularly surprised.'

Armand was still walking briskly alongside the wall, several paces ahead of us. He turned his head to say something to Simon, and glanced idly back at Neil and me, his expression unreadable.

The corners of Neil's mouth tugged upwards. 'We never did get on, Armand and I. It's not your fault.'

I flashed a quick look up at him. 'I don't see that I have anything to do with it.'

'Don't you?' He slanted a kind smile down at me. I struggled for a response, but before I could collect my thoughts, the others ahead of us stopped walking, and I had to step smartly to avoid running over Paul. The vineyard tour was about to begin.

CHAPTER TWELVE

. . . past a hundred doors
To one deep chamber shut from sound,

Armand had led us to a spot halfway along the imposing wall, where the rows of stunted vines began their orderly climb to the crest of the hill. The noise of the passing traffic was muted here, a muffled humming on the far side of the wall, and nothing more. There was only the deep green hill, and the great sundrenched sky with its speckling of cotton wool clouds, and at our backs, the ever-watchful presence of Château Chinon. The modern world seemed but a distant dream.

'Of course,' Armand was saying to Simon, 'you know that it was an American, like yourself, who nearly ruined the wine-making in France?'

'We're Canadians.'

'But that is the same thing, surely?'

Paul stepped in once again to keep the peace, his calm voice riding smoothly over Simon's ruffled feathers. 'What did the American do?'

'He ate our vines,' Armand replied, then to our puzzled faces he explained how the tiny phylloxera beetle, nearly a century and a half ago, had crossed the wide Atlantic aboard the newly-invented steamship, and landed like a conqueror upon the shores of France. In the 1860s, Armand told us, that one microscopic pest, undetected, had ravaged vineyard after vineyard, bringing the noblest of estates near to ruin. The French wine industry had very nearly collapsed, until it was discovered that by grafting French vine stalks onto American roots – immune by nature to phylloxera – the devastator could be held at bay.

'It is a truce only,' Armand admitted, fingering a broad leaf. 'We must still graft, and spray, and be on guard. The danger, it has not entirely disappeared.'

Paul peered closely at the base of one of the gnarled vines. 'These have American roots, then?' he asked. 'All of them?'

Armand nodded. 'Yes. In my father's time, such grafting was done by hand, but now we have a machine to do the work.'

'Wouldn't it be simpler,' I put in, 'just to grow American vines?'

Armand grinned at that. 'The native vines of North America, Mademoiselle, produce the wine like vinegar. Even the roots, they change somewhat the character of our grafted vines, but,' he added, philosophically, 'we must make sacrifices sometimes, to preserve a way of life. And what lies beneath the surface, no one sees.'

Still conscious of Neil standing close behind me, I took the opportunity to move away a few steps, venturing into the row of vines. 'What kind of grapes are these?'

'They are the Cabernet Franc,' Armand said. 'That is the grape of Chinon's wines, the red wines.'

'But there aren't any grapes,' Simon complained, as though he'd been somehow cheated.

'No, we have already harvested, last week. I had a . . . how do you say it . . . a hunch that there would be rain, and at this time the rain can be most harmful to the grapes. The water rises through the roots, you understand, and swells the grapes, and so the wine it has no colour, no substance – it is spoiled.'

Simon, who had only come to see the cellar anyway, lost interest quickly after that. When Armand led us in between the vines, Simon wandered after us, hands in his pockets, his mind on other things.

The vines stood chest-high on the men and reached very nearly to my shoulders, their spreading branches trained around strong wires strung between short posts. Trained, I thought, was the operative word, for despite the twisting tangle there was pristine order here. The rows climbed the sloping hill like soldiers, each vine pruned with such precision that when I looked out across the field of fluttering green I might have been looking out across a level, square-clipped hedge.

Neil walked behind me, silently, and seemed content to listen while Armand explained the workings of the vineyard. Paul was the only one of us who truly paid attention. His intelligent questions pleased Armand, who took his time in answering them, his technical language punctuated by beautifully expressive gestures.

I had thought Armand Valcourt in his element when I'd seen him in his home last night, but here in the fragrant hush of the vineyard another aspect of his being came quietly to the surface, surprising me with its intensity. He spoke proudly of the superior qualities of the *Clos des Cloches* – the south-facing slopes that captured each ray of the summer sun, the limestone soil that kept those slopes well-drained, the age of the vines themselves . . . 'The *appellation contrôlée* requires that a vine be four years old before wine can be made from it, but we wait until our vines have eight years.'

'What is the *appellation contrôlée?*' Paul wanted to know, and Neil's voice drifted lazily over my head.

'A kind of committee that sets the standards for the making of French wine.'

Armand accepted the definition, adding only that the rules were very strict. 'We must not harvest before a certain date, nor after a certain date. We must grow a certain variety of grape, and then we may call our wines Chinon. If not, if we choose to break these rules, the penalties are hard. There are heavy fines, and they will come and uproot our vines.' He shrugged. 'It is truly the end of the world, I think.'

That was the farmer talking, not the aristocrat, just as it was the farmer who knelt now among the vines to demonstrate to Paul how each gnarled branch was pruned by hand to catch the sunlight.

'I am sorry,' he was saying, to Paul, 'that I cannot spare the time today to show you how our wine is made, but I can at least show you the result. It is the most important

150

thing, I think. The process of wine-making, the machines we use, these are things you can learn from a book, but the wine . . .' He gave a pointed shrug. 'The wine, it is like life itself. It must be tasted at the source.'

Simon perked up behind us. 'So we're going to see the cellar now?'

'Yes. I have set out a few good vintages for you to taste.'

'Terrific.' The bounce was back in Simon's step. Moving past us, he assumed the lead, his eyes fixed with a hunter's single-mindedness upon the huge white house.

I wished I could share his enthusiasm. Wine cellars might be interesting places, and impressive, but underground was underground no matter how one viewed it, and the French didn't call their cellars *'caves'* for nothing. The only thing that cheered me was that Harry wasn't here to announce to everyone that I was phobic. 'She has a thing,' he would have told them, 'about going underground.' He always said it just like that, as if it were some random illness, inexplicable, and though I sometimes did remind him of the day he'd locked me in the neighbour's bomb shelter, Harry never would admit he was to blame. 'I shot an arrow at you, too,' he'd once retorted, 'and you didn't develop a phobia about *that.'*

He had a point, I thought. Given the choice between facing a field of archers or spending an hour in someone's basement, I'd pick the archers every time. But now, without a single bowman in sight, I found myself with no real option but to take a deep breath and follow along with the tour.

The cellars of the *Clos des Cloches* lay deep within the cliffs beneath the house. They were enormous, high-arched and spacious like the soaring nave of some fantastic cathedral. The ghostly limestone caught the light and cast it back upon us, and when I let my breath go I inhaled the sweeter scent of oak and wine above the dank aroma of the stone. Along one curving wall the bottles ran in ranks, neatly stacked, awaiting labels, their glass dark green beneath the thickly sifted dust. But the barrels dwarfed them easily.

They were everywhere, those barrels – great monstrous ones that might have served Gargantua himself, and row on row of smaller ones that seemed to stretch for ever, an aisle of darkened oak illumined softly on all sides by countless burning candles whiter than the walls. The candles, set with care upon the rim of every barrel, seemed to be the main source of light in this medieval hall of wonder. Beyond their reach the shadows crept, to claim the farther corners and the dimly rising stacks of bottled wine.

In the middle of it all stood François, tall and grey and elegant, arranging polished glasses on a small table that already groaned beneath the weight of several vintages. He looked round as we came in, his inscrutable face relaxing as he noticed me beside Armand. Only a statue could have failed to be flattered by his smile. 'Mademoiselle,' he greeted me, in French, 'it is indeed a pleasure to see you again.'

To my surprise he welcomed Neil with similar warmth, framing his words in halting English. There was no hint of the bitterness, the tension, that had marked Neil's conversation with Armand. In fact, I thought, they spoke like friends.

Paul, at my shoulder, waited patiently to be introduced, gazing at the arching dome of the *cave's* ceiling with eyes half-closed in rapt appreciation. I'd only known him two days, but I fancied that I recognised that look already.

'Go on, then,' I teased him, with a nudge. 'Shatter me. What's the word for this place?'

He smiled. 'That obvious, eh?'

Armand looked sideways at the two of us. 'The word . . . ?'

'Oh,' said Simon, 'it's just this kind of game Paul plays, trying to find the perfect word to describe a place. He's pretty good, most of the time, except he hasn't got the word for Château Chinon, yet.'

'Yes he does,' I said. 'It's "tragic".'

Armand studied Paul's face closely, as though he hadn't seen him properly, before. 'That is indeed the perfect word. Tragic . . .' He tasted the feel of it, on his tongue. 'And my *caves*?' he asked. 'How would you call them?'

Paul looked a shade embarrassed, but he met the challenge squarely. 'Clandestine,' he said, in his quiet voice.

'So,' Armand said, softly. 'So . . . a place for intrigue, yes? Or secret lovers.' His eyes slid past me, smiling, and came to rest on François. 'Well, who can say you are not right? There is much history here, and in my family there are many secrets.' François glanced up, and Armand looked away again. 'The making of wine,' he said to Paul, 'it is an art wrapped well in secrets. As in your game of words, one tries to find the essence of each vintage, removing that which complicates. Come, I will show you.'

It was more work than I'd imagined, tasting wine. With François guiding me, I sampled the estate's great vintages, trying to follow each instruction – how to hold the glass,

153

how to inhale the wine's 'nose' – there were so many things a true wine-lover ought to notice.

And I did try, really I did. I swirled and sniffed and scrutinised, and in truth I very nearly saw the purple edge that Armand said was such a telling characteristic of his clear red wine. But when he spoke of complex structure and of 'legs', and breathed the scents of strawberries and vanillan oak, I had to admit my own deficiencies. It was a lovely wine, I thought, a great one even, but to my untutored palate it tasted . . . well, like *wine*. And the more I drank the more like wine it tasted.

Neil knew. His eyes touched mine and held, smiling, and the faintest shiver crawled between my shoulders.

'Cold?' Paul checked, missing nothing. He was well into the fourth vintage. Paul, I felt sure, could see with ease the violet edge, and catch the scent of strawberries. I shook my head, and shrugged to clear the shiver.

'No, not really.'

Simon looked at Armand, his expression casual. 'How old,' he asked him, 'would your cellars be?'

Armand shrugged. 'Older than the house. Our *cave*, our cellar, it was once used by the kings who stayed at the château.'

Paul eyed his brother warningly over the rim of his wine glass, but Simon had already seized the opening. 'Really? So this was connected to the château, somehow?'

I might have imagined the flickering glance François sent his employer, and the careful pause before Armand replied. 'Yes. The kings built many *souterrains,* or tunnels, as you call them. Ours is among the oldest, I believe.'

'It still exists?' Simon feigned surprise. 'You mean you have a tunnel that goes straight to the château?'

Before Armand could answer that, Neil set his own glass on the table. 'I haven't seen the *souterrain* in years,' he said. 'Perhaps, Simon, if you ask him very nicely, Monsieur Valcourt will show it to us.' There was a sort of challenge in his voice, and in the way his level eyes met those of our host.

'It is kept locked,' Armand said, finally.

Neil smiled his quiet smile, and the challenge became a dare. 'Surely, just this once.'

There was a moment's silence, then Armand's mouth hardened and he picked the gauntlet up. 'Why not?' He turned to François. 'Do you have the keys?'

I would have preferred not to go with them. The *cave*, at least, was brightly lit and full of air, and I could half convince myself I wasn't underground. But once again, I didn't have much choice. The others swept me with them, through the *cave* and past a small group of incurious workmen, to a darker narrow passageway behind.

Above our heads the pallid rock, its surface scarred and pitted by the chisels of ancient craftsmen, closed round us like a tomb. The smell of damp was stronger here, and Neil was forced to duck his head. There were at least a dozen doorways bolted shut on either side of the passage.

Simon stopped, excited, at the first one. 'Is this the entrance to a tunnel?'

'No.' Armand laughed, and shook his head, it is a . . . how do you call it? A broom cupboard. This,' he told us, walking a few steps on and fitting his key into a lock, '*this* is the door you want.'

155

The tunnel was just that – a tunnel, hung with cobwebs, strewn with dirt, and smelling of decay. I took one look and stepped back hastily, bumping into Neil. He kindly took no notice.

'But it's stone,' said Simon. He sounded disappointed, and I realised he'd expected to see walls of earth or clay. One didn't, as a rule, dig holes in solid rock to bury treasure. 'Is it stone all the way through?'

Armand assured him that it was.

'Can I go in?'

'I am afraid,' Armand replied, 'that I cannot allow it. This *souterrain* is old, and there is now a road overhead that weakens it. To use it now would not be wise.' He swung the door shut and the key in the lock clicked firmly. 'It is not safe.'

Nothing underground was safe, I thought. It was a relief to surface once more into sunlight, and to feel the whisper of the wind upon my face. I stood a moment enjoying the sensation, while the boys walked on ahead with Neil. Armand hung back as well, his face expectant. 'So, how do you like my vineyard?'

I told him it was fascinating, and he looked pleased. 'It is my pride, you understand. This estate has come to me from many generations of Valcourts, and one day it will belong to Lucie.' He looked out, as I had done earlier, across the flat-topped vines. 'The greatest part of me lies in this place,' he told me. 'I'm glad it fascinates you.'

Simon turned ahead of us. He appeared to have recovered quickly from his setback in the cellar, and having ruled out Armand's tunnel as a hiding place for Isabelle's lost treasure, he was eager to get on to other things. He beckoned me impatiently. 'Emily, come on. We're going to the Echo next.'

Armand's eyes narrowed, sliding sideways. 'He has much energy, that young man.'

'Yes.' I couldn't help the smile. Armand walked with me to the gates, and after a confusing criss-cross of handshakes and thank-yous, he turned to take my hand.

'You must come back another time.' *Alone,* his dancing eyes said, and his smile was a sinful thing. 'And you must tell me how you enjoy seeing our Echo. It is quite unique.'

I wasn't entirely sure how one could see an Echo in the first place, but everyone promised me that it was indeed possible, and that there was a lovely view from the Echo, and that I would be suitably impressed.

And so I kept an open mind as I followed my companions through the gates. Neil left us there. 'Sorry, but I promised to meet someone,' was his excuse, and looking like a man well pleased with the day's work, he strolled away, head bent and humming to himself.

Simon, happy to be back in charge, turned sharply in the opposite direction and, keeping his shoulder to the high wall of the *Clos des Cloches,* led Paul and me around a curve of deserted road to a desolate place where the wind wept softly through the long grass. 'Here it is,' he announced, proudly.

There was no mistaking it – a sign posted to one side of a raised viewing platform clearly read: *Ici l'Echo,* and the platform itself, though small, looked rather official.

'It really does work,' said Paul. 'Just stand up there and yell something.'

I climbed the few steps obediently and turned around. The view, as I'd been promised, was a postcard panorama stretching from the château on the one side, out across the silver river and the patchwork roofs and gardens, to the distant hills beyond. Closer than that, across the road, treetops and a tiled roof peeked above an unkempt, rambling hedge. 'But I'll be yelling into someone's yard,' I protested, and Simon hopped up beside me with a laugh.

'It's OK, really. People do it all the time. Here, I'll show you.' And he bellowed out an enthusiastic yodel that would have done credit to a native of the Swiss Alps. The sound soared out and came back, crashing loud against the green hills and the ruined walls of the château, like waves striking rocks on a wild shore.

'Neat, eh?' Simon grinned. 'You can even ask it questions, like this . . .' Again he filled his lungs, and yelled: 'Will I ever get Paul to leave Chinon?'

The answer flowed back, faintly questioning in itself: '*Non . . .*'

'Very funny,' said Paul. 'Why don't you let Emily give it a try?'

I smiled. 'I wouldn't know what to say.'

But they weren't about to let me off that easily. Put on the spot, I closed my eyes tightly and tried to think of something clever. Perhaps I ought to call out Armand's name, I thought wryly, in case he was standing on the other side of the vineyard wall, listening. It might be good for his ego. But the dark eyes that smiled at me in my thoughts were not Armand Valcourt's. I tried to push the image from my mind. Oh, damn and blast, I thought. Oh, *help*. So that

158

was what I yelled, in French. *'Au secours!'*

It was a foolish thing to do. If I'd been in a public place, I might have caused a panic – people hurrying to help me; cries for the police.

But here, I only startled Paul, who turned to stare at me while Echo stirred in far-off fields and called back her advice.

'Cours,' was what she told me.

Run.

CHAPTER THIRTEEN

From out a common vein of memory . . .

'The day gets better and better,' Simon said, as we filed out between the houses at the foot of the cobbled stair. I saw straight away what had pleased him.

It was already afternoon, and the sun had grown uncertain, but Thierry, in a burst of optimism, had set the hotel's tables out around the fountain square. It made a cheery showing, the bright white tables and red chairs. And directly ahead of us, at a table beside the fountain, sat Martine Muret. She was so lovely, so strikingly lovely, with her fashion-model features and cropped black hair. Neil had said that Armand's wife had looked like that, and pushing back another pang of jealousy I looked more closely at Martine, with eyes that sought to see beyond her to a woman three years dead. Had Brigitte Valcourt's hair been short as well? The cut certainly suited Martine, and her simple dark clothes set off her beauty as a plain frame enhances an exquisite painting. Head up, she sat watching the idle activity of the square through expensive sunglasses that hid the expression of her eyes. She looked entirely unapproachable.

Undaunted, Simon raised one hand in cheerful greeting and blazed a path across the square towards her.

Paul looked at me. 'He never gives up.'

'Well, one can't really blame him.' I stopped, and bent to tie my shoe, tipping my face up towards him. 'Paul, what does Martine Muret do?'

'What do you mean?'

'For a living. Does she work, or . . .'

'Oh. She owns the local gallery.'

'Art gallery?'

He nodded. 'Yeah. It's just around the corner there, in one of the smaller squares.' He pointed off to one side of the hotel. 'You can't miss it. There's a Christian Rand self-portrait in the window.'

'They're a couple, then, I take it?' I tried to ask the question quite as if I didn't care, as if it hardly mattered which of the hotel guests Martine had been out with, when Lucie had wandered off.

Paul shrugged. 'I wouldn't say so, no. In fact I'm sure they're not. Good friends, I think – that's all.'

'Oh.' I yanked on my shoelace, tying it too tightly. *Which one was it?* I'd heard Armand ask Martine, last night. *The German or the Englishman?* And I'd been hoping, for some foolish reason, that it was the German. I sighed and stood, and looked again at that lovely face. The face that reminded Neil of Brigitte Valcourt. 'I wonder if she chose that chair on purpose?' I asked.

'Why?'

'Well, she's sitting next to Beauty.'

'What? Oh, the Graces, you mean.' He scrutinised the fountain sculpture. 'How can you tell which one's which?'

'Neil named them, last night. He thought Splendour faced the sunset, and that one there was Beauty, and Joy had the biggest smile.'

'That makes sense.'

I folded my arms and frowned. 'Only they're not smiling, are they?'

'Of course they are. That's what—'

'—Graces do. I know.' Still, try as I might, the only smile I saw belonged to Martine Muret herself. And even that smile looked faintly strained.

'So,' she said, as we descended on her table. 'Simon tells me you have toured the *Clos des Cloches*. And how did you enjoy it?'

Simon grinned. 'It was great, thanks. Mind if we join you?' His arm was promptly nudged from behind, and he turned round, frowning. 'What?' he demanded of Paul.

'I think she has company already, that's all.'

There was no one with her at that moment, but it was obvious from the glasses on the table that she hadn't been drinking alone. Her glass held red wine, but whoever had been with her had been drinking *Pernod*. Martine hesitated for a moment, only a moment, then shook her head. 'No, it is all right. Please,' she moved her hand, inviting us to sit down.

I took the chair facing the fountain, where I could watch

the spring-fed water tumble gently past the bowing Graces like a jewelled transparent veil. Across the table from me Martine Muret smiled pleasantly, expectantly.

'So, what did Armand show you?'

Simon summarised our tour. He didn't mention anything about the tunnel, though, which surprised me, until I remembered that Paul had termed his brother 'paranoid'. Perhaps, I reasoned, Simon was afraid to talk about the treasure in case someone else started looking for it. When he came to the end of his animated account, he leaned back in his chair and raked the hair back from his forehead. 'But I could really use a coffee,' he concluded. 'He gave us these huge glasses to taste with. I always thought wine-tasting meant an inch of wine in the bottom of the glass. Who knew?'

Martine's laugh was a tinkling echo of the fountain spilling down behind her. 'So Armand has made you drunk, today?'

'Well, he certainly tried to,' said Paul. 'But I've still got room for a beer. Emily?'

I shook my head. 'You don't have to buy me a drink, it's quite all right.' But Paul insisted, and he would have kept right on insisting if I hadn't finally given in and opted for my favourite drink of white wine and blackcurrant cordial. 'I'll have a *kir*, then, please.'

My own wine-tasting flush seemed to have worn off, but Thierry, when he came over to take our order, wasn't altogether convinced. He sent me a piercing, faintly paternal look. 'You have eaten lunch, Mademoiselle?' he asked me.

'Well, not exactly.'

He shook his head, disapproving. 'No food at all?'

'Well, no, but—'

'It is not good,' he chastised me, 'to drink the wine without food first.' But he brought me my *kir* in the end, along with a small dish of peanuts that he'd smuggled from behind the bar. 'These are for you,' he said, setting the dish down in front of me. 'Do not let Simon steal them.'

Simon sent him a wounded look. 'You never bring me peanuts,' he complained.

'This is true,' agreed Thierry, without apology. 'Is there anything else your table is missing? No? Then I leave you to enjoy. I have promised to Monsieur Grantham that I will find for him my little stereo so he can listen to his tapes.'

Martine frowned. 'Did he not have a stereo already?'

'My big one, yes,' said Thierry with a wistful nod. 'But this morning, it has broken, and so . . .' His shrug was resigned. 'He is lucky it is only the machine that breaks, and not his violin. I warned him of this yesterday.'

When I asked him what he meant by that, he shrugged again and grinned. 'Only that he plays every day his . . . how do you say it in English . . . *les gammes?*'

'Scales,' said Paul and I, in unison.

'Yes, his scales, and then the symphony by Beethoven. But yesterday,' he shook his head, 'yesterday, he also plays the song of love, and Isabelle, she does not like to hear such songs.'

I heard the sharp clattering of a glass against the tabletop. Across from me, Martine Muret quickly righted her wine glass and reached for a paper napkin to mop up the small spill. 'How stupid of me! No, it is all right, it is nothing . . .'

165

His offer of help refused, Simon took advantage of the moment of confusion to sneak a handful of peanuts from the dish in front of me. 'Queen Isabelle, you mean?' he asked Thierry, showing off his knowledge, but the bartender shook his head emphatically.

'She is no queen, this Isabelle. She is our *fantôme.*' He cast his eyes upwards, searching for the English word. 'Our ghost.'

'No kidding?'

'I do not kid,' he said to Simon, stiffly. 'She lived here, in the last war.'

Definitely not Isabelle of Angoulême, I thought. Not King John's young and tragic queen, but someone else, some later Isabelle, who couldn't bear to hear Neil play a love song. I felt a sharper twinge of curiosity. 'Have you ever seen her, this ghost?'

'Of course he hasn't,' said Simon, mumbling through his mouthful of peanuts. 'There are no ghosts.'

'Ah,' said Thierry, 'are there not?' He slanted a superior eye down on this upstart sceptic from the New World. 'Then it will not upset you to know that you sleep each night in the room where Isabelle died.'

'Isabelle.' Madame Chamond curled herself gracefully onto the seat opposite me and tilted her head to one side, smiling faintly. She was a lovely woman, tall and dark and elegant, with all her husband's grace and charm and then some. 'But this is such a sad story to tell, Simon, and I do not wish to spoil the evening for everyone.'

Which was a rather hollow argument, I thought,

considering what a sorry-looking bunch we were, the lot of us. The boys and I had just come back from dinner at the *Coeur de Lion,* and the food had made me drowsy. Paul, too, was leaning back with half-closed eyes, while beside him Neil lounged in his corner seat, unmoving. Even Christian Rand, who'd dropped in for a nightcap at the bar, looked rather like he might fall off his stool from sheer exhaustion. Simon appeared normal enough, but then nothing seemed to tire Simon. And Garland Whitaker, recovered from her headache, was back in full voice, snuggled like a kitten on the chair beside her husband.

She smiled a faintly pouting smile of encouragement at Madame Chamond. 'You won't spoil our evening one bit. Anyway, you've got us all curious now, about this Isabelle person.'

'Think of how I feel,' Simon chimed in. 'She died in our room, for Pete's sake.'

Behind me, at the bar, I heard Monsieur Chamond's low and pleasant laugh. 'Isabelle did not die in your room,' he said. 'Who told you this?'

'Thierry.'

'Ah.' Our host nodded. 'Well, he does not know the story very well. Even I do not remember all of it. It was so long ago, before I myself was born, you understand . . .'

'She was a Chinon girl,' Madame Chamond began, relenting. 'She worked here as a chamber maid, during the war, the occupation.'

Garland raised her eyebrows. 'Occupation? I thought France collaborated.'

'Not all of France. Not Chinon,' Madame Chamond

167

answered firmly. 'We were occupied. This hotel was used to garrison . . . that is the right word? . . . garrison the German officers. And that is how Isabelle met her Hans.'

'A romance!' Garland's eyes gleamed victoriously. 'Oh, how wonderful! I always *love* a wartime romance, don't you? That's how Jim's parents met, when his father was stationed in . . . where was it, darling?'

Jim Whitaker balanced his second double Scotch with care on his outstretched knee. 'Normandy.'

Madame Chamond smiled rather gently. 'This was happy for your parents, that they could find each other. But war is not so kind to many people. Not to Hans and Isabelle.'

Cradling her wine glass, she settled back against the cushions, warming to the tale. 'They met in 1944, in the spring. They say that Isabelle was very beautiful, a beauty one does not forget, though she had only sixteen years. The German officers noticed this, of course, but Isabelle guarded well her reputation. She had no love of Nazis. Her older brother had joined already the *Maquis,* the Resistance. In time Isabelle might herself have joined them. But instead, she met Hans.

'He came from a good family, Hans. He spoke French and English also, not just German. He was educated. The other officers would bother Isabelle when she was working, say things to her, but not Hans. Always to Isabelle he was a gentleman, a quiet handsome gentleman. She did not wish to think of him, but . . .' Her shrug was philosophical. 'Life does not always let us choose. And so they fell in love, the French girl and the German officer. For both of them the risks were very great. Always they would meet in secret, for an hour of stolen happiness that could not last.'

Madame Chamond paused to sip her drink, quite calmly, though she must have known she had drawn every one of us into the web of her story. Like an audience waiting for the curtain to rise on the second act, we sat in silence until the wine glass was lowered and once more that lovely, lulling voice took up the narrative. I leaned back, listening, my eyes fixed on the dancing flame of the candle on the low table in front of me, and as Madame Chamond went on speaking, my own mind conjured up the images like something seen through darkened glass. I saw young Isabelle, alone and waiting, listening for the familiar footsteps of her lover. And I saw the German officer slip through the sleeping town, heart pounding . . . saw him reach the cliffs and find again the hidden door behind the fall of rock . . .

He turned the corner of the tunnel, blindly. Six steps on, and then another right . . . He counted off the paces in his mind. It wasn't safe to use the torch, not yet – the faintest glimmering of light, the smallest shadow, would bring the sentries running. The tunnels had made them all nervous at first. They'd made him nervous, too, the thought of them, the thought that underneath his feet the earth was riddled with the things, with hollow caves and passages that twisted off, unseen, into the darkness. But now he knew the tunnels well, and welcomed them, and on this night he was more worried about meeting one of his own men than he was afraid of the *Maquis*.

Two paces more, then left . . . he switched the torch on,

blinking in the sudden brightness of the ghostly limestone walls that curved round him like the walls of a tomb.

'Hans?' Her voice, uncertain. 'Oh, God, I was so worried . . .'

How could he have known life before, without her in his arms? He pulled back, smiling . . . touched her face. 'You must be brave for me.'

'I don't want to be brave.' Her eyes seemed very large, there in the darkness.

'Please. For me.' They would both have need of bravery, he knew, before the month was over. It had been weeks now since the enemy had come ashore upon the Norman beaches to the north. Weeks, and still the Reich was fool enough to stand its ground. They knew, they all knew, it was over. Just last night, Jurgen – strong solid Jurgen who had been there longer than anyone – had turned world-weary eyes on Hans above his glass of whisky. 'We're finished, you know,' Jurgen had told him. 'Finished. Only the Führer won't admit it. He thinks we'll win it back for him, the fool.' It was treason to talk like that, but Hans hadn't said anything. Jurgen had looked at him again, and smiled wryly. 'Ah well, I've lived enough, I think, and there is no one left at home to miss me when I'm gone. Tell me, do you still see that girl?'

'What girl?'

'I do have eyes, you know. Do you still see her?'

'Yes.'

Above the whisky glass the weary eyes had grown curious, and almost kind. 'Do you love her?'

'Yes.'

A moment longer Jurgen had watched him, and then he'd thrown something on the table, a small black bag of velvet cloth, tied with a cord. It rattled when it landed, like a sack of shifting pebbles. 'Then give her these. I have no use for them.'

'What are they?' he had asked.

He'd been stunned, then, and even tonight his hand shook slightly as he felt inside his jacket for that same small velvet bag. 'I have brought something for you,' he said to Isabelle. He held out the bag and she looked at him.

'I don't need anything.'

'This is not anything. It's diamonds.'

She echoed the word back at him, her dark eyes flashing disbelief. 'But where would you get diamonds?'

'From a friend. He was given orders to bury them below the hotel, for safety. So they will be there when our Army comes back.' Again he touched her face, he couldn't help himself. 'Only, we won't be coming back

'Don't.'

'I said you must be brave. I do not plan to die, my love.' His smile was a promise. 'I will come back when this is over. I will come back for you.'

He felt the longing in her kiss, and the dampness of her tears against his own skin, but when he opened his eyes she was smiling. He murmured something soft, in German, that she couldn't understand, and closed his fingers over hers, around the velvet bag. 'You keep these safe, for us,' he told her. 'They are our future.'

Our future, he thought sadly, and he reached for her again . . .

The night was nearly over when he wound his way back through the tunnels. Six steps on, then left . . . this must be how the blind felt, he thought, with the darkness thick against his face and the sound of his own breathing harsh in that still space. It was a despairing sort of feeling. Fourteen steps . . . he put out his hand, trailing it along the dry and dusty stone, feeling for the iron ring of the door. His hand touched cloth instead.

Warm cloth, that breathed.

He felt the fingers groping at his throat, cutting off his choking gasp of surprise, but five years of army life had made his own reactions swift and automatic. This was no fellow soldier, standing sentry – the shirt he felt was soft, not stiff. Not a uniform. And the words of hate were hissed in French, not German. Deprived of breath, Hans moved from instinct. Up came his own hands, feeling, finding, then one sharp twisting motion and a sickening crack. The fingers at his throat relaxed, fell away, and he breathed a painful breath.

This time he found the iron ring and wrenched the thick door open, letting in a singing rush of air. Beyond the door the road and roofs were silent. Nothing stirred. The sky was something less than black, a creeping greyness edging out the stars, but still he had to risk the torch to see the body at his feet. The yellow light touched a torn shirt, and brown long-fingered hands, and travelled upwards to the staring face.

Her face. Oh, God. Her brother's face. She'd shown him once, a photograph. 'You wouldn't get along,' she'd said.

'Isabelle . . .' His hand jerked and the torch fell from it, shattering upon the ancient stone.

CHAPTER FOURTEEN

Before me shower'd the rose in flakes;
behind I heard the puffd pursuer;

Beside me, Jim Whitaker bent his head to light a cigar, and the scrape of the match sounded loud in the quiet room.

Garland shifted in her seat, her eyes gleaming like the eyes of a satisfied cat. 'Oooh, it's just like something out of a movie. He really killed her brother? How exciting.'

It was not, I thought, the word I would have chosen. Not exciting. It was, as Madame Chamond had warned us, a story of great sadness. Of all the fighters of the French Resistance, why did it have to be Isabelle's own brother who met Hans in that dark tunnel? Fate had a heartless sense of humour, sometimes. One death, I thought, and three lives ruined. So it had been with John and Isabelle, more than seven hundred years earlier, when young Arthur of Brittany's murder had brought John's great empire crashing to the ground. How many times had they relived those moments, John and Hans, and wished the deed undone?

Two men in separate centuries, both loving Isabelles, bound by a single destiny that sent its unrelenting echo down the years.

A tiny chill swept fleeting through the room, and Simon fidgeted, unable to stand the suspense. 'So what happened?' he asked Madame Chamond. 'What happened to Hans and Isabelle?'

'Ah, well, it was most difficult. A few days later came the liberation and everything was changed. Hans I think was killed, or captured, in the fighting, and Isabelle . . .'

Simon reacted sharply. 'She killed herself? In our room?'

'No, not in your room,' said Monsieur Chamond, unable to mask his quick smile. 'No, Isabelle drowned herself, did she not, in the river?' He looked to his wife for confirmation. 'At least, that is what I have heard. No one has ever died in this hotel, not like that.'

Neil turned in his chair. 'And what became of the diamonds?'

'No one knows,' said Christian quietly. It startled me a little, to hear the cadence of the German voice, so soon after surfacing from my imaginings. It was as if Hans himself had spoken to us.

'Diamonds . . .' Garland Whitaker breathed the word like a prayer. 'Wherever did the Germans get diamonds from?'

'From . . . displaced persons.' Christian's eyes touched Simon and Paul for the briefest of moments before he lowered his gaze and went on. 'The Nazis hid many such things during the war. But you know this, you were talking of it at the restaurant on Friday, of the place you lived in Germany.'

174

Garland nodded. 'And no one's ever tried to find these diamonds? Well for heaven's sake, where was this tunnel that Hans and Isabelle used to meet in?'

'I do not know,' Madame Chamond replied, her smile indulgent. 'Chinon is not so large, Madame, but the tunnels, they are everywhere. And it is just a story, after all. It happened many years ago. The diamonds might just be invention, added later to the story. Who can say?'

Jim Whitaker gave his Scotch a swirl. 'So Isabelle left her ghost behind, did she?'

Monsieur Chamond looked over at him from behind the bar. 'If she did, she is a quiet ghost. She does not bother us.'

'She's murder on my electronic equipment,' Neil said drily, and Monsieur Chamond laughed.

'Apart from that.'

Simon sent our host a suspicious look. 'And you're sure she didn't die in our room?'

'Quite sure.'

Paul smiled finally, in his quiet way. 'I thought you said,' he reminded Simon, 'that there were no such things as ghosts.'

'Well, yeah, but—'

'Then it really doesn't matter where she died, does it?'

Neil Grantham's dark eyes moved thoughtfully from Paul to me. 'I think our Miss Braden believes in ghosts, though. Don't you?'

It was quite unsettling, the feel of those eyes on my face, and I answered without looking up. 'On occasion,' I admitted, 'yes, I do. I'd think Isabelle would have every right to haunt this place, after what happened. I mean, war

175

is so futile, isn't it? So inexcusable, the things it does to people's lives.'

Garland widened her eyes. 'Oh, but it's necessary sometimes, Emily. The Germans – excuse me, Christian – but the Germans just had to be put in their place, don't you agree?'

Simon spoke up in my defence. 'But I think I know what Emily is saying. My grandfather never talks about the war. It hurts too much for him to think about it. And that was over fifty years ago.' He looked across at Jim Whitaker, with a vaguely curious expression. 'You said your father fought in Normandy. Does he ever talk about it?'

'No.'

'My father talks,' said Christian, unexpectedly. 'He was a child in the war. He talks in his sleep. He has dreams.'

We were all silent a moment, reflecting on the wreckage of a war that none of us had lived through. For me, the war meant only Granddad's faded ration book and the neighbour's horrid bomb shelter and musty gas masks gathering dust in the cupboard under the stairs. It all seemed so distant from me, really – an hour or so of film in black and white, and stories told by old men at the local, when the winds of November came cold off the Channel.

So distant, and yet . . . for a moment, there in the bar of the Hotel de France, the echoes of the past came calling, calling, and trailed a haunting trace of laughter through the air.

It was Christian who spoke up first, shifting his position at the bar, his soft eyes thoughtful. 'But this war,' he said, 'it is over now, and now we all sit here and talk, French and German and American . . .'

'And Canadian,' said Simon.

'. . . and Canadian. It is strange, is it not?'

Paul smiled at him. 'It's reassuring. Nice to know we can all move forward, once the scars heal over.'

Half swallowed by the shadow in the corner, Neil calmly pointed out that all old scars felt twinges now and then. 'You can't erase the memory altogether, unfortunately.'

After another full minute of thoughtful silence Simon leaned forward, reaching for his beer glass. 'It's kind of sad, really, when you think about it,' he said, 'but I guess for some people the war is never really over, is it?'

It was Jim Whitaker who answered him, but he wasn't looking at Simon. He wasn't looking at any of us. Eyes fixed unseeing on the darkened windows, his voice came absently, almost as if it didn't quite belong to him. 'No,' he said, slowly. 'I don't believe it is.'

I didn't sleep well, tossed by dreams. I heard the tramp of soldiers' feet across the fountain square, the sound of German voices in the rooms below, the lighter running rhythm of a woman's feet along the corridor. I sighed and shifted restlessly upon the bed, the covers tangling round my legs. Isabelle may not have died in the Hotel de France, but she had left her shadow here. I felt it passing over me, as though she stood beside my bed, and then the curtains at my open window fluttered while the fountain's song grew louder, lulling me to dark oblivion.

I woke early, feeling vaguely melancholic and decidedly unsociable. And so I rose and dressed, and went alone to walk beside the river.

Monday mornings in France had a peaceful silence all their own. Most shops stayed closed out of tradition, and people clung a little longer to their pillows. In all my hour's walk, I only met two people in the shuttered winding streets. From the river's edge, I turned along the road and sauntered up around the château walls to where the white house of the *Clos des Cloches* slumbered in its field of green; then round and up again, past the château's entrance tower with its silent bell, to the narrow breach in the cliff wall, where the steps from the fountain square wound their breathless way upwards.

Here I rested, tucking my hands into the pockets of my jeans and lifting my face to the warmth of the morning sun. Below me, in the patchwork jumble of turrets and church steeples, tightly walled gardens and blind shuttered windows, I heard a swallow singing. O *Swallow, Swallow, if I could follow* . . . What was the rest of that poem? I couldn't remember. Tennyson, again, at any rate – I'd read it at school. Something about a prince wanting the swallow to carry a message to his true love, to tell her he was coming.

A bird, perhaps the same one, broke, rustling, from a fruit tree in the garden just beneath me, and went winging out across the town, its dancing flight and joyful song dissolving my clinging mist of melancholy. 'So my prince is coming, is he?' I asked the swallow, just a speck now in the brilliant sky. Well, I wouldn't hold my breath.

But when, a moment later, I heard footsteps coming up the steps below me, that's exactly what I did – I held my breath for no good reason and leaned forward to peer over the wall. My chest relaxed. I exhaled, and it sounded like a sigh.

Not a prince, certainly. Only Garland Whitaker, labouring upwards, her fingernails flashing blood-red on the iron handrail. The auburn hair, I thought, looked artificial in the sunlight – too bright, too tightly curled. She puffed a little, and her face was flushed.

More footsteps echoed to my right, punctuated by a trill of childish laughter. I straightened away from the wall and turned in time to see a tall man coming round the corner further up by the château, with a lively child swinging on his hand. The man's dark head was bent low, to catch the chatter of the little girl. He hadn't seen me yet.

Thinking fast, I ducked my head and scurried off, away from the château, away from the steps, away from all of them. I was *not*, I thought firmly, going to hang about while Garland and Armand bumped into each other, with me in the middle. She was a hopeless gossip, he was a hopeless flirt, and I'd never hear the end of it.

My getaway would have done credit to a bank robber, I moved that quickly, though no doubt a bank robber would have had a better sense of direction. It should have been easy to find my way down into town, but the first sloping crossroad I came to was blocked, completely blocked, by an idling lorry, and instead of waiting for the driver to move on, I decided to walk along the cliff a little further. Surely there'd be other roads, or even stairs . . .

The narrow road curved upwards and became a lane. Still hopeful, I moved briskly between the silent houses and garden walls, past thick falls of fading ivy and red clay-tiled roofs, painted gates and painted shutters. The houses crowded closely on both sides, parting now and then to give a glimpse of the dizzying drop to the terraced gardens on the cliffside, and the quiet river snaking past the rooftops far below.

I appeared to be the only person about, which was just as well, since there wasn't room for two on the narrow strip of pavement. For a short while I enjoyed the solitude, the scent of roses drifting from the gardens, the spectacular view. But when I reached the first cluster of troglodyte caves, I began to feel uneasy.

I blamed it, to begin with, on the caves themselves. They were not the neatly chiselled cliff dwellings pictured in my Loire Valley guide books, cosily supplied with curtains and carved fireplaces. These caves, cut from a thrusting rise of rock, were eerie and abandoned, black windows crumbling over hollow doors, broad chimneys giving way to the grasping growth of weeds and vines that spilled down from the burning cloudless sky. It was an easy thing, in this apocalyptic settlement, to fancy eyes that watched from every yawning door.

All right, I admitted, so maybe it wasn't too clever of me to be walking up here, on my own. When I crossed the next path cutting down from the cliff, I'd descend to the safety of town.

The path that I was on grew more wild and lonely the further I walked. There were few houses now. On my right, a low rubblestone wall, spattered with lichen and moss, was the only barrier between me and a sheer vertical drop through cedar-scented scrub and tangled weeds. Even the roofs of Chinon, far below, seemed somehow less hospitable.

The paved path turned to yellow soil beneath my feet, and a second crumbling cliff of troglodyte dwellings rose from the weed-tangled hill beside me. A warning prickle chased between my shoulder blades. *Oh, bloody hell,* I thought. I turned. The breeze caught a withered leaf and sent it tumbling end over end across the dirt path, until it was trapped by the long waving grass. Nothing else moved. 'Hello?' I called, just to be sure. 'Is anyone there?'

Silence. Slowly I turned around again, pushing on more cautiously. The solitary house that rose blackly from the path ahead did nothing to reassure me. It was an ugly house, unwelcoming, its sagging door wrapped round with barbed wire coils. As I passed by, the wind swept past, rattling the tightly-shuttered windows like a viper's warning to the unwary. Again the shiver struck me and again I turned my head to look behind. The path was empty.

But this time, when I started to walk on, I heard a sound. The faintest shuffling footfall, and a breathing that was nothing like the wind. Behind me in the house some creature flung itself against the door with a savage growl, and I broke into a half run. I stumbled twice on the uneven ground, and my shoulder brushed a trailing vine and loosed a shower of small white petals that clung to my skin, but I didn't slow my pace until I reached a less neglected place.

There were troglodyte houses here, as well – a neat, low line of them, fronted by a level sweep of gravel. But these houses looked inhabited, not ragged and abandoned. At their farthest end one lovely tree spread green against the white stone walls, and beside the tree a carved and ancient archway sheltered a wooden door with heavy iron hinges.

Here, in this oasis of ordered beauty, I stopped running. There was no logic to it, really, but my racing mind said: *Sanctuary*. Here, I knew beyond all reason, I was safe. With trembling legs I leaned against the wall and drew a ragged breath. I didn't move, even when the sound of footsteps rose above the pounding of my heart. This was not the sound that had pursued me down the path. These steps were different, sharper, climbing from the bottom of the cliff, and there was nothing furtive in their measured tread. Stairs, I thought. There must be stairs nearby. My eyes searched out and found the spot. The steps grew louder, mingling with a voice I recognised, and I felt myself relaxing.

I believe I looked quite normal when Martine and Christian finally appeared above the tangled grasses of the cliff edge.

Martine recovered first from the surprise. 'Hello!' Her widow's veil had been emphatically cast aside this morning, in favour of a yellow windcheater so bright it almost hurt one's eyes to look at it, worn over smartly-pressed black denim jeans and a yellow roll-neck jersey. Even in casual clothes, I decided, she outshone me fairly, but the only thing of which I was truly jealous was her smile. She had perfect teeth. I hadn't ever met a person with really perfect teeth before.

I returned the greeting, straightening away from my supporting wall. 'Out for a walk, are you?'

'Yes. Christian is bored with moving,' Martine told me, 'and so he makes today the sketches for his painting.' Which would explain, I thought, the decidedly battered leather satchel he was lugging about with him this morning, its broad strap digging into his hunched shoulder. He looked half-asleep still. Martine, on the other hand, was wide awake and talking brightly. 'You are admiring the chapelle, Mademoiselle?'

'Please,' I said, 'call me Emily.' And then I frowned. 'What chapelle?'

'The Chapelle of Sainte Radegonde, behind you.'

I looked round at the silent wall, the bolted door. 'Is that what this place is? I didn't know.'

'But yes, this is most famous, here in Chinon. Christian often sketches here. You must come in with us, and see it. The chapelle,' she informed me, 'is not to be missed. Is it, Christian?'

'What?' His head came round a quarter turn, the blue eyes vague as he pulled them away from a contemplation of a floating tuft of clouds. 'Oh, yes, of course. You must come.' He didn't sound particularly enthusiastic, but I didn't take it personally. He seemed to move in a solitary world of his own creation, did Christian Rand.

'The chapelle is kept locked, now,' Martine said. 'Most people, they must ask at the Tourist Office if they wish to see inside. But Christian has a key.'

He was fiddling with it now, in the lock – a long, old-fashioned key like something from a Gothic film. At last it turned, but before he opened the door he did a most peculiar thing. He looked at me with a serious expression, and said: 'You will close your eyes, please.'

'I beg your pardon?'

'I am sorry,' he looked half embarrassed, 'but it is . . . you will only have one chance to be seeing this for the first time, and it is better to be surprised. Please.'

I shrugged and stepped up to the door, screwing my eyes tightly shut like a child waiting to receive a present. I heard the creaking of old iron hinges as Christian pushed the great door open, and I caught a gentle breeze upon my upturned face, a breeze that faintly smelled of flowers and warm stone.

'There,' said Christian. 'You may look.'

At first I couldn't seem to move at all, I could only stand there with my face uplifted to the naked sky and stare and stare until my eyes grew moist. Before me, framed by the open doorway, rose two colossal pillars, smooth and richly white. They seemed to soar towards the heavens, supporting on their curving capitals the arched remains of a ruined wall, capped softly by a golden fringe of grass. Tall iron gates set in between the pillars shielded the inner sanctum, within whose cool and sloping shadows slender columns stretched along a sacred aisle, and the eyes of sculpted saints gazed blindly back at me.

Between the saints and me a garden grew, a wild garden, mindless of man's will or rules of order. Here and there the sunken forms of graves spoke of the time when this wild place had been a proper church, with nave and transept, altar and aisles. But the graves were empty now, the bodies moved and buried elsewhere. Above where they had lain the roof had long since fallen and been cleared away, and the once-high walls had crumbled to uneven contours, their jagged stones yet softened by a trailing growth of ivy.

'My God,' I whispered.

Christian seemed to understand. 'It is most beautiful, this place.'

I scarcely heard him. I finally managed to free my frozen limbs and take a cautious step inside the door.

Here a bay tree arched above a broken baptismal font, and delicate wild flowers quivered at my feet. Everything was green and living, even the soil sprouted moss, and the silent air around me seemed to hum with vital energy.

I nearly didn't see him, to begin with.

He might have been a statue himself, propped against the sunlit wall. The pale hair, the white shirt, both seemed to blend into the ivory stone behind him, and his outstretched legs were buried in a waving sea of green. Only his eyes, when he opened them, commanded attention. They stared, blinked slowly, tried to focus. And then one hand came up to pull the wired headphones from his ears, and I heard the jarring click of a portable tape player being switched off.

'Good morning, everyone,' Neil Grantham said.

CHAPTER FIFTEEN

. . . silent light
Slept on the painted walls . . .

The three of us reacted rather differently, although in my own case it wasn't so much a reaction as a lack of one. I don't think my expression even changed. Martine, beside me, simply laughed, a short delighted laugh, and said, 'Neil, you idiot! How ever did you get in?'

Christian's response was by far the most dramatic. 'You will *not* move!' he ordered, in a forceful tone that sounded not a bit like him.

Neil, who had been leaning forward as if to rise, sank back against the wall and watched benignly while Christian dropped to his knees in the damp earth and swung the bulging satchel from his shoulder, searching through its contents. I'd never seen an artist in action. It was fascinating to watch him clasp an ink pot to the edge of his sketchbook and boldly dash a straight-nibbed pen across the virgin page.

Fascinating to me, at least. No one else took any notice. Martine Muret had doubtless seen it all before, and Neil was looking, not at Christian, but at me. 'You gave me quite a turn just now,' he said, mildly accusing. 'I didn't hear you come in.'

'I'm surprised you didn't hear us opening the door. That lock goes off like a shotgun.'

'I was listening to my music.' The small movement of his head provoked a stern look of reproach from Christian.

'Neil . . .'

'Sorry.' Neil's head stayed very still against the glowing stone, but his eyes swung back to me. 'Thierry loaned me this little machine to replace the one I broke yesterday. It's working rather nicely.'

'At this moment.' Martine came forward, smiling, to stand between the two of us. 'And how did you get in?' she asked again. 'The door, it is kept always locked.'

'I have my methods.' His dark eyes crinkled at the corners.

Christian sighed. 'Martine, please, you block the light. Thank you,' he said shortly, when she'd backed away a step. The pen went scratching across the drawing paper and Christian huddled over it, frowning with the force of his concentration. Neil seemed quite unaffected by all the attention. He didn't stir against the wall, and when his gaze came back to mine it held a quiet resignation.

'It isn't me that interests him,' he said. 'It's something that I'm doing, without knowing it. Isn't that right, Christian?'

The painter looked up, briefly. 'You make this good shadow on the column, just there. This shadow I can use.'

'You see?' Neil smiled at me, vindicated.

Christian lowered his head. 'And also,' he went on, 'you have a quality quite unique that I try to capture. This most amazing stillness.'

'Well, naturally,' said Neil. 'You won't let me move.'

But I knew what Christian meant, and it was something deeper than the seated man's motionless hands or his calm deliberate voice. It was a thing intangible, yet clearly felt – the sense that time was moving round him, past him, leaving him untouched. Even when the drawing was completed and Neil was finally able to stand, rising stiffly from the hard ground and stretching, the aura of stillness clung to him.

Martine smiled. 'You are too old, I think, for climbing walls,' she told him.

'Have a heart, love,' was Neil's reply. 'I've only just turned forty-three – I'm not quite ready for the eventide home.'

Not by a long shot, I agreed, turning my gaze from his boyish face and snugly fitting denim jeans to the crumbling wall above his head, which at its lowest point must still have been some ten or twelve feet tall.

'You climbed that wall?' I asked, incredulous, is that how you got in?'

'Could be.' He smiled again, refusing to appease our curiosity. Turning to Christian, he asked: 'Have you got the keys for this gate with you? Emily might like to see the murals.' He said my name so easily, as though we were old friends, or something more. I thought I saw a flash of curiosity in Martine's sideways glance, but Christian found his keys again and came forward to unlock the towering black grille that sealed the sculpted saints within their inner chamber. They had an odd effect on me, those saints. Though they were trapped in shadows, while I had open sky above me, I felt somehow that it was me, not them, shut in behind the iron bars; that their eyes saw a wider world than mine.

The blind stone faces stared at me as Christian swung the great gate open and we passed into the chapel proper, where our voices echoed as we walked between stone columns soaring high to meet the ceiling many feet above our heads.

'This has been carved from the cliff,' Martine told me. 'You can see here the marks of the chisel. It is very old, this chapelle. Christian,' she said, turning, 'you must tell the story of Sainte Radegonde. I never can remember it properly.'

Christian shrugged uncomfortably and hurried through an abbreviated version. 'She was a German, like myself – a princess. In the sixth of centuries her people were destroyed by the Frankish king, Clotaire, who took Radegonde for his bride. She was then eleven years old. But she was not happy with Clotaire, and so she left him and became a nun. She founded, here at Chinon, a small convent.'

I looked around. 'What, in this spot?'

'No, not here. The hermit Jean was living here, a holy man. I will explain.' He frowned a little, trying to collect his thoughts. He was clearly unaccustomed to the role of tour guide. 'When Radegonde was living at Chinon, there came an order from Clotaire, her former husband, that she should be going south to Poitiers to make a convent, for which he would provide the money. But Radegonde, she was not certain this was good, so she came here to visit Jean the hermit, to ask him what to do.'

'And what did he tell her?'

A second shrug. 'He said that this was a good idea, to go to Poitiers. And so Sainte Radegonde went there, as Clotaire wanted, and built in Poitiers a great church. It is there that she is buried.'

There was an altar of sorts at the end wall, a heavy stone table laid with a white lace covering, set in a hollowed niche that glowed with ancient paintings.

'This mural,' Martine said, pointing to the flaking pigments, rich blue above a deep wine colour, 'this is not the oldest here. This one is only seventeenth-century.'

There were fresh flowers on the altar, and a wooden standing crucifix flanked by bronze candlesticks. Beneath the drape of lace, a broken sculpture bore the likeness of a medieval woman lost in meditative rapture, a royal crown upon her head.

'Is this her?' I asked, bending for a better look, is this Sainte Radegonde?'

Christian nodded. 'Yes. And also this,' he said, showing me a daintier statue that graced a second table in the adjoining painted niche. At the feet of this Radegonde were more cut flowers, and a shallow plate with several coins laid in it. Offerings to the saint, I thought, until Christian set me straight.

'Those are donations to the Friends of Old Chinon,' he said. 'To help with the upkeep of the chapelle.'

Always the practical intruded into the romantic, I reminded myself with a wry smile.

Martine was at my shoulder, pointing. 'The chapelle, it goes even further into the rock, through there.' She showed me a smaller iron gate that spread to fill an opening in the rear wall. There were no saints behind this gate, no kind benevolent eyes, only a few feet of visible stone floor and then an inky darkness. 'There are more caves, and many fine museum items, and an ancient well, from Sainte Radegonde's time. She must see the well, Christian. Do you have the key?'

But the young German shook his head, expressionless. 'No, I have not brought it with me. We can show the well to her another time.'

'But Christian, surely . . .'

'I have not brought the key, Martine.' His tone was firm. 'I am sorry.'

I wasn't overly disappointed, myself. The dank smell of stone that rose from behind the iron gate was acrid and unwelcoming. Besides, my roving gaze had just that moment fallen on a painted frieze at the opposite end of the covered aisle.

'I don't believe it,' I said abruptly. 'There's John.'

Martine, interrupted in her train of thought, looked at the end wall and frowned. 'Yes, that is Jean the hermit,' she said. 'It is a reproduction of his tomb, you understand. The sleeping statue, it is not as old as—'

'No, I didn't mean that,' I broke in. 'I meant the fresco higher up, at the back. That's John Lackland, King of England.'

'Oh, I see. Yes, you are quite right, that is a painting of the Plantagenets.' Her face cleared, and she led us across the neatly swept floor to the corner where the painting was. It was only a fragment of a fresco, really, with a fair chunk missing along the bottom edge, but the colours were brilliant and stunningly true.

'I've seen this before,' I said slowly, admiring the artist's skill. I remembered it from one of Harry's books.

Martine, the art expert, assured me it had been much photographed. 'Many people came to see it thirty years ago, when it was found. It is believed to have been painted when this John came here to marry his queen. That is her there,' she pointed out, 'on the horse behind her husband's. Not the older woman at the back, but the young girl riding in the front.'

Neil came up behind me, closer to the wall, his breath stirring the hair on the top of my head. 'She looks young to be a queen,' he commented. 'And she isn't wearing a crown, is she? The crown is on the older woman.'

'That's Eleanor,' I told him, absently, my eyes fixed on the vibrant painted figures. 'Eleanor of Aquitaine. She was John's mother.' But I wasn't looking at the famous queen. I was looking at the lovely tragic girl in front of her, the great dark eyes that gazed towards the future with such hope . . .

'It was by luck alone that this survived,' Martine was saying. 'Just after it was painted Chinon came to the French king. This John of England, he killed someone, I think, and it was not so nice to have his picture in the church. And so this fresco, it was covered up with plaster. It was not seen again until 1966, when some of the plaster fell down.'

I heard her only dimly. I went on studying the painting, and as my eyes passed over Isabelle it seemed she was now staring straight at *me,* as though she yearned to tell me something. The quiet shadows wrapped cold hands around me, and I quickly looked away. It was, at any rate, the end of the impromptu tour. We wandered back into the sunlight of the walled and roofless yard.

Christian took up a position by the baptismal font, beneath the waving branches of the bay tree, and began to sketch again in ink, his upward glances swift and keen as he traced the broken architecture onto paper. Not wanting to disturb his concentration, I settled myself between Neil and Martine, against the great pillars opposite. I don't believe I did it purposely, sitting between the two of them . . . I don't *believe* I did . . . but then, my actions and reactions where Neil Grantham was concerned were becoming increasingly unpredictable.

He levered his head away from the curved white stone to toss the thick fall of fair hair back out of his eyes, and the noonday sunlight struck him full across the face. 'This is as close to Eden as it gets,' he said. 'I daren't come up here too often, or I'd never get anything accomplished. In fact I'd probably never leave Chinon, come to that.' He started to smile, but my expression stopped him. 'What? What's the matter?'

'Nothing.' I looked away rather quickly. It would sound foolish to tell the truth, to tell him that I'd only just now noticed that his eyes weren't black at all. They were blue, a pure dark blue, deep as the still sea at midnight. Not that it much mattered what colour his eyes were. What mattered was that I'd noticed it at all.

Harry had always laughed at me for noticing men's

eyes. 'I can always tell when you're smitten, my love,' he'd teased me, more than once. 'I only have to ask you what colour his eyes are.' And he was right, as always. If I wasn't interested I answered 'brown', not knowing, but if a man had struck my fancy I could describe his eyes in embarrassing detail.

I felt my face growing warm, but Neil didn't notice. He'd looked away again, towards the far wall, where he'd been sitting earlier. 'There's that bloody bird again,' he said, his voice mildly amused.

Martine, at my other shoulder, turned her head to look. 'What bird?'

'Just over there. The swallow. He was hopping round like mad this morning – made me tired just watching him. He must have his nest around here somewhere.'

I stared at the little fork-tailed bird, and for a moment – just a moment, mind – I almost wanted to believe . . .

Don't be an idiot, I told myself firmly. It wasn't the same swallow I'd seen, it couldn't possibly be, and it certainly hadn't brought me a message from any prince. There were no such things, I reminded myself, as princes. Neil rolled his head sideways again, as if to tell me something, but I pushed myself upright and rose to my feet. 'I think I'll leave my own donation at the altar,' I said, my voice sounding unnaturally bright. 'This is a lovely place, I'd hate to see it go to ruin for lack of funds.'

I wasn't the only one who felt that way, obviously. Beside the statue of Sainte Radegonde, the small chipped saucer held a generous scattering of coins. Among the thin French francs I saw a few larger pieces that proved to be

American, and half hidden below those was a smallish coin of beaten silver . . .

I stared at it a moment, disbelieving. It couldn't be, I thought, it simply couldn't be . . . but there it was, all the same – a small, round coin of tarnished silver, with the image of a dead king raised on one side. The image of King John of England, third of the Plantagenet line.

The breeze blew suddenly chill within the sheltering walls, and I heard again my cousin's laughing voice, and saw him close his fist protectively around that coin, drawing it back and up, out of my reach. 'You might have stopped believing in good luck pieces, Emily Braden,' he'd told me then with an indulgent smile, 'but I haven't. I'd rather lose my right arm than this little chap.'

Numbly, without thinking, I fished the coin from the saucer and closed my fingers round it, pressing it into the soft flesh of my palm until I could feel each contour of its worn surface. It was no longer in its round protective casing, but it was obviously Harry's coin. I wouldn't think too many tourists carried King John coins about. He had been here, then, just recently. I frowned. Harry had been here . . .

My own five-franc piece tumbled with a noisy clatter into the saucer and Martine looked round, blinking in the sunlight. She couldn't have seen me clearly, there in my shadowed corner, but still she asked: 'Something is wrong?'

Beneath the saint's accusing eyes I slipped the coin into my pocket, and shook my head. 'No, nothing's wrong.' Satisfied, Martine turned away again to talk to Neil, and I clenched my trembling hand into a fist. *Nothing's wrong*, I repeated, silently. I only wished I could believe it.

CHAPTER SIXTEEN

Henceforth thou hast a helper, me . . .

It was nearly dark when I left my room and went to look for Paul. I found him sitting alone in the bar, his shoulder to the wall of windows fronting on the square. *Ulysses* lay open on the low table at his knees, the spread pages pinned beneath a heavy glass ashtray.

He looked so peaceful, sitting there, that I hated to disturb him, but there was no help for it. My aunt's telephone had been engaged all afternoon, and when I'd rung my father I'd been greeted by his answering machine. Which left only Paul. I wouldn't have felt comfortable discussing my problems with anyone else, but Paul already seemed an old friend. As I entered the bar he surfaced from his book and sent me a welcoming smile. 'You've got good timing,' he said. 'I was just about to put this down and have a drink.'

'What page are you on now?'

'Five hundred and forty-six.'

'And how many pages are there?'

'Nearly eight hundred,' he admitted, repositioning the ashtray to hold his place while he stretched his cramped shoulders. 'I'm doomed.'

'You could always skip some bits, you know. You'd hardly miss a passage or two, surely, in a book that size.'

'But that would be cheating,' said Paul, as I sat down on the sofa opposite him. 'Besides, I don't do anything half way. Once I start something, I have to see it through – it's just the way I am. I hate leaving anything unfinished.'

'Is it really such a difficult book?'

'Not difficult, no.' He frowned, thinking. 'No, complex would be a better word, I think. There are lots of layers in Joyce's prose, and you can't go too fast or you miss things. For instance,' he said, turning the book towards me with his finger on the open page, 'what would you say that means, exactly?'

I read the passage twice and shook my head. 'I haven't the faintest idea.'

'Neither do I. But I know I'll work it out eventually. That's how you have to read this book, you see. You wade through a few sentences, then stop and think about them, then wade through a few more.'

'Well, you're a better man than I am, Gunga Din.'

'Pardon?'

'You've far more patience than I'll ever have,' I explained.

'Simon wouldn't call it patience,' he said, with a shrug. 'He'd just call it another one of my annoyingly obsessive personality traits. He says I'm a typical physicist, that I always have to force everything to make sense.'

'And do you?'

'Sure.' He grinned at my question, unashamed. 'Because everything does make sense, when you look at it from the right angle. All you have to do is find out what that angle is, for whatever it is you want to understand, and bang, the universe becomes a rational place.'

'Does it really?' I remained unconvinced, sagging back against the seat cushions as I brushed the hair back from my forehead. There was a pink geranium growing in a planter outside the window, behind Paul's shoulder, and I frowned at it without really seeing it. 'Well, I've tried every angle I can think of, and I still don't know what to think.'

'About what?'

Dragging my gaze from the window, I dug into my pocket and held out my hand, palm upwards. 'This.'

Paul frowned. Leaning forward, he took the little coin and raised it to catch the slanting light from the overhead fixture. 'What is it?'

'It's a King John coin.'

'Really? Where on earth did you get this?'

I was ashamed to say I'd stolen it from a donation plate, so instead I told a half truth. 'I found it, up at the Chapelle Sainte Radegonde.'

'Wow.' He turned it slowly, studying the ancient image. 'I can't imagine many people would have one of these.'

'My cousin has one.'

He caught on quickly did young Paul. His upward glance held total comprehension. 'But your cousin isn't supposed to be here yet.'

'I know.'

'So.' He handed the coin back to me, watching my face with careful eyes that were older than his age. 'So you think that this is his, then? That he's been and gone already?'

'I don't know what to think. I rang up the other hotels and they've never heard of him. I checked round the hospitals, but he hasn't been admitted. From all accounts, he hasn't been within ten miles of Chinon. Not recently, at any rate.'

'Did you try the tourist office? They keep the keys, you know, for the Chapelle of Sainte Radegonde.'

I nodded. 'They said no one had asked to see the chapelle for at least a month.' Christian had a key, of course, but if Christian had met Harry he'd have mentioned it to me, surely. My cousin and I were alike enough to be brother and sister, one could hardly miss the resemblance. And while Neil had apparently managed to scale the walls somehow, I doubted whether Harry could have done the same. Harry, for all his energy, was no athlete. 'It's this coin, you see,' I said to Paul, 'this bloody coin, that bothers me.' I rolled it pensively between my fingers. 'His good luck piece, he called it – to help him with the book he was writing. He'd never have left it behind.'

'Maybe he dropped it without knowing.'

I shook my head. 'No, not where I found it. Someone would have had to place it there deliberately. Besides, he couldn't have dropped it loose like this. He carried it round in a plastic case, the kind collectors use.'

'He'd have dropped the whole thing, you mean.'

'Yes. Of course, the obvious answer is that this isn't Harry's coin at all, that it belongs to someone else. But still, it's solid silver, and terribly old, and you'd have to be mad to put it in . . . well, to put it where I found it.'

Paul was silent for a minute. Shaking a cigarette loose from his nearly empty packet he lit it with a thoughtful frown. 'If you're really worried, you could call the police.'

'And tell them what? That I've found a coin that may or may not be my cousin's?' I smiled, knowingly. 'They'd send me packing for wasting their valuable time.'

'So you don't want to bother the police,' Paul summarised. 'OK. There must be some other way of finding out whether he's been here.'

'Well, I can't think of any.'

'You said he was coming here to do some research.'

'Yes.'

'And where would he go to do that?'

I shrugged, a little helplessly. 'I don't know, really. The library, perhaps, or the château . . . no, wait,' I broke off suddenly, remembering. 'He did say he was meeting someone. Some man who'd read one of Harry's articles and was offering some useful information about tunnels.'

'You're sure it was a man?'

I thought back, closing my eyes as I replayed the week-old conversation in my head. 'Yes, positive.'

'Remember his name?'

'No.' I opened my eyes again, faintly frustrated. 'No, I don't. I think he only said the first name.'

'Is he French or English?'

'French,' I said with certainty. 'He wrote his letter in French, I do remember that, only Harry said the fellow must know English because the article – the article about

201

Queen Isabelle's treasure – had been published in an English journal.'

'Right,' said Paul. 'So we're looking for a local history nut who knows the tunnels pretty well and reads British history journals.' He smiled at me above the burning cigarette. 'Sounds like a case for Sherlock Holmes.'

'Impossible, you mean.'

He grinned. 'I mean it's something I could probably look into for you. I don't think there'd be too many guys in Chinon fitting that description, and the few who do must hang around the library. It's just down the street, here,' he nodded out the window. 'I can drop in tomorrow, if you like, and ask around. And if you want to take another look around the chapelle to see if your cousin left anything else there, I'm sure I could sweet-talk Christian into lending me the keys.'

'Would you?'

'Sure. Sweet-talking is one of my specialities.' He smiled, blowing smoke. 'I have to do a lot of it with my brother.'

I smiled back. 'Where is Simon, by the way?'

'Don't know. He took off after lunch, treasure-hunting, and I haven't seen him since. After last night's ghost story, he's been unstoppable, you know – two Isabelles, two hidden treasures, twice the chance of finding something.'

'Look on the bright side,' I told him. 'At least he won't be quite so eager to leave Chinon, now. You'll get to stay a few more days.'

'Longer than that,' he reminded me, sagely. 'Don't you remember? The Echo told Simon he'd never get me to leave.' Leaning back, he stretched his arms above his head.

202

'Listen, do you want a drink or something? Coffee?'

I looked round the deserted room. 'Is the bar open, then?'

'Oh, sure. Thierry's in the back room, doing paperwork.'

'Paperwork?' It seemed an odd thing for the bartender to be doing, and Paul smiled at my reaction.

'Yeah. I think the receptionist, Gabrielle, is helping him.'

'Oh, I see.' I smiled back, as comprehension dawned.

'I'm supposed to whistle if I want anything.'

He had to whistle twice, in fact, before we heard a stirring from the room behind the bar, and a slightly muffled voice said: 'Ho-kay, just a moment.'

Across from me, Paul struck a match to light another cigarette, his eyes faintly apologetic. 'Chain-smoking, I know. My mother would have a fit. But I have to enjoy it while I can, before Simon gets back.'

I bit my lip, thinking. 'Paul . . .'

'Yes?'

'You won't tell anybody, will you, about my cousin's coin?' If he'd asked 'why not?' I would have had a devil of a time explaining. One couldn't very well explain a feeling. And that was all it was – a feeling, an irrational suspicion that things were not quite what they seemed to be among my fellow guests. I'd felt it that first night at dinner, and again last night, here in the bar – that sense of something darker running underneath the surface, some troubled current that I couldn't understand. It reminded me of the time, years ago now, when my father had taken us to London to see a play, only he'd read the tickets wrong and we arrived just as the second interval was ending. I'd sat through the final

203

act in absolute confusion, with the motivating plot-lines of the characters long since laid out and set in motion, so that while I felt their conflict and the atmosphere of tension, I had no idea what was going on.

But whatever the cause of the atmosphere of tension here at the Hotel de France, it didn't seem to have touched Paul Lazarus. 'Of course I won't tell anyone,' he said. 'Not if you don't want me to.'

'Not even Simon?'

'Not even Simon.'

'Thanks,' I told him. 'You're an angel.'

Smiling, he balanced his cigarette on the edge of the ashtray and leaned back in his seat, arms folded complacently across his chest. 'I do my best.'

'Aha!' Simon, coming round the bar door, skewered Paul with a smugly triumphant look. 'I knew I'd catch you at it sooner or later, I just knew it!'

I couldn't resist. I reached innocently across for the lit cigarette and raised it to my own lips, inhaling with perfect nonchalance. 'Catch him at what?' I asked Simon.

His face fell, and even Paul looked faintly shocked, but I managed to hold the innocent expression long enough to convince Simon.

'Nothing,' he said. He glanced uncertainly at Paul. 'I only thought . . .'

He wasn't allowed to finish telling us what he thought. Behind him in the entrance hall the front door blew open and shut and I braced myself as the Whitakers came into the bar, shattering what little remained of the companionable peace that had settled between Paul and myself.

'Why, Emily!' Garland raised her eyebrows in a calculated arc and widened her eyes. 'I didn't know you smoked.'

I didn't, actually. I had given it up three years ago, as part of my more responsible approach to life, and I was somewhat relieved to find it tasted awful, but I sent Garland an almost cheerful shrug. 'Well, we all have to have one vice, don't we? That's what my father says.'

'Only one vice? Darling, how *boring*!' She sank gracefully onto the soft chair nearest the door and gave a tiny, self-satisfied sigh. 'I won't be able to get up again, now,' she pronounced. 'We must have walked a hundred miles.'

'Just over the river and back, actually,' Jim Whitaker put in, as he joined us by the window, 'but my wife's not used to walking. And those shoes don't help.'

Garland lifted one delicately arched foot, the better to examine her tight Italian pumps. 'I know. I really *must* invest in a pair of sensible shoes like yours, Emily,' she said, sending me a smile designed to soften the cutting compliment. 'You English always wear such practical clothes.'

Paul's eyes laughed at me as he positioned the ashtray nearer me, closing his unfinished book and pushing it aside. He looked at Simon, curious. 'And where did you take off to, this afternoon?'

'Oh, nowhere in particular,' Simon answered, swinging his lanky frame into the chair beside me. He whistled a snatch of something through his teeth and looked around. 'Where's Thierry, by the way? Isn't he working?'

'He's in the back, doing paperwork.' The lie came easily

in Paul's unhurried voice. 'He knows we're here, though. He'll be out in a minute or two.'

'Thank God,' said Garland. 'I could certainly use a drink after all that marching around. I prefer places we can drive the car to, you know. What about you, Emily?'

'Oh, I don't mind walking.' I smiled politely, folding what was left of the cigarette into the ashtray with exquisite care. 'I rather enjoy it, actually.'

Garland smiled. 'Like Neil. Honestly, he makes me tired just watching him. Up and down those stairs all day, and he never even breathes hard. It's disgusting. Jim used to be fit like that, didn't you darling? When I first met you. The Army,' she sighed, 'does wonderful things to a man's body. Oh, *there* you are, Thierry, we were beginning to think you'd disappeared.'

Thierry looked rather flushed, and more than a little pleased with himself. Garland mistook his cheerful distraction for an inability to understand.

'We . . . thought . . . you'd . . . disappeared,' she repeated, in a louder voice.

'Ah.' He grinned, and broadening his accent so that he sounded exactly like a music hall actor pretending to be French, he asked her very slowly: 'Would . . . you . . . like . . . a . . . drink?'

Even Jim smiled at that, but Garland missed the joke completely. 'Oh, that's very much better, Thierry,' she congratulated him. 'You see? I told you if you kept on practising, your English would improve in no time.'

Thierry shrugged, a modest little shrug. I didn't trust myself to look up again until after he'd brought the drinks.

For the next half hour I sipped my *kir* and smiled politely. When it became apparent that the Whitakers were rooted to their seats for the remainder of the evening, and that Paul and I would have to wait until breakfast to talk any further about Harry, I excused myself with a rather convincing yawn and started up the winding stairs.

Alone in my room, I closed my fingers thoughtfully round the little silver coin, still nestled deep within my pocket, and wandered over to the window. The night air was thick and full of dampness. In the square below, the street lamps spread warm yellow pools of light upon the smooth black pavement, and water spilled from the fountain like an iridescent rain.

Beside the fountain, the little spotted dog yawned and stretched as the breeze went shivering through the acacias.

The gypsy glanced swiftly upwards, expressionless, at my window, then looked away again and lit a cigarette with unhurried fingers. It was only the darkness, I told myself, that was giving things this air of melodrama. The gypsy had every right to be sitting in a public square, and he might have been looking at anything, really, not just at my window. But still I latched the window firmly, securely, and twitched the heavy curtains closed before I crawled beneath the covers of the wide bed, shutting my eyes tightly into the pillow like a child seeking comfort in the long uncertain night.

CHAPTER SEVENTEEN

'. . . we give you, being strange
A licence: speak, and let the topic die.'

Paul answered my knock at the door next morning with
the telephone slung from one hand and the receiver cradled
close against his cheek. Smiling, he motioned me in, not
missing a beat in his conversation. He was speaking in
French. 'Ah. I see. Yes, I'll wait, it's no problem.' Fingers
cupped round the mouthpiece, he smiled again. 'Come on
in,' he told me. 'Have a seat.'

Which was easier said than done. The boys' room
was the mirror image of my own, except that where I
had one huge bed they had two narrow ones, one neatly
made and strewn with maps, the other rumpled and half
buried beneath a set of curtains, still anchored firmly to
the curtain-rod. Three spreading piles of clothing, sorted by
colour, rose like miniature Alps from the carpet at my feet.
There was very little room to stand, let alone sit.

Paul had solved the problem by sitting on the cluttered

desk, feet braced against a chair that had been buried thick in newspapers. He resumed his seat now, while I made my cautious way around the mounded clothing to perch upon a corner of the neater bed by the window.

Simon, I thought, had a point – the window did look better without curtains. It stood fully open to the morning air, and the jumbled sounds of traffic, talk and fountain drifted upwards from the square beneath, like some discordant modern symphony.

Paul was still on hold, and humming to himself.

'Any joy?' I asked him.

'Sort of. The library isn't open yet, but the staff is there. This guy's just gone to ask the librarian if he knows anyone who—' He broke off suddenly, and bent his head. 'Yes, I'm still here.' A shorter pause, and then: 'Yes. I'm a student, you see, and I'm writing a paper on . . . that's right. And I was told there might be someone here who might be good to talk to. Pardon?' He leaned forward to scribble a few lines on the pad of paper at his side. 'Yes, I've got that. Belliveau, that's B-e-l-l . . . ? You don't have the telephone number, do you? Yes, of course, I understand. Well, I'm sure it won't be a problem. Thanks so much.' He replaced the receiver with a smug expression, and struck a match to light a cigarette. 'Well, that was fun.'

'You want to watch out, Sherlock,' I said drily. 'Big brother might walk in and catch you smoking.'

'Simon,' Paul informed me, savouring the words, 'isn't here. He left half an hour ago, with the Whitakers.'

'Simon's gone off with Jim and Garland?' I couldn't quite believe my ears. 'Why on earth would he do that?'

'Because they were going to Fontevraud, where your Queen Isabelle is buried. Simon thought there might be clues there, as to where she hid her treasure.' Paul shrugged. 'But mostly he went because I reminded him today is Tuesday, our weekly laundry day, and Simon really hates the laundromat.'

I smiled slowly. 'You're a whopping sneak.'

'I know.'

'And how are we supposed to play detective, might I ask, if we have to do your laundry?'

'Thierry and I have it all under control.'

'You didn't tell Thierry?' I asked, startled.

His eyes held soft reproach. 'Of course not. I promised, didn't I? I only told him you and I were taking off to do some sightseeing on our own, and could he help us keep it secret from Simon?'

I smiled. 'Well, that's torn it. He'll be thinking we've gone sneaking off to do something romantic.'

'Nah.' Paul grinned. 'We could do that right here at the hotel. Besides, Thierry knows me better than that.'

'What, I'm too old for you?' I teased him.

He shook his head. 'Hardly. But I'd never hit on someone else's woman.'

'Someone else's . . . ?'

'Anyhow,' he changed the subject, picking up his notepad. 'Do you want to know what I've just found out?'

I stopped frowning and leaned forward. 'Please.'

'Well, the librarian only knows of one man who reads foreign history journals and takes an interest in the tunnels – a local poet by the name of Victor Belliveau.'

'Victor . . .' I tried the name, experimentally.

'Was that the name your cousin mentioned, on the phone, do you think?'

I shook my head. 'I can't remember.'

'Because it sounds like this might be our guy, it really does. Apparently he's been poking around the tunnels for years, making maps and things. Kind of a personal obsession. So if this Belliveau did write your cousin, then your cousin might have met with him when he was here in Chinon. Assuming, of course, that he *was* here. It can't hurt to ask.' Paul checked his notes again. 'He lives just outside Chinon, sort of. I've got the address, but there isn't any phone number. The librarian doesn't think he has a phone. Our Monsieur Belliveau is a true artiste – a little bit eccentric.'

'But you said he doesn't live far from here?'

Paul shook his head. 'Just up the river, past the beach. A fifteen-minute walk, maybe. Do you want to go there first, then? Or would you rather start by taking another look around the Chapelle Sainte Radegonde? I've got the key.'

'How did you manage that?'

Another shrug, more modest than the first. 'I just went round to Christian's house this morning, before breakfast, and asked him for it. Christian's like Neil, he wakes up with the birds, and I figured he wouldn't mind.'

'Well, I'm most impressed, I really am. You've had a busy morning, Sherlock.'

'Morning isn't over, yet,' he reminded me. 'So where do we start? The poet or the chapelle?'

I took a moment to consider the options. The Chapelle

Sainte Radegonde, I thought, was the more appealing prospect, and I was quite certain Harry had been there, but then again . . . I rubbed my thigh unconsciously, recalling the hellish climb along the cliffs, and the endless winding steps that led back down again.

I smiled at Paul. 'The poet, please.'

The house of Victor Belliveau stood on the fringe of the community – a sprawling yellow farmhouse with an aged tile roof, set off by itself with a scattering of crooked trees to guard the boundary fence.

Thierry had confirmed the man's artistic status. 'He was a famous man, this Belliveau,' Thierry had said in response to Paul's casual question. 'Not just in Chinon, but in all of France. I read his poetry at school, in Paris. But now he drinks, you know, and he is not so well respected.'

His property reflected that, I thought. The yard was pitted and unkempt, and the stone barn, built long and low to match the house, was tightly shuttered up. And the rubbish! Peelings rotted everywhere among the weeds, and paper wrappers cartwheeled in the wind to fall exhausted in the rutted muddy lane before us.

'Oh, boy,' said Paul.

'My thoughts exactly.'

'I guess poets don't make much money, do they?' Paul strolled across the road and tried the fastening of Victor Belliveau's gate. It was a long gate, stretched across what might have been a drive, and it was unlocked. One push sent it creaking back on its hinges. The sound spoke of loneliness and isolation, and I'd not have been surprised to see a snarling dog come slinking round a corner, but the only animal that came to greet us was a small black chicken. Keeping its distance, it turned a round and curious eye to watch us cross the lawn towards the house.

It was a farmer's house, square and sturdy. Great blocks of smooth pale stone framed both front windows and the door that stood between them, but the rest of the walls were made of rubble. Much more economical, I supposed. It might have been made quite a pretty house, if someone had cared enough to take the trouble. It only wanted some new roof tiles and a lick of paint on the sagging shutters, perhaps some curtains and a flowerpot or two to brighten things. But I could clearly hear the rattling of the cracked and greying tiles, and on the wall see places where the years had worn away the mortar so the dampness could creep in between the dirty yellow stones. The windows, staring out across the littered yard at the still and shuttered barn, had a blank and empty look.

No-one, I decided, had cared about this house for a very long time.

I had already conjured up a vivid mental picture of Monsieur Victor Belliveau, and so I was completely unprepared for the sight of the man who actually opened the door to Paul's polite knock. This was no unkempt wild-eyed poet, half mad with drink and raving in his solitude. Instead a tidy, dapper little man, with crisp grey hair and a shaven face that smelled of soap, looked back at us in pleasant expectation.

Paul did the talking for us both, in flawless French. He didn't tell the whole truth, mind. He was careful not to contradict the tale he'd spun for the librarian, about being a student working on a paper, only this time he did mention he was trying to find my cousin. 'Braden,' he said. 'Harry Braden. He's from my university. I believe he was here in Chinon last week, doing research, and I thought he might have come to talk to you . . . ?'

Victor Belliveau raked us with a measuring look. 'No, I'm sorry, he did not come here.'

'Oh. You didn't write him a letter, then?'

'No.' Another long and penetrating look. 'You say it is something to do with the tunnels, this paper you are writing?'

'Well,' Paul scuffed his shoe against the step, 'sort of . . .'

'Then perhaps I can help you myself,' said Victor Belliveau, with a rusty smile. He pushed the door a fraction wider. 'Please,' he told us, 'do come in.'

The French did not ask strangers into their homes as a matter of habit, and it would have been unspeakably rude to have refused his invitation. Feeling slightly guilty for intruding on the man's privacy in the first place, I followed Paul across the threshold.

There were only two rooms on the ground floor, a large square kitchen and a second room in which a bed, a coal stove and a sofa were the only furnishings. The far wall of the kitchen groaned beneath the weight of rustic bookshelves, stacked two deep in places, an intriguing mix of paperbacks and expensive-looking volumes leaning wearily on one another. The other walls were bare, with jagged cracks that ran from the ceiling like thunderbolts. In one corner some plant – an ivy branch, it looked like –

had actually worked its way through the heavy plaster and been unceremoniously hacked off for its trouble. Still the rooms, while spartan, were surprisingly clean, and the tile floor had recently been swept.

Victor Belliveau seated us in the kitchen, round a large scrubbed table spread with newspapers. 'Would you like a drink?' he offered. 'Wine? Coffee? No?' He shrugged and poured himself a glass of thick red wine. 'I had some brandy here the other day, but I'm afraid it's gone. They took it,' he said, jerking his head towards the window and the tangled yard outside. 'Damned good taste, if you ask me.'

At Paul's blank look the poet smiled again. 'I'm sorry, of course you wouldn't know. I meant the gypsies,' he explained. 'I have a family of them, usually, living on my land. That's why the yard is such a disaster. Good people, gypsies, but they don't believe in guarding the environment.'

'*Gypsies?*' The word came out rather more sharply than I'd intended, and the bland and guileless eyes shifted from Paul to me.

'Oh, yes. We've plenty of gypsies round here, my dear. Mine stay here several times a year. One's never sure exactly when – they just turn up when the mood strikes, with their caravans. Not everybody likes them, but they don't much trouble me.'

'I see.' The scarred table felt suddenly damp beneath my splayed fingers.

'But what was it you needed to know, about the tunnels?' he asked, his glass trailing moisture on the table as he leaned forward in his own chair, helpfully.

Paul played his part extremely well, I thought. Having

only just left school himself he made a most convincing student – even borrowed pen and paper to make notes, his face attentive, serious. I tried to listen to what Victor Belliveau was telling Paul about the history of the tunnels, but my mind kept wandering off to other things.

Like gypsies, for example. Of course it was coincidence, and nothing more, that Victor Belliveau let gypsies on his land. There must be half a dozen other people living in these parts who had a gypsy caravan parked down their back lane. And besides, I reminded myself, the gypsy with the little dog who haunted the fountain square had nothing at all to do with me. Nothing at all.

'. . . up to the Chapelle Sainte Radegonde,' Belliveau was saying, 'but that has long since fallen in. One has to use imagination . . .'

His mention of the chapelle set my mind wandering again, this time to Harry. Bloody Harry. I ought to have that printed on a T-shirt, I thought. He'd probably be quite amused by all the trouble I was going to, just because I'd found that King John coin. There was bound to be a simple reason why the coin was here and Harry wasn't.

'He died last Wednesday,' Victor Belliveau said, shrugging, and I came back to the conversation with a jolt.

'I beg your pardon?'

'A friend of Monsieur Belliveau's,' explained Paul, for my benefit.

'Well, I knew him, let us say,' the poet qualified drily. 'We were not friends. But this is why the gypsies left, you see. We'd had the police round a few times, asking questions, and gypsies don't much care for that. Not that I was a

217

suspect, or anything,' he said, smiling at his own joke, 'but as I said, I knew the man quite well. It was a sad case. He drank too much.' He shrugged and raised his own glass, which I noticed had been filled again.

Paul raised his eyebrows. 'You don't mean Martine Muret's husband, do you?'

'Yes, Didier Muret. You know them, then?'

'Only Martine,' said Paul. 'I never met her husband. Ex-husband, I should say.'

'Ah, she is a lovely woman, Martine, don't you think? I believe I wrote a sonnet to her, once. But she chose Muret. God knows why,' he said, smiling above his wine glass. 'He was an idiot.'

I frowned. 'Didier Muret – that was his name?'

'Yes, why?'

Didier . . . I turned it round again, concentrating. It rang a bell, that name. I was sure it was the name Harry had mentioned – either that, or something very like it. It was a common enough name. There were probably dozens of Didiers living in Chinon. Still, I thought, it never hurt to try . . .

'He wasn't a historian, by any chance?' I asked.

The poet laughed at that. 'God, no. Didier? He took no interest in such things. He was a clever man, don't get me wrong – he worked once for a lawyer, so he must have had a brain. But I don't think I ever saw him read a book. Now me,' he confessed, 'I have too many books.'

Paul turned to admire the shelves. 'There's no such thing.'

'I have some books, old books, about the history of

218

Chinon, that make some mention of the tunnels. I'm afraid I can't lend them, but if you'd like to look . . .'

It was a good excuse to stand, to bring our rather pointless visit to a close, and I loitered patiently to one side as Paul leafed through the offered books with polite interest.

It was too bad, I thought, that Harry hadn't known about Victor Belliveau. My cousin would have coveted this collection of books – old memoirs, bound in leather rubbed bald at the edges; some odd assorted plays and books of poems; an old edition of *Cyrano de Bergerac*, a copy of a British history journal . . .

I blinked, and peered more closely at the shelf. The journal was a recent one, with a revisionist slant. And there upon the cover, bold as brass, I read my cousin's proper name: *Henry Yates Braden, PhD.*

'What's that?' asked Paul, behind my shoulder. I tilted the cover to show him.

Victor Belliveau leaned in to look as well. 'Ah, yes,' he said, 'that talks about the tunnels, too. I had forgotten . . .' He looked a little closer, and his eyebrows lifted. 'Braden . . . isn't that the man you asked me about? The man from your university?'

Paul nodded. 'Harry Braden, yes.'

'Then I'm sorry he didn't come to visit me,' the poet said, his tone sincere. 'I enjoyed his article very much. He has an interesting mind, I think.'

I put the journal down again, frowning faintly. 'I don't suppose that Didier Muret would have read this article as well?'

The poet shrugged. 'I wouldn't think it likely.'

'Because he didn't read much, you mean?'

'Because he knew no English.' The poet's smile was gentle. He walked us to the door and shook our hands. 'You must come back again, if I can be of any help,' he said. But he didn't linger for a goodbye wave. He closed the door behind us as we stepped onto the grass, and I heard the bolt slide home. The sound seemed to echo back from the abandoned barn opposite, where a padlocked door creaked in the slight wind as Paul and I trudged thoughtfully across the pitted overgrown yard.

'He certainly didn't seem a drunkard,' I remarked.

'Yeah, well,' Paul smiled faintly, 'that doesn't mean anything. My Uncle Aaron soaks up liquor like a sponge, but you'd never know it. He only slurs on days he's stone cold sober.' We'd reached the leaning gate. Paul pulled it open and stood aside to let me pass through first.

I looked at him, curious. 'Do you think he was telling us the truth? About not writing Harry the letter, I mean?'

'Why would he lie?'

Why indeed? I looked back one final time at the dismal yellow farmhouse, at the crumbling walls and sagging roof. The curtains of the kitchen window twitched and then lay still, and the only movement left was that of the lone black chicken, stalking haughtily across the yard through the long and waving grass. I felt a faint cold shiver that I recognised as fear, although I didn't know its cause.

'The chapelle, next,' said Paul, and slammed the gate behind us with a clang that sent the chicken scuttling for cover.

Chapter Eighteen

Two plummets dropt for one to sound the abyss . . .

Paul pulled the jangling ring of keys from the iron lock and swung the great door reverently, as though he hated to disturb the peaceful atmosphere laced with the songs of unseen birds and the whispering of wind in shadowed alcoves. Above the old baptismal font the bay tree rustled gently, while the wild flowers nodded drowsily along the edges of the empty grass-filled graves. Soft weathered faces watched us from each corner of the architecture, from every ledge and pediment and every vaulted niche, and in the shadowed aisle behind the tall black iron gates the pensive saints gazed through the bars as one stares at a lion in its cage.

It should have been unnerving, having all those eyes upon me, but it wasn't. Oddly enough, it was reassuring. I felt again that rush of pure contentment, of childlike wonder, and the sense of beauty stabbed so deeply that I had to blink back tears.

'Wow,' said Paul. 'It doesn't lose its impact, does it, second time around?'

I shook my head. 'You've been here before?'

'Yeah. It was one of the first places we discovered after the château. Simon read about it in a book, I think, and when he found out Christian had a key . . .' He shrugged, and left it at that, moving past me to the soaring grille of iron.

'And what's the word for this place, then? Secluded?' I guessed. 'Sacred?'

He grinned. 'Sanctuary.'

I recalled my own first reaction to the place, and felt an even closer kinship with this quiet young man I'd only met three days ago.

The iron gates swung open, and we stepped into the cloistered aisle with its peeling frescoes and fragile-looking pillars. 'Sacred,' Paul informed me, as he shuffled the ring of keys, 'is just through here.'

'Just through here' lay beyond the altar, beyond the second iron gate – the gate that Christian hadn't had the key to yesterday. The tunnelled passage in behind looked every bit as uninviting as I remembered, and even when Paul had successfully sprung the lock I hung back, hesitating, peering with a coward's eyes into the darkness. 'I haven't brought a torch.'

'A flashlight, you mean? That's OK, I've got one.' It was a pocket torch, a small one, hardly any help at all, but he snapped it on and stepped into the passageway ahead of me. 'I think the main switch is around here somewhere. Yeah, here we go.' A flood of brilliant yellow light dissolved the lurking shadows.

I blinked, surprised. 'Electric light?'

'Sure. This place is kind of a museum, you know. They do take tourists through, during the summer, and I guess they don't want people stumbling around. Here, watch your step.' He guided me over the uneven threshold. The passageway was filled on either side with artefacts and curious equipment, neatly laid out on display. Ancient tools for farming and for wine-making shared equal space with emblems of religion and broken statuary, the whole effect being one of wondrous variety. 'This is where the hermit lived, originally,' said Paul. A few steps on, the passage turned and widened briefly in an arched and empty room of sorts, where more pale statues stared benignly down on us.

My claustrophobia eased a little and I paused to draw a deep and steady breath. 'Is this the sacred part?'

'No. Behind you.'

I turned, and saw what looked like another tunnel running down into the rock, its entrance barred by an ornate black metal barrier, waist-high, anchored in the scarred and worn limestone. Curious, I went as close as the barrier allowed, and peered over it at the flight of crudely chiselled stairs that steeply dropped towards a glowing light. It made me dizzy, looking down. 'Like Jacob's ladder in reverse,' I said to Paul, as he joined me at the railing.

'It's a well,' he said. 'A holy well.'

'But where's the water?'

He smiled. 'Come on. I'll show you.'

I had no great desire to go still deeper underground, but neither did I want to seem a coward. And at least I trusted Paul to bring me safely out again.

Climbing the barrier proved simple enough, no different than climbing a stile back home, but the stairs were a different matter. They were irregular in shape, some only several inches high while others fell two feet or more, and my fingers scrabbled in the dust and chips of rock to find a firmer handhold as I made my slow descent. Paul, who had clearly done this before, went down like a mountain goat, his steps sure and even. I was more ungainly, and brought the dust with me, a great whoofing cloud of it that swirled on even after I had stopped to join Paul on the narrow ledge at the bottom of the stairs.

'This,' he said, 'is the sacred part.' His hushed voice sounded hollow, like the echo round an indoor swimming pool. Intrigued, I braced one hand against the paper-cool stone and leaned forward for a proper look.

The water was there, as he had promised. Clear, holy water, pale turquoise in the glare of an electric light that hung from the stone arch overhead. It was, Paul told me, a Merovingian well, meaning it dated back to the time of the Franks – older, he thought, than Sainte Radegonde herself. The shaft sank deep and straight and true; several metres deep, I would have said, and yet the water was so amazingly clear that I could see the scattering of pebbles at the bottom.

'You can even see the footholds,' Paul said, pointing, 'that the well-diggers used to climb out again, after they'd struck water.' The footholds ran like a makeshift ladder, straight to the bottom of the well – small, even squares the width of one man's boot, gouged in the yielding yellow stone.

I sighed, and the surface of the water shivered. 'Well,' I said, 'at least we know that Harry isn't anywhere down here.'

'A cheerful thought,' Paul smiled. 'But you're right, it'd be pretty hard to hide something in that water. Even a King John coin.' He flipped a tiny half-franc piece into the well to demonstrate, and we watched until it came to rest upon the bottom, clearly visible. 'Here, make a wish,' Paul told me, handing me another coin.

He sounded just like my father, when he said that. For a moment I was five years old again and standing at the rim of the fountain in the courtyard of our house in Italy. But then I caught my own reflection in the water of the well, and the child vanished. I shook my head. 'I don't have anything to wish for.'

'Everyone has something to wish for. Besides, how often do you get a chance to make a wish in holy water?'

'No, honestly, you needn't waste your money . . .'

'Has anyone ever told you you're a terrible cynic?' He grinned and closed his eyes. 'OK, never mind. I'll make a wish for you. There,' he said, and tossed the second coin into the waiting well. It hit the water with a satisfying plunk. End over end my unknown wish tumbled, glittering, and landed close to Paul's one on the smooth and level bottom.

'So what did I wish for?' I asked, curious.

'Bad luck to tell,' he reminded me. Turning, he offered me his hand to help me up the stairs again. 'Right,' he said, 'let's give this place a proper search, and see what we can find.'

We found a treasure trove of slightly dusty artefacts

displayed in every crevice of the caves. We found a smaller chamber at the tunnel's end, where someone evidently lived from time to time. 'There's a caretaker in the summer,' Paul informed me, 'on and off. I think she stays up here.' But no one had been staying here recently. The bed was stripped, the cupboards empty, and dust lay thickly settled on the floor, marked by no sign of footprints save our own. We found a working wine press tucked in one high corner of the largest cave.

What we didn't find, of course, was anything that Harry might have left. There wasn't so much as a chewing-gum wrapper or a shred of tissue dropped in that bright, winding underground maze. I was, by turns, relieved and disappointed. Relieved because I hadn't turned up any evidence that Harry was in trouble, disappointed because I hadn't turned up any evidence that Harry was here at all. There was only that blasted coin.

Paul poked at the donation saucer as we paused before the simple altar on our way back out. 'Is this where you found the King John coin?'

My face flamed with embarrassment, but I didn't bother to deny it. The problem with Paul, I thought, was that he was too damn clever. He had a quiet but persistent way of finding out the truth. 'Yes. I . . . I put in a donation of my own,' I added, as if that made my theft acceptable, but Paul didn't seem to be listening.

'There's got to be an explanation.' That was the physicist talking. He furrowed his brow and stared hard at the plate of jumbled coins. 'There's got to be. We just aren't looking at this from the right angle.'

He was still standing there, thinking, when the faint sound of the noonday bells came drifting up from the town below and broke the peaceful silence of the chapelle. There was nothing more for us to do here, I decided. I tugged at Paul's sleeve. 'Come on, Sherlock, time for lunch.'

'Yeah, OK.' He glanced at his watch. 'I guess I ought to check the laundry, anyway, before Simon gets back. Thierry's probably shrunk everything beyond recognition by now.'

His gloomy fears turned out to be unfounded. From the pristine pile of folded shirts and jeans that met us in the hotel's entrance lobby, it appeared that Thierry had done quite an expert job.

He flashed his quick disarming smile and ran his thumb along a trouser crease. 'I cannot take the credit,' he confessed. 'I gave the clothes to Gabrielle for washing.'

Paul raised his eyebrows. 'Gabrielle?'

'The girl who does reception this week. Me, I am not good at washing things.'

He'd never have to worry about it, I thought, as long as he could aim a smile like that at a member of the opposite sex. It was a difficult smile to resist. I couldn't help but feel a pang of sympathy for Gabrielle – small wonder she was so confused, sometimes. 'You don't play fair,' I said to Thierry.

'*Comment?*'

'She means you take advantage,' Paul explained. 'Is Simon back yet?'

'No, he is still with the Whitakers, I think.' Again the

227

grin. 'It has been quiet here, today.'

Paul turned from the front desk and looked a question at me. 'You sick of my company, yet?'

'Of course not. Why?'

'Feel like having a drink or something? I know I could use one.' Paul glanced back at Thierry. 'The bar is open, isn't it?'

'Of course. You have had a nice time, sightseeing?'

'Very nice.' Paul smiled. 'But don't forget, now, it's a—'

'—secret,' Thierry finished. 'Do not worry, I am good at keeping secrets. If I had a franc for every secret in this hotel,' he said, grinning, 'I would not be needing to work.'

But he condescended to serve us anyway, before vanishing once more into the back rooms. Paul sipped his beer and leaned an elbow on the stack of freshly laundered clothes, which he'd set carefully beside him on his customary window seat. Behind his shoulder I could see the concrete planter outside, with its single pink geranium. It made a pitiful splash of colour against the shadowed backdrop of the busy fountain square.

Paul reached for his cigarettes and offered me the packet. 'Want one?'

'What? Oh, no thanks.' Smiling, I shook my head. 'No, I gave up smoking, years ago. Last night was just a momentary lapse.'

'A momentary lapse that saved my butt,' he pointed out. He lit one for himself and settled back. 'So, what's our next move?'

I gave a faint, defeatist shrug. 'I don't know. I'm rather tired of thinking about Harry, actually.'

'So take a break,' was his advice, 'and drink your drink.'

It was, I decided, sound advice from one so young. I leaned back in my chair and sighed. But I couldn't let it drop entirely. 'What did Martine Muret's ex-husband do for a living, do you know?'

Paul smiled at my obstinacy. 'He was unemployed, I think. Simon actually met the guy once, he might know. Simon didn't like Muret – thought he was a real jerk. He was drunk, you know, when he fell over that railing. That's how he died. And I guess he gave Martine a hell of a rough time when they were married. He didn't hit her or anything, I don't think, but he was . . . well, he was pretty rude. Embarrassing. The kind of guy who likes to play the big shot, you know?'

Like Jim and Garland in reverse, I thought. No wonder Martine hadn't been upset by her ex-husband's death. To her, it must have been almost a deliverance.

Close by, a car door slammed and Paul craned his neck to peer out of the window, beyond my line of vision, towards the hotel's front entrance. 'So much for our quiet drink,' he said, stubbing out his half-smoked cigarette.

'Why? Are they back already?'

'Do you know,' he mused, his dark eyes twinkling, 'I think I'll just slip round to Christian's and give him back that key.'

'Coward,' I teased him. But he just laughed, and winked, and ducked like lightning through the back door as the returning tour party from Fontevraud descended upon the Hotel de France in a blur of sound and motion.

* * *

The transatlantic line hummed thick with static, and it seemed an age before my father picked the phone up at his end. It was suppertime in Uruguay, and I'd obviously caught him in mid-meal. His voice at first was hard to understand.

'Mmwamph,' he said, when I apologised for calling at this hour, and 'Barrrumph-ba' was his comment after that. He cleared his throat, and coughed. 'You're still in France, then, are you?'

'Yes.'

'Still on your own?'

'Yes. Actually, that's why I called . . .' I twined the phone cord round my fingers, then in a rush of explanation told him what I'd found.

'The King John coin? You're sure of that?'

I nodded, not caring that he couldn't see the gesture. 'I've got it right here, in my room. And I don't think he'd have left it anywhere unless he meant to leave it, only that doesn't make much sense, does it?' I sighed, plucking at the coverlet of my bed. 'Honestly, Daddy, I don't know what else I can do.'

'Well, it sounds as though you've handled things quite sensibly.'

'I thought I might just ring Aunt Jane—'

'Good Heavens, no!' My father's voice came booming down the line, emphatic. 'No point getting her upset for nothing – and it may well be for nothing, knowing Harry. No, I think you'd better leave it all with me. I've still got friends you know, in Paris. I'll ask some questions, stir around, see whether they can track him down. All right?'

Which meant, I thought, he'd likely make some notes, then forget all about it before tomorrow morning. I smiled. 'All right.'

'Just leave it all with me,' he said again, in charge now, reassuring. 'And Emily?'

'Yes, Daddy?'

'Don't let it worry you too much, either, will you? Comes sailing clean through any crisis, does Harry. No point in losing sleep over him.'

That, at least, seemed sound advice. I repeated it to myself that night as I lay restless underneath the covers of my bed, my dry eyes fixed upon the mottled shadows dancing on my ceiling. *No point in losing sleep,* I thought firmly, but it didn't help.

Close by, the bell tolled one o'clock, a solemn sound above the chuckling fountain. Through the open window swept a sudden breath of cold night air, and the shadows on my ceiling stilled their motion as the street lamps were extinguished. All the shadows, that is, except one.

It might have been the moon, passing high among the clouds outside, that made the dim reflection on my wall, and what I heard I blamed on my imagination, or the wind. 'Follow,' said the shadow, as it slipped across my bed. 'Follow . . .'

A sudden breath of chill air blew my window open wider, and the curtains flapped and fluttered like a wild tormented ghost. My heart leapt, frightened, to my throat, but I forced it back again. *Fool,* I called myself, as I rose and hugged my blanket round me. *There's nothing there.*

But just to make absolutely certain of that, I leaned

231

across the window sill and looked down at the sleeping square.

The black-and-white cat moved stealthily between the rustling acacias, from shadow into light and back again, carefully avoiding the spray of the glittering fountain. On soundless feet, the cat traversed the empty square and crossed to sniff the planter set beside the hotel door. My gaze followed, and fell and with a startled jolt I saw that I was not the only one awake and watching the cat.

Neil Grantham's hair looked white in moonlight. Ruffled by the night breeze, it was the only thing that moved. His hands lay still upon the railing of the narrow balcony, and beneath the leather jacket his shoulders were immobile, carved of stone. He didn't seem to breathe.

And then his head began to turn and I drew quickly back, away from the window, and the curtains drifted past me on a sigh that was not mine.

CHAPTER NINETEEN

I rose and . . .
Found a still place.

The cat came to me early next morning. How it found me
I'll never know; I'd walked some distance from the hotel to
the hushed and peaceful Promenade, where the plane trees
grew tall and regal by the river's edge. But the black-and-
white cat came to me nonetheless, and curled itself wearily
into my lap with a wide indulgent yawn.

He'd had a hard night, from the looks of it.

He looked, in fact, much like I felt: tired and rumpled
and out of sorts. I always felt like that when I hadn't slept
well. It was an inherited curse, insomnia. My granddad had
it, and my father, and they'd kindly passed it on to me, so
that from time to time I found myself counting sheep into
quadruple digits, while I tried to will my aching brain to
stop its restless thinking. It didn't happen often any more,
but when it did it always brought me to a place like this, a
quiet place where I could watch the sunrise. Things seemed

less important, somehow, once the sun was up.

Behind me, on the cliffs, the château bell sang seven times – they'd just be starting breakfast service back at the hotel. I ought to be getting back. But not just yet, I thought. Not yet. I smiled as I gently stroked the sleeping cat, and lifted vague unfocused eyes to gaze along the Promenade.

Row facing row the plane trees stood, ghostly pale and thick with green, mute sentries from an age long past. Beneath the arching canopy of leaves a raked red gravel path invited idle footsteps, like my own, and garden benches beckoned one to pause and watch the world drift by.

From my own bench I could see clear across the Vienne, past the jutting point of the little island to the darkly wooded shore that lay beyond. And in between, cold and still like a sheet of ice, the river breathed a veil of mist that caught and spread the dawning spears of sunlight.

Earlier I'd watched a yellow kayak cleave that mist, dancing the current down towards the bridge. Earlier still, a woman with a dog had passed me by, her step brisk and purposeful. But now there was only me, and the cat, and the ducks chattering noisily along the riverbank.

My mind had begun to drift idly along with the river when the cat suddenly shifted position, claws pricking through my woollen jumper. I winced, and looked to see the cause of its alarm.

I didn't have to look far. Four trees away a little spotted dog, nose fixed to the ground, came trotting round a metal litter bin. It was obvious that the dog hadn't yet taken note of us, and even more obvious that it posed no immediate danger to my bristling cat – this because the dog was attached by a bright red lead to a man standing, slouched, with his back to the river, his face cast half in shadow by the flat morning light.

The gypsy wasn't alone. Another man had stopped beside him on the blood-red path, a tall long-limbed man with hair so fair it shone in that soft morning light like silver. The gypsy spoke, and gestured, and I saw Neil shake his head, and tossing back some smiling comment he came on towards me.

'Good morning,' he greeted me. 'Mind if I join you?'

There seemed no escaping the man, I thought, despite my best efforts. I shifted to make room for him on the bench and he sat down with a decided thump, angling himself against the armrest so he could look at me. 'You have a thing for cats, I take it? Or are you out to comfort every stray in Chinon?'

'Not every stray. Just this one.'

'Is this your chap from Saturday night, then?' He reached a careful hand to scratch the dirty black-and-white head. The cat, less nervous, subsided into my lap and stared at him through half-closed eyes. 'Well, what do you know.' Neil's own eyes crinkled at the corners. 'He gets about, this one. I think I saw him prowling about last night, as well.' Withdrawing his hand, he stretched his long legs out before him, ankles crossed. 'He seems rather affectionate, for a stray.'

'Yes.' I looked up and past him, to where the gypsy and his dog still loitered. 'What did that man ask you?' I wanted to know.

'He wanted a match, that's all. I didn't have one.'

I set a calming hand upon the deeply purring cat. 'Spoke to you in English, did he?'

'No, French.'

'I thought you didn't speak French.'

He slanted a curious look in my direction. 'I don't, beyond the limits of my Oxford phrasebook,' he said, 'but when a chap comes up to me with an unlit cigarette in his mouth and pantomimes the striking of a match, I've a fair idea what he's wanting.'

'Oh.' My gaze dropped defensively. When I raised my eyes again the path was empty. The gypsy and his dog were nowhere to be seen. I gathered the cat closer and summoned up a cheerful smile to show to Neil. 'I didn't expect to see you up and about this early,' I told him. 'I thought you did your walking in the evenings.'

'Dustmen woke me,' was his excuse. 'Four o'clock in the bloody morning, they come barrelling round the square like it's a parade ground.'

I sympathised. I'd heard them myself, that morning. I'd heard a great many things, actually, from the tiniest rustle of a dead leaf scuttling across the asphalt to the quiet talk and measured footsteps of two gendarmes patrolling on the graveyard shift. Sleeplessness always heightened my senses.

'They wake me every time, those dustmen,' Neil went on. 'Most mornings I just drop off again, but this morning . . .' He shrugged, and fitted his shoulders to the worn back of the bench. 'This is a lovely place, isn't it?'

'Yes, quite lovely.'

'The whole town is, really. I always hate to leave it.'

'Your holiday's almost over, then?' *Blast,* I thought. I

236

could hear the trail of disappointment in my own voice.

'Next week, I think. I'm very nearly back to normal.' He flexed his hand to demonstrate. 'Besides, I'm pushing my luck as it is. I'm not paid a salary to sit around and do nothing.'

'But you've been practising,' I argued in his defence. 'Every day.'

His eyes slid sideways, unconvinced. 'Only for an hour or so.'

'Isn't that long enough?'

'Back home my normal work day lasts six hours, sometimes more. I'm only playing at it, here.'

'Oh. Well, it sounds nice, anyway. I like the sound of a violin.'

He thanked me for the compliment. 'But you'll probably think differently in a few days' time. Even Beethoven loses some of his appeal after the first hundred playings. I'm getting rather bored with him myself, but then I'm only using him for exercise. I know that piece like the back of my hand.'

'You ought to choose something else, then. You're learning something by a new composer, aren't you?'

'I'd never subject the hotel guests to that.' The midnight blue eyes crinkled a second time. 'It's not the nicest piece to listen to, in my opinion – the composer doesn't much like harmony. No, I only listen to the tape of that one, to learn it better, and even then I have to watch my step. The first time I put that tape in Thierry's monster hi-fi I nearly cleared the hotel,' he admitted with a grin. 'Sounded like the whole bloody orchestra was playing in my room, it was that loud. I kept it turned low, after that.'

My mouth curved. 'I'm beginning to think you played the *Salut d'Amour* on purpose on Saturday, so the ghost would break poor Thierry's hi-fi.'

He looked at me with interest. 'I did play it on purpose, actually. But not to upset the ghost.'

I didn't respond to that, but he didn't look away. 'You've just surprised me, Emily Braden. Some people might recognise Bach, or Mozart, but to spot old Elgar takes a certain depth of knowledge.'

'Yes, well,' I glanced down, flushing, 'my mother quite likes classical music. She was always dragging me to concerts. I didn't pay as much attention as I should have, but I do remember what I liked.'

'You've put that in the past tense, I notice. Don't you go to concerts any more?'

I shook my head. 'Terrible, I know, but I never seem to have the time, these days. My mother goes often enough for both of us. Her boyfriend,' I explained, with a dry smile, 'is a conductor.'

'Oh, really? What's his name?'

I told him. 'Do you know him?'

'I know of him, yes. We've never met.' His eyes were mildly curious. 'So then your father—'

'—lives in Uruguay.'

'I see.' He looked away again, but I had the distinct feeling that he *did* see; that he saw rather more than I wanted him to. I tried to steer the conversation back to neutral ground, by asking him which orchestra he played with in Austria – which didn't help much, as I didn't recognise the name.

'That's what everyone says,' he assured me. 'We're

not exactly the Vienna Philharmonic, but we've eighty-six members and we hold our own. And speaking of conductors, ours is just this side of brilliant.'

'You like living in Austria, then?'

'Very much.'

'No desire to move back to England?'

He raised his shoulders in an almost Gallic shrug. 'If you had the choice of living in Austria or Birmingham, which would you choose?'

'If I were a violinist?' I smiled. 'I'm not sure. Birmingham has a cracking good orchestra.'

'And if you weren't a violinist?' He asked the question quietly, and slid his serious eyes to mine, and all of a sudden I felt I'd been tossed into deep water, over my head. I found I couldn't answer him, even in jest, and after a long moment he calmly looked away again, towards the river. 'Damned noisy this morning, those ducks,' was his only comment.

The silence stretched. I was just beginning to think I couldn't bear it any longer, that I'd have to invent an excuse and leave before I did something foolish, when the cat, apparently deciding that I'd suffered long enough, woke from its nap and stirred. Arching its back in a reluctant stretch it dropped gracefully from my lap to the gravel path and stalked off without so much as a backward look, melting like a shadow into the grassy riverbank.

I watched it go. 'Time for breakfast, I suppose,' I said. Standing up, I brushed my hands against my legs to clear off the clinging strands of cat hair, suddenly aware of the rattling hum of traffic from the boulevard behind us. It seemed a harsh intrusion, in the scented stillness of the Promenade.

'I'll walk back with you.' Neil rose and stretched as the cat had done, and fell into step beside me.

The red gravel path led us into the modern world, where cars and lorries lumbered noisily up and down the boulevard. All along the far side of the street the shopkeepers were running through their daily ritual of opening up, polishing windows and scrubbing down awnings and sweeping the pavement in front of their stores.

We kept to the river walk. There were plane trees here, too – not as ancient or peaceful as those of the Promenade, but nearly as tall, and the breeze blowing through them was idle and cool. It had blown the mist from the murmuring river that danced past in sharp sparkling ribbons of light, and the pavement was dappled with shadow and sunlight, both shifting in time with the whispering leaves.

Despite the bustle of the boulevard, no one seemed to hurry on the river walk. Several people had stopped to lean against the low stone wall and watch the yellow kayak I'd seen earlier come smoothly stroking by on its return trip. Further on a young man struggled up a flight of steps in the sloping river wall, fishing rod in one hand and creel in the other, looking well satisfied. And further on still, not far from the steps where Paul usually sat, a little girl skipped down the cobbled boat launch towards the chattering ducks. They let her come quite near, indeed – so near that the older man lounging some distance behind her stirred in mild alarm. Raising his voice, he called her back a few steps from the swift-flowing water.

Beside me, Neil smiled. 'Just like her mother. She has no proper sense of danger.'

My head jerked round before I remembered that he would know Lucie Valcourt. Lucie could hardly have remembered him from his visits to the house – she wouldn't have been more than four years old herself when her mother died, and three more years had passed since then. But she obviously knew Neil now, and knew him well. When she came dancing back happily up the ramp to say hello, she greeted me in singing French but spoke to Neil in clear, if halting, English. 'Good morning, Monsieur Neil,' she said. 'I feed the dukes.'

'Ducks, love. And yes, I see that. No school today?'

The dark curls swung from side to side, emphatically. 'No. It is Wednesday.'

'Wednesday already?' He raised his eyebrows. 'You know in England, children go to school on Wednesday.'

Lucie wrinkled her nose at the thought. It was an expression, I decided, that must have crossed many a French face down through the ages – the civilised person pondering the ways of the barbarian. Even her comment, that she would not like to live in England, was hardly without precedent.

François turned his dry indulgent gaze on Neil. 'But in England, a man like me would have some rest,' he said, also in English. 'Instead this little one, she takes me every Wednesday for a walk, like a dog.'

'I feed the d . . . ducks,' she chimed in, careful with the new pronunciation. She thought of something, looked at me. 'Mademoiselle, you would like also to feed the ducks? I have much bread.'

241

If anybody else had asked me that, I'd have said no, but then I'd never learned the knack of saying no to children. Neil stayed behind with François, and Lucie lapsed into French again as she led me down the broad boat launch, her small feet bouncing on the cobblestones. 'Monsieur Neil is a friend of yours, Mademoiselle?' she asked, and then without giving me a chance to answer, 'He was a friend of my mother's, too. He lives in Austria. Last summer I went there with Aunt Martine, and he came to visit us. He speaks German,' she informed me, 'but he can't speak French. I heard him try to, once, with Aunt Martine, and he got all his words mixed up. It was funny. Do you like him?'

'Yes, I do. He's a very nice man.'

'Is he your boyfriend?'

'No.'

'Oh.' She bounced a little higher. 'He is very pretty, I think. Prettier than my papa.' With the candid eyes of childhood she looked back at Neil who stood, arms folded, talking now to François. 'But he is not perfect.'

I smiled. 'No?' If Neil Grantham had a flaw, I certainly hadn't been able to find it.

'No.' Lucie shook her head. 'He has a space, a little space, between his teeth, right here.' She bared her own front teeth and pointed to the spot. 'He says it is to whistle with.'

'Ah.' Fortunately, I was spared the need for further comment. We had come nearly to the bottom of the ramp now and Lucie tugged at my sleeve, her voice dropping to a solemn whisper. 'François says it is not good to scare the ducks.'

I took the hunk of bread she gave me and began to throw out crumbs in my best non-threatening manner. It was rather like dropping a chip in Trafalgar Square. From everywhere, it seemed, the ducks came flapping. A small Armada of them massed in the shallows of the river while others tumbled over one another on the cobblestones, adding their full-throated pleas to the general mayhem. They fluttered, they splashed, they begged and demanded and, like the pigeons of Trafalgar Square, they didn't show the slightest fear of people. How had Neil put it, exactly? No proper sense of danger . . .

'. . . and this one, this is Jacques,' said Lucie, pointing out her favourite birds among the bunch, 'and that one with the funny legs I call Ar-ree.'

The bird in question did have funny legs, quite long and skinny, together with a rumpled and dishevelled look that reminded me instantly of my cousin. Something unseen broke the surface of the water beside us and sent a spreading wash of ripples out, unstoppable and oddly sinister.

The gawky duck stared at me and I tossed a crumb towards it. 'Why Ar-ree?' I asked, casually.

'It's an English name,' she told me, with a proud upward glance. 'My Uncle Didier, he has an English friend . . . well, he's dead now, of course, but his friend is called Ar-ree. Last week he came to feed the ducks with me, and he said this duck looked just like him.'

I tore the bread between my fingers, with a jerking motion. 'Harry?' I checked. 'Was his name Harry, Lucie?'

'Yes, Ar-ree. It's such a funny name. Are many people in England called this?'

243

'Quite a few.' I frowned, thinking hard. Her Uncle Didier, she'd said. I put the names together in my mind – Didier Muret and Harry. Didier and Harry, *here*. 'Was it last Wednesday that he came to feed the ducks with you?'

She nodded. 'François had a headache last week, so he couldn't walk with me. But after lunch my Uncle Didier said he could take me out, instead. He's dead now,' she said again, quite matter-of-fact. 'He's not as nice as François. François always lets me stay here a long time, and then we have an ice cream. But Uncle Didier had his friend to talk to last week, and he didn't let me give the ducks all my bread. He was in a hurry, he said.'

A duck flapped against my foot and I took an absent step sideways, flinging down another scattering of crumbs. My bread was very nearly finished. 'Your uncle's friend, did he look anything like me?'

'Yes, very English,' she said, squinting up at me to check. 'But his nose was not so straight.'

'I see. What else do you remember about him?'

'He was very funny, and he likes to feed the ducks, like me. *And* he can make his ears wiggle.' Which obviously raised him above the level of the common man, in her opinion. I looked down at the scruffy little duck with the long ungainly legs, and tossed him my last breadcrumb.

He really did remind me of my cousin, that duck. And if Lucie had her story right, then Harry had been here, in Chinon . . . Harry had been *here*.

I wasn't given time to ponder this new piece of information. Lucie grabbed me by the hand and pulled me back up the ramp to where François and Neil waited, chatting like old friends. Neil laughed at something François said, and turned to look at me. 'Still standing, are you, after that attack? We couldn't see the two of you for feathers, from up here.'

Lucie looked up at him, her brown eyes curious. 'Monsieur Neil,' she asked, in careful English, 'do your ears move?'

'I beg your pardon?'

The tone of his voice penetrated my troubled fog of thought, and I smiled in spite of myself. 'I think she's asking if you can wiggle your ears.'

'Oh. Of course I can.' He crouched to Lucie's level, and demonstrated. I leaned against the low wall, next to François. I wanted to ask him about Didier Muret, but I couldn't summon up the courage, so I tried to slide into the questions sideways.

'She is,' I said in French, 'a lovely child.'

'Yes. I'm very fond of Lucie.'

'She talked to me a bit about her uncle. She seems to be taking his death well, for one so young.'

I felt the brush of his eyes and he lifted his shoulders. 'Didier Muret,' he told me, cryptically, 'was not the sort of man one mourns. And anyway, she didn't know him well.'

'Was he a historian?' I kept the question lightly curious. For after all, I thought, we only had Victor Belliveau's word . . .

'A historian?' He turned that time, to look at me directly. 'No, Mademoiselle, he was a clerk – a lawyer's clerk – when he worked at all.'

'Oh. I must have got it wrong, then.' The doubting

flooded back, and what had seemed so certain moments earlier now hovered in the realm of the improbable. Why would an unemployed lawyer's clerk, who reportedly read no English, be interested in a British article on Isabelle of Angoulême, I wondered? It simply made no sense.

François looked back at Neil and Lucie, his weary eyes softening. 'She is just like her father sometimes, very charming. And she doesn't take no for an answer.'

The child was giggling at the moment, a delighted and infectious sound. 'Again,' she commanded, and Neil sighed in mock despair.

'They'll fall off, you know, and then you'll be sorry.'

But he wiggled his ears again, anyway, and was rewarded with another fit of giggles from his appreciative audience. It was a difficult sound to resist. So it was odd that François's smile faded, the lines on his face deepening as though something had pained him.

Concerned, I touched his arm. 'Are you all right?'

I saw the shiver, hastily suppressed, and fancied for a moment that his gaze seemed faintly questing on my face, but when he spoke he looked himself again.

'Yes, I am fine, Mademoiselle. I am an old man, that is all. Sometimes I see the ghosts.'

CHAPTER TWENTY

Thro' her this matter might be sifted clean.

I didn't go straight back to the hotel. Instead I turned along a narrow street and went in search of the smaller square where Martine Muret kept her gallery.

It wasn't difficult to find. A few acacias grew here as well, draped over cobbled stone, well pitted and grown dark with age. The sun shone warmly, cheerfully, upon the clustering of leaning shops and houses, reflected in the gleaming glass front of the little gallery.

Even without Christian's paintings hanging in the window, I believe I would have known the place belonged to Martine. It looked like her, somehow – so smart and neat and elegant, with everything in perfect order. But Christian's oils clinched the matter. They stood out from the other paintings easily, the bolder brush strokes and exquisite play of light and shadow lending them a warm, romantic feel. Stepping closer, I peered with interest at the softly swirled self-portrait Paul had mentioned. Christian, I thought, had a master's touch. He'd shown himself no quarter, tracing every jutting outline of his sharply contoured face, the pale eyes gently sombre and the golden hair uncombed.

He'd breathed similar life into his landscapes. I saw the walls of Château Chinon shiver under storm clouds, and the idle spreading peace of fields flecked liberally with grazing cows, but my favourite of his paintings was the one that showed the river.

He had painted it at sunset, not far from the steps where Paul often sat. The steps themselves were plainly there, beneath the looming silhouette of Rabelais, and on the placid water three ducks drifted round a weathered punt, moored close against the sloping wall, while further off the gleaming arches of the bridge stretched like a golden thread from shore to shore. The only thing missing from that picture, I thought, was Paul himself, sitting halfway down the steps with his back to the traffic above, reading *Ulysses* and smoking an illicit cigarette.

It wasn't often that a painting so transported me, and when Martine herself came out onto the doorstep to greet me, she had to speak twice before I heard her.

'It is a lovely painting, that one, is it not?' She smiled, understanding.

'Very lovely.' I bit my lip. 'Is it very expensive?'

'Not so expensive as his others. It is a smaller canvas, and there are no cows in it. Tourists,' she informed me, 'like the cows, and so the cows have higher prices than the river. But if you like, I have a price list.'

I came inside and waited while she went to fetch the list.

The gallery's interior was bright and white and spotless, meant to show off every sculpture, sketch and painting to advantage. Martine had a clever eye for art, I thought. I didn't see a single work that I would not have wanted to own myself. Still, I fancied most of it was well outside my price range, and when Martine finally found the list and ran her finger down it, I braced myself for the inevitable. Not that it mattered, I consoled myself. I hadn't come to buy a painting, anyway. I'd only come to ask Martine some subtle questions about her ex-husband, Didier Muret.

'Painting number 88,' she said at last. 'Yes, here it is.' The sum she quoted was almost twice what I earned in a month.

I heard a quiet footstep on the polished floor behind me. 'Perhaps Christian will reduce his prices, for a friend.' A man's voice, but the accent was distinctly French, not German. I hadn't seen Armand Valcourt come in. Martine had, though; she didn't bat an eyelid as she shook her head, a smile softening her sigh.

'Christian,' she said, 'would give them all away, I think, these paintings. He has too generous a nature. Always I must watch him and remind him painters, too, must eat.'

I glanced round at Armand, and said good morning. 'I saw your daughter earlier, by the river.'

'Yes.' He smiled. 'This is her morning with François. The ducks, I think, and then the ice cream . . . such a simple way to happiness. She likes her Wednesdays, my Lucie.'

His eyes were quite unhurried as they roamed the quiet gallery, and he didn't seem in any rush to move. So much, I thought, for my chance of a private chat with Martine. I tried to hide my disappointment by asking him how old his daughter was, exactly.

'Lucie? She has nearly seven years.'

'And already she has genius,' said her slightly biased aunt. 'She can tell you every step of how the wine is made, that little one.'

'She is a Valcourt,' Armand said, as if that explained everything. 'It will be hers one day, the *Clos des Cloches*, and so I pass traditions down, as I learned from my father.'

Martine smiled. 'But she is half her mother's child, remember. She likes the vine but also likes the art. Perhaps one day she will begin the home for artists that Brigitte so often talked about.'

'God help us.' Armand shuddered. 'The artist by himself, he can be interesting. A few of them at dinner, when they are not fighting, that also can be interesting. But a house of artists,' his eyes rolled heavenward at the thought. 'They would drive me mad.'

'You will forgive my brother-in-law,' Martine said, her dark eyes teasing. 'He likes only the art on his wine labels.'

Armand looked offended. 'That is not true. I like this painting very much.' He nodded at a watercolour hung behind the cash register, a sweeping vista of a vineyard with a mellow-walled château nestled in the distance. 'This shows great talent.'

'This shows grapes.' Martine's voice was dry. 'But no matter. I'm sorry, Armand, was there something that you needed?'

'No, not really.'

'Oh.' Surprise flashed momentarily across her lovely

fragile face, from which I gathered that Armand Valcourt didn't often visit the gallery without a reason.

'No, I was just passing, and I thought I would come and see what you have done. Lucie says there are sculptures, somewhere, that are new.'

Martine considered; shook her head. 'Not new ones, no. I do not think . . .'

'Ah, well. You know Lucie, she sometimes gets her story wrong.' He didn't seem concerned. Hands in his pockets, he leaned closer to me, his breath feathering my neck as he studied a smaller pen-and-ink drawing on the counter. 'And this is also nice, Martine. It is by Christian, yes?'

She looked, and nodded. 'Yes.'

'It looks like Victor's place.' He reached to pick the drawing up, his arm brushing casually against my shoulder. 'Yes, so it is. I wonder sometimes what Victor does with himself, these days. Do you ever hear from him?'

Martine shook her head. 'Christian sees him, now and then. They have a drink and talk.' She smiled at me, in vague apology. 'This is a friend of ours we speak of, an old friend.'

Victor Belliveau, I nearly said. Of course, they all would know each other from the days when Brigitte Valcourt had held her magnificent parties up at the *Clos des Cloches*. A poet would have been included on the guest list, I decided, alongside musical Neil and clever Christian. I longed to ask Martine about those parties, just as I longed to ask her if her former husband ever talked of history, or of Englishmen named Harry. But even as I tried to summon up the nerve, a telephone rang shrilly in the gallery's back room, and

Martine excused herself to answer it, her heels clicking on the hard tile floor as she walked away.

Armand shifted at my shoulder, looking down at me. After a moment's silence, he cleared his throat and spoke. 'I have a confession.'

'Oh, yes?' I glanced up.

'I have not much interest in art. And sculpture bores me.' He moved around to lean against the counter, facing me, and raised one hand in an automatic gesture before remembering he shouldn't smoke here. The hand went back inside his pocket. 'When I said that I was passing, that was true. But I only stopped because I saw you here.' He grinned. 'It is no easy matter, in a town this size, to find someone.'

Harry always said I had a talent for deducing the obvious, and I displayed it now. 'You were looking for me?'

He shrugged. 'I thought, if you had not made plans already, you might let me buy you lunch.'

'Lunch.' I repeated the word rather stupidly, and he brought his smiling eyes back to mine.

'Yes. Most days my lunch hours are reserved for Lucie. My work, it keeps me very busy, so I try to keep this hour for her, our private time. You understand?' Convinced I did, he carried on. 'But on Wednesdays, François takes Lucie for half the day, and they eat lunch together, so I am left with no one.'

No one? On the contrary, I thought, the women must be queuing up.

'You don't believe me?' His eyes were warm behind the coal-black lashes. 'It is true. I am a rich man, Mademoiselle, but the price one pays for influence is isolation.'

It was a blatant attempt to play upon my sympathies, and while it didn't work, I must confess I couldn't see the harm in having lunch. Besides, I thought, Armand Valcourt had also known Didier Muret. Perhaps I could ask him the questions I had meant to ask Martine.

'All right, then,' I said, on impulse, 'I'd be happy to have lunch with you.'

'Good.' He flashed a smile briefly, raised his eyes, then dropped them to his watch. 'Good, then I shall pick you up at your hotel at noon, if you like?'

My own watch read nine forty-five. 'All right.'

'Good,' he said again, pushing away from the counter. 'In that case I will leave you for the moment, to enjoy the paintings. I have business still to do before we eat. You will excuse me?' His smile was very charming, but it wasn't serious. It didn't mean anything.

He showed the same smile to the rumpled young man who bumped shoulders with him in the doorway. 'Morning,' Simon said cheerfully, as Armand slipped past him into the shaded street. Whistling an aimless happy tune, Simon stepped into the gallery and stopped short at the sight of me. '*There* you are!' From his tone, one would have thought I was some errant schoolgirl, late for lessons. 'Paul's been looking everywhere for you, you know. You missed breakfast.'

'Yes, well—'

'He's back at the hotel now, waiting for you to turn up.'

Martine emerged from the back room, having dealt with her telephone caller. Her dark eyes, dancing, travelled from

Simon's face to mine. 'You are much in demand, I think, this morning. All these men come looking for you.'

Simon, bless his heart, said: 'I'm looking for Christian, actually. Thought you might know where he is.'

She arched a curious eyebrow. 'Christian?'

'Yeah. I wanted to borrow . . . something.'

'If he is not at home . . .'

'He isn't.'

'Then you might try in the next street,' she advised him, 'around this corner. He talked last night about making a drawing there.'

Simon, to my surprise, showed no desire to hang about chatting to Martine. Thanking her, he turned to me. 'You should probably come with me,' he decided, 'so we don't lose you again.'

There was little point in staying, I thought glumly, as heavy footsteps sounded on the front step and an elderly couple entered the gallery, calling out a greeting to Martine. She saw us graciously to the door, her eyes faintly puzzled as they met mine over our handshake. 'Was there something else, Mademoiselle, that you were wanting to ask?'

'No.' The lie fell heavy as a lump of lead.

'It's only that . . .' She stopped, and shook her head, and the bemused expression cleared. 'No matter, it is nothing. Enjoy your day, the both of you.'

The day, I found, had swiftly changed its character. The sun now hung, suppressed, behind a screen of dull grey cloud, and the air smelled faintly of motor oil and coming rain.

Simon took the lead and I followed him, head down and

deep in thought. So deep in thought, in fact, that at the next corner I nearly ploughed straight into Christian Rand without seeing him. Not that it would have mattered to Christian – he probably wouldn't have noticed. The young artist was lost in contemplation of a different kind, staring with half-seeing eyes at the bakery across the road.

Neil Grantham was something of a recurring theme this morning. He was standing next to Christian now, head back and hands on hips, his calm gaze focused on the same building. I looked, saw nothing too remarkable, and offered my apologies to Christian for so nearly tripping over him.

At first I thought he hadn't heard, but then the roughly cropped blonde head dipped forward slightly, in a silent nod of acknowledgement.

'Working, eh?' asked Simon, and again the artist nodded, not moving his eyes.

'I must tear down this building,' he said, slowly, 'it spoils my composition. But how . . . how . . . ?'

I shot Neil a quizzical glance.

'He doesn't mean it,' he assured me. 'He does it all in his head, you see – pulls things down, or lumps them closer together, to make a better picture. Artists can do that sort of thing.'

'Oh.' I hadn't really taken Christian literally, if only because knocking down a building required a physical energy that seemed quite beyond him, somehow – but it always helped to have a proper explanation.

Neil smiled, understanding. 'I only know because my brother paints, and he tears things down all the time. He's very much like Christian, actually, my brother is, though his paintings aren't nearly as good.'

'You've a talented family, then.'

He shrugged. 'It comes from my mother, I suppose. She used to sketch, and teach piano.'

'So what did your father do?' Simon asked drily. 'What was he, a writer? Actor? Opera singer?'

'He worked for British Rail.' The boyish grin was like a flash of light.

I looked away and checked my watch again. 'I'd best find Paul,' I said. 'Excuse me.'

I left the three men standing like a mismatched group of statuary in the middle of the street, with Simon chattering on to Christian about borrowing a shovel and bucket. Rather like a child going to play at the seashore, I thought with a smile. Well, perhaps he'd find his treasure, after all. No harm in trying.

The hotel bar was closed until the lunch hour, but I found Paul sitting in there anyway, reading in the semi-darkness. He put *Ulysses* down when I came in, and stretched, his expression relieved. 'Well, it's about time. I was starting to get worried.'

'Sorry.' I sat down, stretching out my own weary legs. 'I went out rather early, for a walk along the river.' I didn't mention meeting the cat, or Neil – for some reason, that part of my morning seemed private and not for sharing. But I did tell Paul about Lucie Valcourt, and how we'd fed the ducks together earlier, and what she'd said about her uncle's English friend.

'Wow,' he said. Leaning back, he absently rumpled his

hair with one hand. 'So you think Muret might have been the guy who was supposed to meet your cousin here in Chinon?'

'It certainly sounds like it, don't you think? I mean, he could have read the journal article at Victor Belliveau's house. They knew each other.'

'Only everybody so far says he didn't know English.'

'I know.' I frowned. 'And I haven't figured out yet why he would be interested at all in what my cousin wrote about. There are so many questions. I was going to ask Martine about it, actually. I went round to the gallery this morning.' I smiled. 'But it was rather too crowded to talk properly, and I'm not sure I would have had the nerve to ask anything, anyway. I mean, it isn't done, is it? Not when you hardly know a person, and it's her ex-husband you're asking about, and he's only been dead a week. Still,' I told him, brightening, 'I'm having lunch with Armand Valcourt, and he might be able to—'

'I beg your pardon?' Paul cut in, with an incredulous smile. 'You're what?'

'Having lunch with Armand Valcourt,' I repeated. 'And you can wipe that smug look off your face, Paul Lazarus, because I really don't—'

'OK, OK.' Paul lifted both hands in self-defence. 'And it's not a smug look, I'm just jealous, that's all.'

Jealous? Heavens, I thought, he surely didn't think of me that way, did he? 'Paul—'

'Hardly seems fair, you eating lunch with a rich guy while I'm stuck with cheese-on-a-bun and Simon.' He grinned at me. 'Where's he taking you?'

257

'I haven't the faintest idea.'

'Somewhere disgustingly expensive, I'll bet. There are a couple of gourmet restaurants down the rue Voltaire, the kind of restaurants where they have six forks, you know the type. What time are you meeting him?'

'At noon.' I turned my wrist to read my watch. 'Oh, Lord, it's just gone eleven now, and I haven't even showered.'

'Go on then, I'll cover for you.' He leaned back in his seat and reached for the tattered paperback. 'Just remember your mission, Dr Watson.'

'And that is?'

'Get the man drunk and ask him about Didier Muret.'

'Right.' I smiled, and turned to leave. 'Let's hope he tells me something useful, then.'

'Let's hope he doesn't. I, for one, would feel a whole lot happier knowing there was no connection between Martine's husband and your cousin.'

He didn't need to tell me why. My own mind had already gone this route a few hours earlier, and reached the same unsettling impasse: if my suspicions were correct, then Harry had been here in Chinon last Wednesday, feeding ducks with Lucie and chumming with her uncle Didier. And by Thursday morning, Didier Muret was dead.

CHAPTER TWENTY-ONE

. . . call'd mine host
To council, plied him with his richest wines,

He didn't choose a gourmet restaurant, after all, and I only had to muddle through three forks, a simple feat recalled with ease from my days of eating at Embassy dinners. Except for the forks, my lunch with Armand Valcourt bore no resemblance to those plodding Embassy events.

For one thing, the surroundings were more comfortable. The restaurant's dining-room was rustic, whitewashed country French, its deep-silled windows stuffed with flowers blooming pink and red in the slanting midday sunlight. Pine tables, artfully distressed in keeping with the country theme, were set at discreet intervals around the room, and the russet tile floor gleamed warmly mellow, spotless, at our feet.

They'd seated us beside the fireplace. Not yet in use, it too was filled with flowers, shell-pink roses mixed with ferns and feathered pale chrysanthemums. The smell of roses, delicate, seductive, clung to every breath I took. It swirled around the scent of wine, the whiff of garlic, and the tender tempting fragrance of the shellfish jumbled on my plate.

Exquisite food, a charming ambience, and the close, attentive company of a handsome man who, if not exactly an aristocrat, was clearly near the top rung of the social ladder, as evidenced by the quietly respectful service we'd received. It was a shade surreal, the whole affair, which was perhaps why I felt so terribly relaxed. That, or the fact that Armand had twice refilled my wine glass.

He was holding out the bottle now, dividing the remaining wine between our empty glasses as he finished off an anecdote about his daughter and her bicycle.

'She looks like you, you know,' I told him. 'Not feature for feature, but the smile is the same.' We were speaking English, mainly I think because it gave us the illusion of privacy, encircled as we were by three tables of French-speaking patrons.

'Thank you,' he said, and looked at me. 'You have no children?'

'No.'

He didn't push it, didn't pry. 'They are like nothing else, children. Nothing can prepare you for the feelings they create. You would do anything.' He pried a mussel from its shell and chewed it thoughtfully. 'I was not sure, myself, that I wanted a child, but when Lucie was born . . .' He set his fork down with a shrug. 'Everything was changed.'

'It must be difficult, though, raising her alone.'

'Not quite alone.' He smiled, a smile that forgave my

ignorance of the privileged world he lived in. 'There was a nurse, in the beginning, to take care of her. Then, when Brigitte died, Martine came back to live with us. And of course, there is always François.'

'He's been with you a long time, has he, François?'

'A long time, yes. His parents worked for my grandparents, and François himself was born the same year as my father – 1930.' He caught himself and winked at me. 'Don't tell him I told you this. He likes to be most secretive about his age. My wife said always François was like those men in films, you understand, the valet faithful to the family who counts their needs ahead of his.'

I told him I could understand her point. 'He looks the perfect butler, and he does seem rather loyal.'

'Perhaps. But he is more like family, François, and he stays because the vineyard is his home as much as mine. He does not serve without the questions, like the valet of the films, and if he serves at all it is because he likes the person he is serving.'

'He must like you, then.'

Armand smiled above his wine glass. 'I try his patience, sometimes, but this is natural for people who have passed a life together. Lucie he adores.'

I remembered the way François had watched his young charge by the ducks that morning, how his weary eyes had softened on her face. But even as I thought of that another image rose to take its place – of François staring, startled, at the laughing little girl. Seeing ghosts, he'd told me. For a moment I debated asking Armand if Lucie looked very like her mother, but then decided it might be easier to ask him about Didier. If I could only find some plausible excuse, some way of leading him round to the subject . . .

Toying with my glass, I tried the indirect approach. 'You said Martine came back to live with you when . . . when you were widowed. Where did she live before that? Here in Chinon?'

'With her husband, yes. You know that he is dead?' The dark gaze flicked me, moved away. He shrugged. 'One should not be speaking ill of the dead, I know, but he was not a pleasant man, her husband. Already when she came to help with Lucie there were problems with the marriage.'

I nodded, pleased that my tactic had worked. 'Yes, I'd heard they were divorced.'

'Annulled. There is a difference, to the Church.' The wine swirled like liquid gold in his glass as he lifted it and smiled faintly. 'If you believe in that sort of thing.'

'And you don't, I take it?'

'Me? No, I believe in the things that I can touch – my land, my family, old traditions and good wine. And you?'

I had to admit I hadn't the faintest idea. 'I'm a sceptic, I'm afraid.'

'You have no religion?'

'No.'

'People, then. You must believe in people.'

'People aren't permanent,' I answered drily, and he raised his eyebrows in surprise, a slow smile forming at the corners of his mouth.

'You are indeed a sceptic, as you say. Tell me, did you always think this? As a child?'

'Good heavens, no.' I grinned. 'I was the most believing

child that ever lived. I wished on stars and everything.'

'So what has happened?'

'Life.' I gave the answer with a shrug. My last mussel had grown cold in its shell, and I pushed it away with my fork. How had we got on to this subject from Didier, I wondered? The conversation wanted steering back to more productive ground. 'And Martine's husband? What did he believe in?'

'Money,' came the answer, then he tempered his quick judgement with an even-minded shrug. 'That is not fair, perhaps, because I do not know what it is like to be coming from nothing, as Didier did. He had, I think, an ugly childhood. Martine had money, so he married her.'

I found it rather difficult to imagine any man marrying Martine Muret simply for her money, but Armand assured me this was so. 'It is the thinking of most people, of Martine herself. But then,' he admitted, 'most people, they think this is also why I married my wife.'

'You?' I stared, surprised. 'But you're . . .'

'Rich? Yes, now, but when I married things were not so well for the *Clos des Cloches*. I managed badly in the early years, the harvests were not good, and everybody knew this. I'm not surprised that people think I chose Brigitte for money.'

'And did you?' It was too late to withdraw the question, however much I kicked myself for asking it. Already Armand was leaning back, head tilted, considering his answer.

'In part.' He smiled without apology. 'This was no burning passion, between Brigitte and myself. It was more business, an exchange. She wanted a nice house, where she could play the hostess, hold her parties. And me, I wanted a beautiful wife of good family. That she had money was one more attraction. At that moment, we suited one another, but later . . . I was sorry for her death, but I did not suffer with it.' His smile softened. 'Do I shock you? I should keep to the politics in conversation, or you will not come to lunch with me again.'

But he didn't keep to politics. Instead he asked about my family and my childhood, so I favoured him with a few of the better anecdotes I'd gathered growing up a Braden. I finished with the one about the day Harry tried to burn me at the stake. We'd been playing in the garden – Joan of Arc, as I recall – with me strapped to the rose trellis for an added touch of authenticity. The blaze had been spectacular, and for a few long moments, while Harry was off looking for my father's garden hosepipe, I had felt uncomfortably close to poor St Joan.

Most people laughed when I told them that story, but Armand looked rather shocked. 'He is alive still, this cousin of yours? Your father did not kill him?'

'No, he survived. He lectures in history, on and off, in London.'

'I see.' He smiled then, and leaning back he felt for his cigarettes. 'Then I am glad you did not bring him with you. The history of my family, that is one thing, but the wars, the kings and queens . . .' His shrug dismissed such trivialities. 'I find them always boring.'

Here was my opportunity, I thought, to swing the conversation round again. 'Your brother-in-law was quite the historian, though, from what I hear.'

'Didier?' The cigarette lighter clicked shut. Leaning back, Armand narrowed his eyes as the smoke curled upwards. 'A historian? Who has told you this?'

'I don't remember,' I hedged, keeping my voice light. 'Someone at the hotel, I imagine. I thought they said he had a love of history.'

He lifted the cigarette and inhaled smoothly, but I saw the line of his jaw tighten. 'You have been misinformed, I think. My brother-in-law loved nothing but himself. And money. Always money.' His voice sounded hard. Didier Muret, I was learning, had that effect on people. 'He couldn't keep a job, because he stole. Brigitte, my wife, she once found him work with her own lawyer, for Martine's sake, but it was no good. The money went missing there, too. Martine left him after that. She let him stay in the house, but he got no more money from her.'

Well done, Martine, I thought. 'Actually,' I went on, trying to make the white lie sound convincing, 'I think it was young Simon who told me your brother-in-law liked history. They'd met each other once, I think.'

'Simon?' Armand looked sceptical. 'The boy with the long hair, who came to tour my vineyard? But he does not speak French, not like his brother. And Didier, he spoke no English. They might have met, but they could not have talked to one another.'

'I must have got it wrong, then,' I said brightly. Three people had now told me the same story, and three people, I thought, couldn't be mistaken. Which meant that Didier Muret could not have read my cousin's article, would not have had a reason to contact him, had probably never met him. What had Armand said that morning, about his daughter? *Lucie, she sometimes gets her story wrong.* And a duck named 'Ar-ree' was hardly the best evidence, I reminded myself with a wry smile. 'It must have been some other Didier he was talking about. Simon's less than clear in conversation, sometimes.'

Not that I was very much better. I really *must* go easy on the wine while trying to investigate, I thought. It took all my effort, as we left the restaurant, just to walk a straight line without tripping over cobblestones.

I don't think Armand noticed. He strolled easily beside me, along the half-deserted rue Voltaire. I smiled when I saw he walked with one hand in his pocket, his cigarette held loosely in the other. Most French men walked like that. It was a sort of national identity badge, a wholly unconscious habit they acquired at some early age and carried till they died. In my younger days in Paris I'd often passed a lazy hour at the Luxembourg gardens, spotting the *français* among the tourists by the way they walked.

'I have enjoyed this,' Armand said, when we came out into the fountain square. 'I enjoy your company. We should have dinner one night before you leave.'

It was a non-committal sort of invitation, and I responded in kind. 'I'd like that.'

The light goodbye kiss caught me slightly off guard, I must admit. Things naturally progressed this way, of course, among the French: from smiles and nods to handshakes to *la bise*, the friendly double kiss, but they didn't usually progress this quickly. Armand Valcourt, I thought, worked fast.

He was only a flirt, and a harmless one, and I was decidedly single, but still I felt a twist of guilty conscience. I cast a quick glance upwards at the hotel, along the row of empty balconies, to where the tall and graceful windows of Neil's room reflected back the calmly drifting clouds. I thought I saw a flash of something pale behind the glass, but I might have imagined the movement.

I must have imagined it. The château bell was chiming three o'clock when I entered the hotel lobby – it was Neil's normal practise time, but there was no violin this afternoon. There was only Thierry, looking very bored behind the desk. No, he told me, nobody was back yet. There was only him, and the telephone, and . . . He broke off, brightening. 'You would like a drink, Mademoiselle? In the bar?'

I shook my head. 'The last thing I need, Thierry, is a drink. I'm floating as it is. No, I think I'll go upstairs and have a nap.'

He rolled his eyes. 'The naps,' he said, 'are for old women, and for children.'

He was quite wrong, I thought later, buried deep beneath my freshly-ironed sheets and soft wool blanket. An afternoon nap was a glorious indulgence, tucked into the middle of a long and active day, with rich food and fine wine fuzzing round the edges of one's drifting mind. I sighed and snuggled deeper.

Few sounds rose to drown the murmur of the fountain underneath my open window. Now and then a car passed by, or someone shouted to a friend across the square. Nearby a dog barked sharply and was silenced by a quick command. But nothing else disturbed the peace, the perfect peace that filled my shadowed room. The fountain's voice grew louder still, subtly altering pitch, becoming low and deep and lulling like the darkly flowing river to the south.

It was so close, that sound . . . so close . . .

It was beside me. I hardly ever dreamed, not any more, so I was rather surprised to find myself moving in that strange, disjointed way that dreamers do, not in my room but down along the river, where the plane trees wept like mourners in the wind beneath a grey uncertain sky. I moved with no real purpose, no true course. One moment I was standing on the bridge, and then there was no bridge, and I was sitting on the riverbank, my arms hugged tightly round my upraised knees. Across the calm water I could see my cousin Harry, pacing back and forth along the tree-lined shore of the little island. He wanted to cross, but without the bridge it was impossible.

'No point in worrying about Harry,' my father said beside me. Smiling, he reached into his pocket and handed me a King John coin. 'Here, make a wish.'

I took the coin from Daddy's hand, without thinking, and tossed it in the water. It changed, too, as it fell, no longer silver but a diamond, and where it sank the river ran pure red, like blood.

Alarmed, I looked up at the place where I'd seen Harry, but he wasn't there. The only person standing on the far shore was a lean tall man with pale blonde hair, his eyes fixed sadly on my face. He was trying to tell me something – I could see his lips moving, but the wind stole his voice, and all that reached me was a single word: 'Trust . . .'

A cold shadow fell across the grass beside me, and I

looked up to meet the gentle gaze of the old man François. 'Seeing ghosts?' he asked me. Then, incredibly, he raised a violin to his shoulder and began to play Beethoven.

I opened my eyes.

One floor below, Neil stopped his practising a moment, tuned a string, began again. I listened, staring at the ceiling. Ordinarily, I found Beethoven soothing, just the thing to clear my mind of stray and troubling dreams, but this afternoon it proved no help at all.

At length, I simply shut it out. Closing my eyes to the light, I turned my face against the pillow and felt the unexpected trail of tears.

CHAPTER TWENTY-TWO

There moved the multitude, a thousand heads:

'You've got a snail on your sleeve,' Neil pointed out, quite calmly, as if it were an everyday occurrence. I looked down in surprise.

'So I have. Poor little thing. Making a break for it, that's what he's doing.' Gently I detached the clinging creature from the slick material of my windcheater. I ought to have put him back in the bucket with the others, I suppose, but I just couldn't bring myself to do it. Instead I closed my fingers softly round the snail and wandered on, away from the fishmonger's stall. The noisy Thursday market crowd pressed in on all sides, but Neil managed to stay close by my shoulder.

'Thief,' he said, grinning.

'I'm not stealing him, I'm liberating him,' was my stubborn reply. 'Bravery should be rewarded.'

'Well, I'd hardly think that chap back there with the

tattoo and the cleaver would agree with you. He's charging a good penny for his escargots.'

I shrugged. 'Plenty more in the bucket. Do you see a planter anywhere about?'

'Whatever for?'

'I can't put him down here, now can I?' I explained, patiently. 'He'd be trodden on.'

Neil sent me a lopsided smile and lifted his eyes to look over my head. 'Would a flower pot do?' he asked. 'There's a flower seller over there, by the fountain.'

The fountain square was not so crowded, and one of the benches was actually free. Neil sat down with a grateful sigh while I set free my pilfered snail among the potted geraniums.

I was rather glad myself to be out of the crush for a moment. For all its festive fun and colour, the market was a confusing sort of place, with everybody jostling and disagreeing over the price of a bolt of calico or a hunk of cheese, and children coming loose from their parents and being chased down with a stern warning *not* to wander off again, and the vendors themselves doing everything short of a strip-tease to make one stop beneath the bright striped awnings and take notice.

Some of the vendors had gone high tech. With microphones shoved down their shirt-fronts they kept their running patter up and drowned the ragged voices of their neighbours, while from every corner of the Place du Général de Gaulle came blaring music, blending like a weird discordant symphony by some off-beat composer.

I didn't mind the noise – it was the crowd that was a

nuisance. We'd started off in company with Simon and Paul, only to lose them several minutes later. I'd tried myself to lose Neil, once or twice, but it hadn't worked. He was tall enough to see above the milling heads, and my bright blue jumper made me easy to spot. And, to be honest, I hadn't really tried *that* hard.

'I must be getting old,' said Neil. 'I haven't the stamina for market day that I once had.'

'I know what you mean.' I turned, leaning against the bench, and found him watching me. The strong midday sun caught him full in the eyes, making them glow a strange iridescent blue before he narrowed them in reflex.

'How many pets do you have, back in England?'

I stared at him. 'Not a one. Why?'

'I just wondered. Animals do seem to follow you about, don't they? First the cat, and now a snail.' Again the brief and tilting smile. 'I'd have thought your house would be stuffed to the rafters with strays.'

I shook my head. 'No, there's only me.'

'I saw your cat last night, by the way, when I went for my walk. Quite an adventurous chap, isn't he? He'd gone clear across the bridge to the other side of the river, the Quai Danton.'

I heard the hint of admiration in his tone, and glanced up sideways, struck by a sudden thought. 'I don't suppose you ever adopt strays, yourself . . . ?'

Neil intercepted my look with knowing eyes. 'Much as I'm sure your little friend would enjoy the train ride back to Austria, I'm afraid I couldn't take him. My landlady doesn't allow pets.'

I'd been tempted to take the cat home with me to England, only it wouldn't be fair to put him through the quarantine. I thought of winter coming on, and sighed. 'He ought to live in Rome,' I said. 'They have whole colonies of cats there, running wild, with women to feed them.'

'That reminds me,' Neil said, shifting on the bench to dig one hand into the pocket of his jeans. 'I've got a present for you.'

I blinked at him. 'A what?'

'A present. I meant to give it to you at breakfast, but Garland trapped me at my table . . .' He dug deeper, frowning slightly. 'Don't tell me I've bloody lost it, after all that . . . no, there it is.' His face cleared, and he drew the whatever-it-was from his pocket.

It didn't look like anything, at first – I only saw his hand stretched out towards me. And then his fingers moved, and a disc of bright metal glinted between them, and he dropped the coin into my upraised palm.

It was the size of a tuppence but twice as thick, with a gold-coloured centre surrounded by an outer ring of silver. Absently I rubbed my thumb across the bit of braille close to the coin's edge. 'It's Italian,' I said, faintly puzzled.

'Yes, I know. Five hundred lire. Last night at dinner I sat next to a kindly old Italian gent,' he explained, 'who found that for me in the pocket of his overcoat. He charged me rather more than the going rate of exchange, I think, but I simply couldn't let the opportunity pass.'

'You mean you actually bought this from someone?' I stared down at the coin, feeling the weight of it, the warmth. 'For me?'

'You said your father gave you coins to wish with every morning, when you lived in Italy.' He turned his mild gaze upon the dancing spray that veiled the three bronze Graces. 'Different fountain, of course, but I thought if the coin were the proper currency, you might still get your wish.'

I was stunned that he'd remembered such a small thing, that he'd gone to so much trouble. My vision misting, I tucked my head down, mumbling thanks. The spectre of my five-year-old self danced happily beside me. *What should I wish for, Daddy?* And again I heard his answer: *Anything you want.* Anything . . .

I hadn't heard Neil move, and so the touch of his fingers on my face startled me. It was a light touch, warm and sure and faintly comforting, as if he had every right to tip my chin up, to fix me with those understanding eyes and brush his thumb across the curve of my cheekbone, wiping away the single tear that had spilled from my wet lashes. 'It's really not that difficult,' he said. 'Believing.'

'Neil . . .'

'Whenever you're ready.' His smile was strangely gentle. 'It'll keep.' His thumb trailed down my face to touch the corner of my mouth, and then he dropped his hand completely and the midnight eyes slid past me to the crowded market square. 'There they are,' Neil said.

The boys had spotted us as well, but it took them a few minutes to push their way through. I was grateful for the delay. By the time they reached us, I was looking very nearly normal.

Paul's hands were empty, tucked into the pockets of his bright red jacket, but Simon had evidently fallen victim to the vendors. '. . . and you can't tear it or wear it out,' was his final proud pronouncement, as he held up a perfectly ordinary-looking chamois cloth to show us. 'You should have seen it, Emily – the sales guy even set *fire* to it, and nothing happened.'

I agreed that was most impressive. 'But what is it for?'

'Oh, lots of things,' Simon hedged, shoving the miracle cloth back into its bag.

Paul grinned. 'He's pathetic,' he told us. 'He nearly bought a radiator brush, of all things. Every salesman's dream, that's Simon.'

'Mom and Dad have a radiator,' his brother defended himself.

'And I'm sure that's what they've dreamed we'd bring them home from France – a radiator brush.' Paul's voice was dry. 'Have you still got my bread, by the way? I'll need it to feed the ducks.'

'What? Oh, yeah.' Simon rummaged in a carrier bag, tugging out a long piece of baguette. 'I'm surprised those stupid ducks haven't sunk to the bottom of the river, the way you feed them.'

'Ducks need to eat, too.' Paul took the bread and turned to me, his dark eyes slightly quizzical. 'You're welcome to come with me, if you want, unless you'd rather—'

'I'd love to come,' I cut him off, relieved to find my legs would still support me when I stood. Neil settled back against the bench, the soft breeze stirring his golden hair. He met my eyes and smiled. I was running away, and we both knew it, but he didn't try to stop me. He seemed quite content to stay behind with Simon and peruse the bulging carrier bags, while I scuttled like a rabbit after Paul.

The crowd surged in around me, swept me on, and shot me like a cork from a bottle onto the Quai Jeanne d'Arc, where Paul stood waiting at the foot of the Rabelais statue.

We sat on the steps, as we had before, with the sloping stone wall to our backs and the river spread like a glistening blanket before us, stretched wide at either end to the horizon. The ducks were clustered out of sight at the end of the boat launch, but the cacophony of paddle and squawk still rose loudly to our ears, nearly drowning out the constant drone of traffic on the quai. The same flat-bottomed punt bobbed gently to the rhythm of the current at our feet, its chain moorings trailing clots of sodden dead-brown leaves.

Paul reached for his cigarettes, nodding at my hand. 'What have you got there?'

Vaguely surprised, I looked down at my tightly clenched fist. 'Nothing,' I said, a little too quickly. 'Just a coin.' I dropped it loose into my handbag, and heard it fall to the bottom with a reproachful clink. Frowning, I ran a hand through my hair. 'Listen, could I have a cigarette?'

'Sure.' He held the packet out, unquestioning, and struck the match for me. 'That must have been some conversation, back there. He looked like he could have done with a cigarette, too.'

I inhaled gratefully. 'Who did?'

'Who, she says.' Paul shook his head and looked away, smiling through a drifting haze of smoke. 'OK, since you don't want to talk about it . . .'

'There isn't anything to talk about,' I told him, stubbornly. 'We've fifteen years between us, Neil and I,

277

and he lives in a different country. And he's a musician, for heaven's sake.'

'What's wrong with musicians?'

'They're unreliable.' I reached to tap the ash from my cigarette, my expression firm. 'Besides which, he's blonde.'

Paul didn't even waste his breath trying to figure out what *that* fact had to do with anything. He simply looked at me with quiet sympathy, the way a doctor might look at a patient with a terminal disease. 'You're not making sense,' he pointed out.

'Yes, well.' I rubbed my forehead with a weary hand. 'I've not been sleeping, that's the problem. I'm not thinking clearly.'

'That's OK. It's the job of the Great Detective to think clearly,' he said with a wink. 'Trusty sidekicks are always a little muddle-headed, don't you know.'

'Right then.' I leaned back, my eyes half closed. 'What's on the Great Detective's mind this morning?'

'Afternoon,' he corrected me, with a glance at his watch. 'It's twelve-thirty, already. And if you must know, I've been thinking about numbers.'

'Numbers?'

'Twenty-two, in particular.' He smiled. 'There are twenty-two people with the first name Didier listed in the Chinon telephone directory.'

'How do you know that?'

'I stayed up last night, counting them. It's a pretty thin directory. So if the man who wrote to your cousin does live in Chinon, he's probably one of those twenty-two.'

'Twenty-one,' I corrected him. 'Didier Muret is out of it.'

'Is he?' Paul sent a smoke ring wafting through the pregnant air. 'I've been thinking about that, too. I asked Thierry what he knew about Martine's ex-husband, and it's kind of interesting, really.'

I leaned back, hands clasped around my bent knees. 'Oh yes?'

'Yeah. It seems apart from being a colossal drunk, Didier Muret was one of those guys who likes to flash his money around. You know – expensive clothes, expensive car, buying drinks for everybody.'

'So?'

'So where did he get the money from?' Paul asked. 'The lawyer that he used to work for fired him for stealing from the petty cash, and Martine cut him off completely, except for the house. So how could Didier Muret afford his lifestyle?'

I had to admit no easy answer came to mind. 'But I don't see how that connects to my cousin, at all.'

'It doesn't, really. It's just one of those things that I tend to wonder about.'

I smiled, remembering his belief that everything ought to make sense. 'Looking for the angle, are you?'

'Always.'

'What else did Thierry tell you?'

'Oh, lots of things. It's hard to shut Thierry up, once he gets going. He said the death was ruled an accident, but the police originally thought someone else was with Muret that evening, because of the number of wine glasses they found. Which probably explains,' he said, 'why they questioned poor old Victor Belliveau, and people like that.' He rubbed

279

the back of his neck, thoughtfully. 'Your cousin's not a violent person, is he?'

I raised my eyebrows. 'Harry?'

'Suppose he'd been drinking, or someone made him really angry . . .'

I finally caught his meaning, and rose bristling to my cousin's defence. 'Paul, you don't think for one minute that *Harry* killed Martine's ex-husband?'

He shrugged. 'Not really. I just think it's a hell of a coincidence . . .'

'It's ridiculous,' I argued. Harry would never hurt anyone; he hated fighting, and besides, what possible motive would there have been? Even if Didier Muret *had* somehow read that article, and written to Harry, and met with him . . . how could that lead to anything like murder? And even if it was an accident . . . I shook my head. 'Ridiculous,' I told Paul, resolutely. 'Harry's got a great respect for justice. He would never run away from something that he did.'

Paul looked at me, amusement in his eyes, and handed me another cigarette. 'OK, OK. I'm sorry I brought it up.' His smile punctured the balloon of my righteous indignation.

'Well, anyway,' I said, softening, 'the point is moot, isn't it? You said the death was ruled an accident.'

'Accident,' Paul replied, 'is just another word for chance.' But when I asked him what he meant by that he only shrugged, turning his gaze thoughtfully across the river. 'I don't know, exactly. Just a hunch I have. Tell me again about this theory of your cousin's. About the lost treasure of Isabelle of Angoulême.'

I told him, and he listened, quietly, attentively. My father looked like that, I thought, when he was doing crosswords. One could almost hear the wheels at work. 'So what,' I asked him, 'are you thinking?'

'Nothing important.' He lifted his cigarette. 'Like I said, it's just a hunch. Simon's paranoia rubbing off again, most likely. Gypsies, Nazis, treasures in the tunnels . . .' He smiled. 'This really is a case for Sherlock Holmes.'

'Well, don't get too carried away with your investigations,' I implored him. 'I'd hate for you to spoil your whole holiday on my account.'

'Don't worry so much,' was his advice. 'I'm hardly spoiling my holiday. Here.' He handed me a hunk of bread. 'Feed the ducks.'

When all the bread was gone, he stretched and checked his watch. 'I'd better go find my brother. He said something about having lunch with Christian – I don't know. Simon thinks that every German is an expert on the Nazi empire.' Paul smiled. 'He never gives up, my brother. He's bound and determined to find one of those treasures, before we leave.'

'You might never leave, then.'

'Suits me. Hey, are you going back to the hotel? Could you take this with you?' He shrugged his jacket off and held it up to me. 'It's getting kind of warm, with all this sun.'

'Sure. Paul . . .' I frowned. 'I know you like playing detective and all that, but you will be careful, won't you?'

'What could happen?' Paul stood up, pitching his spent cigarette away. The breeze caught it and sent it tumbling down the steps into the brackish water, where it landed with a soft and final hiss. For a brief instant, with the sun at his back, he looked like some young hero from the Old Testament, a David yearning for the battlefield. But then I blinked and there was only Paul, with his black hair flopped untidily across his forehead and his dark eyes deep and quiet as the river at our feet. 'I'll be careful,' he promised. 'Want to meet for drinks in the hotel bar? Say, three o'clock?'

'OK.' I climbed with him to the top of the sloping steps and leaned, half sitting, on the low stone wall, watching him walk back towards the market place. At the other side of the zebra crossing he turned back, grinning, and called out something that I didn't catch. He seemed to be pointing at the Rabelais statue beside me, but I couldn't see anything out of the ordinary. I nodded anyway, and waved. Satisfied, he turned away again and vanished in the crowd.

My cigarette had burned down nearly to the filter. It left an acrid bitter taste upon my tongue, and I bent to crush it out against the wall, holding the torn stub lightly in my fingers while I looked round for a litter bin. There was one not far from me, at the edge of the busy road. Gathering Paul's jacket in my free hand, I pulled myself away from the river wall with a small sigh, and wandered the few steps forward.

The jacket felt a good deal heavier than it ought to have been. It hung awkwardly to one side, and for a moment I thought he'd left his wallet in it, until one pocket gaped to reveal the dog-eared pages of a thickish paperback, with a cracked disfigured cover. I was smiling as I tossed my dead bit of cigarette into the bin.

The prickling at the back of my neck was my only warning. I barely turned in time to see the gypsy step from the shadow of the brooding statue and cross the boulevard, walking back towards the market square. He didn't look at me. I might have been a ghost, invisible. Paranoia, I thought, was a sign of creeping age; and yet I did feel more at ease when man and dog had disappeared, and the shifting sea of faces swirled and flowed to fill the wake behind them.

CHAPTER TWENTY-THREE

. . . the heralds to and fro,
With message and defiance, went and came;

Thierry set my second *kir* on the low table at my knees, propped one foot against the carpeted step up to my section, and picked up his story where he'd left off. '. . . and they cannot eat or bathe, or do anything for pleasure – not until the sun has set, tomorrow night. It is a most important holiday. Paul calls it Yom . . . Yom . . .'

'Yom Kippur?'

'Yes, that is it.' Thierry nodded. 'The Day of Atonement. Paul says it is a day for remembering the dead, and for confessing sins.'

'I see.' I took a sip of my drink. 'And this begins tonight, then, does it?'

'When the sun goes down, yes. Paul and Simon, they will have to eat like giants before then, if they are to fast all day tomorrow.' Thierry placed a sympathetic hand on his own flat stomach. 'I would not like to be a Jew, I think.'

'Didn't you ever fast for Lent?'

His dark eyes danced with mischief. 'My sins, they are so many, Mademoiselle – the fasting, it would do no good. Besides,' he added, 'the Jewish holiday is more than just not eating. Paul says it is forbidden to be angry, or to hold an argument, or to think bad thoughts about someone. It is not possible.' He dismissed the notion with a 'pouf'. 'Not if I must serve Madame Whitaker.'

One level up, the violin ran through a series of scales and then began its mournful song. Thierry frowned. 'He has not listened to me, what I said. He plays today the love song.'

Sure enough, the strains of the *Salut d'Amour* came drifting down the empty stairwell and into the bar. I tried to shut it out, leaning back in my chair. 'Where is Madame Whitaker today, anyway?' I asked Thierry. 'I haven't seen her at all. Does she have another headache?'

He shook his head. 'She has gone with my aunt and uncle, to see the church at Candes-St-Martin. It is a nice church, very old.'

'Did her husband go, as well?'

'I do not think so. But he is also out, somewhere.'

Hiding from his wife, most likely. Happy marriages, I thought, seemed something of a rarity these days. Especially in Chinon.

'Ah.' Thierry glanced upwards, approvingly, as the violin shifted tunes. 'This is the symphony by Beethoven, is it not?'

I listened, and nodded. 'Yes, the Eroica.'

'Comment?'

286

I repeated the name more clearly. 'Beethoven's Third Symphony. He wrote it for Napoleon.'

Thierry raised his eyebrows. 'So it is French, this symphony?'

'Well, in a way. But Napoleon went and had himself crowned Emperor before this piece was finished, and Beethoven wasn't at all pleased about that.' In fact he'd been so disillusioned that he'd changed the dedication – no longer for Napoleon, but simply 'to the memory of a great man'. Every age, I thought, had mourned the loss of heroes.

Thierry smiled. 'You know much about this music, Mademoiselle.'

'Not really. I just remember certain pieces, and the stories that go with them.'

'Me, I do not listen to the type of music Monsieur Grantham plays. I take him into Tours, to the discotheque, so he can hear real music, but . . .' The young bartender shrugged again, amiably. 'He says he likes better the violin.'

Silently, I sided with Neil. 'What time is it now, Thierry, do you know?'

He turned his wrist to look. 'It is just after fifteen hours.' He sighed. 'Two hours more before my work is finished for today.'

Work or no, I thought, the hotel bar wasn't the worst place one could spend an afternoon. The long polished windows stood open to the scented breeze and the glowing sunlight of an autumn afternoon fell warm upon my neck and shoulders. Outside, the market crowds had thinned and I could clearly see the fountain scattering its rain of diamond drops through which the Graces gazed, serene.

287

Thierry was looking out the window, too, and thinking. 'Yesterday, that was Monsieur Valcourt you lunched with, was it not? I did not know you knew him.' The trace of envy in his tone puzzled me, until he went on, 'He has the best car, the very best.'

I smiled, remembering that bright red Porsche that purred like a great cat and gleamed like any young man's dream. 'It is a nice car,' I agreed.

'Madame Muret, she has promised she will take me for a fast drive in this car one day. When Monsieur Valcourt is gone to Paris.'

'Has she really?'

'Yes. He lets her drive the car, when he is gone. She brought it here last week when she came once to see Christian, and she would have given me the ride then,' he confided, 'only I could not leave until my work was finished and by that time the police had telephoned.'

I frowned. 'The police?'

'Yes. To say they had found the body of her husband.' He sighed, shaking his head. 'It was most sad.'

Presumably he meant his thwarted efforts with the Porsche, and not the death of Didier Muret. I sympathised. 'I could ask Monsieur Valcourt, if you like. He might have time to take you for a—'

'No, please,' he broke in hastily. 'It is not so important. And besides, it would be more pleasant, I think, to drive with Madame Muret.'

Et tu, Brute, I thought drily. Were there any men around who *weren't* smitten by Martine? Smiling, I swung my gaze beyond the tumbling fountain. There was that blasted spotted dog again, I thought. Without its owner, this time. It snuffled round the edges of the phone box at the far side of the square. Now who, I wondered, would a gypsy be telephoning?

When the phone behind the bar burst shrilly into life, I think I jumped as high as Thierry did, then caught myself and smiled. Paul was right, I thought. Simon's paranoia was definitely spreading.

'A moment,' Thierry begged the caller, as a trio of customers came through the door from the street. He cupped his hand over the receiver and sent me an imploring look. 'Mademoiselle, I wonder . . . ?'

'Yes?'

'It is a call for Monsieur Grantham, but he is practising, and when he practises he always takes his telephone off the hook. I wonder, would you be so good . . . ?'

'You want me to fetch him for you?'

'Please.' He flashed the charming smile at me, the one the poor receptionist, Gabrielle, had such trouble resisting. I was a little more immune than Gabrielle to Thierry's charms, but his dilemma was very real. The new customers settled themselves at the bar, expecting service. I sighed, and rose half-heartedly to go and break up Neil's practise session.

A shiver struck me on the twisting staircase, but I shook it off again, blaming it on the cool breeze that drifted through the open door to the terrace. On the first floor landing the air felt distinctly chilly. Here the violin was sweeter, stronger, and even though I knocked two times it kept on playing. He couldn't hear me.

My third knock was so forceful that it moved the door itself – the handle hadn't latched properly – and I felt like an intruder as I watched the door swing inward on its hinges. It didn't open all the way, just far enough to show me one angled corner of the room. And Neil.

It was easy to see, then, why he hadn't heard me. I doubt if anyone could have reached him at that moment – he was locked in a world that no one else could touch or even visualise. He looked a different person when he played. His eyes were closed as if it somehow pained him, the fleeting and elusive beauty of the music that would not be held, but slipped past the listener almost before one's ear could register the notes. Neil's hands moved lightly over the familiar strings, sure as a lover's touch and twice as delicate. And the strings responded in a way no human lover could, singing pure and sweet and achingly true. It was disquieting to watch.

The violin faltered, and stopped, and my ears rang in the sudden silence. Neil opened his eyes. They were brilliant and beautiful, unfocused, the eyes of a dreamer surfacing. And then he looked towards the open door and saw me and he smiled, a broad exhausted smile that included me in its happiness. 'Bloody Beethoven,' he said. 'He does make one work for it.'

It was my own fault, I thought later. He'd as much as told me, by the fountain, that whatever happened between us would be up to me, that I would have to come to him. 'Whenever you're ready,' he had said. And now here I was, standing in the doorway of his room, not saying anything, trying desperately to remember what message I'd been sent to deliver, while Neil set down the violin and came towards me. Even when he took my face in his hands, I couldn't say a word. I only stared at him, and thought *He's going to kiss me* . . . and then, in a rush of panic, I remembered. 'You have a telephone call,' I blurted out.

My eyes followed Neil's mouth as it halted its descent. 'I beg your pardon?'

I cleared my throat, and repeated my message. 'Thierry sent me to tell you.'

'I see,' he said. But he didn't take his hands from my face, and he didn't move away. We might have gone on standing there indefinitely, staring at one another, if it hadn't been for Garland Whitaker.

It was difficult to say which sound came first – they seemed to happen all at once, like tracks laid down upon the one recording. I heard the front door slam, and Garland's voice half screaming and half sobbing words without apparent meaning; and then somewhere someone smashed a glass and through Neil's window came the first faint wail of sirens in the fountain square.

CHAPTER TWENTY-FOUR

And some were push'd with lances from the rock,

Neil moved with calm deliberate speed. He was downstairs in the entrance lobby before I'd even reached the stairs, and by the time I followed, he and Thierry had between them coaxed some sense from Garland Whitaker. Her eyes were still half wild in her pale bewildered face, and her voice held traces of a shrill hysteria, but her words came easily enough, between small sobbing breaths. I heard the words, of course, but I didn't for a moment believe them. It simply wasn't possible.

'No.' My voice, half strangled, made Neil pause and turn his head, but for all his swiftness he was not in time to stop me.

I didn't seem to touch the ground. I felt the heavy door swing to my desperate push, and heard the screech of tyres as I dashed across the narrow road. At the edge of the fountain square, where the château steps wound down between the lovely ancient buildings, the bright red ambulance stood waiting, blue light flashing, doors flung wide. The square was crowded, full of people, questioning and murmuring and elbowing each other for a better view. I pushed my way with purpose to the fountain, searching for one face among the many . . .

'What is it?' asked a man, ahead of me, and his companion answered, 'Someone's hurt.' Just hurt, I thought. I knew it. Somehow Garland Whitaker had got the story wrong.

But then my eyes found Simon.

They had moved him to one corner of the square, to one of the benches, where he sat huddled like a child with a blanket round his shoulders. Someone had given him a cup of coffee, and a kind-faced man in uniform knelt by him, talking, but Simon didn't respond. He looked so young, so unutterably young, his frozen face beyond emotion. I shivered in the chill spray of the fountain as the gathered crowd increased the tempo of its murmuring, excited.

The medics were bringing the body down.

'No, don't look.' Firm hands took hold of me and turned me round, away from the spectacle. Above my head Neil's voice spoke low and steady. '*Don't* look.'

Dry-eyed, I focused on the weave of his crisp white cotton shirt, and the tiny frayed bit at the point of his collar, and the way it moved with his breathing. He didn't speak again, didn't try to comfort me or stroke my hair, and yet the comfort flowed out from him anyway and kept me standing still.

Around us the voices swelled, loud and confused. The doors of the ambulance slammed shut, an engine roared and rumbled off, and then it was all over.

Neil let go of my arms, breaking the spell. My gaze shifted upwards from his collar, and our eyes locked. For a long moment we just stood like that, staring.

'He isn't dead,' I said, at last.

His voice was gentle. 'Emily, don't.'

'He isn't dead!' I felt the bitter sting of tears at that, and pushed him off, stumbling blindly up the square towards the château steps. It was a foolish thing to do, I knew, a foolish thing to say. I'd caught a glimpse of the stretcher as they brought it down the steps, and I'd seen as well as anyone the swaddled figure strapped to it. The sheet had been drawn up over the face, which plainly meant . . .

But I couldn't bring myself to even think the words.

The crowd of people on the steps had thinned, and those remaining moved obligingly aside to let me pass. It must have been my face that made them move aside with quiet words and pitying glances. My face, I thought, must look a bit like Simon's: cold and bloodless, empty-eyed. I pushed on, lungs burning, to the uppermost angle of the steps, where the high cliff wall rose stark and merciless in front of me, sharply outlined in the harsh sunlight. A bit of street lamp and a sign peered over the wall's top edge, and at its base the cobblestones spread rough and jagged in the shadows.

There was very little blood on those stones. I consoled myself with that, and with the knowledge that it would have happened quickly. For all it was a wicked drop, he would have fallen faster than his mind could register the fact. It helped a little, thinking that.

There were people talking round me and from both below and overhead the noise of traffic rose and fell, but oddly enough the only sound that truly penetrated was the closer whining of bees – not the portly languid insects so familiar to my garden, but a smaller, nastier-looking variety, as pale as the stone of the high wall behind them. They were everywhere, those bees, drifting amongst the white mist-like flowers of a grasping vine hanging from the weathered stone. The flowers were nasty as well, and the smell of them clawed at the back of my throat. It was an evil putrid scent, like roses left to rot on the rubbish heap.

I turned away from it. Neil was standing two steps down, his shoulders propped against the wall. He straightened as I came back down towards him, but he didn't say a word – he just fell into step beside me, understanding. With one last ragged backward glance, I turned and let him lead me down to the fountain square, away from the place where young Paul Lazarus had died.

The brandy burned. My second sip was much too large, but I coughed a little, forced it down, and raised the glass again. It was odd, I thought, how the mind behaved so differently in times of stress. Mine grasped at detail, any detail, anything that might distract it from the thoughts that brought it pain.

I counted three pink petals clinging to the lone geranium that drooped against the window of the hotel bar. Four cigarette ends jumbled in the ashtray in front of me: two left there by Madame Chamond, edged with rich red lipstick; two taken from the pack I'd found in Paul's coat pocket, stuffed beside *Ulysses*. I had smoked them to the filter, till the paper curled and burned. Another sip of brandy washed the acrid taste away.

The Chamonds had moved off a discreet distance to the cushioned bar stools, respectfully out of earshot, yet near enough to lend support. Madame Chamond had cried. I saw the smudge of shadow at the corner of one eye, and the specks of black mascara that bore witness to her tears. Monsieur Chamond, grim-faced, reached out to shield her hand with his. I looked away.

Across from me the young policeman with the tired eyes made one more scribble in his notebook. He was sitting in the place where Paul usually sat, and I hated him for it. But then, I thought with a sigh, I was tired myself and still in shock and anything but rational. And we'd gone over all these questions once, already.

The policeman glanced up, reading my mood. 'I know, Madame, this must be trying for you, but it's necessary that I ask these questions, you understand. The boy's brother can't tell us much. He was in the château when it happened. And you have spent much time with the . . . with Monsieur Lazarus.'

'Enough time to know he didn't kill himself.' The police, I knew, thought differently. It didn't take an expert to interpret all those questions. Was Paul a happy person? Had he been depressed of late? Did he have a stable family? On and on the questions probed and prodded, dozens of them, variations on a theme. 'He wouldn't kill himself,' I said, to make it absolutely clear. 'He was very happy with his life.'

'I see.'

'He loved his family very much.' I looked away again, and focused on the pink geranium. The sun was nearly gone now, and the light was weak. It would be early afternoon in Canada. Paul's mother would no doubt be busily at work somewhere, preparing for the holy day of Yom Kippur, not knowing that her son . . . I struck a match and the flame trembled as I touched it to my third cigarette. 'I can't believe,' I said, 'that no one saw what happened.'

'It is unfortunate.' He nodded in agreement. 'But this is market day, of course, and most people are down here, in the Centre Ville. They aren't up visiting the château.'

'But there must be residents, surely. People who have houses on that road.'

'They saw only your friend sitting alone on the wall. It's a low wall, where the road is – waist-height, but on the other side . . .' He shrugged, and let the image form itself. Not that I needed reminding. I'd seen the deadly drop, myself – I knew the likelihood of somebody surviving.

'If he did not jump, this friend of yours,' said the policeman, 'then he must have fallen. Perhaps he lost his balance, sitting there.'

'Or perhaps someone pushed him.'

'Perhaps. It is my job to look at all the possibilities.' His face looked almost kind at that moment, and I gathered my courage, drawing a deep breath so that my next words came out on a kind of endless rushing current.

'Then you might want to ask questions of another man, Monsieur. A gypsy, with a dog, who often hangs about the fountain square.'

'Oh, yes?' The pencil halted on the page, and he raised his eyebrows expectantly. 'And why would I wish to question him?'

I told him everything, beginning with the man who'd written to Harry – the man Paul had believed was Didier Muret – and ending with our final conversation by the river, just that morning, when the gypsy had followed Paul into the market-day crowd. The young policeman took notes politely. He even asked me, once or twice, to clarify a point. But it was plain from his expression, so carefully-schooled, so bland about the eyes, that he thought I was off my trolley.

'I see.' He flipped back a page in his notebook. 'You say your cousin left a message, Madame? And that you did not worry about him, at first, because it was his habit to change his mind, is that correct?'

'Yes.'

'Ah.' The single syllable spoke volumes. 'I can make enquiries, if you like, about your cousin. And I know this gypsy well, I'll talk to him, although I don't think he will tell me much. I know he looks rough, but he doesn't make much trouble.' He glanced at me. 'Perhaps, Madame, your cousin's absence . . .'

'Disappearance.'

'. . . has made you, how shall I say, sensitive to things that are not there?'

I swallowed that small rebuke, along with a mouthful of brandy, and felt the muscles of my jaw tighten. No point in wasting my breath, I told myself. It was obvious that my suspicions hadn't been taken very seriously. I watched in silence while he made a final entry in his notebook and flipped it closed.

'I must thank you, Madame, for your time and for your patience. You've been most helpful.' It was a lie, I knew, but he told it well. I hadn't helped at all, unless he counted holes poked in his suicide theory as evidence of my helpfulness. I smiled faintly at him and he nodded, rising to take his leave of the Chamonds with both respect and muted sympathy.

He hadn't been gone from the bar thirty seconds when Garland Whitaker swept in, looking rather like Lady Macbeth, with just the proper touch of *déshabillé* and an air of drama hanging over her. Behind her Jim moved silently, tall and stoic.

Garland took the chair the young policeman had been sitting in. Paul's chair. She leaned in closer, placing one hand on my sleeve in a gesture that was meant to be comforting. 'Oh, Emily, how *awful* for you,' she sympathised. 'I simply couldn't have done it, not this soon after . . . Well, you know. Did he ask very many questions?'

I looked sideways, at the wide blue eyes so greedy for a breath of scandal, and felt my patience slipping from me. 'No,' I said, 'he didn't.' Something of my contempt must have shown in my face, because she dropped her hand and shifted a little further away from me on the plump cushions.

Madame Chamond crossed over from the bar and took a seat, her warm low voice like balm upon my blistered nerves. 'You must be tired,' she said. 'And you have finished your brandy. Edouard . . .' Turning, she called her husband's attention to my empty glass, and in an instant he was at my side as well, bottle in hand. He had brought

300

glasses for his wife and the Whitakers as well, but when Garland urged him to take a seat he straightened up with a courteous shake of his head, and tightened his grip on the brandy bottle.

'No, I cannot stay. I must go back and see how Simon is, if you will please excuse me.'

He went out through the door behind the bar, into the passageway that led back past the office to the Chamonds' private quarters. 'Simon spends this night with us,' Madame Chamond explained. 'We could not leave him in that room alone. Tonight he sleeps in Thierry's room, and Thierry keeps him company.'

'Poor kid.' Jim Whitaker frowned. 'Shame it had to be him that found the body.'

'Another five minutes,' his wife said, 'and it would have been *me,* darling. Oh, what a horrible thought.' She shuddered with feeling, and I looked at her again.

'What were you doing on the steps?' I asked her. 'I thought you were in Candes-St-Martin.'

'I was. Monsieur Chamond wanted to stop in at the hardware store, you see, to do some shopping, so I said they should let me off at the château, and I'd walk back. It's not far, I said, not when you use the steps. And I thought Jim might be lonely.' She sent her husband a vaguely questing look. 'But of course, you weren't even here, were you darling?'

'No.'

I thought she hesitated, waiting for some explanation, but it was clear Jim Whitaker was not in a communicative mood. 'Well, anyway,' she went on, 'I started down the

301

steps and ran smack into Simon and . . . well, you know. It was a horrible shock, let me tell you.'

For a brief moment I thought I caught the faintest glimmer of distaste in Madame Chamond's normally immaculate expression. 'It is a shock for all of us.'

'It just doesn't seem real, does it?' Garland went on, unable to leave the wound unprobed. 'I mean, one minute you're talking to someone, and the next . . .' Her eyes moved to the low round table at her side, and her train of thought was interrupted. 'Isn't that Paul's book?' She reached to grasp *Ulysses*. I'd had to pull it from the pocket of Paul's jacket to get at the cigarettes.

Garland didn't ask how the book had come to be there. She simply turned it over, with a sigh. 'I guess he'll never finish this, now. Not that it really matters. Poor Paul, I can't believe—'

'For God's sake, Garland.' Jim Whitaker leaned back against the window wall, and rubbed his forehead with a weary hand. 'Just shut up.' He spoke the words quietly, as though he had exhausted all his energy. To my surprise, it worked. Garland actually stopped talking, but her jaw compressed with irritation and I knew she'd give him hell come morning.

I held out my hand. 'I'll take that, please.'

She handed the book over in silence with a small uncaring sniff and, rising, said good night to us and left.

Jim sighed, a heavy sigh. 'I'm sorry,' he said simply. 'Truly sorry.' And pushing himself to his feet, he followed his wife out into the hall.

With downcast eyes I trailed my fingers across the

lettering of the book's cover, blinking hard. *Not that it really matters,* Garland had said. But it did matter. It had mattered to Paul. I saw again his flashing smile, and heard his cheerful voice telling me: 'It's kind of become an obsession. I won't be able to rest until I've finished the damn thing.'

Madame Chamond leaned forward, concerned. 'You haven't touched your brandy. Would you prefer another drink?'

'No, that's all right.' I looked out the window again, at the darkening sky. The sun was gone. Yom Kippur had begun. A time for fasting, Paul had told Thierry – for remembering the dead. 'I really don't want anything. I think I'll just sit up for a while on my own.'

My hostess looked in silence from my face to the book, and back again, pressed my shoulder with a gentle hand and rose with the grace of a dancer, leaving me alone in the quiet bar. I heard her talking to someone in the entrance hall, and then I heard the lower timbre of Neil's voice, and then they both moved on and there was only silence.

My fingers found the turned-down corner on the page where Paul had stopped. The book wanted concentration, so I curled myself against the seat and did my best.

I sat there all night, reading.

At four o'clock the dustmen rumbled in the darkness round the square, but I paid them no heed. The first pale streaks of dawn had just begun to split the steel-grey sky when I finally closed the worn covers of the book and lowered it to my lap. It was done, now. Finished. I spoke the word again, out loud, though there was no one there to hear me: 'Finished.' No more labours for Ulysses, no more voyages to make. Paul, wherever he had gone to, could find rest.

I felt the warmth of tears upon my face, and my body ached with a hollow weariness that was almost more than I could bear, but I felt better, all the same.

Wiping the wetness from my cheeks, I turned my head. Outside the window, the three pink petals clung and trembled on the bowing geranium, the only spot of colour in that grey and dreary morning. The wind was rising from the distant river, chasing the wall of cloud before it. It caught a handful of dry twisted leaves and sent them scuttling across the deserted fountain square. It caught the lone geranium as well, and set the pale pink petals dancing.

And as I sat there watching, one by one they, too, were torn away, swirling past my window out of sight, until only the stripped and naked stem remained.

CHAPTER TWENTY-FIVE

That morning in the presence room I stood . . .

I had met death before, in different forms – I knew quite well the pattern of my grieving. First came shock, and then the tears, and then a bitter anger, followed by a softer grief that time would wear away. As I stood alone now on the steps to the château, looking down on the spot where Paul had died, I felt the anger come creeping up inside me. The Jews might call it a sin, being angry on their Day of Atonement, but I welcomed the emotion. It was something real, at least – something warm and hard and tangible, where before there had been nothing, only numbness.

Someone had washed the step, since yesterday. A crumpled mass of yellow leaves lay rotting in the crease between the stone steps and the wall, and except for a few spots of darker colour in their midst everything was as it had been before. It might have been imagined, what I'd seen here yesterday afternoon, and Paul himself might never have existed.

'It isn't fair,' I said. There was no one there to hear me. It was too early yet for anyone to be wandering about. Back at the hotel, the kitchen staff would be only just beginning now to set the breakfast tables and brew the first pot of morning coffee. I was thankful not to be there. It would have only made me angrier still, to watch the daily routine unfold with all its petty rituals, as if nothing had happened. It had to be that way, of course, I knew that – but understanding something didn't make it easier.

It was strange, I thought. On a different level, I'd faced the same grim tangle of emotions when my parents had divorced, five years ago. I'd grieved then, too. But where that loss had deadened me, killed dreams and hope together, losing Paul had sparked some part of me to burning life.

Don't get involved. It had become my motto, almost, that small phrase. Safer not to care too much, and better not to love at all than risk a disappointment. But with Paul, I thought, how could one help but care?

'Damn,' I whispered.

I don't know how long I stood there, looking down at the unspeaking stone. I had no way of telling time. The sky, I thought, grew faintly brighter, but the sun stayed tucked behind its veil of clouds and the wind on my face promised rain. After what seemed a minor lifetime I raised my eyes and, turning, climbed the final flight of steps up to the road.

The château bell began to strike the hour and I turned to watch it ringing, a small black swaying silhouette high in the narrow wedge-shaped tower that loomed at the bend of the road. Seven times the bell rang out; the last note hung and quivered on the morning air.

It wasn't difficult to find the place where Paul had been sitting. The wall here was indeed the perfect height for sitting on, its broad top capped with rougher stone. There was a sign here, slightly dented, warning people that the road ahead was not for common use. Paul must have sat beneath that sign for some time. Three spent cigarettes lay clustered at the base of the wall, their frayed ends showing that he'd stubbed them out against the stone, as was his habit. He had sat here, and smoked, and then . . .

I forced myself to take the short step forward, to the wall, and gazed down at the sheer relentless drop to the hard steps below. It was more difficult to look at than I'd thought. I took a hasty step back from the low wall, shoving my hands in my pockets in a gesture that was unconsciously defensive. I was wearing Paul's red jacket over yesterday's rumpled clothes, and although I'd left *Ulysses* in the bar, the left-hand pocket still held something firm and full of angles. My fingers brushed it, recognised it. Cigarettes. There couldn't be too many left, after my self-destructive binge last night. I drew them from my pocket now, not because I craved one but because a tiny thought was troubling me.

If Paul had left his cigarettes behind, forgotten for the moment in the pocket of his coat, then how had he smoked three here yesterday afternoon? He might, I thought, have simply bought another packet, but then he would have bought the same brand, surely? It was a popular French brand, sold at every corner store – a longish cigarette with a plain white paper filter and the brand name stamped in simple black. I'd never seen Paul smoke a different type.

And yet here before me was the evidence – the three spent ends on the pavement had dark spotted yellow filters. I picked one up to look, but there was no clear name or logo visible. Not only were the cigarettes a stranger's brand, but there were no match stubs anywhere. Paul had always used matches, and I thought it unlikely he'd have bought himself a lighter all of a sudden. Not impossible, of course, but decidedly unlikely.

Which meant, to me, that someone else had given Paul those cigarettes; that someone else had held the lighter for him. That no matter what the witnesses had said to the police, Paul hadn't been alone here yesterday, not all the time. He hadn't been alone.

Knowing this myself was one thing; telling it to the police was quite another. In my mind I could already hear the quiet tolerance, the kind but oh, so firm dismissal by the weary young inspector. If only someone else could speak for me, instead – someone with a bit more clout, and knowledge of the system. The Chamonds, perhaps, or maybe even . . .

I bit my lip. What was it that Armand Valcourt had said to me in Martine's gallery? 'The price one pays for influence is isolation.' Influence . . .

The bell below me in the town began to chime the hour, a tardy echo of the older peal from the château. With thoughtful eyes I raised my head again to look along the steeply rising road.

If François thought the hour an early one for visitors, he gave no indication of it. 'You may wait here,' he said, politely. 'He will not be long.'

I thanked him and he withdrew, leaving me alone in the quiet room. This was not the glittering sitting-room into which I'd been shown on my first visit to the *Clos des Cloches*. The windows here were thickly curtained, and the room itself was small. It appeared to be a study of sorts, or an office, with richly panelled walls and shelves for books. A writing desk stood angled in one corner, and on its surface, neatly dusted, a row of framed photographs stood waiting for inspection.

The photographs were all of Lucie, at different ages, solemn and smiling. There was no one else. I moved closer to examine them, brushing the glass of one with wondering fingertips. My mind drifted back, I don't know why, to the argument I'd overheard last Saturday, between Armand and Martine. 'What do you know of love?' she'd taunted him. Lord, I thought, how could she ask that, having seen these photographs?

Behind me the door to the study opened and closed again, quietly. I spun round, hands laced nervously behind my back, to face him.

He'd obviously been dragged from the course of his morning routine. His hair was damp from the shower, and he hadn't finished buttoning his shirt, but I fancied he looked more presentable than I did. He, at least, had slept. The memory of that sleep still lingered round his heavy-lidded eyes, and the way he looked at me was unconsciously intimate.

'I'm sorry,' I began, speaking French from instinct. 'I shouldn't have bothered you, this early.'

'It is no problem.' He fastened the last few shirt buttons.

'What did you want to talk to me about?'

'My friend is dead.' To my dismay, I felt the tears come burning up behind my eyes. I blinked them back, determined not to cry, but Armand saw them anyway. He stepped quickly away from the door, muttering a soft recrimination that was, I gathered, directed at himself.

'I didn't think,' he said. 'I'm sorry. That was the young boy yesterday, who fell, yes? I didn't realise—' He broke off, stiffly. 'It must be very difficult.'

I nodded dumbly, and took the chair he offered me. He didn't sit behind the desk, but pulled a second chair across the carpet, facing mine, and sat so that his knees were only inches from my own. His dark eyes gently searched my face. 'You have not slept.'

He had dropped the formal manner of address, and used the more familiar '*tu*' instead of '*vous*'. It was not a change that the French made lightly, signifying as it did a deepening of one's relationship. At any other time I might have noticed, and been flattered, but today it scarcely registered.

'No,' I said, 'I couldn't sleep. Too many thoughts.'

'I understand. Myself, I've worried many times about Lucie playing near that wall. I was afraid that such an accident might happen.'

'But it wasn't an accident, that's just it.' I took a breath and squared my shoulders. 'Someone pushed him.'

He stared, incredulous. 'What?'

'I . . . I'm not sure who did it, but I think I do know why, only the police wouldn't listen. They were very polite, and all that, but they wouldn't listen.' My voice was bitter, laced with more emotion than I'd heard in it for years. 'Somebody pushed Paul.'

He studied me. 'You saw this happen?'

'No.'

'Then how can you be sure?'

I sighed, and looked away. 'It's a long story.'

'I have time.' He smiled, faintly. 'Have you eaten, yet?'

'Yes,' I lied.

'Well, I have not. So I will find François, and while I eat my breakfast you will tell me this long story of yours. All right?'

It didn't take as long as I'd imagined, after all. I'd finished talking by the time he pushed his plate away. We had moved into the sitting-room, to the same dining table where we'd shared our first meal on Saturday. Across the table from me, Armand lit a cigarette in contemplative silence. He smoked a yellow-filtered brand, I noticed. But then, so did half the population of France.

'Your cousin is in danger, you think?'

'I don't know what to think,' I answered honestly. 'I only know that Paul was trying to help me find him. And now Paul's dead.'

'Like Didier.' He lowered his gaze to the tablecloth in brow-knit concentration. 'So this is why you asked so many questions about Didier, last time we met.'

'Yes.'

'You might have told me then, that you were worried for your cousin.'

'It's not the sort-of thing one drops on strangers, is it?' I replied. 'And anyway, you seemed so sure that Didier could not have known Harry.'

311

'I'm not perfect,' he said quietly. 'And I'd hardly call us strangers, you and I.' He lifted his eyes, then, and I met them squarely, aware that in the hard pale light of day I must look something less than human. 'You have told this to the police, you said?'

'Every word.'

'And they did not think it serious.'

'Yes, well,' I shrugged, 'that's why I've come to you. I thought, perhaps, if you could talk to them, a man of your standing . . .'

His mouth twisted. 'You overestimate my influence, I think.'

'Then you won't help?'

'I didn't say that.' He turned his head and spoke over his shoulder. 'François.'

The older man appeared around the doorway with such alacrity that I didn't wonder Armand's wife had thought François the classic flawless butler come to life. 'Yes, Monsieur?'

'Would you telephone to the police station, and tell them that I wish to speak to . . .' He paused to look at me. 'This, policeman that you met, was he young? A tall young man, dark-haired? Inspector Fortier, then, François. I'll wait until he's on the line.'

'Thank you,' I said, as François quietly left the room. 'You're very kind.'

'You're very young,' he told me, smiling. Leaning forward, he reached across the table and smoothed a wayward strand of hair behind my ear. 'It's nothing to do with kindness.'

312

A small cough sounded in the doorway behind us, and Armand lowered his hand from my face, turning. 'Inspector Fortier is not there,' said François, 'but there is a Chief Inspector Prieur who would be pleased to speak with you.'

'Prieur.' Armand searched his memory for the name. 'He is not local, surely?'

'No, Monsieur. He says he comes from Paris.'

'Oh, yes?' Armand pushed back his chair. 'Thank you, François, I will use the telephone in my study.'

He wasn't gone long. When he came back he didn't sit; he lit another cigarette and sent me a self-deprecating shrug. 'You did not need me, after all. Inspector Fortier seems to share your doubts. He has begun a full investigation and he's out now looking for your gypsy friend, to ask him questions.'

'You're joking.'

He assured me that he never joked. 'And I will look myself for this gypsy, so you may stop worrying so much and try to get some rest.' He glanced at his watch. 'I will drive you back to your hotel. But first, I must make one more phone call, a business call – it may take some minutes. Will you be all right if I leave you here with François?'

'I'll be quite all right.'

'Good.' He smiled, a slow and charming smile that warmed his shadowed eyes. 'I won't be long.'

In the silence that followed his departure, while the pressing weight I'd felt earlier slowly eased with the relief of burdens shared, François moved forward to clear away the remains of Armand's breakfast, his eyes concerned and watchful on my tired face. 'I'm very sorry, Mademoiselle.'

I knew what he meant. 'Thank you.'

'Death is always difficult, but the death of the young . . .' He sighed, and set the dishes on the sideboard. 'There is no justice in it.'

'No.'

He slanted a look down at my empty plate. 'You do not wish a cup of coffee, Mademoiselle?'

'No, thank you.'

'A piece of toast?'

I shook my head. There was no easy way to explain that I couldn't eat, that I was fasting for Paul, so I simply said: 'I'm just not very hungry.'

'I know, it's very difficult, but the dead, they are beyond our care. It is to life that we must turn our energy.' He fixed me with a philosophical eye. 'You must still sleep, and guard your health. And you must eat.'

It was his tone, and not his words, that made my mouth curve, and though I quickly dipped my head his eyes were keen enough to spot the smile, just the same.

'It's only that you sound so much like my mother,' I explained, with a shake of my head. 'She used to talk to me like that.'

'Ah. Well.' He looked faintly embarrassed. 'With you I'm always too familiar, I know. Please forgive me. Sometimes I look at you and see instead my sister – you are very like her. She also had this sadness that does not belong in one so young.' His eyes grew soft, remembering. 'Life was not always very kind to Isabelle.'

My smile died. A faint prescient shiver chased along my spine. 'Isabelle?'

314

François nodded. 'My sister. There were three of us, born in this house: myself, and Isabelle, and Jean-Pierre, my brother. I was the youngest, and the only one to carry on in service to the family Valcourt. My brother died in the final days of the last war, and my sister . . .' He shrugged, and looked away. 'She left Chinon not long after the liberation.'

It seemed too wild a thought, but having lived enough to know the world could be quite small at times, I asked the question anyway. 'Did your sister ever work at the Hotel de France, Monsieur?'

'Why, yes, but how did you . . . ?' His eyebrows lifted and then fell again with a sudden nod of comprehension. 'Of course, you're staying there. You will have heard the story about Isabelle and Hans. It is romantic, don't you think? I thought so myself, when I was a boy.'

I agreed that it was most romantic. Except for the ending, I added silently. 'Where did she go, your sister,' I asked him, 'when she left Chinon?'

'She went away.' A door closed, firmly, and I didn't venture further. Instead I asked him whether the diamonds had really existed. 'Oh yes,' he told me, 'they were real diamonds. My sister showed them to me.'

'And they've never been found?'

'Isabelle hid them well.' His mouth quirked slightly, with a hint of pride. 'Monsieur Muret, he always said that he would find the diamonds. It was for him an obsession, the thought of money. He dug everywhere little holes, down in the cellars and up on the hills, looking for that fistful of jewels, but of course he never found them.'

315

I sent François a curious look. 'Why, "of course"?' I asked him.

He smiled cryptically, and shrugged. 'Isabelle hid them well,' he said again. 'She was very clever, my sister.'

'And very beautiful, I'm told.'

'Yes.' He cleared the coffee pot away and set it with the dishes on the sideboard. 'I could find you a photograph, if you would like to see one. Perhaps you will see then why I am reminded of Isabelle, when I look at you.'

'I'd like that,' I said. 'I've a fondness for old photographs.'

'Then I shall find one for you,' he promised me. 'Perhaps tomorrow, when I have time to sort through my albums.'

'I believe,' I told him, slowly, 'that I've already seen your sister, in a way.'

He arched an eyebrow. 'Yes?'

'Yes. She haunts the hotel corridors.'

His eyes forgave my superstition. 'That is a legend, Mademoiselle, nothing more. And it is quite impossible. There are no ghosts.'

I wasn't so sure. I saw again that gentle shadow drifting past my bed, its soft voice urging me to 'Follow . . .' Follow what?

'Unless,' said François, reconsidering, 'you count the living. Then I would have to say that you were right.' His lined face softened as he looked at me. 'The Hotel de France this week is filled with ghosts.'

CHAPTER TWENTY-SIX

. . . notice of a change in the dark world
Was lispt about the acacias,

The hotel's entrance lobby seemed dim and deserted for the time of day. Most mornings, cleaners bustled round the bar and breakfast room, the hoover doing battle with both typewriter and telephone to see which of the three could outperform the others. But this morning there was silence. Thierry, slouched behind the reception desk, was the only sign of life.

His eyes were strained and rimmed with red, and when he greeted me his voice sounded rough, as though his throat were hurting him. I wanted to say some word of comfort, but my own nerves were still raw and vulnerable and I was much too tired for tears. Besides, I thought, we each of us knew how the other felt. There was no need to say the words. 'You're on your own again, are you?' I asked him. 'Where have your aunt and uncle gone?'

'They take Simon up to Paris, to meet his parents at the

airport. They will be back tonight, I think.' He paused a moment. 'The police came here at breakfast. They have taken everything of Paul's, everything but this.' He reached beneath the counter and lifted the forgotten item up, to show me. It was Paul's copy of *Ulysses*. 'I found this in the bar. My aunt said that you finished reading it. You finished it for Paul.'

My own throat felt rather painful, just then. I coughed to clear it. 'Yes.'

'I wondered, maybe . . . do you want to keep it? Because, if you do not, then I would like . . .' He broke off, frowning, and tried again. 'I thought that I might like to read this book. To learn the English better.'

I didn't bother telling him that Joyce's tangled prose was not the best source for a student of the language. It wouldn't have mattered anyway, not to Thierry. I knew what he was struggling to say. 'You keep it, Thierry,' I said gently. 'I think Paul would have liked that.'

'Thank you.' He tucked the book away again, out of sight behind the overhanging counter. He didn't meet my eyes.

'Where are the others?' I asked him.

'I don't know.' He shrugged, uncaring. 'Out.'

Thank heaven for that, I thought. Aloud I said: 'I'll just go on upstairs, then. If anyone asks, tell them I'm sleeping, will you?'

'Yes, of course.' He pulled himself back with an effort, and showed me a smile that held a hint of his old cockiness. 'Don't worry,' he assured me, 'I will see that you are not disturbed.'

* * *

I did sleep, as it happened – a restless sleep of troubled dreams that ended as the sun was striking full upon my window. My first thought was that the château bell had woken me, because even as I turned my face from the light I heard the deeper echo of the sister chime from City Hall.

It didn't penetrate too fully. The memory of sleep lingered like a drug, tangling my thoughts and weighting me to the wide bed. I was still lying there, listening to the fourth and final chime fade ringing through the rooftops, when I heard somebody moving in the room next door. A faint thump, followed by the unmistakeable crash of a curtain rod falling from its hooks. I smiled faintly into the pillow, and thought: *The boys are back*. And then, in a painful rush that burned like blood returning to a frozen limb, I remembered.

I opened my eyes.

The noises in the next room had grown louder, now. I heard a scuffling footfall and a burst of boyish laughter, and the creaking of the window swinging inward on its ageing hinges. Stumbling to my feet, I tugged on jeans and a loose sweater and went out into the hall to investigate. I'd probably not have done it if I'd been awake; but I wasn't awake, not really, and this tiny part of me still hoped . . . still hoped that . . .

'Yes?' The door to the boys' room opened to my knock and a tall young woman, blonde and florid and full of life, peered politely out at me. 'Can I help you?' She spoke in English, but it wasn't her first language. Swedish, I decided, or perhaps Danish. Something Scandinavian.

I shook my head, my smile an unconvincing cover for

the stab of disappointment. 'No, I . . . I was looking for someone else. I'm sorry.'

That only made it worse. She looked at me with feminine suspicion. 'There is only my husband.'

I rushed to fix the blunder. 'Oh, no, I meant that I must have the wrong room. Sorry to have bothered you.'

I don't think I completely reassured her. The round blue eyes were rather glacial when she finally shut the door, and I felt a twinge of guilt. Her husband, poor chap, was no doubt going to be called upon to answer a question or two. Stupid, I chided myself. What had I been expecting? Some sort of miracle, that's what – Paul Lazarus . . . Lazarus, risen from death . . . only I was old enough to know that miracles didn't happen.

I suddenly felt very much alone.

Downstairs, the cool and shadowed bar was empty. On the radio, a folk-rock balladeer was strumming out a sad poetic tune, and the candles burned for no one on the low round tables. The tall glass doors stood open to the afternoon breeze. I walked on through and crossed into the fountain square, into the sunlight, where the bright white tables and red chairs were clustered, waiting, underneath the acacias.

I wanted to sit alone, but Garland wouldn't hear of it. She all but dragged me to the table she was sharing with her husband, and I was much too tired to argue with her. Apart from which, I rather liked Jim Whitaker. He smiled kindly at me as I took the chair beside him. 'Can we buy you a drink?' he asked.

'No, thank you. I'm quite fine.'

'Well, I could use another,' he confessed, raising his hand to catch the server's eye. To my surprise it wasn't Thierry who came over, but the flustered pretty Gabrielle.

'Such a bother,' Garland said, as Gabrielle went off to fetch Jim's *Pernod*, 'when Thierry isn't working. I mean, he's a pain sometimes, but at least he gets your order straight. I ask you, does this look like a Manhattan?'

I confessed I'd never seen one. 'Where is Thierry?' I asked.

She took a look around, leaned forward and stage-whispered the answer: '*Police*. They came to get him after lunch, to ask him questions. About Paul. Do you know,' she leaned in closer, 'they've started an investigation. That's what Martine said. They don't think that it *was* an accident, Paul falling off that wall.'

'Garland . . .' Jim warned.

'What? It's common knowledge, dear, she's bound to hear about it. Nazis,' she said, turning back to me.

'I beg your pardon?'

'That's who did it, just you watch. They've come back for the diamonds, the way they did in Germany, where Jim and I used to live. Don't you remember? I told you all about—' She paused, distracted by a scene just past my shoulder at the entrance to the rue Voltaire. 'Well, well, *well*, isn't this interesting? Look who's here.'

Jim and I turned to look, as we were meant to. In front of the phone box, two police cars had drawn up to park against the curb. The drivers got out first, young officers in uniform who both deferred respectfully to an older plain-clothed colleague whose calm unhurried movements marked him as a man of high authority.

'His name's Prieur,' said Garland, when I asked. 'I think he's a Chief Superintendent, or something – someone important, anyway. From Paris. He came to the hotel this morning, during breakfast, to ask us all some questions about Paul. *Very* nice man,' was her considered opinion. 'Real class, if you know what I mean. And he *smiles* at you when he's talking, not like those other policemen. I gather,' she added, leaning towards me, 'that the local boys aren't too happy to have him sticking his nose into their investigation.'

I glanced again at the two young officers. They didn't look disgruntled, but appearances meant nothing. One of them was walking back towards the second patrol car. 'But surely,' I said, frowning, 'if they called the poor man down from Paris, they'd be pleased to have him here.'

'Well, that's just it, darling. They didn't call him down. He was already here, at his country house . . . where did he say it was, Jim, do you remember? Oh well, anyway, it's near Chinon. And he heard about Paul's accident, and thought he'd see if he could be of any help. It's because of him,' she told me, 'that they started the investigation. Or at least, that's what I hear.'

I didn't think to question where she'd heard it. Women like Garland Whitaker always seemed able to tap into the local grapevine with shocking efficiency, unhindered by barriers of language and culture. She'd been kept well occupied, this morning. 'This Prieur man,' she went on, having fortified herself with a sip of her unsatisfactory Manhattan, 'was the fellow who came to drag away poor Thierry, for questioning.'

Her husband smiled. 'Come on now, honey, I'd hardly call that dragging. The man was pretty polite about it, from what I could see.'

'Well,' Garland sniffed, 'Thierry didn't want to go, you could tell. And anyhow, my *point* was that since Mr Prieur was the one who came for Thierry, I'd have thought that he'd be busy right now asking Thierry questions, but it looks as though he's found some other person now . . . look, just who is *that,* I wonder?'

She meant the middle-aged man climbing from the rear of the second patrol car, straightening his back with a motion that spoke of weariness and apprehension. I could have told her, from that distance, who the man was. I could have said: 'That's Victor Belliveau. He's a poet, quite a famous poet, and he lives just up the river.' It might have been my own distaste for gossip that kept me silent, or the fact that it satisfied me knowing and not telling her, denying her that bit of information. Whatever the reason, I said nothing.

'He must be *somebody.*' Garland lifted her chin like a hound sniffing the quarry's elusive scent. 'A suspect, maybe, do you think? Really, it's just so exciting, to be in the middle of a murder case.'

'If it was murder.' Her husband took the rational point of view. 'In which case, we're probably all under suspicion. Even you.'

She looked vaguely surprised at the thought. 'Me? Oh, I don't think so, darling.' The four men had moved off now, out of sight, along the rue Voltaire. Deprived of her entertainment, Garland sighed and turned round again in her chair, facing me across the table. She was drawing breath to speak when voices raised in argument came filtering down through the feathery branches of the acacias, from an open hotel window. The voices spoke neither English nor French, and so I didn't understand a word of what they said, but the passionate delivery promised some fresh scandal, and Garland tipped her head appreciatively. 'That sounds like the young couple that just arrived. The ones that Gabrielle put into the boys' room – and Thierry isn't going to like *that,* I can tell you, there'll be feathers flying when he finds out what she's done. But like I said to Jim, it's just a room, and you can't keep shrines when you're supposed to be making a profit.' She paused, and listened to a few more lines of unintelligible arguing, and clucked her tongue. 'Such a shame, they were a cute couple. Swedes, I think she said. On honeymoon. I wonder what she's mad about.'

I rather suspected she was giving the poor chap the devil on my account, demanding to know why some other woman had come knocking at the door, but I kept my suspicions to myself. Fortunately, Garland Whitaker wasn't seeking my opinion.

'Maybe it's the room that's unlucky,' she mused. 'Maybe Thierry was right after all, about that French girl killing herself in that room at the end of the war. You know, we only have Monsieur Chamond's word for it that there isn't a ghost. I think . . .' A glimpse of movement through the windows of the hotel bar interrupted her train of thought. I twisted round and saw, as Garland did, the tall proud figure of the Swedish woman, seating herself at the deserted bar with an indignant flip of her long pale hair. Garland's eyes grew predatory. 'Will you excuse me for a minute? I think I need to freshen up my drink.'

She bustled off, clutching her empty glass with purpose. Across the table, Jim Whitaker's gaze held kind apology. 'She can't help it,' he said. 'It fascinates her, other people's lives.'

I summoned up a smile for him. They were very different, Jim and Garland. I'd rarely met a couple so ill-matched. The stray thought made me look again towards the open window of the room beside my own, where the honeymooning husband was presumably now sitting by himself.

'She's wrong about the room, you know,' I said, remembering what François had told me earlier about his luckless sister. 'Isabelle didn't kill herself there. In fact, I don't believe she killed herself at all.'

'I know.' He lifted his drink, slowly. 'She died of cancer in Savannah, Georgia, twenty years ago.' Above the glass, his eyes swung calmly round to lock with mine. 'She was my mother.'

CHAPTER TWENTY-SEVEN

See that there be no traitors in your camp:

'It made a nice enough story,' said Jim Whitaker, 'in the bar, the other night. And it was accurate, for the most part – all except the ending. Hans may have died at the end of the war, but Isabelle . . .' He shook his head. 'She wanted to, she thought about it, but she couldn't bring herself to offend God any more than she had already. So she did the next best thing. She married my father.'

Above our heads the sunlight filtered through a cool and trembling canopy of green and set the shadows swaying, and the fountain sprayed the pavement beside us. The chattering confusion of the patrons at the other tables blended into one soft muted background, like an artist's wash upon a coloured canvas. And Jim Whitaker, who'd always seemed to me so bland, so indistinct, now stood out clearly in relief.

'He met her just after the liberation,' he went on, still in that calm and quiet voice. 'Here in Chinon. He felt sorry for her, I think. The French didn't have much sympathy for collaborators of any kind, and everyone knew that my mother had been fooling around with a German officer. She didn't have an easy time of it. My father offered her an out. He married her in private, took her home to the States, and that was that.'

The dappled sunlight danced across my face, and I shaded my eyes as I looked at him. 'So the story has a happy ending, then.'

'In some ways, yes. She lived a good life – three children, a nice home, a husband who took care of her. But I'm not sure that I'd ever have called my mother happy.' He slung one leg over the other and leaned back in his chair, considering. 'I don't know – is happiness a thing we choose, I wonder? Or is it something handed out to some, and not to others?'

'A bit of both, I should think.'

'My mother would have said that it was God's will she and Hans were separated. But I'm not so sure.' His gaze swung gently to the open door of the hotel bar, through which he could plainly see his wife's sharp silhouette bent close in conversation with the Swedish bride. 'I think we all make choices in our lives that set us down the road to happiness or disappointment. It's just that we can't always see where the road is leading us until we're halfway there.' There was a hint of regret in his calm voice; regret, too, in the way he dragged his eyes around to look at me. 'My mother chose her road.'

Somebody laughed beside us and the breeze blew past

a fleeting whiff of roses. I breathed it in and sighed a little sigh. 'She must have missed it terribly, this place.'

'I guess.' His shrug was very French. 'She never talked about it, not to me. I didn't know a thing about my mother's past until she died. The day of the funeral my Dad got drunk, and the whole damn story came pouring out of him.' He narrowed his eyes in remembrance. 'Since then, I've always wanted to come here, to see the place where it all happened. I should have done it years ago. I was stationed at a base in Germany back then – it would have been so easy just to hop on a train, but . . .' His smile also held regret. 'I just never got around to it, somehow. I kept on saying next year, next year . . . and then last spring Garland said that she was bored with going to the Mediterranean, she wanted to vacation someplace else, so I said what about Chinon.' Again his gaze searched out the animated figure of his wife. 'She doesn't know,' he added. 'Garland, I mean. I've never told her about my mother.'

I stared at him. 'But . . . I mean, you've just told *me*.'

'Yes. It doesn't make much sense, I know, but it's different somehow, telling you. There were times, and I hope you won't take this wrong, but there have been times this past week when you've made me think of her. Of my mother. I don't know what it is, exactly, but there's a resemblance.'

I smiled. 'You're the second person who's told me that today.'

'Oh, really? Who was the first?'

'This man I know, up at the vineyard . . . Heavens,' I broke off suddenly, as the realization struck me, 'he'd be your uncle, I suppose. Your mother's younger brother, a rather nice old man named—'

'François. Uncle François, yes.' He nodded. 'Yes, he used to write us letters, when I was a kid. And then Mom died and the letters stopped coming. I thought he must be dead himself.' He shrugged, self-consciously. 'I'm still working up my courage to go and see him. There are questions I want to ask, about my mother but . . .' He looked down. 'Fifty years is a long time.'

'Well, you needn't worry about François. He's sharp as a tack and he speaks very fondly of your mother. I'm sure he'd love to meet you. In fact,' I said, 'I think he knows already that you're here.' And I told him what François had told me earlier that day, about the Hotel de France being full of ghosts.

The silver eyebrows rose a fraction. 'And you think that he meant me?'

'You're the only person here with ties to Hans and Isabelle.'

'Am I?' He frowned and squinted briefly upwards at the canopy of green. 'I wonder,' he mused, so quietly I almost didn't catch it. 'Yes, I wonder . . .'

A flash of motion from the hotel bar distracted him. Garland had moved to the open doorway and was beckoning her husband to come inside and join her at the bar. He caught her eye and nodded slightly, exhaling on a tight-lipped sigh. 'Excuse me please,' he told me, 'I'm being summoned. Listen, I'd hate for her to know . . .'

'I won't say anything, I promise.'

'It isn't just the privacy, you know. It's self-preservation.

Especially after that storytelling session Sunday night.' A smile faintly creased the corners of his mouth. 'If Garland ever knew that the Isabelle we talked about was my mother, I'd never have a moment's peace.'

'Why not?'

'The diamonds, honey.' His tone was dry. 'Garland has a thing for diamonds. She'd be like a dog with a bone – she'd never let it go. She'd have me out there digging little holes in the hills, hoping to find the damn things.'

Like Simon, I thought. 'Your mother never told anyone . . . I mean, she never mentioned—'

'Where they were?' He smiled sadly and pushed himself to his feet. 'She told my father they were stained with blood, they'd only bring unhappiness to anyone who touched them. She didn't want them to be found.'

I watched him walk across to the hotel, his shoulders very straight as though he'd braced himself to carry something heavy. It must be difficult, I decided, for a man like that to spend his life with Garland. He seemed to have no peace at all – she hadn't even left him alone long enough to finish his drink. His glass was still half full of *Pernod*. I looked at it, my forehead creasing in a slight frown. I'd seen a glass like that just recently, I thought. Now where . . . ?

And then I remembered. I remembered coming down from the *Clos des Cloches* on Sunday afternoon with Paul and Simon, and finding Martine Muret sitting all alone beside the fountain. There had been a glass of *Pernod* on her table, then – half finished, just like this one. And Garland . . . my eyes moved thoughtfully to the shadowed figures in the hotel bar . . . Garland had been in bed with one of her headaches, as she had been on Saturday night. The night Lucie Valcourt slipped away from Martine and her 'man friend'. 'He stays at this hotel,' Lucie had told me. And I'd assumed that it was Neil, or Christian . . . but I'd never thought of Jim.

The puzzle pieces slid and fitted, locked in place, and I felt the oddest sense of satisfaction, to think that Jim might find some happiness in spite of Garland. He was right, I thought, not to tell her the truth about his mother. Garland was the sort of woman who'd be dazzled by the thought of diamonds, the promise of riches. Like Didier Muret, who'd married for money.

I frowned again. There was something else that Jim had said, that also made me think of Didier Muret. Now what on earth . . . ? *Digging little holes in the hills*, that was it. François had said that, too, this morning – he'd said Didier had dug holes everywhere, looking for the diamonds. An obsession, François had called it. Only Didier hadn't found them.

Or had he?

A sudden, creeping thought took hold and turned within my troubled mind. Everything makes sense if you look at it from the right angle, that's what Paul had promised me. And Paul, last time I'd seen him, had been searching for the right angle from which to view Didier Muret. Unpleasant out-of-work Didier Muret, who still had money left to throw around. That's what had bothered Paul. But then if Didier *had* found the diamonds, that might explain a great deal. Where he got his money from, for one thing, and maybe . . . maybe even why he'd died, last Wednesday.

I heard again Garland Whitaker's decided voice, saying 'Nazis'. I'd thought her foolish at the time, but now it seemed less fanciful. Not Nazis, necessarily, but someone who had known the tale of Hans and Isabelle, someone who had come to find the diamonds, and found that Didier Muret had been there already. People did murders for less, I knew, and greed was a powerful force.

Paul, I recalled, had thought that Harry might have been with Didier last Wednesday night – the night Didier died. And if it had not been an accident, if someone had pushed the unpleasant Monsieur Muret down the stairs . . . what then? Had Harry seen the culprit? Was he now himself in danger, and had he dropped his King John coin on purpose, as a warning to me? And Paul . . . had Paul perhaps guessed all this yesterday, and pressed too close upon the murderer? I pressed my fingers to my forehead, trying to make sense of things.

A crowd of young men came jostling around the corner and funnelled into the hotel bar, their voices raised in energetic conversation. They were mostly blonde, and their words weren't French. Germans, I identified them. It all kept coming back to Germans, and the Hotel de France.

The Hotel de France was full of ghosts, this week, so François said. Living ghosts. Like Isabelle's son, who might have had his own good reasons for wanting Didier Muret out of the way; who might have come back for the diamonds; who had been out somewhere, alone, when Paul was killed. But I couldn't cast Jim Whitaker as a murderer, somehow, and I doubted he'd have told me who his mother was if he'd wanted to avoid suspicion.

My thoughts turned over, slowly. If Isabelle was here in spirit, through her son, then what of Hans? Was he here, too? In Christian, maybe – of an age to be his grandson, to have heard about the diamonds. It couldn't be Neil, I thought, with a feeling of relief I preferred not to analyze. Neil's father worked for British Rail, he'd said. And anyway, he'd been in his room when Paul was killed. I'd seen him there, I'd heard him playing the Beethoven. It couldn't have been Neil.

The thought was still resonating in my head like the final quavering note of a sonata, when Neil himself came out of the hotel – not through the main door, but the small, half-hidden door beside the garage. The same door I had used last Saturday, when I'd fallen asleep on the terrace and found myself locked out. It made a rather handy escape route, actually – if I hadn't been looking straight at that corner, I might not have noticed Neil at all.

As it was, he didn't notice me. Head down, his movements purposeful, he passed by swiftly on the far side of the fountain and vanished up the rue Voltaire, beyond my line of vision. I was unprepared for the sudden stab of longing that twisted in my chest at the sight of his long tall figure, pale hair ruffled by the wind, his hands tucked deep within the pockets of the weathered leather jacket. Oh, *hell,* I thought. I hadn't asked for that, it simply wasn't fair, it wasn't . . . I broke off suddenly, in mid-thought, as the significance of what I had just seen finally penetrated.

Turning, I stared hard at the hotel, at the wall by the garage, at the little door. I nearly hadn't seen him, I reminded myself. He had left the hotel, and I nearly hadn't seen him. Which meant that someone from the hotel could have done the same thing yesterday . . . could have climbed the steps, to where Paul sat . . .

I rose and crossed the square. The door creaked inwards at my touch, then gently closed behind me as I started up the winding stone stairs. I had just set foot upon the broad deserted terrace when the violin rose suddenly in plaintive song, from inside the hotel. And then, as unexpectedly as it had started, the tune was silenced. A prickling shiver struck between my shoulders. There were no such things as ghosts, I reminded myself . . . and yet, that couldn't be Neil playing, because I'd just seen Neil leaving the hotel.

I heard a snapping sound, a whir, and then the eerie performance was repeated – two bars of music, and a queer unfinished ending.

Gathering my courage, I moved to look around the corner of the open terrace door. Neil's door was also open, but he wasn't in his room. Instead it was Thierry who looked up as I came to stand in the doorway.

'Hi,' he greeted me, looking none the worse for wear from his afternoon of being questioned by the police. 'You are looking for Monsieur Neil?'

'I thought I heard the violin.'

'That was just me.' He held up a cassette tape, to show me. 'I am looking for the tape I gave for Monsieur Neil to listen to. My friend Alain, he wants to make the copy.' There was a small stack of home-recorded tapes piled neatly on the dressing table beside the sprawling hi-fi, and Thierry shuffled through them with a frown. 'I thought that I had found it, but no . . . maybe this one . . .' Choosing another from the stack, he slotted it into the machine and pushed the play button. A full orchestra sounded the opening strains of a Strauss waltz at an alarming volume, and Thierry quickly punched 'stop', his frown deepening.

I took a small step forward, staring at the hi-fi. 'I thought this was broken.'

'What?' He glanced up. 'No, I fix it for him two days ago. Ah!' His hand closed round the errant tape with satisfaction. '*This* one, this is mine.' A brief sound check confirmed the fact, and he returned the first recording to its rightful place in the tape player. '*Bien*, I put everything back as it was, and Monsieur Neil will not be missing my tape, I think.'

'Thierry,' I asked him, slowly, 'could you play that one again, just for a moment?'

'Sure.' He touched the button, and the stirring strains of Beethoven's *Eroica* swept past me into the hallway. Not the full, orchestral version, but a solo violin – the part Neil practised nearly every afternoon. The part he'd told me he knew like the back of his hand.

'He likes to play it loud, yes?' Thierry raised his voice above the piercing sound, and I nodded. Only that was somehow wrong, I thought. Neil didn't like to play it loud. *Can't set the volume higher than three, or it makes your ears bleed,* he'd complained. Thierry went on talking, proudly. 'It gives a good sound, this stereo. It sounds exactly like Monsieur Neil playing, does it not?'

It did, at that – exactly like Neil. I hugged myself, trying to ward off the cold cloud of suspicion, refusing to admit the possibility. 'All right,' I said to Thierry. 'That's enough.'

336

Flashing me the irrepressible grin, he switched the recording off. He looked round suddenly, remembering something. 'Oh, there is a message for you, downstairs.'

'A message?'

'Yes, an envelope. The man who brought it, he came while you were sleeping, and he said I should not wake you up. He said it was not urgent.'

'Who was it, do you know?' I asked, cautiously.

Thierry shrugged. 'The valet from the *Clos des Cloches*. I do not know his name.'

François? Hugging myself tighter, I followed Thierry downstairs. I could hear Garland, still sitting in the bar, her high-pitched laughter grating like a nail drawn down a blackboard. But her laughter was the only sound that rose above the din of German voices – all those young men, I thought, that I'd seen from outside. Thierry rolled his eyes at the noise. 'There is a . . . how do you say it? A congress this week, here in Chinon. These men do not like the bar at their hotel, so they come here instead. Poor Gabrielle, she should have Neil here, yes? To take the orders for her. Neil speaks good German,' Thierry told me. 'Christian says so. But me, I do not like to learn that language. It is not pretty.'

Not pretty, no, but powerful. I started feeling cold again and closed my eyes a moment, letting the jangle of voices mixed with laughter swell around and over me. These walls, I thought, had heard those sounds before: the voices of the German officers who'd lived here in the war. Like living ghosts, the German tourists went on talking, laughing . . .

'Ah,' said Thierry, jolting me back to the present. 'Here is your message.'

It was in truth from François. Not so much a message as a bit of handwriting wrapped round a faded photograph. *I thought that this might interest you,* the writing read, in French. *You see how you resemble her.*

There were two people in the photograph, a man and a young woman. The woman was laughing, looking off to one side as though the photographer hadn't been able to hold her attention long. The picture was black and white, a little scuffed and taken on an angle, but the image was very clear. I had to admit that I did look a bit like Isabelle. We weren't by any stretch of the imagination twins, but there was something similar about our eyes, the way we held our heads, the line of our noses.

But it wasn't Isabelle's face that made me stare. It was the face of the man beside her.

'My God,' I said.

It might have been a portrait taken yesterday. He was gazing straight into the camera lens, his dark eyes calm and composed, and although in the faded photograph his close-cropped hair looked white, I knew it wasn't. It was blonde. Just as I knew those dark, dark eyes were blue.

With shaking hands, I turned the picture over and read the pencilled line of writing on the back: *Hans and Isabelle, June, 1944.*

I had forgotten Thierry. He looked across the desk at me, vaguely puzzled. 'Mademoiselle?'

'Thierry,' I said slowly, 'where is Monsieur Grantham, do you know?'

'I do not know. He went, I think, to the police station to talk to Monsieur Belliveau. The poet – you remember?

When I was leaving from the police, they had just brought Monsieur Belliveau for questioning. Not about Paul, you understand. It was about some Englishman who had gone missing. And Monsieur Neil, he tries to help because they were friends, once.'

Of course they were friends. Neil and Victor Belliveau and Christian Rand: they'd all been part of Brigitte Valcourt's grand artistic parties at the *Clos des Cloches*. And Belliveau now shared his land with gypsies, so no doubt Neil had met the gypsy with the dog – the one who followed me. 'My God,' I said, again. Blinking back the foolish senseless tears of shock, I stared down at the damning photograph. Neil's own eyes smiled up at me, from the face of another man, his image nearly creased beneath the pressure of my fingers.

There must have been a reason why he hadn't mentioned his relationship to Hans. Just as there was a reason why he'd put that tape in Thierry's hi-fi, and set it at a volume that he couldn't stand. Because it *had* been Neil playing the Beethoven, it *had* . . . I'd seen him. At the end of his practise session, perhaps, but nonetheless . . . And it was a difficult piece to play – that's why he'd looked so exhausted when I'd interrupted him; why his hair had been so damp around his face; why he'd been breathing with such effort, as if he'd just been running . . . running . . .

'Ah,' said Thierry, glancing beyond my shoulder. 'You see? You speak of the wolf, and you see his tail. Here comes Monsieur Neil.'

I looked round wildly, and then, to Thierry's sheer astonishment, I dropped the photograph and ran. I ran like a rabbit pursued by a hawk, up the curving stairway to the first floor landing, and out onto the empty terrace through the door that still stood open, as it had been open on the afternoon that Paul had died. I ran across the terrace and down the narrow stairs and out of the little door into the crowded square. No one paid me any attention. They kept on sipping wine and drinking coffee at their tables round the fountain while I turned and bolted up the breakneck steps to the château.

I didn't stop running until I'd reached the top, and I only stopped then because I thought my lungs would burst if I went one step further. With my back to the low wall I slumped forward, hands on my knees, drawing in deep, sobbing, painful breaths of air.

The sudden scraping of a match in front of me brought my head up with a jerk, in time to see the gypsy's black eyes smiling at me as, against the cliff face opposite, he touched the brief flame to his yellow-filtered cigarette.

CHAPTER TWENTY-EIGHT

'Would rather we had never come! I dread
His wildness, and the chances of the dark.'

The match flared in the breeze and died abruptly.

'It is not safe, Mademoiselle,' he told me, in coarsened English, 'to stand so near the edge.'

I was gathering breath to cry blue murder when he moved. But he didn't move towards me. Instead he turned and started slowly up the road, towards the château, with the little mongrel dog trotting on ahead of him.

I hadn't expected that.

Stunned, I let my breath escape without a sound and felt my fear flip over into fascination. By the time he'd gone ten paces from me I had found my voice again. 'Wait!' I called after him. 'Please wait!'

He stopped walking, looked back. The dog stopped too, impatiently, close by his master's feet. I cleared my throat and asked the question.

'You know what happened to him, don't you? You were here.'

It was a rather ambiguous question, but he didn't pretend to misunderstand me. He met my eyes and nodded slowly. 'But I,' he said, 'was not the one who pushed him, Mademoiselle.'

At that he turned away again and walked on a few steps to where a wooden door hung scarred and derelict in the face of the yellow cliff. Through that door both dog and gypsy went without a backward glance. 'Wait!' I cried again, but it was too late. They were gone. A swiftly moving cloud passed over the sinking sun and in its shadow the breeze struck chill upon my face. 'Follow,' the wind whispered, swirling against the ancient stone. 'Follow . . .'

My brain resisted. *Don't be an idiot,* it told me. *Go right back down those stairs, my girl, and straight to the police* . . . But the unseen forces calling me, compelling me, did not respond to rationality. They pulled me numbly to that door and sent me through it like Alice on the trail of the White Rabbit. The door swung wide, and in a slanting triangle of light showed me a shallow flight of steps descending into darkness, a darkness that grew palpable as the door creaked gently to behind me.

Oh, hell, I thought. Why did it have to be a cellar? I held my breath, and swallowed down the cowardly swell of panic. Think of Paul, I told myself. The gypsy knows what happened . . .

There were only six steps in all. I counted them as I went down, with a hand braced on the cool stone wall to guide me – six steps and then a level stretch. The wall at my hand fell away, and I moved onward cautiously, only to be brought up short by another wall directly to the front.

Confused, I took a small step backwards, reaching out my hands to feel the inky blackness that surrounded me. Deprived of sight, my other senses rose to fill the void. The lingering smell of the gypsy's cigarette bit sharply at my nostrils, as did the dank sweet smell of stone that never sees the sun. Above the rasp of my own breathing my straining ears picked out the faintest clicking of the little dog's toenails on the stone floor, a sound that echoed and receded steadily along the passage to my right.

My groping hands touched chiselled stone above my head, as dry as parchment, brushed with dirt, a ceiling arched and rounded like the one I'd seen in Armand's cellars. And then I knew, with a strange instinctive certainty, where I was. Not a cellar, I corrected myself. This was no ordinary cliff house. I was in the tunnels.

My first thought was to turn back while the door was still just steps behind me. A labyrinth, that's what everyone I'd met had called the tunnels of Chinon. A labyrinth of twisting passageways that burrowed through the hills, unsafe, uncharted, half of them forgotten and collapsed through lack of use. *You'll get lost,* warned the nagging little voice inside my head. *You'll get lost down here and no one will ever find you.* The wave of panic swelled again and I hesitated, heart pounding.

Some distance off, the clicking footsteps of the dog paused in their progress, as if the beast had sensed my indecision. The gypsy whistled softly and that echoed, too, along the stone walls back to me. '*Allez!*' he ordered. Come along! He was speaking to the dog, I knew, but nonetheless the single command shifted me. I set my face in that direction, squared my shoulders, and plunged on into the darkness.

I didn't stumble, which surprised me, since the floor was anything but even. I slid one hand along the wall, to keep my bearings as best I could, and strained my ears to hear the gypsy's steps in front of me. He knew I was following. I fancied that he kept his pace deliberately slow to aid me, and just before I reached a turning in the tunnel where I might have lost my way, the gypsy started whistling in the darkness up ahead, drawing me onward as a beacon draws a ship.

For the most part, though, the tunnel ran straight on with neither bend nor break, and only the straining muscles of my legs to tell me when we sank deeper into the rock or rose again towards the surface.

We were rising now. Ahead of me the little dog's staccato rhythm altered to a sort of surging scrabble and the gypsy's boots fell heavily with measured sureness on the stone. My brain, attuned to darkness, told me: *Stairs, they're climbing stairs*. I slowed my pace expectantly. My searching hand trailed off the wall and into emptiness, and a sudden spear of light came hurtling down to trap me where I stood.

My ears had not deceived me. I had reached the bottom of a long and narrow flight of stairs, like cellar stairs, that stretched invitingly towards the world above. Someone was standing on the upper landing, poised against the open door – the gypsy, I presumed, although he was at best a silhouette. I couldn't see his face. He pushed the door wide and left it open, passing through into whatever lay beyond.

It had seemed a good idea at the time, I reminded myself as I climbed the stairs – now, I wasn't so sure. God knows

344

where I would find myself when I emerged, and what would happen to me there. My feet dragged just a little up the final few steps. And then I thought again of Paul, and why I'd followed in the first place, and squaring my shoulders I stepped across the threshold.

I was completely unprepared, coming from the cold and ancient darkness of the tunnels, to find myself standing in a one-roomed house with fridge and cook-stove and a cheery fire burning in the fireplace. I'd expected a cave, I think, some sort of wild dungeon of a place, with sullen eyes that peered at me from the corners. But this was no cave, and the only eyes I saw belonged to the gypsy, the dog, and the young man lying on a bed in the far corner. A pale and rumpled young man who smiled and sent the gypsy a look of congratulation.

'Oh, well done, Jean,' my cousin said. 'You found her.'

'Feel better now?'

I pressed my fingers to my forehead and nodded, refusing the gypsy's offer of a stout brandy and water. Harry settled back against his pillows with the air of a penitent. 'I didn't think . . .'

'You never do.'

'Well, how was I to know you'd go all weak-kneed on me? You're not the swooning type, my love.'

'Yes, well,' I pushed my hand through my hair with a tired sigh. No point in telling Harry I'd been fasting, either, I decided. He'd only try to feed me something. Instead I opted for a general explanation. 'It's been a devil of a week.'

'My fault, I expect.'

'Mostly.' I looked at him. 'Harry, what on earth—'

'I can explain,' he promised, cutting me off with an upraised hand. 'I suppose it's easiest to start at the beginning, when I arrived in Chinon.'

'Last Wednesday morning, was it?'

He gave me a curious look. 'Yes. I drove up overnight from Bordeaux, and got here shortly after breakfast. Rather proud of myself, I was, arriving two whole days before you.'

'But you didn't go to the hotel.'

'Well, no.' His tone implied it was an odd suggestion. 'It's not as if I was expected, after all. Our reservations didn't start till Friday. And one doesn't usually check into hotels at breakfast time, Emily love. Not when the tourist season's over with, and rooms are easy to come by. I figured there was no real hurry, so I parked the car and went to find this chap who'd written to me.'

'Didier Muret.'

'That's right. How did you . . . ?'

'Just go on. I presume you found him?'

'Yes. He wasn't at home, but his neighbour said I should look down by the river. Said he'd gone out with his niece to—'

'Feed the ducks,' I finished calmly.

'Yes.' He sent me a faintly irritated, sideways glance before continuing. 'Anyhow, I found him, but it didn't take me long to figure out he'd got it all wrong, somehow. He didn't read English, you see, he'd only seen the journal article in someone else's house, and read the title: *Isabelle's Lost Treasure* – I guess one could translate that easily enough – and so he'd written to me. Only it wasn't Isabelle

346

of Angoulême he was interested in, it was—'

'—another Isabelle. I know.'

Harry's eyes narrowed on my face. 'Perhaps you'd like to tell the story.'

The gypsy laughed, a soft laugh, at my shoulder, and hitched a second chair up to the bedside next to mine. 'I told you,' he said, 'she has been well occupied, this past week. She might have found you on her own, without my help.'

'No doubt.' My cousin's voice was dry.

'I only know,' I said in self-defence, 'that Didier Muret was after diamonds. A stash of diamonds, hidden at the end of the last war by a girl named Isabelle. I'd assumed he found what he was looking for, only . . .' I paused, frowning. 'Only if he had, he wouldn't have needed you.'

'Well, I can't have been much use to him, as it was,' Harry confessed. 'He kept asking me about the tunnels under the *Clos des Cloches,* and I hadn't a clue. He'd said, in his letter, that he had information to give to *me,* but it certainly felt the other way around. Still, I felt bad about it – not being able to help him, I mean. I even rang your father, from a public call box.'

'But he wasn't home.'

'How the devil do you know that?'

'He rang back, wanting to know why you called. I confess, I was rather curious myself.'

'Well, no great mystery. Your father's got a network strung through Europe that would put our Secret Service men to shame, you know. I thought he might know someone who knew someone who could be of some assistance to this Didier fellow.'

'But you left the hotel's number on Daddy's answering machine.'

'I thought I'd *be* in the hotel by lunchtime, didn't I?' he told me, patiently. 'Only Didier Muret insisted that I lunch with him, and he seemed so damned disappointed by the treasure mix-up that I couldn't very well refuse. So I went back to his house, had a drink.' He flashed his old familiar smile. 'A few drinks, actually. I tried to cheer him up. And then, before I knew it, there it was suppertime, and I offered to go and get a take-away for the two of us. And on the way back, with my pizza,' he told me, 'I got this.'

He tilted his head to one side, showing me a patch of bruising that spread darkly underneath the fair hair just behind his ear.

I stared. 'He hit you?'

'No.' My cousin smiled. 'It's rather complicated, actually, I'd better let Jean tell it.'

The gypsy leaned back in his chair and lit a cigarette. It was odd, I thought, to be sitting here so calmly with a man that I'd been trying to avoid these past few days. A man I'd suspected of murder. His voice, when he spoke, was coarse but musical, his English remarkably good. 'That night,' he said, 'the night Monsieur Muret was killed, I am walking with Bruno,' his dark eyes glanced downwards, at the little dog, 'and I see that the door to Muret's garden, it is open. This is luck, I think. Muret, he keeps much whisky in the house, and the street is very dark there.' His shrug was casual, as though thieving were a wholly respectable pastime. 'So Bruno and I, we go into the yard, but before we are in the house we hear voices. Loud voices. I look in

348

the window, and I see the two of them arguing. So I wait. I watch. Muret and the other, they go upstairs. Muret is very angry. Then . . .' He made a violent gesture with a hand across his throat. It was quite ugly. 'Muret he falls, and I see that he is dead. The other man, he sees this too. He comes out of the house, out the back door, into the garden where it is very dark. He does not see Bruno and me – we hide up by the wall – but your cousin,' he paused, and smiled at Harry. 'Your cousin, he comes at that moment through the garden door, with his pizza.'

'Bad timing,' Harry admitted.

'There is a little light from the house. And so the killer, he looks at your cousin. Your cousin, he looks at the killer. And—' Again a telling movement of the hand. 'He is badly hurt, your cousin. He says to me: "Hotel de France", and so I try to help him there, but when we turn the corner I see the car, the killer's car, and so I bring your cousin to my family, where he will be safe.'

I looked at Harry. 'So you saw him, then. The man who murdered Didier Muret.'

'That's just it – I didn't. It was too bloody dark, and the lights of the house were behind him. I couldn't see a thing. He knocked me on the head for nothing.' Harry rubbed his bruises ruefully.

My gaze swung back to the gypsy. 'But you saw him.'

'Yes.'

'And the man who murdered Paul.'

'Yes.'

I had to ask the question, even though I knew the answer. 'The same man?'

'Yes.'

'And you didn't go to the police?'

He looked at me as though I had two heads. 'The police? This is not England, Mademoiselle. The police, they will not listen to a man like me. They think I tell the lies. And your cousin, he did not see the man who hit him. So . . .' He shrugged, and blew a puff of smoke. 'We talk, we think, we wait.'

'You might have come to me,' I said, a shade reproachfully. I would have known then not to get involved with Neil. I wouldn't feel this aching emptiness inside me, as though my heart had shrivelled to a useless lump of ice. And Paul . . . Paul might yet be alive.

'I tried this,' was the gypsy's calm response. 'Your cousin, he is not so good the first few days – he cannot keep awake. But he keeps saying "the Hotel de France", and "Emily", and in his wallet I find this picture.' He showed me a less-than-flattering snapshot of myself, a few years out of date. 'And so I go to the Hotel de France. I look for you. On Friday, finally, you arrive, but it is not possible to speak to you. And so I wait until you go to dinner, I telephone to the hotel, I pretend to be your cousin.'

'Why?'

My cousin answered that. 'Jean had to think rather fast that day, I'm afraid. He had to come up with a story that would keep you from worrying, without tipping off the murderer. So he left a message that I'd been delayed – brilliant, really, considering he hardly knew me – and then he kept an eye on you, to see that you weren't harmed.'

The gypsy smiled. 'We frighten you, Bruno and I, I see

this. But it is difficult, you understand. Always the killer he is very close to you.'

'Yes, I know.' I looked away more sharply than I meant to. A log fell into the fire with a hiss, and it was an ugly mocking sound, like an old woman's wheezing laugh in that stale room. My eyes stung and I blinked the wetness back.

'I see the way you smile at him,' the gypsy said, 'and I think no, she will not believe me.'

'Well, you're wrong.' I felt the stubborn lifting of my jaw. 'And you could have warned me when I first arrived, you know. I hadn't met him, then.'

The gypsy frowned. 'But . . .'

Behind us, on the bed, my cousin shifted. 'My dear girl,' he said, quite clearly, 'of course you'd met him. The bastard dropped you off at your hotel.'

CHAPTER TWENTY-NINE

. . . the gates were closed
At sunset,

'It didn't half give me a shock, I can tell you,' my cousin went on, shaking his head. 'I mean, of all the bloody people for you to meet, your first day out!'

I slowly turned to stare at him, feeling rather stunned, like a racing driver who'd gone almost round the course at top speed only to slam into a brick wall at the final bend. 'But it can't be Armand.'

The two men shared a knowing look. 'Look, love,' said Harry, 'I know you like the man, but—'

'No, it isn't that.' I shook my head, impatient to make him understand. 'It's just that I know who killed Paul, you see, and it wasn't Armand Valcourt. It was Neil.' There, I thought, I'd said it; I'd finally put a voice to the painful thought. I stilled the treacherous quivering of my mouth, aware both men were staring at me. Couldn't they see, I thought, how much I wanted to believe . . . ?

My cousin frowned. 'Who the devil is Neil?'

'Neil Grantham. He's a violinist, staying at my hotel.'

'Ah.'

'Only he wasn't playing the violin yesterday, it was a tape, and the opening allegro to Beethoven's Third is at least fifteen minutes long, so he had heaps of time to run up the steps and push Paul off . . . I doubt if it takes me more than a couple of minutes myself to climb those steps, and I'm not nearly as fit as Neil.'

'Ah,' Harry said again, as if my explanation were perfectly clear. 'And why would this violinist want to push a Canadian kid off the château steps, pray tell?'

'Because . . . because . . .' My chin trembled, and I realised the motive was no longer clear, not after what the gypsy Jean had told me.

'You're way off beam, love,' Harry told me, gently. 'It was Valcourt who did the killing.'

I didn't take that in, at first – I only felt relief that nearly shook my body in a deep and swelling surge. *It wasn't Neil,* my inner voice rejoiced, but I was half afraid to listen to it. I turned to the gypsy. 'You're absolutely sure?'

He nodded, his black eyes calm and certain. 'Yesterday afternoon,' he explained, 'I am coming down from here to the town, through the *souterrains,* the tunnels. I stop at the door in the cliff. There is a space between the boards in the door, and so I look, like always, to make sure the way is safe.' He drew one finger along the line of his eyebrow, frowning. 'But it is not safe. *He* is there.'

'Monsieur Valcourt?'

His nod this time held sadness. 'He is sitting on the wall,

354

beside your friend, the young *canadien*. They smoke, they talk – they talk like friends. But the boy, he is not on his guard. He is not watching Valcourt's face, as I am, so he does not see the danger. When Valcourt gives to him another cigarette, the boy lifts up both hands to light it, and . . .' No brutal gesture, this time, just a small regretful shrug. 'It is so quick, there is no time for noise. The boy falls and Valcourt walks very fast towards the château. When I cannot see him any more I open my door, I come out. It is terrible, what I have just seen, you understand?' A brief pause while he lit another cigarette himself, still frowning. 'I go down at once to see if the boy . . . but he is dead. He is dead.' The gypsy glumly shook his head, and sighed a spreading pall of smoke.

There was something unfinished about that story, I thought, but I couldn't quite put my finger on it. The little dog Bruno yawned with gusto and jumped onto my cousin's bed, stretching himself into the blankets. And then I remembered. I remembered very clearly how I'd seen that dog the afternoon before, outside the phone box at the corner of the fountain square. Spurred by that memory, I took a stab in the dark. 'So you went down and telephoned Monsieur Grantham, didn't you?'

'To Monsieur . . . ? Ah, the one who plays the violin. No, I do not telephone to him, Mademoiselle. I telephone to the police, to say there has been an accident.' He shrugged. 'And then I leave as quickly as I can. I come back here, to tell your cousin.'

'I was asleep, I'm afraid,' Harry said, with a regretful smile, 'and by the time I'd heard the tale from Jean all hell had broken loose at your hotel, which made it rather difficult to contact you.' His eyes were very gentle as he met my gaze. 'I am a selfish bastard, aren't I, love? I was so busy feeling sorry for myself I didn't stop to think you might yourself be in some danger. I thought you'd be quite safe with Jean to keep an eye on you, and from what I heard I gathered Valcourt rather fancied you. I thought,' he said, a little sadly, 'that it would be all right, you see. But when Jean told me Valcourt had just pushed your friend right down the château steps, I realised I was wrong. Of course, by then,' he went on, pushing himself upright on the pillows, 'the word was out that the police were looking everywhere for Jean. His sister came to tell us that. So I could hardly send him down . . .'

'I told you,' said the gypsy, 'that your cousin, she would come to us.' He shrugged with the complacency of one who trusts the mystic course of fate.

Harry smiled. 'So you did.'

It hardly mattered, I thought, whether I'd found them or they'd found me. What mattered was what all of us intended doing now. For, in spite of Harry's evidently weakened state . . .

I looked more closely at him. 'God, I never thought. Were you very badly hurt? Do you need a doctor?'

'No,' he told me, rather quickly, hitching higher up in bed. Although he looked more tired than normal, he really didn't appear too ill. 'No, I don't need a doctor.'

The gypsy also clearly thought the question daft. 'My sister, she has seen him,' he explained. 'She is better than a doctor. She finds us this empty house, to keep him hidden, and she comes each day to make for him the medicine. It is not good, she says, for him to move around too much.'

Even so, it seemed to me unthinkable to simply sit here and do nothing. Two men were dead already, and my cousin's life was hardly safe from harm. I frowned and cleared my throat and was about to speak when I was interrupted by a gentle, furtive tapping sound, like the faint patter of a branch blown by the wind against a window pane.

Jean scraped his chair back on the floorboards and rose to answer the door. A different door than the one I'd entered the house by, but then the tapping sound had not come from the tunnels. It had come from the outside.

The door swung open and I saw for the first time just where I was – the slanting view of narrow path and waving grasses and the smudge of rooftops far below was unmistakeable. I must have walked straight past this house, I thought, when I'd come up that first day alone and by accident to the Chapelle of Sainte Radegonde, and again when I'd returned to search with Paul. I would have to see the house from the outside, of course, to know just where along the path it stood, but all the same I knew that I was on the cliffs and just a stone's throw from the lovely ruined chapelle. The tunnels had brought me this far.

I'd scarcely registered the fact before my attention shifted to the woman standing in the doorway. She was quite young, with an arresting face and a figure that begged the word 'voluptuous'. Had I met her on the street, I would have thought her looks exotic – Italian, perhaps, or even Turkish, dark hair and eyes and olive skin – but I'd not have taken her for a gypsy. She looked so . . . well, so modern, really, in her stylish jeans and jumper; so unlike my own conception of a gypsy, and yet seeing her beside her brother Jean one couldn't possibly mistake the family likeness.

This was, I thought, without a doubt Jean's helpful sister with the healing hands, who came every day to nurse my cousin's wounded head. Which probably explained why Harry had been so content to stay hidden, I thought drily. Already he had slumped again, wanting sympathy, assuming his most appealing little-boy-lost expression as he turned to face this newest visitor.

From the exchange of greetings that followed I learned the woman's name was Danielle. We were introduced, but she was clearly too preoccupied with other things to spare me more than a few words and a distracted nod. 'They have taken Victor to be questioned,' she announced, her lovely face clouded with worry.

Her brother nodded. 'Yes, I know.'

'You know? And yet you are still here? What kind of man are you, to let your friend face trouble in your place?'

'They will let him go.'

'Oh, will they?' She tossed her head, eyes very bright. 'That isn't what I hear. I hear they think he murdered this one here,' a jerk of the jaw towards Harry, 'and that he tries to hide the evidence.'

My cousin sat bolt upright. 'What?'

'Victor Belliveau?' I checked, and the woman Danielle turned her wild eyes on me.

'Yes. They think he is a murderer because I hide the car in his old barn,' she said.

My cousin's car, I thought. Of course, it would have had to be hidden somewhere. I remembered the decrepit stone barn that faced Belliveau's house, and how the locked door had moaned and rattled in the wind.

Danielle went on, with feeling. 'He doesn't even know about the car, poor Victor. That barn, he never uses it – I thought it would be safe. It is my fault,' she cursed herself. 'And he has always been so good to us. And you refuse to help him.'

'It is too great a risk . . .' began the gypsy, but my cousin cut him off.

'All right,' said Harry, in a tone I recognised from countless lost arguments, 'that's it. I'm going down.'

And he began to lever himself out of the bed, wincing with the effort, though I couldn't be sure how much of that was for Danielle's benefit. I knew better than to try to stop him, but Jean wasn't privy to my years of experience with Harry's moods.

'The police, they will not listen—'

'Then we'll just have to make them listen.' Harry swung his feet to the floor and reached for his shoes. He had been resting fully clothed in bed, no doubt to guard against the creeping autumn chill that soaked through even these stone walls. His dusty jeans and crumpled shirt, together with his week-long growth of beard, made him look the sort of person one normally found skulking under bridges with a bottle of cheap wine – not at all respectable; yet through the rough exterior, my cousin's odd heroic quality still shone, brilliant and compelling.

Danielle moved to his side, drawn less perhaps by his

heroic brilliance than by a practical and simple fear that he might fall and hit his head again. Certainly he seemed a little less than steady on his feet, although the obstinate determination in his face showed plainly that he had the will to override his weakness. If he *was* truly weak, I amended the thought, not missing his brief smile when Danielle took firm hold of his arm to help him balance.

Jean sighed. 'I will come too.'

'No.' Harry shook his head. 'No, you should stay up here I think, and out of sight, until I have a chance to clear this whole thing up with the police. Danielle can help me,' he said, brightening. 'We can take the tunnel, like you do. Danielle knows the tunnels, doesn't she?'

'As well as Jean.' The woman raised her chin with pride. 'I can guide you.'

Oh, wonderful, I thought. Aloud, I said: 'Shall I stay here, then?'

Harry frowned. 'Well, if you like. Although I would have thought . . . oh, right,' he realised, suddenly. 'Tunnels. I quite forgot. My cousin,' he informed the others, predictably, 'has a thing about tunnels. Why don't you take the outside path, instead? It's not the nicest of neighbourhoods, I'm afraid, but it is still light outside and I'm sure you'd find the way back with no trouble. You could meet up with us outside the château, where the tunnel door comes out. All right?'

'All right.' I nodded. A trace of apprehension must have seeped into my voice because Danielle looked up to meet my eyes across the room, her hands protective on my cousin's arm.

360

'Do not worry,' she told me. 'I will take good care of him.'

I thought that Harry looked distinctly pleased with the situation as his self-appointed nurse steered him to the cellar door. A moment later I could hear their footsteps slowly moving down the narrow stairway that led down into the darkness of the tunnels. I shuddered at the memory of that darkness, and turned my back on it. The gypsy Jean misread my action.

'They will be fine,' he told me. 'It is an easy walk down there, easier than along the cliff, and no one will see them until they have reached the safety of the town.' He walked with me to the front door, keeping to the shadows as he held the door open for me to pass through. 'Take care, Mademoiselle,' was the only advice he gave me. And then the door was bolted once more behind me and I found myself alone on the cliff path, between the château and the Chapelle of Sainte Radegonde, with the hollow eyes of half-decayed troglodyte dwellings staring at me blackly through a tangled web of weeds and sunbleached grasses.

The house looked larger, seen from the outside. It was unremarkable in design, like a child's drawing of a house – four walls, peaked roof, two windows and a red brick chimney, with no frivolous decoration to relieve the solid severe lines. Two storeys tall it rose, which meant two rooms; two narrow rooms, at that, and yet it still looked somehow larger, perhaps because there were no other buildings nearby to lend it proper scale. There was only the hill rising up behind it and the gaping crumbled cliff dwellings snaking off on either side, and behind me the treacherous drop to the grey roofs of Chinon.

I remembered this house, from my first foray up the path last Monday – the day I'd felt I was being followed. I'd felt afraid, outside this house. I remembered the barbed wire, and the leaning door, and the barking dog and the sound of the wind. How differently might things have turned out, I wondered, if I had knocked at the door of the house that day, instead of running? Had I found Harry then, we might be safely home in England, he and I, while the Chinon police dealt with Armand Valcourt and left Victor Belliveau alone. And Paul would be fasting with his brother, observing the holy day of Yom Kippur.

Hindsight, I thought, was like a punishment, remorseless in its clarity and painfully unable to change what had gone before.

Turning from the house, I pressed on down the path towards the château, which I knew lay some ten minutes' walk away, although I couldn't see it from here.

Since I'd first gone into the tunnel after the gypsy earlier that evening, the wind had shifted subtly and the clouds were drifting in to catch the brilliance of the sinking sun. The air was cold and singing past my ears. A strand of hair whipped stinging in my eyes, blinding me for a moment until I could push it back and blink the tears away. I tucked my chin into my collar, dug my hands deeper in the pockets of Paul's red jacket, and hurried on.

The path wound round and down and up again, past caves and staring houses that hunched shoulder to shoulder to watch me scurry by. And then the houses blended to a single wall that guided me along the rising slope towards the narrow, soaring clock tower at the château's gate. I bustled upwards, feeling the now-familiar burning of my laboured lungs, and glanced at my wristwatch to check the time.

Surprisingly, the walk had taken less than ten minutes – it was just past seven, which meant that, even though Harry and Danielle had started first, I was likely to arrive at the meeting place ahead of them, considering my cousin wasn't moving at top speed and was moving in the dark, on top of that. I slowed my pace a little, to ease the pressure on my pounding heart.

And then my heart, quite suddenly, seemed not to beat at all.

Ahead of me, almost at the very spot where Paul had fallen yesterday, a man was sitting on the low stone wall. He sat with body angled forward, elbows braced on knees, head bent to contemplate his loose-linked fingers. He was frowning.

Behind the pensive figure of Armand Valcourt, the château cast a stark and stretching shadow on the smooth deserted pavement. Deserted now, but not for long. At any moment now my cousin and his gypsy nurse would shuffle up the steps from the dank tunnel, and walk through that door just there . . . just *there* . . .

My gaze swung past Armand's bent shoulders to the cliff face further up the road. Fighting back the rising tide of panic, I struggled to reassure myself. There was a gap between the boards, so Jean had said, a gap that one could look through, to make sure the way was safe. *Oh, dear God, let them have the sense to look,* I prayed, in the

363

fervent way that non-believers pray, when they hope to be proved wrong.

I wasn't the least bit worried, at that moment, for my own safety. Armand might be a killer, but he hadn't struck me as a psychopath. He must have suspected, from the very first, that I was somehow linked to Harry, to the man who'd seen him leaving the scene of Didier Muret's murder. He'd seen Harry's face, after all; any fool would have noticed the resemblance between my cousin and myself. And Armand Valcourt was no fool.

And yet, he'd always been a perfect gentleman. He didn't know I knew, I thought – that was the key. And as long as I kept up a normal front I doubted he would try to harm me now. After all, I reasoned, there was no way Armand could know that I'd just come from seeing Harry, not unless I told him myself, and I was hardly about to do that. I could just tell him I'd been walking on the cliff path – hardly a suspicious activity – and he'd have no cause to think anything had changed between us. No, he wouldn't harm me, I decided, steadying my lurching pulse with a concerted effort.

But if he came face to face with Harry, now, and Harry barely able to stand up straight, let alone defend himself . . .

A crowd of tourists would have made the roadway safe, but it was suppertime and no one was about, not even a straggling student or a local resident – not one soul, just as it had been the afternoon before. I flicked another watchful glance towards the door set in the cliff face, and squared my shoulders. History, Harry always said, went round and round, repeating – but the tragedy of yesterday would not be replayed tonight, not while I had the power left to stop it. Forming a smile that felt natural upon my face, I took a bold step forward, and another.

He was so deep in contemplation that he didn't hear my footsteps drawing closer, and when I finally spoke to him his head came up with a startled jerk.

'A penny for your thoughts,' was what I said. What thoughts did killers think, in private?

He turned towards me, no longer frowning, his preoccupied expression fading to a warmer look of welcome. 'My thoughts aren't worth a penny,' he said evenly, in French. 'You've been walking? By yourself?'

'Just as far as the chapelle.'

'The Chapelle Sainte Radegonde?' His eyebrows lifted a degree. 'It's not the safest walk, that, for a woman on her own.'

'Quite safe in daylight, I should think.' So many things, I thought, were safe by daylight. Even talking to murderers. Or at least, that's what I hoped. Mind you, there wasn't that much daylight left, and I was running out of time to think of some way to make Armand Valcourt move from where he sat, leaving the way clear for Harry to get down to the police.

Think, damn you, think, I ordered my racing mind, but no ideas came. My hands shook ever so slightly, and I tucked them back in my pockets to keep them still.

Armand noticed. 'You are cold?'

'No. No, it's just—' And then it finally struck me, what excuse to use. 'It's just this place,' I said, quite honestly. 'It's difficult to stand here, so soon after . . .'

'*Dieu*, I didn't think. I'm sorry.' He sent a brief look up the road and raked his hair with one lean hand, then met my eyes again and smiled. 'Have you ever seen the sunset from the walls of the château?'

The château, I thought. Public place, with lots of people. Perfect. Trying to keep the relief from showing in my voice, I replied that I had not. 'Is it very lovely?'

'It is something to be remembered.'

The walk up the hill was a short one, but to me it seemed to take an age. I held my breath as we passed the door that hid the tunnel's entrance, and fancied that I heard somebody stir behind the wooden panels, but it might have been imagination, or the wind. The wind had risen sharply with the sinking of the sun, and it caught now in my throat as I quickened my step to keep pace with Armand's longer strides.

The young guide at the château admission booth looked faintly surprised when we appeared. Her wide eyes swung from me to Armand, and she cleared her throat. 'Monsieur . . .'

Armand reached for his wallet. 'Two adults.'

'But Monsieur . . .'

'We wish to see the sunset,' he explained. He passed a bill across the narrow counter, with its tumbled stacks of coloured brochures and souvenirs. I didn't see the exact denomination of the note, but it was rather more than the price of our admission. The girl took it slowly from his hand and looked at it, hesitating, then took two pink tickets from below the counter and handed them to Armand.

I frowned as we walked up along the gravel path, past

the Royal Apartments on our way to the far western wall. 'Why the bribe?' I asked him, casually. The only other visitors I could see were heading in the opposite direction, so I'd already half guessed what Armand's answer would be. And I was right.

'The château closes to the public at this hour,' he said, with an uncaring shrug. 'But it's no problem. The workers stay on for a while yet, to finish up the closing, and they know me well. We're neighbours.' He stepped aside to let me go ahead across the short bridge spanning the dry moat that split the grounds. Directly in front of me, the ruined Moulin Tower rose like a sentinel at the château's westernmost edge, its jagged, roofless silhouette a foil for the brilliant wash of colour on the billowed clouds behind.

It looked as though the very sky was burning.

'It will be still more splendid in a moment.' I heard the click of Armand's cigarette lighter and smelled the drifting smoke as he moved up to join me. 'I hope you found your cousin well?'

My mouth went dry as dust. 'What?'

'You have,' he said, 'a most revealing face.'

Some distance off a set of ancient hinges creaked a protest that was silenced by a final-sounding thud. They were closing the gates to the château.

'It was bound to happen, I suppose,' Armand went on, lifting one hand to gently touch my hair, 'but I'm still sorry he had to tell you.'

CHAPTER THIRTY

It needs must be for honour if at all:

I felt the change in my own eyes. He dropped his hand.

'You are afraid of me,' he said. 'I didn't want that. I didn't want . . .' The dark eyes angled downwards, shutting me out, and he pulled sharply at his cigarette.

My heartbeat lurched arhythmically and for a second time I steadied it. Don't panic, I thought, just stay calm. Surely Harry would by now have reached the meeting place, the place where the steps started down to the fountain square, and he would not wait long before deciding something must have happened to me. Unlike Harry, I was never late.

No, I reassured myself, he'd realise something had gone wrong and he'd go straight to the police, as he'd intended. And then the police would telephone the château where, somewhere, a handful of straggling staff members were still working through their closing duties, and the police would ask if anyone had noticed me upon the road, and then someone was bound to tell them . . . Yes, I thought, trying desperately to convince myself, that's how it would happen. If I only kept my head and kept Armand in conversation, then everything would be all right. It was only a matter of time before someone came for me.

He will come . . . The promise, in a voice not quite my own, flowed, through my mind and over me and filled me with an oddly quiet calmness. I cleared my throat. 'May I please have a cigarette?'

I was breaking faith with Paul, I knew. *Nothing for pleasure,* that's what Thierry had said was the rule of Yom Kippur. No food, no drink, and certainly no cigarettes. And yet my request was not for pleasure, it was purposeful. It bought me time. If Armand found it odd that someone shut into a deserted ruin with a murderer would think of smoking, he didn't let on. His face remained impassive as he handed me the packet and the lighter.

The wind rose wilder up the tower walls. It took me several tries to light the cigarette, the flame kept blowing out.

Armand stood watching me. 'I wouldn't have hurt you,' he said.

Past tense, I noticed. Lovely. My own voice, to my surprise, was nearly normal. 'So what happens now?'

'I don't know.' He looked suddenly an old man, very tired. 'It's . . . difficult, this business. And so much, I think, depends on you.'

'On me?'

'What you decide.'

'I see.' I felt a fleeting stab of warmth upon my cheek

from the dying sun. 'Well, I don't see how I can decide anything. I haven't heard your side of things.'

'And do you want to hear?'

'Of course.'

He looked at me a long moment. 'I don't believe you.'

'Believe what you like.'

'No, you're only saying this because you're frightened . . .'

'Well, of course I'm bloody frightened!' I shot back, against my best intentions. 'You've killed two people that I know of – maybe you killed your wife too, I don't know. My God, Armand, I'd be a fool not to be frightened!' I broke off suddenly, horrified by my outburst. Never antagonise your attacker, that's what all the advice columns said, and never let him see your fear. My heart sank miserably as I waited for Armand's reaction.

He was watching his own cigarette glow crimson in the angry wind. He flicked the end and loosed a swirl of sparks that quickly died. 'I didn't, as it happens, kill my wife.' His smile was very tight, and brief. 'I thought about it, off and on. She was most . . . irritating, sometimes, and there were days she pushed me almost to my limit, but in the end she died quite naturally – her heart . . .' He raised his eyes then, looked away. The hand that held the cigarette was very steady. 'Then Didier, my loving brother-in-law, he came to me and asked me if I knew about the will. Brigitte's will. Not the one she'd made when we were married, but the one she'd written out herself the week before her death. Didier, he was a clerk for Brigitte's lawyer, then – he'd seen the envelope addressed by her one morning in the office post, and being curious he opened it. It was a legal will, he told me, signed and witnessed, everything. Brigitte,' he said, 'had left me every cent she owned, on the condition that I turn my house, my land, into an institute for her damned artists. God!' The word came out with all the bitterness that lingered still within him. 'Without her money, I was lost – I had so little of my own. And yet, to get the money she would make me give up all I *did* own. She would have robbed her daughter of the legacy we Valcourts have been born to since before the Revolution. No,' he said, his voice low and determined, 'the money, it was Brigitte's, but the land . . . the land is *mine*. It will be Lucie's land when I am gone, and no one has a right to steal that from her. No one,' he repeated. I glimpsed a violence in the deep black eyes, a quiet violence, carefully contained, but even as his gaze swung round to lock with mine it vanished like a thing imagined. 'Didier, he knew how I would feel. He'd counted on it. He had kept the will locked in his desk; the lawyer hadn't seen it. A little bit of money to destroy it, that's what he'd been after, and when Brigitte died, well . . . he knew he could ask for any price, and I would pay it.'

'But surely, the people who witnessed the will . . .'

'Ah yes. Your Monsieur Grantham, he was a witness, did you know? And he asked me, when Brigitte died, what happened to the will. I told him she had changed her mind, and Didier, he told this story also.'

'But he didn't keep his promise. To destroy the will.'

'No.' He shook his head, looked down again. 'No, at every turning there it was, that damned will, waved in my face. A most convenient blackmail scheme, I must admit.'

'You might have gone to the police. Explained what happened. Maybe they could—'

'No. No, you can't understand. You don't have children, Emily,' he told me softly, accusingly. It was the first time he had called me by my name. 'Children, they are everything. We owe to them a name they can be proud of, and a future with no shadows in it. Lucie deserves that much from me. I couldn't risk a scandal.'

I challenged him. 'Is that why you killed Didier?'

'It's cold,' he said. His cigarette was dead and he reached in his pocket for another. 'The wind, it's cold. You must be frozen.'

'I'm fine.'

'You're shaking. Come, let's sit down.'

The only place I saw to sit was on the broad low wall that jutted from the west face of the Moulin Tower. Beyond that wall the sun had flattened on a purple haze of hills, spilling its brilliance into the darkly flowing river, and the wind had turned electric with the threat of a coming storm. I slowly shook my head, staring at the crumbled wall and thinking of the sheer and plunging drop it masked on the other side. I was thinking, oddly enough, not of Paul being pushed from the cliff but of my mother, years ago on a family trip to Cornwall, chasing me constantly down the sea spray-slicked footpaths and warning me: 'Don't go near the edge!' She would be proud of me, I thought, for finally heeding her advice.

'No,' I said. 'I don't want to sit down.' *Stay in the open,* I told myself, *don't drop your guard.*

Armand smiled, tightly. 'Not on the wall. Just there,

beside the tower. By the door.' There was a sort of trench-like entryway that led up to the Moulin Tower's wooden door. The leaves lay thick upon the pavement there, unmoving, proof that the ivy-choked walls on either side blocked out the wind with ease, and against one wall, nestled in the ivy, was a narrow concrete bench. It offered shelter, but not safety. Safety lay in staying out upon the lawn, where anyone might see us.

Again I shook my head. 'I'm fine.' I hugged my arms around my waist to stop the trembling. 'You were going to tell me about Didier.'

'Ah, well,' he shrugged, as the flame of the lighter danced behind his cupped hand, 'that was an accident. Not that I regret it, but it was not meant to happen. I was that week in Paris, meeting buyers, but each lunch hour I telephoned Lucie, to talk. She likes for me to ring her when I'm out of town. Most days we talked of school, of François, but on that Wednesday Lucie asked me could she have a shovel.' His jaw tightened a little, remembering. 'I asked her why, and she said Uncle Didier was going to go digging for treasure with a man, an English man. She said she'd heard them talking just that morning, by the river, and she thought it sounded fun. Fun.' His smile held no humour. 'I felt like I'd been punched. I'd warned Didier once, you understand – I'd paid him well not to dig on my land, to ruin my vines, looking for those foolish diamonds. I told him if he ever tried again to touch my land, my daughter's land, I'd kill him. I didn't mean it,' he qualified. 'I don't believe I meant it. But I had to make quite sure he understood. So when I heard from Lucie, what was going on, it made me angry.'

Only Lucie, I thought, had got the story wrong, as usual. She'd heard Didier and Harry talking about tunnels, about digging for treasure, God knows what. And Didier, who had hoped to learn from Harry some new clue to help him find the diamonds, had no doubt been rather stunned himself to learn he'd wasted his effort. Small problems of communication, I thought, that had led to murder.

Armand shrugged. 'I had to talk to Didier, to stop him, so I hired a car and drove to Chinon. He was alone and drunk, when I caught up with him. He laughed at me . . . he *laughed* . . . and so I told him that I'd had enough, that I wasn't going to give in any longer. That I didn't think he even had the will any more. I hadn't seen it for months. That made him angry.' I saw his faint smile glimmer in the gathering dusk. 'Didier, he didn't like to be called a liar. Said he'd show me I was wrong. He went upstairs, and so at last I knew where he kept Brigitte's will. I only meant to take it back, to burn it – but Didier, he tried to stop me . . .'

'So you killed him.'

'He was very drunk. It was easy to take the will from him, but he came after me, attacked me on the first floor landing. I pushed him off – not hard, but he went back over the railing.' Armand shrugged, a short and callous shrug without remorse. 'There was nothing I could have done.'

'You could have reported it. It was an accident, for heaven's sake.'

'But why? Why let that bastard draw me into an enquiry, headlines in the newspapers, gossip in the cafes? He was dead, I owed him nothing, so I left him where he was. I don't regret what I did. If I had to do it again, I would

375

still have left the house, only,' he admitted, 'I'd have left it by the front door, not the back. I thought the back door would be safer, not so many windows facing me, and the lane beside is always dark. I hadn't counted on your cousin coming up the path.'

'He didn't see you,' I informed him.

'Did he not? I was so certain that he did. I thought I'd killed him, too, but I did not have time to check. I could not risk a neighbour looking out and seeing me.' He lifted the cigarette, his mouth twisting. 'The next day, when Martine called me in Paris to tell me Didier was dead, I learned no other body had been found. The man who'd seen me, he was still alive, and though he had not talked to the police, he was a danger. I could not risk another blackmailer, you understand. So I came back to Chinon. And then,' he said, quite simply, 'I saw you.'

So I'd been right, I thought. He'd seen the resemblance from the very beginning. 'Is that why you sent me the invitation?' I asked. 'Because you wanted me to lead you to my cousin?'

'I wanted to find out who you were,' was his reply. 'And when I learned you had no brother, that you were in Chinon by yourself, I thought it must be just coincidence, that you looked so much like him. I was surprised, at lunch, when you mentioned a cousin – I hadn't thought of cousins – but then you said this cousin lived in England, so . . .' He shrugged, a little sadly. 'I did not know, for sure, until this morning. When you told me.'

'I see.'

He watched my face a moment, mulling something over.

'You said your cousin did not see me. And yet you knew,' he mused. 'Who told you?'

'You were seen.'

'The gypsy,' he decided, his mind sifting through what I'd told him that morning. He was very sharp, I thought. 'It was the gypsy with the dog, was it not? The one who follows you around. So, it is just this gypsy's word against my own, then.' The knowledge seemed to please him, and I kicked myself for having told him anything.

'My word as well,' I said, lifting my chin with a courage I didn't quite feel. 'You shouldn't be telling me this.'

'You won't repeat it.'

My belly crawled with sudden cold. 'Oh? And why not?'

'Because of this.' I guessed his intent even as he reached for me, but I didn't have the time to move away. The kiss was hard, and yet it scarcely registered – I was past feeling anything. I simply stood and let him kiss me, unresponsive. At length he drew back, touched my cheek. 'We have this still between us, you and I,' he said. 'From the moment I first saw you . . .'

When he bent to me again, my mind stayed stoically detached and analytical. Past Armand's shoulder I could see the little ivy-shrouded bench, with dead leaves drifted underneath it. I saw the wooden doorway to the Moulin Tower, bound firm with iron hinges, and I watched it shifting inwards as the wind went rushing past it. Impossible, I told myself. The tower was off limits, closed to tourists, it was always locked. The door could not have moved.

Armand drew back a second time and, frowning, lit a cigarette. He smoked too much, I thought absently. Like

377

Paul . . . And suddenly my thoughts weren't absent any more. The feeling came back in a searing flood that scalded every nerve to painful rawness.

I didn't move, but mentally I took five paces back, away from Armand. I could perhaps forgive him for the death of Didier – a tragic accident, unplanned, partly orchestrated by the victim – I could forgive him that, and as for Brigitte's will I understood a father's drive to shield the future of his daughter, however much I disapproved of his methods. But Paul . . . No, I decided firmly – never. Day of Atonement notwithstanding, I could never forgive him for Paul.

'You are thinking of the boy,' said Armand. He hadn't lied about my expressive face. 'Two people, you said – I have killed two people. Did the gypsy see that as well?'

I didn't tell him, this time, but he read the answer anyway, in my stoic silence.

'Ah.' He accepted this new information calmly. 'I am sorry. Not about being seen, you understand, but about . . . I didn't know he was so close a friend.'

'Would that have made a difference?'

'No.' The black eyes touched mine briefly, honestly, and slid away. 'No, it wouldn't. I could not have let him live.'

My throat had begun to hurt. 'Why not?'

'He was too smart, your friend. Too clever. But I didn't know how clever until yesterday, when we met quite by chance upon the road, just outside there.' A nod in the direction of the sturdy château gates. 'He asked me questions, then, about Didier. About when Didier was working for the lawyer. Now, if the other boy had asked me, I might just have thought he asked from curiosity – he

378

likes Martine, that one. I'd not have thought it strange. But this boy Paul, his questions made me curious myself. And so I sat with him, offered him a cigarette and asked him why he wanted to know about my brother-in-law. Do you know,' Armand said, unable to keep a trace of disbelieving admiration from seeping into his voice, 'he'd worked the whole thing out: the blackmail, the struggle by the stairs, the whole thing. Blackmail, he said, was the only thing that could explain how Didier got all his money, and more than likely the blackmail was connected to Didier's days as a lawyer's clerk. Your friend, he told me he thought Didier had not been by himself that night, that someone else was with him, maybe someone who had pushed him down the stairs . . .' Armand broke off and shook his head, incredulous. 'Too clever, that's what this boy was. Oh, he didn't know that it was me, of course. And he didn't bring the Englishman . . . your cousin . . . into it.'

'Yes, well, he wouldn't have,' I told him. 'Paul had promised, on his honour, that he wouldn't tell anyone else we were looking for Harry.'

'On his honour,' Armand echoed, with a faint and distant smile. 'Then I should have had him promise me he wouldn't talk of Didier at the hotel. I couldn't let him do that, couldn't let him talk of blackmailers and lawyers . . . it was too dangerous.'

I didn't understand, and told him so.

'Because of Neil. Because he would remember, maybe, Brigitte's will. He would ask questions. It was too dangerous,' he said again. The last word seemed to echo from the ruined walls around us, and I turned my head away in time to see a shadow moving past the gaping window of the Moulin Tower. The shadow vanished as I looked, and yet I caught the motion at the corner of my eye. And underneath the window, as the wind swirled fiercely by, the heavy wooden door creaked further inward on its ancient hinges, beckoning.

I judged the distance silently, between the tower and myself, and knew that with a running start I might just make it. I could bolt the door behind me. I'd be safe then, till they came to find me, if they came at all . . .

Behind us, in the high and narrow confines of the clock tower that guarded the château's entrance, the great medieval bell began to toll the time. Half past seven. Hunching deeper in my jacket, I swung my troubled gaze around to watch the outline of the ringing bell. 'Who's that coming now?' I asked Armand.

And when he raised his head to look, I ran.

I heard him swear; I heard him pounding close behind me, but I ran as one possessed and when I reached the door I still had time to turn and slam it shut behind me. The only problem was, there was no bolt. Not on the inside. 'Damn,' I breathed. I couldn't hope to hold it, by myself. Already I could hear the scrape of steps upon the stone outside, I saw the heavy handle start to turn . . .

My eyes were not adjusted to the darkness, and I stumbled as I dragged myself across the barren room to where the ghostly suggestion of a staircase curled its way upwards against the wall. The door crashed open behind me.

'Emily! For God's sake, don't be stupid. I won't hurt you . . .'

I had reached the stairs. With one hand trailing on the curved stone wall to guide my steps, I started up. The stone felt damp and full of dirt – the smell of it burned sharply in my nostrils, but I was climbing far too rapidly to register the full range of sensation. I burst with trembling legs into the upper chamber, open to the sky, and groped my way around the wall in search of some place, any place, to hide. The gathered clouds, tinged still with crimson, gazed down at me with pity.

The light was nearly gone now, and the wind seemed everywhere around me. It had a voice, that wind, half human and half demon, that numbed the mind and turned the soul to stone. I'd reached the end, with nowhere left to go. A slash of brightness showed in the wall a few feet on and with desperate hands I clawed my way around to it. I found a window . . . well, an arrow slit – a crumbling gaping arrow slit my height and width, with jagged edges framing an impressive view across the roofs of Chinon's old and peaceful heart.

In ages past an archer would have stood here, poised with watchful eyes to hold the castle keep against all challengers from the darkening hill below. And nearly eight centuries ago a frightened girl of fifteen years might well have stood in this same spot, watching the spreading fires of the rebel barons camped around the château walls. I could almost see the fires myself, tonight – the rue Voltaire below me was a blaze of light, and I fancied that I saw a line of torches winding up the cliff. *Oh, God,* I prayed, *please let him come.*

'I'm coming up,' Armand announced, below me. He

was on the stairs. 'Do you hear me, Emily? I'm coming up. Don't move.'

I slid away, along the wall, and pressed myself into the dripping stone. Armand moved very slowly, with deliberate purpose. His steps fell loud upon the worn stone. 'Please, Emily, I promise I won't hurt you. I could never . . .' His voice trailed off, and clearing his throat he tried again. 'Just don't move. The walls are weak in places, they're not safe. Please . . .'

I could see his outline now, at the top of the stairs. A few more steps, and he would be beside me. Panic froze my limbs, keeping me anchored to the stone while Armand edged his way towards me, past the arrow slit.

Then, in one flashing second, my whole world seemed to explode. The sudden stab of brilliant light came slashing through the arrow slit like lightning, and caught Armand full square upon the face. He tried to move and turned against the wall, and, frozen still, I heard the horrifying sound of grinding mortar giving way, and watched while Armand lurched to one side, out of sight. The light that had so blinded him kept shining, unconcerned, upon the settling dust and pebbles. It reflected even on the thick clouds moving low above the sharp and ragged edges of the roofless chamber I stood in.

And then I realised what had happened. The sunset, now, was nearly over. They had turned the floodlights on.

Armand hadn't fallen, not completely. With one hand he kept a death grip on the stone ledge where the arrow slit had been. Half stunned, I sidled round and watched him while he scrabbled for a foothold. He couldn't find one, but he managed to bring his other hand up to strengthen his grasp. And there he hung, suspended, muscles straining as he gathered all his energy to pull himself back up and in.

His fingers clung mere inches from my feet – I could have stepped on them, kicked at them, sent him to his death. It would, I thought, be no less than the man deserved. He'd killed Paul, hadn't he? But even as I thought of Paul I knew I couldn't do it, for in my mind I saw again Paul's gentle face, his dark eyes gazing out across the darkly flowing river, and I heard again his voice telling me sadly: 'People hate too much, you know?'

I knew.

And anyway, I thought, it was a sin to hate someone on Yom Kippur. I slowly crouched and braced myself with one hand against what remained of the wall, and stretched the other hand to take firm hold of Armand's wrist. He raised his head to look at me. With all the floodlights angled up behind him I could only see a darkened outline of his face, I couldn't see his eyes, and yet for some strange reason I believed I saw him smile at me. He turned his own hand slightly in my grasp until his fingers closed with mine. And then he just let go.

They told me later that when Armand fell, my group of would-be rescuers had only just arrived within the château grounds – that Harry was, in fact, still causing some kind of disturbance at the entrance booth. But somehow, when I spun away from the gaping, light-filled hole, Neil was there to catch me, his solid body shielding me from danger while his arms came round me strongly, firmly, warm as life itself.

I clung to him while, overhead, the clouds burst forth

a final brilliant streak of golden red, as if the gates of heaven themselves had briefly opened, and closed again. My trembling stilled; the wind seemed to fall silent, and some weight I didn't fully understand, a melancholy ages old, was lifted from my sobbing chest and drifted like an answered prayer into the darkness.

'It's all right, don't be frightened, now,' Neil said, his mouth moving down against my hair. 'I'm here.'

CHAPTER THIRTY-ONE

. . . the long fantastic night
With all its doings had and had not been,
And all things were and were not.

Inspector Prieur proved to be a decent man. I'd thought as much the moment I'd first met him, when he'd come walking across the château yard, calm in the midst of the confusion, and gently coaxed me out of Neil's protective hold. He'd looked like someone's grandfather come down for sports day, with a vacuum flask in one hand and a dark wool blanket in the other. 'You must be cold,' he'd said to me. 'I've brought you coffee.' And then, when I was ready, he'd begun to ask me questions, but even that had been relaxed – less an interrogation than an undemanding chat. When it was finished, he had looked at me with understanding. 'There is a child, they tell me. A little girl.'

'Yes.'

The old inspector, weary-eyed, had fixed his gaze upon the Moulin Tower. 'It can be difficult, a case like this. It can be difficult to prove. The suspect dead, and just one witness – no real evidence. And if the witness should rescind his statement, or refuse to testify . . .' The sentence hung unfinished, and he had raised his shoulders in a philosophical shrug. 'Sometimes, the scales of justice find a level of their own, without our help,' he'd said. 'And sometimes, in seeking justice, we don't always serve it. Do you understand?' Not trusting my voice, I'd nodded carefully. 'Good. Then I will see what I can do. There will be rumours, you understand; talk around the town. I can't stop that. And if, when she is grown up, she chooses to come looking for the truth, then she will find it. But perhaps,' he'd said, his grey eyes very kind, 'she will not look. It is better, I think, for a child to keep her heroes.'

A decent man, I thought again. I had blinked the tears back, smiled at him. 'Thank you.' And suddenly I'd felt a crawling sense of déjà-vu. A memory of a younger man in uniform, much larger, who had smiled at me in just that way . . . 'I'm sorry,' I had said. 'This may sound foolish, but I wonder . . .'

He'd looked pleased. 'Your father said you would remember. I told him no, that you were such a little girl in those days, but he was very sure.'

I'd blinked. 'My father?'

So he'd kept his promise, after all. He'd promised me he'd ask his friends in Paris to enquire after Harry, stir around, but I hadn't expected him to do anything. I certainly hadn't expected him to send a chief inspector straight to Chinon. Harry'd put it rather well, I thought: *Your father's got a network strung through Europe that would put our Secret Service men to shame.* I was just a

386

bit surprised he'd actually remembered.

I'd felt an old and automatic need to apologise to the inspector for the trouble he had gone to on my family's account; for the interruption of his holiday; for everything. He'd merely smiled, and shrugged it all aside.

'Your father is an old friend,' he had told me. 'He was worried. And when Andrew Braden worries, it is rarely without reason.' Then against a blurring backdrop of black sky and brilliant lights he had tucked the blanket tighter round my shoulders, and left me with the vacuum flask of strong reviving coffee.

I could have done with that coffee now, I thought, as I nestled deeper into the cushions of my seat in the hotel bar and stiffened my jaws to smother a yawn.

For the second time that week, the bar of the Hotel de France was blazing light long after its official closing time. One would have thought it was the cocktail hour and not past midnight. How far past midnight I could not be sure – I seemed to have lost my wristwatch – but when last I'd asked Jim Whitaker the time he'd told me it was going on for one, and that had been before Monsieur Chamond brought out the second bottle of Calvados.

We were well down in that bottle now. Monsieur Chamond had abandoned his bartending duties to settle on the stool beside his wife, leaving Thierry with the job of keeping all our glasses full. Thierry, for his part, was deep in some debate with Christian Rand, and had filled his own glass rather more often than ours. It was a smashing Calvados, well aged and mellow, resplendent with the golden warmth of apples from the finest fields of Normandy.

387

After going twenty-four hours without food, that warmth had spread through all my aching limbs, and I'd long since given up my efforts to make sense of what was going on around me.

François was there . . . now, that was strange. I wanted several times to ask him how and why he came to be there, but my tired brain kept stumbling on the question, and no one else seemed interested, so I just let it pass. I was having enough trouble getting used to seeing Harry lounging opposite among the potted palms, his lean face animated while he chatted on to Neil as though the night had been a normal one, like any other. My cousin's health had greatly improved, I'd noticed, since the gypsy woman Danielle had left us to go round to the police station, where her brother and the Chief Inspector were still sorting out the matter of official statements.

I didn't doubt they'd get it sorted. Certainly everyone here had entered the conspiracy of sympathetic silence. Oh, we could talk about it now, between ourselves, but come the morning I knew even Thierry, facing questions from his friends, would simply shrug and shake his head and say: 'A tragic accident' like the rest of us. He felt cheated by Armand's death, I could sense that – it had robbed him of the chance to take his personal revenge upon Paul's killer. But even Thierry couldn't transfer all that hatred to Lucie Valcourt. A child shouldn't suffer for her father's sins.

Martine, I thought, would see she didn't suffer. Martine had looked like a different person, up at the château, her face composed and elegant, expressionless, while she'd listened very quietly to Inspector Prieur's explanations. And then with equal calm she'd asked him: 'And my niece?'

'One of our officers is with her now. We haven't told her anything.'

'I see. Thank you.' She had nodded. 'Thank you very much. I will take care of her.' Lucie was in good hands.

Beside me, François stirred and said something to Jim. I pulled my thoughts back just in time to catch the final sentence. '. . . am looking forward,' he was saying, in his musical English, 'to showing you, while you are here. Perhaps your wife—'

'My wife will not be staying,' Jim said quietly. 'She's going on to Paris, and then home.'

I'd thought it odd that Garland hadn't joined us, but at some point between my third and fourth glasses of Calvados it had ceased to be important. Now I looked at Jim and thought: *He told her, that's what happened. He told her about Martine.*

Jim shrugged. 'But I'll be here for quite some time, I think. As long as I'm needed.'

Christian made some comment, low, in German, and I saw a warm approving smile flash across Neil's face, his dark eyes crinkling at the corners. I quickly looked away again before he caught me staring. Not that it would have made a difference if he had, I told myself. Unless of course he'd turned that smile on me, and then . . . and then . . .

I sighed. Well, that was the whole problem, wasn't it? I didn't know just what would happen then. I only knew I'd been avoiding him since we'd come down from the château, feeling uncertain without knowing what I wasn't certain *of*. It all came, I supposed, of having someone charge to your rescue like a bloody-minded prince out of a fairy tale; of having someone take you in his arms the way a lover might, as though you really *mattered*.

I felt my cousin watching me, his blue eyes frankly curious, and with a silent curse upon all men I sipped my drink, ignoring him.

It didn't work. Instead, he turned his curiosity on Neil. 'My cousin was convinced you were the culprit,' he said cheerfully.

Neil raised an eyebrow. 'Really?'

'Mm. Something about Nazis, I think, and diamonds. I'm afraid I didn't follow it all, but then she never does make sense when she's upset.'

'Ah,' said Neil.

François looked on, benevolent. 'My fault, I think. The photograph . . .'

'God, yes.' Neil grinned. 'Wherever did you dig that up? It's quite a damning likeness, that.'

Christian swivelled round upon his stool, addressing Neil in a mild voice. 'I am very angry with you. All these years you are a German, like myself, and I am never knowing this.'

'Half German. My mum's pure English, through and through. Dad moved to England when the war was over, and she met him there.'

Madame Chamond frowned prettily. 'Except your name,' she said. 'Grantham. It does not sound a German name.'

'Dad wasn't very proud of being German in those

days. He took the name of the place he moved to first, in Lincolnshire.'

'Oh, right,' said Harry, smiling. 'I've gone through Grantham dozens of times on the train. It's on the main line north to York, isn't it?'

Neil nodded. 'Mum and Dad still live there, actually, and my brother Ron.'

I tried to recall what he'd told me of his family. 'The painter?'

'No, the chemist.' Again the grin. I had to look away. 'Michael, he's the painter, lives in London. Then there's Isabelle. My sister,' he explained, as Jim and François both reacted. 'So you see, he didn't quite forget.'

Jim Whitaker frowned thoughtfully. 'But he didn't come back for her, did he, like he promised?'

'He was afraid, I think, that she would hate him. I used to think it terribly romantic, as a boy – like something out of Shakespeare.'

François smiled softly. 'That is why you came to Chinon in the first place, was it not? To do what your father could not?'

'I put it down to destiny,' said Neil.

'Ah, yes,' said François, 'destiny has played a part. It was destiny, I think, that your old friend Brigitte married Armand, that she came to live in my house, and that she invited you to visit her.'

'Destiny, too,' Madame Chamond put in, looking from Neil to Jim to François, 'that the three of you should be together, here at our hotel.'

Jim smiled. 'That's true.'

'Although,' Neil qualified, 'if you want to be technical, that was Emily's doing.'

'Me?' I did look at him that time, eyes widening. 'What on earth did I have to do with it?'

'Well, you took off like a rabbit when you saw me coming, and no one knew where you had gone. Poor Thierry was beside himself.'

Thierry looked up suspiciously from his post behind the bar. '*Comment?*'

'You were concerned.'

'Ah. Yes, I showed to Monsieur Neil the photograph, a photograph of him, I was thinking, and he asks me where it came from, and I told him—'

'So I rang up François,' Neil went on, recapturing his narrative. 'I thought you might have gone up there, to have a word with him, but of course he hadn't seen you.'

'And then I am worried,' François said in turn. 'Because I'm told that you were most upset, and so I called someone to come and stay with Lucie, and I came down here.'

'Where he met me,' said Jim. 'So you see, Emily, it really was your doing.'

And the rest, I knew, had happened pretty much as I had thought it would. Danielle and Harry, on arriving at the meeting place to find I wasn't there, had marched post-haste to the police station where, from all accounts, my cousin had stirred up a minor riot. The police in turn had telephoned the hotel to check my whereabouts. Naturally, that only raised the level of confusion as, with torches waving, everyone had formed a siege force the like of which had not been seen in Chinon since medieval times.

In all, I'd heard, some fifteen people had swarmed up the château steps to rescue me. Odd, I thought – I'd noticed only one.

Monsieur Chamond poured out the last of the Calvados and clucked his tongue regretfully. 'Another bottle gone,' he said. 'Thierry, would you mind . . . ?'

'Not at all.' Thierry could hold his liquor rather better than the rest of us, I thought. He walked with little effort to the door behind the bar, then swore with feeling as he bumped against some unseen object in his path.

'Be careful,' Christian warned him, craning forward, 'that is fragile.'

'So is my foot. You should give it to her . . .'

'Now is not a good time, I am thinking.'

I caught the furtive sideways glance and sensed they were discussing me again. 'What should Christian give me, Thierry?'

For an answer Thierry hoisted up a flat brown paper parcel, two feet square. 'This.'

A painting, I thought. It could only be a painting. And I knew which one it was before the paper fell away beneath my clumsy hands. Christian watched my face, uncertain. Everyone, it seemed, was watching me. My fingers hardly shook as I pushed back the torn paper so that nothing obscured my full view of the lovely painting. Painting number 88, the river steps, with Rabelais a sleeping shadow in the background.

Christian cleared his throat. 'Martine, she told me that you liked that one, so I thought . . .' He knew why I liked it, too – his smile showed me that. It was a tight smile, almost forced. And then he put it into words. 'I should have painted Paul there, yes? On the steps.'

I shook my head, and touched the fifth step lovingly. 'No need,' I told him, honestly. 'He's there already.'

Harry was the only one who didn't fully understand. He frowned and looked across at me. *I'll tell you later,* my eyes promised him, *only please don't ask me now.* Still frowning, he reached out a hand. 'Can I see it?'

'God, it's brilliant, Chris,' Neil breathed, looking over Harry's shoulder. 'That river really moves.'

Jim Whitaker leaned forward, too, to look. 'It's too bad,' he said finally, 'that Didier Muret was never told what really happened to the diamonds. Think of all the trouble that it night have saved.'

François looked shocked. 'You cannot mean that.'

'Sure. If he had known she threw them in the river, he'd have never tried to find them, would he?'

'The river?' François raised his eyebrows. 'Who told you Isabelle did this?'

Jim faltered, thinking back. 'Well, she did. At least, she told my father . . .'

'What did she tell him, exactly?'

'I'm not sure, it was so long ago. I always thought . . .'

'*Not* the river,' François said, with certainty. 'She might have said "the water", but not "the river".'

His tone, his words, had finally penetrated past my fog of Calvados. I turned in my seat to stare at him. 'Do you mean . . . you don't mean that you *know* where the diamonds are?'

'Of course.' He smiled. 'I helped her, I was there. She

told me they were stained with blood, those diamonds, and she knew only one way to make them pure.' He shrugged, and looked an apology at Jim. 'She didn't throw them in the river Vienne,' he said. 'She gave them back to God.'

CHAPTER THIRTY-TWO

. . . all the past
Melts mist-like into this bright hour,

The ancient door swung open with a heavy groan as Christian's key turned creaking in the lock. A shaft of torchlight caught a pillar's gleaming edge, then travelled up to where the grasses waved upon the ruined wall. Beneath the clouds that raced across the moon, the Chapelle of Sainte Radegonde slept still and peaceful, sacrosanct. Nothing moved.

And then the silence blinked.

Christian's keys dropped jangling to the ground and at the muttered German curse my cousin swung the torch around to help. 'Just there,' Harry pointed out the keys, 'beside the . . . no, beside that clump of flowers. Right.'

'This would be easier,' said Christian, 'in the daylight.'

Harry grinned. 'Well, we're here now, so there's no point having second thoughts. Besides, it's all well and good for Jim and François to put off exploring until morning –

they're old men. They've lost their sense of adventure. Not like us.'

'Jim Whitaker's not old,' I contradicted.

'Of course he is. He must be over forty, surely.'

'Thanks,' said Neil, behind my shoulder. 'I'll just stop here and have a nap then, shall I?'

'I didn't mean . . .'

'I know you didn't.' Neil's smile forgave my cousin's blunder. 'Emily, my dear, could you just shine your torch in that direction, so Christian doesn't trip on anything? Thanks, that's lovely.'

Christian walked ahead, pinned by the torchlight like a cabaret performer in a follow spot. His shadow loomed macabre on the frescoed wall behind the sturdy iron grille. Again he clanked the ring of keys, selecting one to fit the lock. 'Let us hope that Sainte Radegonde does not mind to be awakened.'

'She won't mind.' Harry's tone was confident. 'And anyway, it's not as if we're doing anything we oughtn't. We're just having a bit of a peek, that's all. Giving in to normal curiosity.'

Still, I half expected the saint's statue to be frowning at me, disapproving, as I passed between the iron gates and entered the hushed chapel proper, where the cave-like walls arched up to rest upon the ghostly row of pillars. But when I glanced at Radegonde's stone face she looked back benignly. Evidently, I thought, even saints could understand the pull of curiosity.

Thierry would be terribly put out when he learned we'd come up without him, but he'd gone to bed before us – it was really his own fault. The Chamonds, too, had given in to weariness, and Jim as well, and François had gone back up to the *Clos,* to help with Lucie. Which had only left the four of us – Harry, Christian, Neil and me – quite pleasantly awash in Calvados and irretrievably beyond the point of being tired.

I had, for my own part, reached that magical plane of inebriation in which time begins to float and anything seems possible, which went a long way towards explaining why, when Harry had leaned forward and said: 'Listen, *I've* got an idea . . .' instead of running in the opposite direction as experience would warrant, I had donned my jacket and trailed after him. Completely sober, I'd have had more sense. And I would never have come up that cliff path in the dark, alone or no.

'I've got it open,' Christian announced, twisting the key to the third and final gate. Harry'd wandered down the aisle to stand below the Plantagenet fresco, his torchlight angled up to catch the vibrant figures of young Isabelle and John. 'Well done,' he said, in absent tones. He stood a moment longer, looking up. 'I was afraid it might have changed, since I last saw it.'

I raised my eyebrows. 'Changed? In one week? Hardly likely.'

'Not one week, love. It's been at least two years since I've been up here, to the chapelle. Had I known my hiding place was quite so close I might have tried to sneak in another visit. One forgets how very beautiful—'

'Hold on,' I stopped him, frowning. 'You were here last week. You must have been. That's how I knew that you were missing in the first place – you left your coin, your King John coin, there on the altar, as an offering.'

'No chance.'

'You did.' My chin rose stubbornly. 'Or at least, if you didn't leave it there yourself, perhaps the gypsies . . .'

'Darling Emily.' My cousin strolled towards me, hand in pocket. 'I'm not all that daft, you know. I mean, they're lovely people, gypsies, but they will take things unless you're careful. My watch is gone, and my wallet . . . but they haven't taken this.' He held his hand out, with the coin upon it, to show me. 'With this, I was very careful.'

I stared. It was the King John coin, without mistake, safe in its plastic case. I opened my own wallet, just to be sure, and drew out the matching coin. Harry stabbed it with a beam of light.

'How curious,' he said. 'I wonder how on earth it got there.'

'I don't know.'

Christian leaned in closer for a better look. 'It is very old, yes? Somebody must have found it on the ground here, near the tombs perhaps, and put it with the other coins as tribute to Sainte Radegonde.'

'Y-yes, I suppose that's how it could have happened.'

'You don't sound terribly convinced,' said Harry, grinning. 'What other explanation is there – Sainte Radegonde herself, perhaps? A helping hand from beyond? Don't tell me that you've found religion, Em.'

'Of course not.' And I meant it, only . . . only . . .

Behind the altar, lovely pale Sainte Radegonde just went on gazing at nothing in particular, her blind, carved

400

eyes serene and peaceful. I put the coin back in her dish of offerings, and pushed it well down, frowning. Neil moved up behind my shoulder, and his breath brushed warm on my neck. 'The world would be dead boring, don't you think, if everything were easy to explain?'

My cousin grinned. 'The true Romantic viewpoint,' he pronounced. 'Come on then, are we ready? Tunnels again, Emily. You'll have to cope. She has a tunnel thing,' he told Neil, confidingly.

'Oh, yes?' Neil glanced my way. 'I'll have to remember that.'

Beyond the second gate the glare of harsh electric light seemed almost an intrusion. The chapel caves cried out for candles, I thought, or the flicker of a burning torch. The hanging bulbs and switches took away much of the mystery, and it wasn't until we'd reached the steep and crooked steps that dropped down to the holy well that I felt again the ancient and eternal sense of wonder shared by all explorers.

Harry must have drunk more than I'd thought. By the time the rest of us had slid with caution down the steps my cousin had stripped neatly to his underpants.

'What *are* you doing?' I demanded.

'Well, you can't see anything from here. Just pebbles, really. If I've come all this way to see diamonds, then I want to bloody see them, don't I?'

I looked down at the narrow shaft of clear blue water, plunging several metres deep into the rock. 'You can't be serious.'

He just grinned, stepped cleanly off the ledge and dropped feet-first into the well. The spray that came up after him was cold as ice. Neil knelt beside me, one arm braced against the pale stone wall to see I didn't accidentally topple in myself. 'We'll fish him out again,' he promised. 'Never fear.' The three of us peered over the edge, to watch as Harry forced himself towards the bottom, his hands splayed out in search of the elusive diamonds. 'Runs in your family, does it?' Neil asked idly. 'This sort of behaviour?'

'Well, yes, it seems to.'

'Ah.'

I might have asked him why he wanted to know, but our situation was already intimate beyond the comfort level, and at any rate there wasn't time. My cousin broke the surface of the water in a burst of triumph, gasping air.

'He was right,' he called up to us. 'Old François was right. Just look!' And spreading out his fingers he stretched up his hand, palm upwards, to the light. I saw the glittering before I saw the stones themselves.

'*Mein Gott*,' breathed Christian.

'Precisely.'

And then for some few minutes we were silent, all of us. I thought of Isabelle – Jim's mother, François's sister – standing here that summer evening while her world fell in around her, holding diamonds stained with blood no human hand could wash away. I thought of Hans . . . where had he been that night, I wondered? Miles away, by then. He'd sought redemption too, in different ways. He had surrendered, left his country, changed his name. Well, it was over now, I thought. Time everyone forgot, forgave, let be. Yom Kippur might have ended with the sunset, but the message of the

402

Jewish holiday remained. *People hate too much.*

'There are some coins down there,' said Harry. 'Not old ones, but . . .'

Paul's wishing coins. 'Just let them lie,' I told him.

'Yes, Mum.' He grinned. 'And these as well, I think.' He tipped his hand to let the diamonds tumble back into the turquoise water. 'Bad luck to steal things from a holy well. Sainte Radegonde would have my head.'

I watched the flashing glitter of the gems descending. They vanished at the bottom, amid a scattering of what looked like pebbles. How many diamonds had there been? I didn't want to know. After all, they were nothing more than stones, small bits of stone that someone thought were pretty, and in that illusion lay their value. In the greater scheme of life, I thought, they didn't matter a damn. Maybe all that mattered was the tangible, however fleeting – friends and family, feelings . . .

'Oh, sod it,' Harry bit out. 'Damn, I think I broke my finger.' He'd made his way to the sheer wall of the well and had begun to climb up, using the row of footholds gouged by the well-diggers centuries earlier. He pulled his hand free, flexing it.

He was still several feet below us, and I had to lean to look. 'It doesn't look broken.'

'Well, maybe not, but it might have been. There's something jammed in here – a block of wood, it feels like.' Far more gingerly now, he placed his injured fingers back within the recessed foothold just above the surface of the water. 'Hang on,' he said, 'it isn't wood at all. In fact it feels like . . . I'll be damned.'

'What is it?' Christian leant down, curious, as Harry finally tugged the object free. I only saw a small dark square the size of Harry's hand. He passed it up to Christian. 'You tell me.'

It was filthy dirty, for one thing. My cousin's hand left black marks on the stone as he swung himself up the few remaining feet to join us on the narrow ledge above the well. Christian had turned the packet over, sniffing. 'Oil,' he pronounced. 'It has been oiled.'

'Waxed as well.' Harry pointed to the great untidy splotch of black that held the packet closed. 'Somebody didn't want this getting wet.' He was dripping water himself, but that didn't seem to bother him. He slicked his hair back, glanced at me. 'Emily, love, would you toss me my trousers? Thanks.' He rummaged for his pocket knife and prised the battered blade open. It was rather tricky, since the packet seemed to crumble when he touched it, but at length he'd sliced the wax seal through and gently, oh so gently, coaxed the stiffened edges apart.

The squares of parchment had been folded up so tightly for so long that they were nearly solid lumps, and Harry didn't try to force them open. He knew better. There were specialists who did that sort of thing. But he did forget his training long enough to turn the parchment in his still-damp fingers, searching for a scrap of writing, anything. 'Oh, my God,' he said.

I looked at him, and caught some measure of his own excitement. 'What?'

'You ought to know that signature,' he told me, stretching out his hand towards me. I looked. I blinked, a long blink,

404

looked again. And then I raised my head to stare at him.

I couldn't even speak.

Neil slid his gaze from me to Harry. 'What are they?'

'Letters.' My cousin's voice had roughened slightly, as it always did when he became emotional. It echoed back from the still water of the well. 'Love letters, I expect. Written by a king eight hundred years ago.'

Christian stroked a corner of the crumbling oiled packet. 'Eight hundred years? Incredible.'

My cousin looked at me. '"A treasure beyond price,"' he quoted, and his eyes grew moist. 'That's what the chronicle said Queen Isabelle hid, here at Chinon. Only it wasn't jewels, or money. Damn, who would have known . . . ?' He shook his head, his dreamy gaze returning to the crudely-chiselled footholds in the soft, unspeaking stone. And then, as if he'd suddenly remembered Neil and Christian wouldn't have the foggiest idea what he was talking about, which meant that they were fair game for a classic lecture, Henry Yates Braden, PhD, promptly cleared his throat. 'You see,' he began, 'there was another Isabelle . . .'

Chapter Thirty-Three

. . . lift thine eyes; my doubts are dead,

'What, no lectures?' Harry asked me, as we paused before the altar. Christian swung the iron gate shut and the sound disturbed my thoughts. I turned unfocused eyes towards my cousin.

'I'm sorry?'

'About how I shouldn't steal things from historic sites,' he clarified. 'You're rather puritan about the subject, as I recall. You read me the Riot Act that day I nicked a pebble from Tintagel.'

'That wasn't a pebble, it was a building stone, and if everybody did that there wouldn't be a castle left to . . .' I saw his smile forming and broke off with a heavy sigh. 'Anyhow, I suppose I can't talk, can I? I stole a coin from an offering plate, for heaven's sake.'

'You brought it back.'

'And you said yourself you're going to give the letters to the University of Paris.'

'Right. Just as soon as I have a chance to look at them.'

My gaze narrowed. 'Harry . . .'

'Well, have a heart! You can't expect me to just turn the damn things over without looking at them first. Christ, I'm not a saint, you know.' His eyes flicked sideways to where Radegonde's calm statue stood behind the altar, as if he half expected to be flattened by a lightning bolt. 'Besides,' he went on, in a lower voice, 'since no one else even knows that the letters exist, it stands to reason that no one will miss them for a few days, will they?'

'A few days?'

'Well, a month maybe.'

'And then you'll send them on to Paris?'

'On my honour.' He swore the oath with hand upraised.

Past redemption, I thought – that's what Harry was. On his honour indeed. I smiled and looked away, out past the iron grille to where the gentle fingers of the breaking dawn touched softly on the bay tree standing sentinel beside the chapelle's door.

'Cold?' Harry asked me.

'No.'

'Then why the shiver?' And then he followed the direction of my gaze, and said quite simply: 'Ah.'

I turned around. 'What do you mean, "Ah"?'

'Just "Ah".'

He saw things rather more clearly than I liked, I thought. More clearly, sometimes, than I myself could see. I felt the colour stain my cheeks and turned my head away again, looking back towards the bay tree and the man who sat beneath it.

He was sitting comfortably stretched out against the outer wall, one leg drawn up on which to rest his injured hand. The hand hung stiffly, as though it hurt him, and I remembered Harry telling me how Neil had climbed the château walls to get inside. Actually climbed the walls. They must have been a good twenty feet high, even at their lowest point around the gates. Less than that on the inside, naturally, where the ground level was higher, but even so. He simply hadn't wanted to wait, so Harry said, for the main gates to be unlocked. It must have been a different Neil Grantham, I decided, who'd shown such a lack of patience.

It could not have been this quiet man, lost in a serenity so deep he scarcely seemed to breathe, with the faint light trickling through the bay leaves turning his hair a pale and softly radiant gold. He might have been Christ contemplating the sunrise over Gethsemene. All else was darkness compared to him, and though he neither moved nor spoke his very stillness drew the eye more effectively than motion – drew it and held it until I felt myself being pulled into the glowing centre of its reverent, breathless peace.

Harry watched me, eyebrows raised. 'I like him, if it matters.'

I faced him with a flat expression. 'I don't know what you're talking about.'

'Right.' My cousin turned to Christian, with a smile. 'Sorry to have kept you from your bed, but I really am grateful for this. And for these.' He patted the lumpy parcel wrapped with care inside his jacket.

Christian shrugged. 'It is no trouble. And now,' he announced, brushing his forehead with one hand, 'I will make for everyone some coffee, yes? So much excitement in one night, it makes the head ache.'

'Coffee,' Neil agreed, 'sounds wonderful.' He rolled his head against the stone wall to smile at us, and moved to stand up, wincing a little. 'It isn't so much the excitement,' he explained, 'as the drink. Bloody Calvados. I feel like there's a herd of horses dancing on my skull.'

My cousin laughed. 'That's age for you. You ready, Em?'

No, I thought, I wasn't ready. That was the whole problem, wasn't it? I trailed along the cliff path after them, too busy with my own confusing thoughts to join the conversation. I had some vague memory of passing by the house where Harry had kept hidden, and of brushing through the fragrant clutch of pine, and then of starting our descent into the town, but I was still surprised to find myself upon the pavement outside Christian's house, with all the houses round still shuttered tight against the pale and spreading light of day.

I looked at Harry, and at Neil, and suddenly I felt a little stifled. 'Actually,' I said, 'I don't feel much like coffee. I'd rather get some sleep.'

Harry's eyes were gently sceptical. 'Oh, yes?'

'Yes. I think I'll just go back to the hotel.'

Neil smiled at me, faintly, seeing too much, as he always did. I tried my best to make a graceful exit, but in truth it took all my effort not to break into a run as I wound my way through the narrow sleeping streets. Each window seemed to stare at me, accusing me of cowardice, and even when I reached the fountain square the elegantly entwined Graces looked less than approving. I wrapped my arms around myself defensively, moving across to stand at the fountain's edge.

Splendour, Joy and bloody Beauty – they looked as stern as ever, those three faces. Unless . . . was that a quirk I saw, just there? I squinted through the tumbling rain of water droplets, glistening like diamonds in the slant of morning sun. No, I decided, it was nothing. And yet, I had the feeling that the statues were trying to tell me something.

'It would never work,' I answered them aloud. I wanted to tell them that the fairy tales were lies, all lies, but it was difficult to say the words when above me Château Chinon rose resplendent in the sunshine, looking every inch the castle of a fairy tale. Difficult, too, to deny the existence of Prince Charmings when one had just last night come charging to my rescue. Damn, I thought. And happy endings? A sweet wind whispered through the leaves of the acacias, and I thought I heard Jim Whitaker's voice asking me a second time, 'Is happiness a thing we choose, I wonder?'

I wondered, too, and found no answer.

My hands were cold. I rummaged in my handbag for a pair of gloves and saw a flashing glimmer at the bottom, in amongst the jumbled clutter. Gloves forgotten, I reached in deeper, and closed my fingers round the two-toned coin. Not a French coin, but an Italian one – five hundred lire, to be exact. I seemed to see Neil's eyes before me, watching me, quietly urging me to make a wish. *Whenever you're ready*, he'd told me. *Whenever you're ready.*

411

It had been years since I'd performed the tiny ritual, yet in the end it came so naturally. I took a deep breath, kissed the coin, and sent it tumbling with a wish into the icy water of the fountain.

I was so intent on watching it fall that I didn't notice the cat, at first. The little creature had rubbed past my legs twice before I surfaced from my thoughts and looked down. The cat blinked up at me. It came into my arms without hesitation when I bent to pick it up, and nestled underneath my chin, purring like a motor-boat.

Behind me, Neil's voice warned: 'You'll get fleas.'

I stiffened, then relaxed, not looking back. 'I don't care.' How long he had been standing there, I didn't know – I hadn't heard his footsteps. But I heard them now, crisp and even on the pavement as he came across the square to join me at the fountain's edge. I went on looking at the water, and my hands upon the cat were almost steady. Almost.

Neil glanced into the water, too, then turned his quiet gaze on me. 'I see you've used your coin,' he commented.

'Yes.'

'You didn't wish for the cat to find a home, did you?'

I looked at him then, and saw that his eyes weren't quiet at all. They were alive, intense with some unnamed emotion, and a question lurked within their midnight depths. Slowly, I shook my head.

The question vanished and he smiled. 'Thank God for that,' he said. 'I thought you might have wasted it.' And then he raised a hand to touch my face, a touch of promise, warm and sure, and as I struggled to smile back at him he

412

kissed me. It felt so very right, so beautiful; tears pricked behind my lashes as life flowed through all my hollow limbs, and I lost all sense of place and time. It might have been a minute or an hour later when he moved, slanting a thoughtful look down at the black-and-white bundle of fur in my arms. The cat stared back at him, a trifle smugly.

'I suppose,' said Neil, 'that this beast will have to come with us?'

Just like that. I stared up at him. 'I thought you said your landlady hated cats?'

'Yes, well, she doesn't much like other women, either, but I fancy she'll get used to both of you. Even Austrian landladies,' he informed me, 'recognise the hand of destiny at work.' His own hand felt very warm as he smoothed my hair back. 'Still, we'd better see to it the little fleabag gets his injections. Have you named him yet?'

I hadn't really thought about it, but quite suddenly I knew there was just one name that would fit. 'Ulysses,' I told Neil. 'His name's Ulysses.'

A flash of understanding passed between us, and his dark eyes smiled down at me. 'Right. Put Ulysses down, then, will you?'

'Why?'

'Just put him down.'

The cat yawned grumpily as I lowered him to the pavement. A stiff breeze scattered the fountain's spray around the three bronze Graces, and the cat leapt safely out of range, moving to resume his nap beneath the nearest bench. The fountain's spray struck me as well, as cold as ice, but I didn't really mind it. Neil's eyes, his smile, his touch, were warmth enough. Maybe he was right, I thought – it might not be so difficult, believing. I lifted my own hand to touch his face, his hair, to bring his head lower. And in the moment just before he kissed me, I could have sworn that, past his shoulder, Splendour smiled.

Author's Note

If you walk the streets of Chinon, you will find each setting and each building mentioned in this story. Because of this, I wish to remind the reader that while the places may be real, the people who inhabit them are entirely fictional.

To the Chinonais, I offer my apologies, for moving their *gendarmerie*. To Paul Rhoads, who became my guide, and to Dorothee Kleinmann, who shared her Chapelle with me, I give my heartfelt thanks.

And to all my friends at the Hotel de France, both past and present, I dedicate this book.